Across the Blue Ridge Mountains is a deeply researched novel firmly based in history that captures how a woman, regardless of time period, has to live by the fateful decisions she makes and how resilience and showing up to the table are her only way forward. Through her life's journey, a stream of characters appear that reflects the best and worst in her but inevitably forces her to grow in ways she may not be ready for. Ultimately, her inner strength must rise to meet many challenges.

Early Praise for Across the Blue Ridge Mountains

"An ambitious, important, and beautifully written first novel by a gifted new writer. Maggie Marangione deeply knows the Virginia mountain towns she writes of and the hard lives within. In Mary Dodson, she has created a clear voiced, brave, and unforgettable heroine equal to the myriad challenges she faces. I read this book in blazing gulps, and thought about it for days after I finished the last page"— *Tom Barbash, author of The Dakota Winters*

"Across the Blue Ridge Mountains paints a picture of the life and times in the Blue Ridge Mountains just before the coming of Shenandoah National Park like no other book I've read. It transports me there with accurate details in an immersive saga."—*Sue Eisenfeld, Author of Shenandoah: A Story of Conservation and Betrayal*

ACROSS THE BLUE RIDGE MOUNTAINS

M. S. Marangione

Moonshine Cove Publishing, LLC

Abbeville, South Carolina U.S.A.

First Moonshine Cove Edition August 2022

ISBN: 9781952439391

Library of Congress LCCN: 2022909522

Cover image by Colleen Pendry; Colleenpendry.com Colleenpendry@gmail.com; interior design by Moonshine Cove staff.

To the memory of the families, and their descendants, who were removed from their lands to create the Shenandoah National Park.

Acknowledgment

I would like to thank authors Martha Woodroof, Sue Eisenfeld, and Tom Barbash for their encouragement and support, as well as Cynthia Mora and Gene's team for their copy editing

ACROSS THE BLUE RIDGE MOUNTAINS

"I remember there were days, many days, that I walked in the sun."
—*Mary Dodson, Shenandoah National Park Oral History Archives,*
James Madison University, 1971

Chapter 1

Elkton, Virginia
The Shenandoah Valley at the foothills of the Blue Ridge Mountains,
1918

I met Halsom at Court Days in Harrisonburg, Virginia the autumn of the year that I turned fifteen and, in some ways, he was more influential on my life than my parents, because I didn't listen to them. Instead, I chose to follow Halsom across the Alleghenies in the pitch black of a no-moon night, traveling west along Swift Run Gap. This was the same road my parents and I were now bumping along on that September day when I was still blameless. I regarded maple, oak, beech, and dogwood holding onto some of their green leaves, the wild pink Virginia roses still spilling forth along the fence lines, and the second bloom of honeysuckle dripping yellow, orange, and white. Like me, they were on the edge of change.

I would not have been motoring to Court Days if my Daddy were not a responsible man who had inherited a tannery from my grandfather, who inherited it from his father, who built the business straight off the boat from Ireland with the cash his family had sent with him to America. A tannery is a smelly business with big vats for animal hides that get processed into leather. My mama wished Daddy did something a bit *cleaner* as she used to say. But that fragrant business had built her a three-story grand Queen Anne house on Elm Street, with white cupolas, delicate gingerbread trim, patterned bay windows, sixteen double columns holding up the wrap around porch, forced air heat from the basement, gas powered lighting and a three-foot-tall white picket fence with concrete ornamental pineapples stationed on the fence posts.

She spent considerable money on decorating this house with store-bought lace curtains, multicolored Oriental rugs, marble-topped tables and carved dark brown walnut furniture that felt like it could eat you. My mother wanted to have a concrete example that distanced her from family, which had struggled following the devastation of the Civil War. She also collected porcelain dolls, which scared me, and I never played with them yet that didn't stop my mother from buying them. I think she wished those dolls was her daughter, as they were ideal in their perfection and could not talk but stare dumbly at her with their dead eyes.

Because my mother was of a nervous disposition that made her yell a lot, I took refuge in walking the deer trails that serpentine around Elk Run Creek, and I would follow those deer trails clear to the top of Tanners Ridge, finding peace at the top of the mountain. If there is a heaven, I thought, it is a carpet of iridescent moss glistening beside a stream with the only sounds being the squirrels chattering or a pileated woodpecker's call and smells that are fresh, cool, and light like freshly cut grass, young stems, conifer trees and lily of the valley. My mother's house and church smelled like mothballs and old ladies. I was not from mountain people my mother always reminded me when I came home trailing leaves and fresh air.

"If you don't watch out, you'll end up like them." She would spit out these words at me. Swinging my bucket of blackberries, bird feathers or whatever I had gathered and toted home, I'd holler, "I rather be a mountain person and free than stuck in town putting on airs." Then I would get slapped. My father would just pull his newspaper higher over his head and continue to sip his evening whiskey.

Motoring to Court Days and seated in the back seat of my father's Packard sedan, I was wearing my favorite dress, yellow with a white lace overlay. It brought out the gold in my almond shaped eyes and complimented my tawny complexion that my mother said I *didn't* inherit from her side of the family but "from that mixed bag of Irish genes on your father's side." As my father steered the car around a pothole, she told him, "This car will be the death of me. I just know it." Staring at the back of her head, I thought unchristian thoughts.

With the snare drum sound of the engine rat-a-tat-tatting, it seemed to me that Daddy drove like he was driving a toy train around the Christmas tree. We headed down the streets to Harrisonburg so fast that I could not make out the faces of my neighbors as they waved from their porches and I wondered if they talked about how the car cost more than most people made in a year, which made me feel self-conscious about the displays of our money. Mama and I held our hats on our heads as our hair swirled around our faces. It was exhilarating, but she struggled against the wind to keep her hair in place.

"I don't think these cars are progress for women," she shouted as we hit another pothole and she landed splay-legged, half on the seat with her dress flying up above her knees. I looked out at the Massanutten Ridge and wished I could climb it on that sweet and warm Indian summer day. Our valley was so pretty with the Shenandoah River a light blue gray, keeping the fertile, green pastures company like a best friend, always constant. I often felt that the Blue Ridge Mountains to the east and the Alleghenies to the west were like two protective fathers. The Blue Ridge Mountains, why, they glowed blue in the sunrise and twilight and were like a father who could read you a bedtime story. The Western Alleghenies, protecting untamed West Virginia, glowed orange and were higher and daunting in their beauty, like a father who loved you, but you were afraid of, too.

Daddy didn't shift to a lower gear until we began the long slow descent into Court Square and the houses got closer together and the busyness of the street increased. My daddy's car was one among many, but there were also horses, wagons, people on foot, livestock for sale, produce vendors, dogs running to the other side of the street, and smiling county politicians skirmishing around through the crowds eager to shake hands with everybody. The sidewalks were also covered with old furniture, farm implements, buggy harnesses and other items for sale or trade. There was a minister preaching on a soapbox, a blind fiddler playing a jig, children darting around horses and wagons, and people everywhere. The smell of exhaust, manure, wood smoke and roasting peanuts and popcorn from the peddlers hung in the air.

People from all the neighboring counties—Augusta, Shenandoah, Page, some even from Franklin, West Virginia, would come to the county seat, and I could remember my grandfather saying they used to sell slaves, too. The slave block was still there in front of the courthouse with people sitting on it like it never bore witness to any misery at all. All of this would be too much for me, so exciting and overwhelming, especially after a kidney-jarring two-hour motoring. Yet, my mother seemed to come alive, smiling, chatting, practically glowing as she shopped with her considerable allowance.

"Here, Mary," said Daddy, "you get yourself an ice cream or soda." He pressed a dollar into my palm and while I was staring at it wondering what I wanted, my parents sauntered away. Suddenly, a shadow crossed over me and I swung my head around to see where it came from.

"What's your name, sweetie pie?" I looked for my parents; they were nowhere to be seen. They had evaporated just as he had appeared. His gray eyes were admiring my father's car and, it seemed, me. I could not stop staring at them as they held me fast. His eyes were the color of the slate in the mountains, and then there was his confidence. He walked right over as if he knew me. Maybe in cities men were that bold, but not in the valley unless they were common. He stretched out his hand for me and helped me out of the car. I took his hand like I knew him. Blushing, feeling both shy and adventurous, I looked at his face and quickly lowered my gaze.

"My name is Mary."

He was taller than I and slight, with a smile that curved up on one corner and made his eyes dance as if he was lit up from within. A dimple cleft his chin. I admired his thick and curly dark brown hair, big strong hands and his white shirt which was unbuttoned so I could see dark hair escaping from his chest and tickling the hollow of his throat. I caught the faint wisp of spice, bay and rum and I breathed in deeply.

As I stepped gingerly beside him, we began strolling down the street side by side.

"Well, it's a pleasure to meet you. My name is Halsom, and I hope I haven't scared you, but you're just so captivating in that pretty dress."

"I don't scare easily." I wanted to win his confidence and appear a woman of the world.

"You know, it does me good to have such a beautiful woman on my arm for a stroll today."

No one had ever referred to me as a woman before.

"Where are your people from Halsom?" I asked directly, sounding like my mother.

"I'm from up North, but don't let that worry you because I'm a man who thinks a great disservice was done to the South. Every day that I spend in this Valley, I feel lucky that good fortune brought me down here."

"What is it that you do? What brought you down here?" *A Yankee...Oh my God.*

"Opportunity and a chance to get out of New York City. That is the truth, and I feel I can tell you my heart. There's something about you. You're like no woman I have met before. Maybe it's those eyes. They remind me of the eyes of the Asian women I met when I was working on the railroad out west."

He began spinning his tales about cities, barrooms, shipyards, that were far away from the woods of the mountain and my small-town life, and his stories carried me to worlds and people that I had imagined and read about in my father's *Atlantic, Washington Post* and *National Geographic.* Halsom quickened in me my desire to see it all. Elkton seemed very small and trivial. Halsom's stories made me feel like I had been in the desert without water.

The more he talked with his deep baritone voice rolling up and down, the more entranced I became by his stories till I no longer was paying attention to any of the activity around me. Stories were the *only* reason I would go to my mother's sewing circles, because I hated to sew and could not get ten stitches to an inch. The stories the women told were also enchanting, in a comforting and soothing way, with their sweet lilting voices keeping time to their sewing, they sewed tales of their days, weeks, months, and years that would make me sleepy, probably because they were so comforting but tedious. Halsom's stories made me feel alive all over as if an electric current were running up my spine.

"...and I have ridden the logs from Shenandoah to Front Royal—those massive oaks, maples, hickories, and chestnuts coming from the mountains, hauled down by the mountain people."

"I've seen them too, going right past my daddy's tannery and down to Island Ford where the men lash those timbers into rafts."

Come to think of it, those river riders were the only exposure I had to anything colorful or different. The river riders were not the shy and silly boys who dunked our pigtails in the ink wells like idiots. These men would look into the rapids with determination and devilry, throwing their heads back and howling a Rebel Yell when the swells of the river got big. In the summer, they stripped off their shirts revealing tan skin, shoulder and arm muscles and stomach muscles that looked like my mother's washboard. My best friend, Ethel, and I would walk down to the river bridge and wave to them, and then we would turn to each other, covering our mouths and giggling wildly when they shouted back to us and called for us to join them. I wanted to go down to the river's edge and talk to them, but Ethel would drag me away.

"Your daddy owns that tannery in Elkton?" Halsom leaned his head back to look me square in the face.

I nodded eagerly.

"You don't say..." he seemed to consider this. "You got any brothers? Sisters, as pretty as you?" he grinned at me.

"Just me."

He was quiet for a moment.

"So... you probably know all about the hole in that river that can eat raft boats alive, you know the one, to river left after the Elkton Bridge?"

He grabbed me by the wrist to scare me, and I giggled because I didn't know what else to do. Of course, I knew of it.

"Why, after the flood last year, that river swirled and churned from blue to brown and white caps higher than I ever seen till you could not see the boulders or holes till you were up on them. What usually took three days to get to Front Royal took us only two. And at Newport, I watched those waves curl backwards like something you only see on the ocean."

Seeing my interest in adventure and our common knowledge of the Shenandoah, he went on.

"One spring, we came around a bend and a mighty sycamore had fallen across half of the river. That tree had to have been 30 feet long and try as we might, we couldn't turn that boat to river left. We braced ourselves but when we hit that tree, this young boy we had with us was sent over the raft as if he was shot out of a cannon. He got dragged under by the current, churned by the backward rolling hydraulics, and got crushed by the raft and pounded by the water and rocks and the cold. That happened to me once, but I had enough sense to pull up into a ball, cover my head and I swam under the current."

I pictured myself as a river man, living a life dangerous and free, drinking that homemade wine, brandy, and moonshine brought down from the mountaineers. As if reading my mind, Halsom pulled a flask out of his pocket and held it out to me. Looking around quickly to see if anyone was watching, I hid behind his shoulder and took a quick swig. My eyes watered, my throat burned, I let out a cough and a sputter. I had never had whiskey before. Well, Ethel and I once sipped sherry from her mother's cabinet. Halsom smiled.

"You're my type of gal." He took a long swig before placing it in his breast pocket.

I was his type of gal. He was as hazardous as the buried tree limbs and strainers that trapped a man beneath the swells and currents of the river. But, oh, how handsome he was even with a shadow of a beard. He didn't have the smooth baby face of Johnathan Abel, who was being forced by both of our parents to court me. Halsom made me feel like I was in a spell and ready to do anything. Leaning into me so closely I could feel the heat from his body and his breath tickling my ear, his arm circled my waist, placing pressure on my hip, which made me feel like I was going to break out in a sweat. I felt like I was ready for anything.

By comparison, being with Johnathan Abel felt like being covered in a damp blanket. My parents would usher Johnathan Abel, the preacher's son, into our sitting room as if Jesus himself had stepped off the cross. I held a special grudge against his father, who whipped me in front of the Sunday school class for simply saying, *"Preacher Dean, with all due respect, it makes no sense how Noah got onto that ark with all those animals, given how many animals there are all over the world, and I know because my Daddy gets National Geographic."* Sometimes, Johnathan Abel and I went walking after Sunday supper, and sometimes I would let him kiss me to see if I would like it. I didn't know much, but I knew Johnathan Abel was doing it all wrong. I was always wiping great strands of saliva off my face.

Preacher Dean and his son came to dinner *every Wednesday evening* after his mother died of some tumor in her stomach, and he wasn't so much of a Bible-believing Preacher Man when he hauled his dying wife up to Sandy Bottom to the witch woman, Granny Hite. She gave Preacher Dean a simple, which is a mixture of herbs, and told him to put it under her bed. But neither Jesus nor Granny Hite could save Preacher Dean's wife.

After they would leave of an evening, my mother would always remark on how nice Johnathan Abel was, how nice Preacher Dean was, how nice, nice, nice.

"Young lady, you better start thinking real long and hard about what nice really is or you will find yourself on the wrong ends of things. Mark my words." But I knew if I married Johnathan Abel, I would have to numb myself with cough syrup every day for the rest of my life.

Halsom picked up a curl of my light brown hair and twirled it around his finger.

"You've got the prettiest hair I've ever seen... kind of honey-colored, amber."

"Maybe I'll trap you with my amber-colored hair the way real amber catches a fly." I could not believe this came out of my mouth. Those were flirting words, the likes of such I had only read in dime store novels. The liquor had loosened my tongue.

As he ran his finger down the side of my face and over my lips, I cautiously pulled away from being touched, nervous by what I had encouraged.

"You've caught me all right, sweet girl. Do you figure that's how Mary caught Joseph with a baby that wasn't his?"

While I didn't quite know what he meant by that, I thought I was going to melt like a summer ice cream cone from the feeling of his finger caressing my face. About that time, a group of Negroes leading some mules they were selling came past, and one bay colored mule was jumping sideways and rearing. Halsom, who was walking on the outside, where a gentleman should, circled his arm around my waist and gently guided me past them. I realized we had walked away from the courthouse a fair distance and were down by the icehouses, meat processing buildings and railroad yards. Panicked at being so far from the car, I recognized I was with a complete stranger. This overrode my desire to stay with him.

"I best be getting back. My mama..."

"If you want to go back to your mother we can. I was just so enjoying your company. When can I see you again?" He held both my hands now and had stopped me from walking so he could face me directly.

"I don't know." I tried to pull away from him. He held me so fast it hurt.

"Well, I know. I'll find you, and I'm going to see you again and you're going to see me, with or without your parent's permission. What do you think of that?"

He wanted me. With complete certainty, I knew I wanted him. Halsom was my ticket out—to someplace or something besides the long dull tunnel of existence in a small town. He loosened his grip, and I rubbed my arm where he had grabbed it, but I let him hold my hand as we walked back. I had given him my answer. When we reached my parents, my mother glared at me.

"Get in this vehicle this instant!"

Halsom turned to my mother, holding her with a long smile, tipping his cap while keeping her gaze and grinning like he knew a deep dark secret, maybe about her. My mother's face softened.

"It was nice meeting you, Mary," he said turning to me. My mother's hand fluttered to her throat as she looked at him while motioning for me to get in the car.

My father, oblivious, continued talking business with James Roudabush.

"I'm telling you, we have got to be prepared. Change is coming to our business. Everything's going to be built like Ford's assembly line."

"I'm sure you're probably right, but I know if I don't get my women folks home directly there will be hell to pay." He touched the tip of his fedora as he got in the car, where my mother and I were waiting, and he pulled the car onto Main Street.

Turning my head to look back, I saw Halsom and James Roudabush watching us drive away, and between my mother glaring at me with her no-lip face, my father's whistling and my chest hurting from something I couldn't explain, I considered hurling myself out of the car. But I didn't because I knew my adventure was just beginning.

Chapter 2

It was over two weeks before I saw Halsom again and I when I did, my heart exploded in my chest at the sight of him. Ethel and I had been in the schoolroom helping Miss Halfyard, our schoolteacher, with the straightening up after school let out. Some of the boys had stayed after, too, as a load of wood for our stove had been dropped off. They were splitting and stacking it. One of the families, whose children went to the school, would just bring wood; it would be delivered without a word being said, like magic.

Our schoolhouse was built many, many years ago by the Crawford family. There were benches lined up in rows like soldiers, and the inside smelled of wood or coal, with three windows and a door in front and back, and pegs at the entrance for our coats. It was as simple as a pioneer cabin but with white clapboard and a tin roof. The teacher's desk had an ink well and there was a chalkboard behind it. The floors always seemed dusty no matter how many times they were swept. In fact, that fateful day Halsom came to fetch me, I had just finished sweeping it and had gone out the door with the dustpan.

Ethel was scolding the Baugher boys for not stacking the wood properly. "That wood will never dry and will not burn good, and I don't plan on freezing all winter." Ethel had her hands on her hips. She was bossy for a fifteen-year-old girl.

Yet, amidst this normalcy, my eyes were abruptly drawn to the woods, and there stood my Halsom at the edge of the tree line looking straight at me as if he had materialized from the mountain itself. He stood in the shadow of the forest where only I seemed to see him.

"Come on children, you all did well this afternoon." Miss Halfyard, who was built like a turnip, brought out a busy day cake for us.

We went to the steps of the schoolhouse to eat our cake in the sun. Halsom stood in the shadows of the forest watching us. The boys were cutting up and acting foolish, pushing each other around. Ethel whispered in my ear about how cute Osaba was, and it was clear he liked Ethel. His face would turn beet red when he looked at her. Suddenly, Halsom was standing in the schoolyard materializing out of the thin air. My friends stopped their foolishness and looked up.

"Why, who is that?" Miss Halfyard stood up as crumbs fell from her generous bosom. Halsom strode toward us. The boys shuffled nervously, and Ethel elbowed me. "Who *is* that?"

"Hello there," he said to the group with his broad smile covering us all. "Seems like you all have been doing a pile of work. You boys split all that wood?"

"Yes, sir." The boys looked at him and then down at their shoes.

"Hmmm, and green wood at that. You boys must have some gunpowder in you to split all that green wood."

"Well, we are lucky to have that wood. The Farmers' Almanac says we will have an early winter, and I'm lucky to have these boys." Miss Halfyard cast one of her infrequent smiles in their direction.

"And what do you have these pretty girls doing for you today? Or are you girls just here to tease these boys?"

Ethel giggled and hid her head in my shoulder like a fool. For a minute I was just too stupefied to say anything, but before Miss Halfyard could reply, I said, "I help Miss Halfyard correct some of the schoolwork, especially the writing. Ethel helps with the math. Miss Halfyard concentrates on the penmanship. She is all about the penmanship. God forbid your cursive isn't like the McGuffey reader, you'll be sitting in that room writing instead of eating lunch."

"Well, really, Mary. Writing clearly is the way of being civilized, and Lord knows most of you need some refinement, especially you."

She punctuated this with a rap on the top of my head, hard, with her ruler, which she must have kept in a belt loop or maybe she pulled it out of her hair, because it would appear like a magician's wand. Out of the corner of my eye, I saw Halsom wince. I was blushing now, and the boys were pleased by it because they didn't like me. Ethel said they didn't like me because I was different, *odd*, and that I looked funny.

They sometimes called me *pancake face* because my face was fairly flat, with high cheekbones. Once I made my Daddy show me my birth certificate because I looked so different from my parents, but I was their daughter.

"I'm sure you have your work cut out for you here." Halsom smiled as he put his foot on the steps, leaning into Miss Halfyard like a vine looking for a trellis.

"I sure do, and what about you? You're not from around here, are you? Are you the man who is supposed to bring me my new readers?"

"I'm afraid I'm not that man. Do you need someone to check on them for you? I would be more than happy to do that for you." Oh, how he dripped honey, and Miss Halfyard was squirming under his steady gaze.

"No, no. that is quite all right," she stammered, for he had made her blush too.

"I'm here to walk Mary home; I'm a friend of the family," he said so smooth.

I felt Ethel pinching me hard on my waist.

"Well, let me get my books," I said jumping up.

"And don't forget the fireside poets," said Miss Halfyard turning to me. I was copying out some of the poems so that we had enough for the class. Mama would cluck to her friends about my helping Miss Halfyard, as if I were working for the President or something. Miss Halfyard would sometimes slip me some of my favorite lemon drops when no one was looking. She kind of liked me but then seem to be more annoyed with me, too, like many.

I flew through the door and gathered up my things like one possessed. Halsom gave me his arm and the boys parted for us like the Red Sea, shuffling their feet backwards.

"You boys keep up that work for your teacher. It will make you good and strong."

He winked at them, and the boys smiled from under their hair falling across their eyes, as if they were too afraid to know what Halsom meant.

Ethel, whom I had known all my life, was looking at me as if she didn't recognize me. I took Halsom's arm and walked away from the schoolhouse and into the woods without looking back.

Chapter 3

The sun rose up same as always and the sun set the same over the Valley, but I was not the same once Halsom started courting me. I had not realized how much I was missing in my life until I met him and how I was expecting a miracle to occur that would catapult me into a more exciting future, a future beyond my mother, Johnathan Abel, and Elkton. Looking out my window, the leaves having fallen off the trees that lined Elm Street, I noticed that two more cars had shown up on our street, yet horses pulling wagons of ice, milk and wood still clumped on by like we were caught between two worlds. I didn't know what to do with myself. I felt a rising anxiety in between Halsom's visits, like a panic in me that had no name. I thought I would never be right. All I could think about was his hand on my waist and his eyes and his voice.

Sitting at dinner after Halsom showed up at the schoolhouse, I was listening to Mama tell Daddy about meeting up with Ida Cash at the women's garden club. Pushing Brussel sprouts around my plate, I thought to myself with dread. *"Will this be my fate too, a life like my mother's?"* I looked up from my plate and burst into tears, pushing myself away from the table and almost dragging the white Irish lace tablecloth with me. I ran upstairs to my bedroom.

My bedroom window faced the river westward. The wallpaper had a teeny tiny pink rose pattern that I got to pick out. I threw myself onto the goose down mattress that had been ordered from the Sears Roebuck catalogue. I fell onto my bed as if falling into a grave.

My parents were silent for a while, but then they commenced to talking again like it was any other day. Later that night, my mother came up to see me, where I was lying on my bed, staring up at the ceiling and at my ceiling fan that was still and silent.

"What is ailing you?" She stood by my bedside with her arms crossed.

How could I tell her? How could I tell her that if I didn't see Halsom again and had to spend the rest of my life in this town I would start walking west and not stop until I walked into the Pacific Ocean? So silly. It was silly to say it and it was just as silly to think about it, but it was what I felt in my heart.

"I don't know, Mama. I'm just sad."

She looked at me, hard. "Well, you just don't have enough to keep yourself busy. We have spoiled you; I tell your father that at least every other day. Tomorrow is Saturday. You'll go to work with your daddy and see some of those mountain families and think about what you've got and stop all that dreaming and moping around. Then, when you get home, we will do your hair up in pin curls for church." Pin curls for church. Mama was a firm believer that a pin curls and a little rouge would fix everything, but I went to work on Saturday morning with my daddy just the same.

The tannery was a busy place, and I suppose she was right in that I could not sit and stew in my own juices with so many people coming in and out and doing business. Daddy had a pile of men working for him, breaking down the wood, running the vats and processing the hides. Of course, he didn't get dirty. He was a businessman, and his job was just to keep it all running smoothly. I would sometimes help with the bookkeeping, letter writing, and office work. Because it was such a busy place, people could be selling apples or baskets, trade a horse and just talking, talking, talking. They did that the most. As I got out the clean white paper to commence writing a letter, the people all got quiet and started craning their necks and looking outside the door. Hearing a big commotion, I stepped out of the office, and what did we all see getting ready to head up the mountain but a big, new, shiny black cookstove. The driver jumped off the wagon.

"Any of you know the King of Free State Holler?" He was reading a scrap of paper.

Do we know the King of Free State Holler? In my fifteen years, I had heard of him but never seen him.

"Ole Abe Peterson?" said Mr. Shifflett, who had brought over a load of wood with his two mules.

"I guess. I was just told to bring this here stove to the tannery where he would pick it up. It's paid for. He bought it."

The men hanging around the tannery shifted and smiled and were a bit worried because they were all figuring in their heads how to unload it.

Well," Daddy said, "if he said he was coming for it, he'll be here."

Abe Peterson and his clan had lived on their mountain, down towards Luray, since the Revolutionary War, and The King of Free State Holler liked to spread his arms wide and tell everyone he owned from mountain to mountain. He was born before the Civil War, had fought in the Union and was the fourth generation of Petersons to live in those mountains along the Hughes River. His house was large with two stories and two stone chimneys on either end. A well built and maintained stone wall surrounded his many gardens and orchards. The generations of Petersons lived in peace and plenty around this patriarch, and they had to depend on no one for their survival. The men farmed, hunted, trapped, gathered ginseng, lumbered, did stonemasonry and carpentry, and ran stills with the main supply routes to Adams's Skyland resort and Nethers. Hundreds of gallons of apple brandy came out of that hollow each year, with people paying two dollars a gallon. Those men would take it to settlements twenty-five miles away. And believe you me, people moved out of the way for them when they were coming down the mountain with keg-laden mules and rifles cradled by Petersons in front and in back.

Their women were blessed too with strong and tall and healthy children and flowers all along their front porches. They even built a school and paid a schoolteacher. They were Biblical.

Daddy was closing up his shop and paying his men when the Peterson wagon came down the mountain with Abe Peterson himself driving it and his five sons walking beside it. It is a shame that there was only me, Daddy, and the driver, who brought the stove, to see what happened next, because this sight stayed with me forever. Without saying a word, those Peterson men pulled out huge log poles from that wagon and commenced to sliding those poles under the stove. The driver jumped up.

"You ain't gonna tell me them boys are going to carry that stove up that mountain?"

It was hard to say where the King of Free State Hollow was looking because his big black hat was shading his eyes. All you could see were his snow-white beard and long white hair. "Last time I looked, they weren't boys." That is all he said. He tipped his hat to my father and me.

"Hello, Abe," said Daddy.

I couldn't believe it. My daddy knew him. I was looking from the King to daddy and those men who were slowly and quietly lifting that stove onto their shoulders and commencing to walk up that mountain. The King clucked to his team of bay horses and swung the wagon behind those boys, leaving us all silent and watching.

The King of Free State Hollow was a man among men. Now, he would have run an out and out war against those government people in the 1930s when over a thousand mountain families were forced off the Blue Ridge to make way for a park. The King of Free Sate Hollow would have run them all back to Washington, D. C.

"Those are real men," said Daddy watching them go and not just because they could lift a 1,200-pound stove.

By the time the government came to the mountains in the 1930s, many were living on lean times, what with the Depression and all, and the chestnut trees dead and prohibition turning lawful men into outlaws. But, of course, those federal agents tried to tell the Petersons that they didn't own a pebble, let alone from mountaintop to mountaintop like Abe Peterson said, though they had been living there since the 1700s. Why, they were descended from a Hessian soldier who switched sides during the Revolutionary War when General George Washington offered those Hessians land for doing so. Buttons from their military coats were found between the house beams. Yet, by 1928, two hundred years later, the federal government was offering people a pittance, mind you, to leave their home places and all that history.

Government people ran the mountaineers off from five counties in the Blue Ridge Mountains with lies. First, they told the families that they could stay and that they would build the Shenandoah National Park around them. Then, they told the families that they could stay awhile and keep on living there until the park came. Then, they told them they had to get out and those that resisted the government got burned out.

When that time of the burning came, in the early 1930s, many families asked if they could take the fence boards or windows or logs since the government people were going to burn it and, well, the families did own it. But the government people said, *No. You cannot have a thing except your personal belongings.* Can you imagine how it would feel to live so close, watching every penny, and then watch your whole life and the lives of all your ancestors burn up before your eyes? The government people were not saving or re-using. They were burning and taking and burning and taking. Just like Sherman.

But in 1918, before all that came to pass, my world was about mooning over Halsom and my life as a young girl in Elkton and watching the King of Free State Hollow drive his team back home across Swift Run Gap when both he and I still ruled our worlds.

The next day Daddy took me down to the apple butter boiling way up in Red Gate to get me away from my mother who was in a dark mood and in bed with a sick headache. It was the best fun in the world, though I hate apple butter. It would take days and days to get the apples ready, let alone the years to get the trees full of apples. There were apples that tasted like pears, and apples so purple they looked black. Winesaps, Sweetins, Black Giants, Stamens, Pippins, and Milams, they just grew here on these mountains. Every home place had apples in those days, and people would bring their extra apples by the cartful.

We got up so early that morning, the house was not yet warm, though I could smell the coffee on the stove. When Daddy made coffee, he put a pinch of cinnamon in it, and I could smell that too. I rolled over in bed, warm under my quilts, which were all scrunched up in my hands. I slept with fists after I started sparking with Halsom. I looked out the window at the leaves a rainbow of colors and that sweet sugar frost on the grass and steam rising from the river so that the world looked like fairyland.

"Come on, Mary. The coffee's ready. We got to get going," Daddy called up the stairs in a whisper so as not to wake Mama.

"I'm coming."

Daddy and I stopped in town so he could check the tire pressure before we headed out on our journey. The first Elkton car garage had opened a few months earlier, and one of the mechanics came out to say hello. "Mr. Jenkins, are you and Mary headed out for a drive on this nice day?"

"Yes, we are. Just checking the pressure. Don't want to get too far along and have a tire go low."

"Of course not. Let me do that for you." He reached around for the pump. "You know, there's been a man come round here asking questions about your tannery and describing your daughter."

I froze.

"Hmmm," said Daddy, "...well?"

"That's it, I reckon, but I thought you should know. He ain't from around here. Talks like he is from up North."

Daddy nodded. "Well, you know where to send him, Clive."

"You two have a good day." He put his rag, stained with oil and gasoline, in the back of his trousers looking at me with an expression that made me squirm.

Chapter 4

Halsom tracked me down for the second time at the schoolyard when the autumn leaves turned brown and were curling on the dead grass. As soon as we got out far enough away from the school and the keen eyes of Miss Halfyard, Ethel, and the boys, who might seem slow-witted but really were not, I turned to him. "How did you know where to find me?"

"I have my ways."

I held his arm tighter, and I felt him pulling me closer to him. "Do my parents know you come for me?"

He looked at me so slow and sweet. "They will."

I felt the surety of his words and the sense that I was riding down the river on one of those logs with a sense of freedom and a sense of recklessness. We walked down the old schoolhouse road. Even though people used the big wagon road, there was still a nice path, no bigger than a deer trail, running through the woods and down to town. We scared up a covey of grouse that burst through the underbrush like shotgun pellets. I watched them scatter and disappear into the trees as if they were never there.

"Let's sit for a moment," he said.

We took a seat on an old maple log that was covered with moss and rock tripe, a kind of mushroom you can eat, I suppose, if you're starving to death. I smoothed my skirt out underneath me, careful to keep my legs covered.

"I'm not able to get you out of my mind, my sweet Mary. I think about you all the time. All the time." He gathered up my hand and began rubbing the back of my hand with his long, tan, and rough fingers.

I swallowed hard. My throat was dry. "I think about you, too," I finally whispered. I longed for him like I longed for the woods and the mountains, with a yearning so bad I felt I could jump out of my skin if it was not satisfied.

"Well, that's good." He laughed. "I'll be staying in Elkton for a while, and I was hoping we would see each other regular."

I was sneaking glances at his face. "Yes," I said, sealing my fate.

"Good." He lifted my chin, and I knew what was coming.

My heart and body melted with a warmth, sting, prickle, and quiver that made me feel dizzy, like all the blood was rushing out of my head and pooling in some place lower. I kissed him back, and it felt as natural as brushing my hair. He chewed and sucked on my lip and played with the curls of my hair. Then his tongue, like a serpent, flicked into my mouth and danced with my own tongue both teasing, and hard and I think I blacked out. Oh, I felt very bad for feeling like I was on fire, but I wanted more of whatever he had.

Being enchanted by him was so incredible and yet I felt so alone by it, and what made it worse is that feeling tied me to him because I thought it was all tied up in him, and I thought it was love. His kisses continued on so very, very soft. Later, his lips on my body were like a caress. His kisses on my places that I didn't know could be kissed made the world stop moving. And that is all I'm going to say about it.

He smoothed back my hair, putting a lock of it behind my ear, and ran his finger down the side of my face. "Let me walk you home and see your parents."

All at the same time, I was giddy and excited and thinking that was the worst idea in the world. We got up from the forest floor, and he swooped me up in his arms carrying me like a child, and I placed my arms around his neck and buried my head into his chest. His shirt was open and the skin on his chest smelled so good. It was a deep musky and satisfying smell that filled me. Like the woods itself, he smelled both strong like oak leaves and the green notes of newly cut hay. When he put me down, I reached up to kiss him again.

At the foot of my parents' house, I was so filled with him that I ran in the door, slamming it against the wall.

"Mama," I called, "Mama, I have someone I want you to meet." I went through the parlor and on out through the kitchen and back out through the back door, because she was taking clothes off the line by the summer kitchen.

"Stop shouting, the neighbors will hear you. And come help me."

"But I have got someone I want you to meet, and he is standing on our porch."

"What are you talking about? And stop pulling me. Here, take this basket."

We walked into the house, and I put the basket down by the ironing board in the kitchen. My mother smoothed out her hair and took off her apron.

"Who is here?" She straightened out her dress as we walked to the parlor.

"You'll see," I said this as if I was bringing home the prodigal son, and, I suppose, I was, but not ours.

She was half annoyed and half curious, and she swung open the front door and I saw her back straighten and her shoulders go rigid as soon as she saw him.

"How do you do, Mrs. Jenkins." He bowed a bit to her and stuck out his hand. "I'm Halsom Redding, and I'm here to court your daughter."

My mother looked at me as if she was struck by the Rapture. She looked back at him, and she raised her hand a bit as if her good manners could not but help her from shaking Halsom's hand that was held out to her.

"I...well..." Her shoulders relaxed down a bit as Halsom kept his gaze and smile upon her steady. I watched him snake charm my mother. It reminded me of an osprey catching a fish on the river, smooth, direct, and deliberate, with more grace than cunning, but ever so swift. He was so close to her, holding her hand softly, and gazing at her steadily with that smile that must have made my mother feel she was the most important person in his universe; I watched with awe and jealousy, as I thought that look had just been for me.

"Well, I guess... well, come in, Mr. Redding," she finally said, and he was invited in, and he crossed over the threshold of the house.

My mother was very proud of her parlor, though she would not consider herself vain, and she would never confess it. Daddy had sent to Charlottesville for furniture covered in maroon velvet. Intricately carved woodwork covered the back and sides of the claw-footed sofa, loveseat, and chair. The rug was *oriental,* she told people, and was white, red, and blue in patterns that I would stare at when Johnathan Abel and his father came over to visit. Following the patterns made me dizzy but in a good way. Gas lamps and two marble tables sat prominently in the room. The walls alternated between wainscoting and brocade wallpaper, and the windows had heavy drapes that my mother tied back every morning.

"What fine taste you have. Is your rug from Peking?" Halsom looked around and settled his eyes again on my mother. He had an air of self-assurance as if he knew everything about rugs from Peking, and he strode around the room, shoulders back, and fingering the velvet, letting his hands glide over the furniture as he kept his eyes steadily on my mother.

"Why, yes. I do believe it may have come from there, but my husband believes it is from Turkey."

My mother was returning to herself. She sat on the edge of her red velvet chair, and Halsom and I sat on the couch, a respectable distance between us. Halsom positioned himself closest to her.

"You have a very pretty daughter, and I can see where she gets her beautiful hair from."

My mother's hand fluttered to her face. "Yes, I suppose," she said brightening, "We Dove girls were known for our hair!"

Who was this woman? I thought to myself, but I didn't waste much time thinking about that. I was watching Halsom devour my mother.

"I knew Quentin Dove a few years back. I believe his family came from Eaton Hollow. Do you know him?" Something in me made me feel like he was making this up.

"I don't believe that I do."

"Well, Mrs. Jenkins, I can see that we caught you in the middle of your wash day, so I'm not going to waste any of your time. I'm sure you have your irons sitting on the stove right now."

He said, *we.* I stopped watching him like he was in a movie. Coming right back into myself and my body. *I'm going to die right now, I'm so happy.*

"I would be very pleased if you'd let me call on your daughter. I realize you don't know me, but I can assure you I have noble intentions. For some things," he added with a laugh, "and I'd just like the privilege of spending time with your daughter, under your supervision, of course."

"I don't know. I mean, I need to discuss this with her father. Where are you from, Mr. Redding?" she looked intently at him now.

"I'm from... "

I was on the edge of my seat, too.

"...New York."

He might as well have said he was from Hell.

"New York?!" My mother cried out, and for a moment, I thought all was lost.

Halsom chuckled and inched to the edge of the sofa so he could be closer to my mother. He took up both of her hands. My mother straightened up but didn't pull them away. He told her about his heartbreak over the War and fighting brother against brother, his plans for a lumber business, and his admiration for my father's successful enterprise.

"You're right, Mr. Redding. He is known up and down this valley. You know both our families have been in this valley since before The War. My grandfather fought in The War at the battle of Port Republic. We remember The War here, Mr. Redding."

Good grief, I thought to myself rolling my eyes.

"I know you do. A terrible thing Sherman did to the Valley. All that burning. Unforgiveable. I know God will never forgive us for fighting brother against brother."

He was in, I thought to myself.

"You are so right."

And just then, my father walked through the door as he did every afternoon at the civilized hour of 5:00 p. m., carrying the paper under his arm. He was momentarily surprised to see us in the front room so early in the evening.

"Why, John, I'm so glad you are home." My father looked at my mother amused and surprised.

"Yes?" he said looking at me and Halsom. It was obvious neither one of them remembered him from Court Square. Halsom was a conjurer for sure.

"John, this is Mr. Halsom Redding. He is here to start a business. He is in the lumber trade." She smiled at him with a look I had never seen before. My father looked unperturbed.

"Oh, how do you do?" he tucked the paper under his arm and held out his hand. "Are you looking to do business here in Elkton, because we already have..."

"No, sir. I'm looking down towards Waynesboro, maybe as far down as Buchanan."

"Ah, good. There's a lot of business to be had down there, what with the new rail lines and timber companies."

"Yes, there is," said Halsom

"So, what can we do for you Mr. Redding?" asked my father.

"Well, John, he would like to call on our daughter."

My father nodded and looked at me, and my pleading face, and at my mother, then back at Halsom. "What would you like, Missy?"

"John!" said my mother. She turned to Halsom. "I will discuss this proposition with my husband, Mr. Halsom. I mean, Mr. Redding."

"I completely understand. You just let me know. I'm staying down at the Elkton Inn." Halsom stood up to leave.

"Mr. Redding," my mother called after him.

"Yes?" Halsom turned back to regard mother.

"May I inquire as to your age?"

"I'm..."

We all were looking at him now,

"...Twenty-eight. Good night Mr. Jenkins, Mrs. Jenkins." He tipped his hat and bowed a bit in my mother's direction.

Watching my mother warily, I could not read her. I stood up with Halsom and walked him outside. Night had fallen, but I could make out his face.

"I'll be back. Mark my words, I'm coming for you."

"Please come back, even if they don't let you," I whispered.

"Don't worry. They'll let me."

I watched him put his hat back on his head and saunter away wanting to run after him. I felt like a child left in the woods, alone, frightened, scared, and panicked. I couldn't bear going into that house where I felt more alone than I did in church, and the man who made me feel wanted had vanished into the night air. I put my hand on the oak tree in our front yard and pressed my head against its bark, trying to pull strength from it and taking comfort in its steadfastness. *He will be back, he will be back;* I was hoping to make it true by thinking it.

When I came inside, my mother was back at her ironing and my daddy was sitting with his dram of whiskey, reading the paper as if it were *any other day of the year.* My mother didn't look at me.

"Here, Mama, I will do the ironing for you. You just go and rest."

She shot me a glance, pursed her lips, and wiped her hands on her apron, which she had put back on.

"You just best be careful, Missy. I just don't know, and what will the minister think of this? Our neighbors? I know *my* mother was fifteen years younger than daddy, but ...this is just—"

"But Mama, I don't like Johnathan Abel. Daddy," I pleaded in his direction.

"You just settle down."

"What's the matter, Alma?" my father shouted from the parlor.

"You stay here and finish this." My mother closed the kitchen door and went into the parlor.

I could hear the rustling of my father's paper as he put it down to face my mother.

"John, I just don't know about this." Of course, I was *not* doing the ironing but had pressed my ear to the door. Now, I realize, my mother was wrestling in her mind with two devils, and I think one was maybe being free of me. "She has got no sense, and she is headstrong, thanks to you, and this man is not from around here."

"Well, Alma, there are plenty of people not from around here, and we both know the world is changing. There is good money to be made if you have a head for it."

I was peering through the keyhole and could see my father's knees and my mother's back as she sat catty corner facing him.

"I think he's a rogue," she said.

"Humph. What gives you that impression?" my father picked up his paper.

"I'm not sure. I just have a feeling about him. New York! Who *are* his people? And his age."

"A feeling, Alma? So, if women get the vote are you going to elect the next President of the United States based on a feeling?"

My mother stood up and she was mad. "Well, I expect you to make some inquiries. Do you hear me, John?"

"I expect I will."

I jumped back from the door and spun around to realize I had left that big hot iron on my white shirtdress. Panicked, I leapt for the iron, grabbing it with my bare hand. I screamed as my mother came through the door. I was horrified from the pain and the anticipated wrath for burning my white chemise. Tears were flowing down my face as my mother looked from my hand to the dress, and back to my hand.

"Good grief, Mary, I cannot turn my back on you for a second." She grabbed my arm and yanked me to the water spicket as she began a long fast monologue on the ills of her life and me. As the cold water fell over my hand, I looked into my mother's eyes, which held complete contempt for me. She was so angry that her whole body shook. "I swear, you should have temptation written on your right hand."

She was right. She slathered my hand in honey, but it blistered anyway. The skin never completely healed even though my mother sent away for some special and expensive skin healing cream because she was worried that I wouldn't have the hands of a lady. In a way, I did have temptation written on my hand from that day forward.

I went to school with it bandaged like a white baseball glove. It was my right hand, my writing hand, and that hand was the slippery slope to the end of my school days. No more copying or schoolwork for me. Yet, I did have a bit of celebrity among the girls, but for the boys, Halsom sealed my fate, especially with Johnathan Abel and Preacher Dean. I was *other* now, more so than before. Miss Halfyard regarded me with disdain, half sad, and now convinced that my hand and Halsom proved the point of my inherent waywardness.

Miss Halfyard had made a choice. She was a spinster, committed to it with zeal, and appeared happy in that decision despite its challenges. I wanted to not end up like her or my mother who was mean, dissatisfied, and had sick headaches. But I didn't know how to be the woman I wanted to be which was, basically, to be free like a man.

When Halsom first saw me with my bandaged hand, he said. "How am I going to hold your hand?"

"I guess you will just have to hold the other hand."

"I guess I will just have to think of something else." With a cunning smile, he pulled me to him and pressed his body to mine as his hands ran the length of my back and cupped my bottom, making gentle methodic pulses as I became lightheaded.

Chapter 5

My father didn't see or report any trouble with a *businessman* calling on me. My mother was not so sure. She may have married my father at seventeen, but when it came to sizing people up, she was a good study. It took a long time for me to know what my mother was seeing, what she was afraid of, and how love and marriage are two completely opposite ideas. My mother had often brought up to me that she could have and wanted to marry Maurice Templeton who rode through the Civil War Remembrance Day Parade on his horse making it rear and tipping his hat to the crowds. She, instead, chose my steadfast, unassuming and book reading father, who, I believe, may have been an atheist. He once confessed to me that he could not believe in a God that could harm children, but my mother didn't quibble about such issues. My father showed up to church at weddings and funerals, and my mother made her twice weekly appearances; they were both content.

My parents had another daughter before I was born who sickened and died just shy of her twelfth birthday. This was a child that they begot during their first year of marriage when they still were in love. This girl was as a ghost to me, because I was a late life baby born when my parents were forty. Still, twenty years after her child's death, my mother had pictures of her all over the house. Once, on her death anniversary, my mother told me that she could not believe that she was pregnant with me until the doctor confirmed it at five months. She thought she had stomach cancer. When she was in her dark moods, she reminded me of it often and that I was the one she got when the one she wanted had died.

My dad was briefly in the army, and that was how he met my mother. He was stationed at Fort Pickett and my mother was visiting family when they met at a drug store soda fountain. My mother made him give her his watch so that she knew he would come back to see her.

I heard from my grandmother, her own mother, that my mother used to sneak out her bedroom window to go see him. My father, on the other hand, kept getting his sergeant stripes pulled off for not returning to the base when he was supposed to. So, I get a double dose of impulse, from both of them, though to look at them now you would *never* think my mother sneaked out of anything, let alone her bedroom window. I don't know what my father was thinking when he set eyes on my mother besides her good looks, but I liked knowing that they were both once alive.

I once asked my mother, "Do you love Daddy?"

"You learn to love, Mary, but don't marry a man you have fallen head over heels with. It will be your ruination. It's better if they love you more than you love them. *And* remember, men won't buy the cow if they can get milk for free."

I may not have known much about men, but I could tell the difference with how I felt for Halsom and how I felt with the preacher's son, and being with Halsom was like a first bite of candy. How oatmeal tasted is how it felt to be with Johnathan Abel. My parents' marriage seemed like it would taste like sausage gravy, what you expect, but hard on the stomach. So, it was hard to know what to do, because I had no guidance in these matters.

I thought a lot about love, God, fire, men, and the sensations of my body when I was near Halsom. There has got to be something unnatural when I couldn't remember my own name when he kissed me, but whom could I talk to about this? Ethel? She would have been shocked, as I knew she had only been kissed once. What is this ache that I'm feeling all over as if it is in my very bones? I wanted to walk till the fire and the longing left me. I felt like a hollow deer antler that the mice of the forest had eaten all the marrow out of.

Waiting for Halsom to return one evening, I walked out of the woods on Elk Street by the river, gazing at the peeling paint that resembled skin shingles on the square, squat house of Widow Cubbage's home. I regarded her dark windows. Widow Cubbage was addicted to laudanum, and to see her at the apothecary getting her medicine was to see a once beautiful woman, pale and glassy-eyed vacant, but also burning and unnatural. I have heard it referred to as ghost sickness. I was addicted to Halsom and aching to see him so bad I felt sick and puny. This is what she must feel like in some way. My judgment of her turned into compassion.

I turned my face to the sky, finding delight in catching the first snowflakes of winter on my tongue. The twilight of the winter sky was barren, yet beautiful, providing the twirling flakes of snow a stage as if they were ballerinas. Quietly gliding into my house, I saw Daddy acknowledge me from his paper, and I tiptoed up the stairs so as not to alert my mother, but on the tenth step, there was a crack in the walnut flooring, and I momentarily lost my balance and stepped full on it. The creak was like a bad pull on a violin.

"Mary!"

Freezing, like a statue, my breath was suspended in anticipation of what would come next. "Clean up and set the table or I *will* volunteer you for cleaning the church on Saturday. And for good measure, I 'll have you read the Bible to old lady Wilcox who has got the gout."

"I'll be down in a minute," I called, turning on the light in my room. The lamp cast a soft and comforting glow, and I was glad to be home. I noticed a piece of paper on my bedside table, folded neatly and held in place by my hairbrush which had been moved off of my vanity table. Curious, I gingerly approached it, revealing the words, *tonight-where the cornfield meets the river.* How in the world did this get here? I looked around as my room now felt strange and foreign. My heart was pounding. I tucked Halsom's note into my chemise, next to my left breast and planned my escape as my heart continued to pound in my ears.

Chapter 6

That night, Halsom's kisses were as far removed from reading to old ladies as I could ever get. Our romance progressed, the regularity of his visits gave me some comfort, and he had a lot of money to spend. When we were not meeting in the dark of the night, he would show up to the house with a gift for me and good tobacco for my father or candied almonds for my mother. He came to the house just often enough to give me messages as to where to meet him. Sometimes that would be down by the river, by the rolling green banks covered with meadow grass, the dried stalks of red Indian paintbrush and Sweet Annie. Sometimes I would meet him in the woods, where the world smelled like earth and pine, but it was cold now.

"Progress is coming to this Godforsaken backwards place," he told me.

And I didn't need a crystal ball to see the world was changing, with zippers, toasters, the silent movies, and automobiles giving people the movement of the Gods.

"I've been doing some speculating, and I'm going to make me a pile of money in this valley. I wonder if your father would like to invest in a business venture?" Halsom looked at me.

I was not quite sure what a venture was or how this was actually going to happen. My father never talked business to my mother, and she never asked. But business ventures and money were not the only things on Halsom's mind.

During a warm spell, a time out of time, the air felt almost balmy, and the winter sun on my face felt as if spring might not have forgotten the world. I was even wearing my spring coat as it was too warm for my winter coat, and no mittens or itchy wool hat, either. Halsom and I walked the woods at the foot of the mountain. Finding a deer path, no wider than six inches, I led him up the mountain till we got to the panther ledge that overlooked a mountain valley between two ridge lines. I had come up here many a time but never with anyone. I was showing him all my secret places.

"Where are you leading me, little girl?" he stopped to catch his breath.

"To the edge of the world."

The panther ledge was a ten-foot ledge made of granite, rock, and shale and, when we finally reached it and the warm sunshine hit our faces, he let out a wide grin as he surveyed the expanse of my beautiful Virginia that lay spread out before him. The pale yellow of the sun contrasted with all the ashen bark of the trees. The boulders glowed blue-gray like the color of Halsom's eyes. We were staring down into a valley inside the mountains that was all woods as far as the eye could see. I could hear my heart pumping in my head from the uphill climb, and I caught Halsom gasping for air even as he lit a cigarette and pitched the match over the ledge. I was surprised that it bothered me.

"I wonder if this is what the Indians lived in and the first settlers," I said turning to him, "all wilderness—no house, church, street..." My voice trailed off, as this sight always took my breath away.

He looked at me. "Come here." He pulled his damp shirt off of his back and threw it to the side of the ledge. "Take your dress off and feel the sweet sun on your skin." Just then a breeze blew over the ledge and it brought goose bumps up over my arms. "Here, I'll help you."

He undressed me and let my clothes fall down to my ankles. I stepped out of the pile of my skirts and chemise and over to him as naked as I ever was, but instead of scared or frightened or ashamed, I was completely and totally full of power and awe. As the wind swirled around me and the warmth of the sun heated my skin, my breasts, and my legs and back, I looked over my universe and my bare-chested man and felt like a goddess.

Just then, a red-tailed hawk flew out of the tree behind us, startling us both as it took flight.

"It would take us hours to reach the valley, and look, he's already there." Halsom studied on this, and a darkness came over his face. "Damn bird," he said.

"Come here." He grabbed my hand and pulled me to him.

The hair on his chest felt foreign to my skin and against my own breasts and I melted into him just the same, running my left hand over the taut muscles of his arms. I could not stop myself from touching him or wanting him to touch me.

He pulled away from me and undid his trousers, letting them fall and we were now both standing naked on the panther ledge. Slyly, I let my eyes run over his body. So, this is what a man looks like.

I kissed him and closed my eyes to let myself better feel what his kisses were doing to me. He laid me down on those hard rocks, and he cleaved me in two. My scream rocked and echoed from hill to hill, and I was more alive than I had ever been in my life. My head rocked back, and my spine arched so I could thrust my hips closer to him. I was overtaken by a force so much bigger than myself that somehow this force contained him and the whole forest and mountains, and I was no longer in my body but a part of the entire universe.

Even though it hurt, I wanted to do it again and again and again. So, we did, till we were both pale, spent, cold, and half dead.

When we finally left the panther ledge, the air was getting cool, and the sun had moved west. We were both in a bit of daze, love-drunk. I tried to focus on a maple tree that was sheltered and still had most of its leaves, but the colors were so bright that when I beheld it, I felt I had died inside a rainbow. The call of the circling hawk, the crunching of the leaves under our feet, and Halsom's breathing were the only sounds I could hear, and they were all throbbing in my ears. The blood moon was rising in the night sky. I wanted him to carry me, to absorb me into himself so that I didn't have to be Mary ever again.

"Tell me about New York," I said to break our silence.

"Nothing to tell. It's crowded and noisy and dirty. It has more people than you can fancy in your life. And they are always aching and rushing to go someplace, pushing into you on the sidewalks. People of all different shapes and sizes and talking different languages, people from as far away as Asia or Africa. There're a lot of smells, too. You can buy hot roasted chestnuts on the street in winter and can smell coal and wood smoke in the air. If you go to Central Park, you see where the rich people live with fancy carriages, and the women wear fur coats when they go out. Then you get down to the Lower East Side where I'm from, and that's different."

"How different?"

"It smells different, piss and cooking, garbage rotting in the streets. I had to scrape to get by and grew up learning how to use my fists and smarts or I wouldn't make it. I remember seeing a nine-year-old girl get run over by a horse and wagon on the Bowery. Her parents didn't shed a tear but went to court over getting insurance money."

I didn't know what to say to that. "Are your mom and dad still there? Your family?"

"The only family I need now is you," he said drawing me to him.

Chapter 7

I didn't see him again for over two weeks, and when he returned to me, he was not so lovey-dovey. His face was like stone and his eyes were so dark that they looked black like a snake's eyes with no pupils.

"What's wrong, Halsom?"

He didn't answer.

"Are you mad at me? Did I do something?"

"A woman is always doing something to aggravate a man. Stop talking."

What did I know of the problems of men? I tried to make him laugh, but when that didn't work, I just worried right on beside him. He seemed beyond cheering. I asked about who was doing him wrong, because there always seemed to be someone or something at the root of his anger. He ignored me.

We were in the parlor of my home, and both my parents were gone as it was my mother's Tuesday Bridge Club and my Daddy's long workday.

"I know what would make me feel better." He said this to me without a smile and pulled my dress off my shoulders without soft sweet kisses and kicked my legs open while pushing me down on my mother's maroon velvet couch. This didn't feel like love or anything, and as his heaviness overpowered me, I heard my mother's voice. *Mary, once you have intimacies with a man you cannot go back to holding hands.*

"Halsom, Stop! My parents could come home." I tried to push him off me, but it was no use and this time the whole business was over quick, and I didn't feel a part of anything.

As he tucked his shirt back in his trousers, he studied me, as it was obvious to him that I wasn't feeling in love at that moment.

"Come here." But I did not. "You're such a little girl; you don't understand nothing. Grow up."

I watched him rolling a cigarette and getting ready to step outside to smoke. "Come here," he said again and when I didn't move, he came to me and grabbed me up and kissed me with such force my lips hurt.

"You love me?" he asked.

I nodded, but I wasn't so sure.

"Good."

As he got ready to open the front door, he turned to me. "Now, have you mentioned to your daddy about my investments? I want to talk to him, man-to-man about it. Got it?"

I nodded.

He leaned back and regarded me. Smiling, he tipped his hat to me, which was an odd gesture. The lace curtain fluttered as he slammed the front door, and I got busy picking up my mother's throw pillows and doilies. Running myself a hot bath, I couldn't get the water hot enough to make myself feel better.

My mother eyed me when she walked in the door, pulling off her fur collared coat, removing her kidskin gloves and placing them, with her hat, on the table by the front door.

"Mary, did you see that they are building onto the girls' college in Harrisonburg?" Daddy asked as he waved his newspaper at me.

"Go put on your blue dress; we have company for dinner tonight," my mother said, not even looking at me. "Johnathan Abel and his father are coming for supper. Now, clean up and brush your hair."

"Mama..."

"Do as I say and do not sass." Her eyes cut into me and after Halsom manhandling me, I had a funny feeling as if I was invisible, and didn't know who or what I was, not belonging to anyone or anything. Muttering "damn her," under my breath, I climbed the stairs.

"What did you say?" my mother yelled.

I turned back and looked at my father who was smirking. "Just hope I can get this knot out of my hair."

"That had better be all that you said because you are not too old to have your mouth washed out. You hear me, Missy?" my mother called up the stairs.

I snickered as I went to my room thinking my mother was as out of touch with me, my life, and the universe in general. But she got her revenge.

Chapter 8

The gas lights flickered as my mother brought out her roast chicken, a company meal, biscuits and gravy, fried apples, and green tomato preserves. A vanilla pound cake was for dessert, which she was serving with coffee. My mother was an excellent cook and, though she would not admit it, she took pride in her cooking, and she could cook a meal, so everything was ready at the same time. As Daddy, Preacher Dean, Johnathan Abel, and I sat at my mother's table, Preacher Dean said a forever grace, meaning it goes on forever.

"Be present at our table, Lord. Be here and everywhere adored. Your mercies bless, and grant that we may feast in Paradise with Thee, and may strengthened for thy service be. Bless the Lord, O my soul, and all that is within me, bless his holy name. Bless the Lord, O my soul, and forget not all his benefits. Blessed be God, eternal king, for these and all his good gifts to us. Our Dear Heavenly Father, we thank Thee for this food. Feed our souls on the bread of life and help us to do our part in kind words and loving deeds..."

What felt like thirteen lifetimes later, this grace ended, and my father carved the chicken, passing around the plates. I did notice that Johnathan Able was not looking at me as he usually did. In fact, he didn't glance my way at all. Well, that was fine with me, one less worry. Actually, this gave me the opportunity to study him. I suppose he was nice enough looking, yet I knew if I married him, I would be very unhappy. I would be lying to him and to myself because, I didn't believe in the Bible word for word like they did. I didn't want to be the woman the Bible kept pushing women to be and being in church was like being suffocated, slowly. I knew, like I knew the color of my eyes, that being with him was not the road God gave me to walk, or the desire to do it, or the attraction.

After dinner, we all sat around the parlor, and still, he would not look at me. I have got to admit I was beginning to wonder what was going on. I wasn't going to let a sleeping dog lie.

"Mary, can you go fix us our coffee and slice that cake for me?" my mother asked. "Johnathan Abel, you go on and help her."

We rose obediently, our parents smiling after us. As I began getting down the cake plates from the side table, I turned to him, "What's wrong with you, Johnathan Abel? Cat got your tongue?"

"Nothing," he said simply and firmly, but there was a tone and a feeling I got when he said it that made me know there was something. A woman should always pay attention to her intuition.

"Something's wrong. You got a stomachache?" I turned to him.

"I got an ache all right." He pushed up against me, grabbed my hand and put it on his pants. I jumped back so surprised and a bit scared; it was like I had been burned all over.

"What's wrong with you?"

He sneered at me. "Well, you give it away to him you can give it to me too."

My face got flaming hot and I turned my back on him. I fumbled with the plates and holding my head down, I pushed past him and into the parlor. My mother glanced at me looking at my face, but I turned from her and ran back into the kitchen. "Bring out those cups and saucers." My eyes were averted from him.

I came back out with the beautiful yellow pound cake, which smelled like butter and vanilla and was dusted with sugar.

"Please slice the cake for us."

The grown-ups' talk was buzzing in my ears. I felt hot and sweaty and chilled all at the same time. I also felt a bit sick to my stomach, and I didn't cut myself a nice big slice of that pound cake. My world turned that night and would never be the same ever again. To this day, when I think about it, I get a bit queasy.

Later that night, when Johnathan Abel and his daddy had left, I had finished clearing the table, helping my mother with the dishes, and putting her dining room back right again, I laid in bed with my hands on my stomach. A gnawing worry was growing within me. I searched my room in the darkness and this dread was building and filling up all of the air in the room. I threw the quilt back and opened up the window letting the cold winter air slap me in the face, and I took long draughts of it, filling my lungs.

I grew up that night, all right. I went from a young girl holding the world by the tail to what, at the time, felt like an old woman. It was the night my spirit first shook. I knew in my head and my heart I had jumped off the railroad tracks, and I would be off the rail lines for the remainder of my days.

Chapter 9

The full knowledge of my fate was known to me as the world prepared to celebrate Christmas and the birth of light. The town had decorated the streetlamps with evergreens and red ribbons. This was the only time of the year my mother condoned my wood-walking. I left the house early and made trips back and forth to the woods to bring my mother pine boughs, creeping cedar, and holly branches with bright red berries, and she would put bayberry candles in the windows. I went through these motions as if I were sleepwalking, and I didn't wake up until I saw Halsom on Christmas Eve. When he twirled my hair in his fingers, I was safe.

My parents were always up by 6:30 am., which meant that they were in their separate bedrooms by 8:30 every evening except summer. Halsom and I would wait until we could not hear the creaking of floorboards upstairs and then, lying back and into Halsom's arms, I would feel the warmth of his body right there in my parents' parlor. As we watched the candles flicker and the sweet, piney, and bitter smell of bayberry fill the room, I wished I could die right then and there and know peace forever, but that was not to be. I took a deep breath.

"Halsom, I'm pregnant."

For a moment, time stood still. I'm sure of it. He raised himself on his elbow to look at me while my parents slept on. "Is that a fact," he said calmly.

I nodded.

"How do I know it's mine?"

I sucked in air like I had been punched in the stomach and my jaw dropped open in shock.

"Well?" He looked at me seriously, straight on and without a smile. I couldn't talk, as I never even dreamed such a though could even cross his mind. Big fat tears dripped off my face and splashed onto my hands, which I had placed demurely in my lap.

Taking that as my answer, he said, "Let me think on this."

We sat on the love seat quietly for what seemed like a very long time. "I guess I best getting on my way." He rose and walked out the door.

I'm not sure what I expected. I climbed the walnut staircase and could barely lift my feet, covering my mouth with my hands so my parents could not hear my sobs. I went to bed but didn't sleep, and the morning light hit me like a sword directly from God's hand.

"Hello, Missy," my precious, beautiful daddy said to me the next day while he was drinking his morning coffee, and I could not bear it. I burst into tears and ran straight away to my room, where I could hear my parent's voices through the heating grate.

"Oh, dear," he said to my mother as he tapped his soft-boiled egg, "I think we have our first broken heart." I could imagine my mother looking up from her sewing, which was something she always did in the morning because she said she was *fresh* and had the patience for it. "Good riddance."

I hated her, but the terror of the situation I was in outweighed even my long-standing hate.

I went to school and did my chores in a world that didn't resemble my world anymore. Half of me tried to pretend everything was fine, and it was not really happening, and half of me thought about jumping into the river with rocks in all my pockets. And all of me strained for any sign of him.

It was about two weeks later, on one of those God-awful Wednesdays, when Johnathan Abel and his dad were over. We were all sitting around the table, and I was moving food from one side of my plate to the other. Thankfully, my mother was too prideful and aware of proper behavior to call anyone's attention to me though she shot me a glance when she saw me hide my peas under my mashed potatoes.

"I hear that our speculator has cleared out of town," said Preacher Dean, wiping his lips.

"Which one is that?" asked Daddy. "We have so many these days."

"That carpetbagger that was sparking around your daughter," he said laughing.

"He did say he was looking for timber tracts below Waynesboro. He seemed to know what he was talking about. You can't fault a man for trying to start a business. I'm damn lucky my great-granddaddy knew what he was doing and started this tannery. A turn-key business practically runs itself when it's managed right."

"John..." my mother said.

"Oh, excuse me, Preacher."

I was digging my fingernails into the flesh of my thighs to keep from screaming. "Mama, I need to be excused. I don't feel well." I jumped up from the table sending the whole table into spasms.

"Mary, really!"

I hurried through the kitchen and looked out past the red and white kitchen curtains to the dark night. I could still hear them talking.

"Young girls, Preacher. Be thankful that you have yourself a boy with a good head on his shoulders," my mother said.

"I am. Perhaps now our Mary will settle down and get her head out of the clouds. John Abel, why don't you go see to her and make this an opportunity for yourself," said his father. "Maybe we can forget all this foolishness and just worry about planning a nice June wedding. Marriage will settle that girl down. Mark my words, as said in Ephesians 5:22."

"I do believe you're right. Mary has always had her head on fanciful things. I believe her father has been too permissive with her letting her run wild in the woods and read the *Washington Post,* for goodness' sake. Filled her head up."

"Alma, really," Daddy said.

"The only thing a woman needs to read is the Bible and maybe the *Elkton News Gazette.*" Preacher Dean said with a laugh.

I heard my mother reply, "Amen," as I pushed open the kitchen door and went out into the dark night.

Right on my heels, the door squeaked open again. I turned on Johnathan Abel like a caged animal when I saw him. "Get away from me."

"What's the matter?" he said softly.

I couldn't reply to that.

"You know he was not right for you. He was too old, for one thing, and from New York. He probably can have a ton of fancy women. He probably *has* a ton of fancy woman. You just need to get your head out of the clouds and face the facts. We are right for each other, and our parents feel we should get hitched before you get yourself into more trouble."

I flew at him with fists flying in a rage born of the first rages of women. He bore my fists and blows and screams and tears with stoicism. His shoulders were big enough, as my grandmother used to say, but I hated him. Finally, he grabbed my arms and I collapsed into grief filled sobs.

"I'll still have you."

That undid me. I was not so special anymore. He held me and patted my head like I was a baby.

"There, there, now, Mary. It's going to be just fine."

I thought about it later that night as I was lying in my bed, if that was expected or unexpected? But regardless of whatever heart space it came from inside of him, I seemed to think his offer reflected a weakness and not undying love. But I'm no saint. In the dark hours that followed that night, I admit, I considered it, especially as I wondered if my mother would poison me when she found out, as she would not be able to live through the shame and embarrassment. I would rather be dead then face my father, and I buried my head in the pillow to stifle my sobs. Terror shaking my body, I started pacing my room thinking I could probably convince them all to get us married next month, and Johnathan Abel would not be the first man to not know his baby, and even if he did, he would never mention it. The horror of that life married to Johnathan Abel, smiling at church three days a week, visiting the congregation, and pretending I wanted to be there, having to bare him heaving on me, I considered it with all my other options.

Terrified, I began to think how I could commit suicide, but that would bring shame to my father. Pleating my nightgown with nervous fingers, I hung on to the hope that Halsom was coming, and I willed my thoughts to him, *come back, come back, come back,* like I was reciting a spell. Hour after hour, my bedside clock ticked on as I chewed my fingers to bloody shreds and my brain spun out of control like a snake eating its tail. By morning, I decided I could not do it, deceive Johnathan Abel, and live a lie, but every time I thought about facing my daddy, I died a thousand deaths.

And then it came to me, I would go see Granny Hite in Beldor Hollow.

Chapter 10

The next morning, I dressed for a long walk, because I really didn't know where I was heading, just east and then up the mountain and back into Sandy Bottom on the south side of Swift Run Gap. The stories I heard about Beldor and Sandy Bottom didn't scare me away, because I was desperate, and I was already walking with my sin, so it all didn't matter. I was careful to skirt in and out of the woods so that I would not be spied by anyone, and once I got past the old Lam house, I knew I was free from town, and the mountain people would not tell tales to my people. Walking uphill and all that huffing and puffing in the cold made me perspire and gave me chills all at the same time. Then, when I got a moment's break from that, the dry heaves would come on me and I would begin coughing spittle and sour bile. I was sure I was being punished and rightly so. I stood bent over and gasping, trying to catch my breath.

Rising up, I looked around me, the magnificence of the mountain, as pure as the virgin herself, had me in awe. The trees looked like crepe paper, and a hoary frost had sugarcoated the leaves and branches. Lichen glowed green as if lit up from within, and the thundering of a pileated woodpecker was the only sound breaking the silence. It felt like a cathedral, and I knew this was the only way I could ever find God; for a brief moment I was as safe as a baby in a cradle.

Yet, even with the sense of peace and solitude, quiet, and walking, without a soul or home place or even a chipmunk to rest my eyes on for comfort, I knew I was and had always been this alone. I wondered if this is what it feels like when we are born and when we die.

Up, down, over tree limb, stick, boulder, washed away trail and feeling every rock and pebble under my shoe, I walked till I got to the clapboard Mennonite church in Sandy Bottom. Can you believe those Mennonites missioned into the mountains to try and convert the mountaineers? I guess I don't need to tell you how successful that was, but some of those Mennonites, with their old-timey clothes, stayed in the mountain. I sat on the steps of that church for a while to rest, wondering if I had made an even bigger mistake coming up here. I started crying like a ninny. I had been walking for almost four hours.

The woods were so hushed. Flakes of snow had been fluttering down hit and miss all day. The snowflakes looked like bits of cotton candy, which made me think of the times my daddy took me to the fair, me holding his hand and feeling like I had the world by the tail. Cotton candy, candy apples and my pretty pink dress and little lace-up brown shoes. The horror, the desperation of the predicament I was in was too much for me to bear, and I prayed to God that if he was truly merciful, he would just let me freeze to death; I could take it, but spare my daddy. I have only felt this soul-crushing despair three times in my life, and being pregnant on that church step was one of them. Feeling so much hopelessness is a feeling I would not wish on my worst enemy, not even Halsom, whom I blamed for leaving me and not even looking back.

I heard a horse snort and my head whirled around. Through the snowfall I saw the outline of a man emerge from the tree line. Dressed all in black with hat, oilskin coat falling to his feet, and a jet-black horse, he seemed a forest spirit. I jumped up. He wheeled his horse around beside me, and his horse bellowed gray plumes in my direction.

"I don't mean to be trespassing. I'm just looking for Granny Hite." I was met with silence. "Can you tell me which direction to go?"

The church sat at a tee. I could take the road that ran along the base of the mountain heading southward, or I could take the road that went straight up the mountain eastward. I was wondering if he heard me or was deaf or feeble minded.

"You'll find her that way," he finally said motioning his head to the east. "Her kin live along here." He nodded his head towards some small houses behind the church.

I looked in the direction of the jutted road heading up and into the mountain with bent and leafless trees shading and darkening each side. "How far up?" I asked.

He shrugged his shoulders. "Far enough. I'm going past there. Here, get up." He held out his gloved hand to me. I regarded him. I did the opposite of what my heart was telling me to do, just like when I met Halsom.

"No, I'll walk."

"Suit yourself." He wheeled his horse around behind me and I started walking up that road, now more worried about that horse and him than my business at hand. I turned around to shoot him a look and nearly fell flat on my face tripping over the rocks.

"Maybe I'll take that ride." I tried not to cry, as my knee burned where I had fallen on it. I was sniveling again and wiping snow and mud from my knees.

"Maybe I won't give you one now," he said, without a bit of humor.

I knew then and there I had no business being here. These mountains and these people were another country. And with that, I watched his horse's big rump move on up the trail past me and into the tree-lined darkness of the woods. I had walked so far, I could not turn back now, but I was starting to panic; I wanted to bolt like a rabbit. Then, I just did what I learned to do on that day for the rest of my life, put one foot in front of the other, slowly, deliberately. I told myself, *just get through the next five minutes.*

After a good two hours of walking and tripping, I began to see some lumber cuts, and I was hoping that perhaps I was getting closer, and if I wasn't, I was prepared to freeze to death and die. I could not imagine anyone choosing to live so far up and into a mountain, especially an old woman. The road opened into a clearing, and the snow was falling heavier now. I heard a high-pitched scream, and my hair stood up on the back of my neck. Spinning around wildly, I picked up a stick, twirling it above my head like a magic wand.

It was the scream of a panther. Talk about something that would make your hair stand on end; I was terrified in the dark of a mountain and hearing a panther scream. The government said they were extinct, but as we know, the government doesn't know everything. My eyes searched the woods around me. I was so done up by this time, I could have ripped a panther apart with my bare hands. I continued on, grabbing another stick so that I was double armed, and I continued my trek up the mountain, intensely aware of every noise and shadow, ready to meet whatever crossed my path.

I relaxed when I spied the little odd-shaped house sitting in the clearing of a meadow framed by the mountain on three sides. The fence that surrounded the house was as lopsided as the house. I heard a sound and spun around to look. A goat stood eyeing me warily with its head sticking out of a lean-to. I marched up to the dark little cabin, completely determined now, with my footsteps sounding as loud as kettle drums as I climbed the porch steps. I would have thought she would have come to the door. She had to know someone was out here. What if she is dead and I find her? That would just be a hateful turn of events for me all around.

She was not dead. The door opened and revealed the meanest, sourest-looking old woman I had ever seen. How could this woman look at me with such hate when she does not even know me?

"Granny Hite?" I said. Oh God, what is wrong with these mountain people? Her face was severely crinkled, and her doll-like eyes expressionless.

"Who are you?"

"I'm Mary."

"Carrie?"

"Mary, like Jesus's mother, like Mary Magdalene."

Her eyes softened and she stepped aside, and I walked into her house, the door latching behind me. The first thing I felt was the warmth from the small and modest fire burning in her fireplace. The crane held a steaming kettle and a pot. She motioned for me to sit down. I had not realized how numb and cold my feet were as the pain in my toes suddenly became unbearable. She again motioned for me to pull my chair closer to the fire and I did, loosening my coat and scarf.

"Take them off." She pointed to my coat and scarf. "Or you will not be able to make it down the mountain."

Not taking her eyes off me for a minute, I felt like a burglar. I suppose I was. I looked around. A little bed sat next to the wall of the fireplace covered in layers of crazy quilts, yet she had a feather mattress. A big pine table took up most of the space in the middle of the cabin where I sat in one chair, and her chair, at the head of the table, was draped with a red and brown shawl. On a few pegs near the fireplace hung a dress, an apron, and a linen petticoat. Two kerosene lanterns, one on the table and one on the sill of the window, glowed with a bright yellow flame, yet it was kind of hard to see as it seemed like a dreamy twilight inside that cabin.

Garlands of dried apples and string beans, squash, and little tomatoes, some faded red and some yellow hung from the rafters and fireplace mantle along with bouquets of leaves and flowers and stemmy things. About a dozen crocks, placed like soldiers against the wall, with cheesecloth and string tied around the top, were stationed around the cabin. Side meat sat on the table on a walnut cutting board, along with the oldest pair of scissors I had ever seen and a bone-handled knife. This was not a thing like my home, or Ethel's home or Johnathan Abel's or anyone that I ever knew, not even my grandparents, and they were old. On her mantle was a big, beautiful serving plate with flowers of green and pink and gold threading around it. This was as fine as anything Mama had ever owned. Two orange striped cats jumped up from somewhere and sat at my feet looking at me. *She really exists, and she is a by God honest to goodness witch. It is all true.*

"Here, eat this." She swung the crane out and with a rag and opened up the pot ladling out some cornmeal mush which she put in a bowl and slid across the table to me. The warmth of the bowl and steam rising to my face felt so good. I was starving, and I ate it greedily burning the roof of my mouth. She watched me.

"How did you get up here?"
"I walked."
"From where?

"Elm Street."

She was silent for a while, studying me.

"How did you know where to find me?"

"I just walked, and I had a hunch."

"A hunch?" Her eyes bored into me.

"And I heard tales, I mean, some conversations I've heard from people when I go to Daddy's tannery."

"You John Jenkins's daughter?"

"Yes ma'am."

"I know your daddy."

"You do?" I think my eyes must have jumped out of my head.

She nodded. "He's a good man." I nodded, bursting into tears and burying my face in my hands. As I finished blubbering, I wiped my nose and face with the bottom of my skirt. She waited; she had all the time in the world.

"What did you walk so far up this mountain for?"

"I need some help."

"I expect you do. How far along are you?"

"I don't.... I think about three months."

"Who then? or don't you know?" I simply could not believe that old woman had said that to me. "Of course, I know. Who do you think I am?" She gave me her first smile. "You're a spitfire, aren't you? I suppose that's what got you into this way in the first place. At least, that's what got you up this mountain."

I told her of Halsom.

We sat for a while in the quiet of that cabin, the only noise the spitting of the fire as the flames and cinders danced up the chimney. One cat purred. I looked at Granny Hite's hands as they rested on the table, peaceful and quiet. They had no spots on them like I had seen of other old people, but they were a bit gnarled and twisted up like the trunks of old tulip popular trees when they have grown over thirty feet high, and their canopy stretches out above the forest. I have seen those trunks get so big that they crack open, and you can crawl inside and still they live on. Like the trees, the skin on her palms was cleft all over with deep rivers of lines. We sat so long in that silence I wasn't sure she would ever talk again. She had a lot of patience, that old woman. I think she was going to wait for however long it took.

"I want you to give me something that will make it like it never happened," I finally said.

"And you think that is going to make it like it never happened?"

"No," I replied softly. And the deep sadness that I had forgotten in her cabin and in her presence came back over me. "I do believe I'm done for now. It'll never be the same. I will never be the same. I'm ruined." I didn't realize how long I had been holding my breath till I finally said it.

Just then we heard boots scraping on the porch stairs and the heavy steps of those boots on the porch. She never turned around, but my eyes were fixed on that front door, which swung wide open letting in a gust of cold and snow. The snoring cat jumped up, annoyed, and ran under the bed while another cat, a gold one, ran in as if on fire as the black spirit with the red beard came in. "So, she made it up here. I figured she would," he said closing the door.

"You know her?" asked Granny Hite.

"Saw her at the church. Passed her in the woods. Not much stirring in these woods today with that snow falling but I brought you these." He laid three headless, gutted, and skinned squirrels on the table.

"Why, thank yea, warm yourself now." She turned to me. "We best be getting you on your way."

Panic set over me, panic on leaving that cabin, panic on leaving without a chance. She stood up and began shuffling around to the herbs hanging from the rafters, studying them carefully. Walking to her tall maple Flanders cabinet she picked up her scissors and then opened a drawer to a dresser by her bed. Sliding it open she took out a piece of green and black plaid cloth. As she moved around the cabin, my eyes following her every move, she placed her hand on the man's shoulder gently and kissed the top of his head with such love and tenderness I thought I would crack in two for the want of it myself. He regarded me silently. She took the old scissors and snipped some leaves off a bundle of twigs hanging on the wall surveying some jars that were stacked in row on a sideboard, opening, sniffing, crumbling until she found one that satisfied her. Going over to her great wheel, she pulled white and gray Cotswold wool from the spindle, tied the cloth closed, and handed this bundle to me.

I stood up so ashamed and disgraced. The man cocked his head and squinted his eyes at me. I couldn't swallow. Pressing it into my hands and closing my fingers around the bundle she said, "I have no power over God's order of things. It will be what it will be. Make up a strong tea of this and stir it with a knife. Your mother will know the smell so be smart and use your head. This may or may not break the graft." Turning to the man she said, "Do me a favor and take her back down the mountain."

"I expect she can get down the way she got up, but I will do as you ask." He had never taken off his coat, gloves, or hat. Icicles hung from his beard and mustache. I wondered if he was cold or if he was not human, one of those fairy men my grandmother had told me about that look like a human man but are impervious to human discomfort, so part of the woods they are and not of the human race. Reluctantly, I followed him out to the porch, and the swirling snow hit me on the face like catching your hand in a drawer after the warmth of the cabin.

"Can I stay here? With you?" I turned to Granny Hite in a panic, but she was already closing the door behind me; I didn't ever want to leave that mountain.

"Come on, get on the back, behind the saddle." He led me up to this big boned black horse. He got on first and grabbed hold of my arm and lifted me onto the horse's back behind him in one fell swoop. I could not believe he had lifted all of me like I was a little bit, because I was not; I was five-foot-six in my stocking feet. His horse rocked back on its hocks and lunged forward. That big smooth black Tennessee Walker covered the miles down that mountain as if he were walking over the clouds themselves. It didn't trip, not even once, even with balls of snow clodded up in its hooves. I held onto this stranger's jacket, balancing for dear life, as I rolled from one side to the other of the horse's flank. He said not a word to me until we were back at the crossroads of Swift Run, covering what had taken me two hours to walk in what felt like a few minutes.

"This is as far as I'm taking you. You're on your own from here." He grabbed my arm to balance me as I slid off the horse. "I expect you will do just fine."

I couldn't tell if he was grinning at me or not because of his hat shading his eyes and beard concealing his mouth. He swung his horse around, and then he was gone, back the way he had come, into the mountain and the swirling snow.

I hurried down Spotswood Road and to my house. It was dark, and my mother was looking out the window.

"Where have you been? You have *not* been at school all day."

"I was playing in the snow." She slapped me so hard I staggered backwards. I grabbed my face. It was burning. I ran up to my room, closed the door and locked it. She knew, somehow, she knew it all.

"Alma, what did you have to do that for?" I heard my father ask. I wondered if he had lowered his paper.

Later that night, I crept downstairs to the kitchen. There were enough banked coals in the stove to warm some water. I placed the pot directly on the coals, praying it would not scorch the bottom. I sprinkled Granny Hite's leaves in the water and said a prayer. I'm not sure who I said a prayer to, but I prayed anyway. Of course, I checked on the pot every few minutes, which did me no good, letting out the heat. I swished the water around with a knife as she had told me to do. As I waited, I looked out through the dark and shadows feeling almost like a ghost myself. I felt so old and so tired and now I was dead to the girl I was before Halsom. Just months away from my sixteenth birthday, I thought how it could have been filled with a cake party and a new dress, and the cameo my mother had promised to give me that came with her family from across the water and which was given to her, and her mother and her mother before in a line of women stretching further back than time itself. I had broken the chain with disgrace and dishonor.

I looked out into the dark nighttime sky and the brightness of the falling snow, willing my thoughts to Halsom wherever he was, begging him back from living it up with fancy women in big cities or speculating on business ventures, or sitting in barrooms. He could afford loud and easy laughter. As I sent my soul out to search for him, try as I might, I could not distill any sign of him. What greeted me was the dark, cold, lonely silence of my mother's kitchen. My crystal ball was an empty vessel.

When I could not wait any more, with my usual impatience, I got the lukewarm infusion off the coals and poured it into a cup. The bitter minty taste of the herbs overpowered the sweeter leaves. I wondered what Granny meant about my mother knowing the smell. How did my father know the old woman, from the tannery? Well, my father knew everybody, so I should not have been surprised at that. Maybe she meant my mother would know because my mother knew everything. I could not ever imagine that my mother would know Granny Hite, or lower herself to go up the mountain, but maybe she did. And why? My mother was a woman who had tried to keep her distance from farming and the mountain.

As I drained the tea, I swallowed a few leaves though Granny had told me not too. Then I went to bed, hugging my stuffed teddy bear like the child I no longer was.

I felt the same the next morning as I had for every morning since I come to the realization of what had happened to me, trapped. My mother met me immediately as I came down the stairs. She grabbed my ear and dragged me to the table and my oatmeal.

"I don't know what you are up to, but I'll tell you one thing. If you disgrace my family with your shenanigans, I'll send you so far away you will never find your way back. Do you hear me? Mark my words, there are places for girls like you. You better stop acting like a spoiled twelve-year-old and begin acting like the lady you were raised to be. And another thing, I don't care what your father says, your days of traipsing around the woods like some mountain girl are over. Do you hear me?"

Her face was so close to mine, and she had twisted my ear so severely that she damaged the cartilage, because it was lumpy, red, and swollen from that day onwards. But I knew what was at stake for all of us. I nodded mutely. Later that day at school, I excused myself to go to the outhouse. Imagine my joy when on my white drawers was a smear of blood. I started jumping up and down to help matters, coming down hard on the ground with all my force and energy. No more bleeding followed that little spot, but that didn't matter, because within twenty-four hours of coming out of that outhouse, Halsom was at my parents' front door.

My mother pounced on him, and for the first time in my life I heard her raise her voice to someone who was not family. She had always told me that ladies do not raise their voices because they can get much more accomplished in different ways. A scene ensued in her beautiful Victorian parlor with me begging her to stop, and my father finally putting down his paper and stepping in, separating the whole lot of us.

"I'll take care of this Alma, now calm yourself before you get a sick headache. Mr. Redding, it is best that you don't come around here anymore. I'm not a man who likes to make any threats, but I do believe if I see you here again, I will be obliged to keep my wife from hysteria, and if that means calling the sheriff I will. Do you understand me?"

"Yes, sir, I do. May I at least say goodbye to your daughter, and give her this gift that I brought her?" My father nodded and motioned for us to go on the porch.

"My sweet, sweet Mary." Halsom smiled looking into my eyes with a grin so big I felt my heart would burst from happiness. "Did you think I would not come back for you?"

I nodded because I could not talk. "Now, your mother is looking out the curtains, so we need to be quick. You meet me tonight at midnight by the river, over where the landing is. Pack a few things that you may need. I'll buy you anything when we get where we are going."

"Where we going?"

"Across the Alleghenies." He nodded at me and left, pressing a small velvet box into my hand. I inhaled sharply. I was going west into the wilderness. I was too stupid to be anything but excited.

As I went back into the house and shut the door behind me, my mother was waiting for me. "So, what did your carpetbagger bring you?"

I hated her all over again, but I sat down on the sofa and gingerly opened the box. Inside the velvet box was a thin gold chain with a heart shaped locket. My mother eyed it suspiciously. I had to admit I was a bit disappointed, thinking it was a ring, but I put it on around my neck happily nonetheless, and went upstairs triumphantly.

"Don't worry, Alma. I gave word to the Sherriff when I saw him at the Lodge last week. He and his deputies are prepared to run him out of town if they see him. I expect everything will settle down shortly."

"If the Sheriff doesn't, I will. And Redding better hope that he meets up with the Sherriff instead of me."

"Alma," my father said chuckling, "you'd best make yourself a cup of tea or better yet, a brandy, and calm yourself. I do believe you are forgetting your hard-won refinement."

When the house was quiet and still, I stole away from home. There was no moon to see by that night because it was waning, but my eyes were so good back then I could see in a cave. I took one last look at my girlhood room, and for an instant, I was filled with a foreboding, but I quickly pushed it away. I had only one choice now, and as I knew, I would follow Halsom anywhere, even to Hell, which is precisely where he took me.

He was waiting by the river as he promised, silhouetted atop a small horse, a relief against the frozen silver Shenandoah. He held the reins of another horse. He didn't dismount. "Put your stuff in the roan's saddlebags and get up. Come on! Quick!" I did as he told me. "Come on!" he shouted.

I struggled with my skirts, and finally got my foot in the saddle and mounted fearing his palatable impatience. We rode all night, stopping only so we could relieve ourselves, and finally sleeping with blankets on a pile of leaves and pine boughs the second day. The few questions I asked him were answered with grunts or *you'll see.* I was scared, tired and sore, and when we finally reached the foothills of West Virginia three days later, I was sure I was going to slip off that brave little pony that would stop his trot every time he felt me sliding sideways. I could ride, of course, having ridden at my grandparent's farm, but no woman was meant to ride like that. And so began a life of learning to endure that which could not be changed.

Chapter 11

Fayette Coal Camp, West Virginia, March 1918

I'm in the den of the damned.

Fires burn on the mountain and in the tipple; mud, smoke, and coal dust has consumed me. This is not the quaint little town of my childhood. This town is the devil's playground and there is no way out. Halsom and I aren't married, though he keeps promising that he'll marry me. Then, when he is drunk, he says, *I've taken you under my robe*, implying that living with him should be good enough, or some such Biblical nonsense. Even now, decades later, I cannot bear to think about that time in the Coal Camp, and when I do, a black, bleak gloom settles on me like the coal dust that used to cover everything. But just like that coal dust, which would settle in every crack and crevice of my house, and in men's hair, skin and lungs, no matter how I tried to get rid of it, I never could.

The coal camp was a world unto itself, and it didn't run like the regular world. Well, maybe the company had its own ways of living and rules. I had to figure that out, and I had to figure out Halsom's rules which, at least to me, felt like they had no rhyme or reason. He didn't want me to leave the house yet would yell at me if I hadn't gotten any coal for the stove. *Write to your Daddy and get some of that money,* he would yell, and then the next day, he would say, *I'm your family now don't ever write them.* My head would spin like a top, trying to keep pace with everything, including my growing belly, which didn't seem real to me. My baby, whom I named Colin, after my daddy's father, was born in early June. The birth was the most horrible pain that could be endured without dying outright, and when the midwife gave me the child, I regarded it coolly. Motherhood felt like another unreality, and I kept hoping I was dreaming, but I was not.

I remember walking through the coal camp, following behind Halsom, who had not held my hand since we were courting in Elkton, and staring from side to side like I was at a circus. Such sights I had never seen those itty-bitty slap-shod houses all close together; the dirty, muddy coal black puddle oozing streets; and the mountains stripped of trees and belching smoke, and occasionally, fire. Rough looking children played in the streets, hitting each other, and girls carried one-legged dolls through the mud. The women looked at you with hatred, and the men looked at you worse.

The house—well you could hardly call it that—the two rooms we lived in, was tiny and had holes in the walls and a black stove with coal littered all around it and ground into the floor. The wind whipped through the cracks. We had to share an outhouse with other houses on the row, and I'm telling you, it was a filthy mess. I cleaned and scrubbed those two rooms because it was my place with Halsom, and in the beginning, he would work and come home, but then he wouldn't come home.

"You best watch your man," a neighbor woman said. "I hear he is out sparking over in Rum Alley."

Or, even worse, the company thugs would come looking for him, all dressed clean, with dark suits and bowler hats and riding skinny brown horses with rifles tied to the saddles and guns in their holsters like we were in the wild West.

"I don't know where he is." I would say, and that was the God's honest truth.

When he was home, he wouldn't talk to me much, and I would think it was because he was tired. "Halsom, I made soup." And he would walk by me like I was not even there, not even looking at me. Sometimes he was in a really bad mood so that he would come home on a Friday and not leave the bed till Sunday. I kept thinking I must be doing something wrong, and that he was angry with me. There would be times when we would run out of coal, and I would knock on that bedroom door.

"Halsom? Honey? The door would remain shut and locked. "Halsom, we're out of coal for the stove. Halsom?"

Then, in the rain, snow, or sleet, I would walk the streets, at first big and pregnant, then later with little Colin in a sling, picking up any bits and pieces of coal from the gutters and putting it in my apron, with shame and despair, as people looked at me quickly before looking away.

Even so, the first time I went to the company store, I was so proud that Halsom decided to take me out. The company store was the only place we could shop because no one in the row had a car or a mule, and town was a long, long way away. I knew enough though to see that the prices were high for everything. Why, coffee that cost 47 cents a pound in Elkton cost 68 cents in the camp. And those miners didn't make much money, had to pay for their tools and they were always getting hurt. The coal company advanced pay to the workers in something called script, and if you wanted actual dollars, you only got 75 cents to your dollar of script. On payday, the men, or their families, would line up, and once the company had deducted for rent, mining tools, food, or anything else a miner may have bought at the store, there was a big fat zero, or less than zero.

After Colin was born, Halsom got even more distant and wouldn't talk or look at me. "Halsom?" I was bouncing Colin on my knee, as he was now three months old. His eyes lifted from the cabbage that he was eating, looking at me stone faced. "Um, Halsom... why are you not talking to me? Is there anything I can do?" I reached for his hand that was on the table. He withdrew it as if I had leprosy.

His eyes were black and without pupils. "You could die. Yep, that's what you can do." I had a sudden intake of breath. He pushed his chair back getting up from the table.

"Oh, Halsom," I said running over to him and desperately grabbing his arm. "What did I...." but I didn't have a chance to finish. In a flash, he struck me so hard I slid across that floor and into the wall. I sat there a minute, not believing what had just happened. *Oh*, I thought, *oh*. Walking into the bedroom without looking back, he closed the door.

He will kill me. I thought I knew it as certainly as I knew my name. I was not going to live staying with him. I was not his future but a hindrance to his future. With the passion he used to have for loving me, he now was revolted by me. But I kept thinking if I just tried harder and was more careful with my words and actions, I could make him love me again, maybe even like me. I learned to watch him very carefully and watch his moods. I watched his eyes, too, because they would go blank when his darkness was descending.

One of the benefits, I guess, of his ignoring me, and not coming home unless he had to sleep off a drunk, was that I had to fend for myself, which was an odd sort of freedom. I started helping a woman, Maria, with her washing. She was an Italian woman, and she birthed my baby. Maria bore witness to my life and my bruises but never spoke of it. Through her, I became acquainted with her family and neighbors, and being with people cheered me a bit. Maria's family lived, with the other foreigners, on Mott Street, farther down the mountain from us. There were so many people at those camps, and I had never heard those languages spoken before. I fancied it was kind of like being in the middle of New York City. These women showed me how to cook things like lentils and beans, which my mother had never made.

Do you know when Maria came to this country, she didn't speak a lick of English and she was the only one of her people to learn to speak English within two months. It made me sad, though, that the coal camp was all she saw or knew of America. We would tell each other stories of where we grew up, she in a little town of Leporano by the sea. She did most of the talking, because talking about Elkton would make me feel very, very bad, like with no hope and only despair for a companion. She told me stories about her family's gardens, or Campano, and her grandfather bringing home pheasants and little birds to eat. She also told me that she would run away from school and go to the beach. You can see why we got along. Sometimes we would go together to the company store to shop.

"Listen to me. Don't ever come here by yourself. "Maria said.

"Why not?"

She stopped walking and looked around as if searching for words. She turned and faced me directly and put both of her hands on my shoulders. "You should always go with somebody if you don't want the company men to mess with you." I nodded like I knew, but I didn't know.

Yet, having to fend for myself and now my baby, one morning I decided that I was going to do my shopping by myself like a grown-up woman, because I had my own money. I was grown up all right. I washed and brushed my hair and got put on a dress that was so faded and worn I was darning it every week. I thought of my mother and how she dressed when she left the house with her clothes new and pressed. I pushed my homesickness away. I cleaned up my little Colin and put on his cap. Walking gingerly, to avoid the mud, and trying to stay on the wood planks that people had laid down across some of the deeper trenches and rivulets in the road, I made my way to the company store.

It was quiet during the day, though the men worked in shifts, and there were some miners with their families and some women with gaggles of children around them, but as I got closer the store was empty of customers. I climbed the steps of the Whipple Company Store with determination and my little grocery list in hand. How I mulled over that list, crossed things out, rewrote other items. What did I need? What did I want? What could wait till next wash day? That was half of the excitement. It was almost like a game seeing how far I could make the money go.

The door had a little bell that jingled when I entered. I lingered at the counter, admiring a bottle of perfume called First Kiss.

"Whatcha looking at, girlie?"

I whirled around, almost dropping the perfume. The company man was real close to me, so close I could smell his breath, which smelled sour, and I pressed myself to the counter. I stammered, "I was just looking at the perfume. Excuse me." I pushed past him.

I turned to the shopkeeper. "I would like a quarter of a pound of coffee, half a pound of cornmeal, a quarter of a pound of kidney beans."

"We cut your husband off. No credit. He owes the store eighteen dollars and twelve cents." The shopkeeper looked me straight in the eye.

I blinked. My heart began thumping and I heard it in my ears like the coal shovels coming down again and again on the side of the mountain. I had four dollars and eighty-five cents.

"You know," said the company man now standing so close behind I could feel his chest against my back, "we might be able to work something out."

"I can work. I used to do my daddy's bookkeeping back home at his tannery and doing the ordering. I can stock shelves and sweep and ...." My voice trailed off. The man didn't say anything. The shopkeeper was suddenly gone. "Come on. I'll take you upstairs to the offices," said the company man.

We entered an office that was not empty. One man had his feet up on the desk, a gun on his side, and another man was facing him, drinking coffee, and smoking a cigarette. They didn't move when I entered.

"Lookey here, gentlemen, it seems we have a young lady who might want to strike a deal." The two men looked at me. "Well, little lady. You heard of *Esau*?" said one of the men.

"From the Bible? He sold his birthright to his brother."

He grinned. "It's a way to get a little credit at the store."

"I was hoping to work for some money so I wouldn't need to use credit...I used to—"

He cut me off mid-sentence. The stale smoke made it hard to breathe. I looked for an open window.

"We don't care what you used to do. No money exchanges hands here, but we can give you this." He handed me a small piece of stained paper with the word *Esau* scrawled on it as if written by a child. I looked at them and then back to the paper. The man behind the desk stood up. His hand went to his belt, which he started to unbuckle.

"Oh, no." I moved backwards so fast that I tripped and fell to my knees over the first man's feet. They laughed. The floor was so dirty. I scrambled to my feet clutching Colin and tried to push past them but one of them blocked my way. I darted right, but he darted right, their laughter roaring in my ears. Colin started whimpering. Putting my shoulder to the company man's chest I pushed on him with all my force, stumbling down the steps and grabbing the banister so I would not tumble down the stairs.

"She'll be back," I heard them say after me. I heard more laughter.

I was covered in a sweat as I wiped my hands on my dress, smudging brown stains down the side of it. As I ran out of the store, the heel broke off my shoe, causing me to scream in pain as my ankle twisted. I turned to look back at the store. The first man with the gun was out on the porch smoking and leaning against the railing. He was smoking slowly, like he had all the time in the world, as he looked off to the coal smoke belching from the mountain. His hand moved to his mouth where he removed a piece of tobacco and flicked it over the porch. After stretching long and wide, he went back inside.

I held my broken shoe in my hands and stared at it. Short anxious breaths escaped my throat. I looked up at the sky, contemplating a bit of robin's egg blue through the parting clouds. There was one scoop of coal left at the house, no beans, no cornmeal, and definitely no sugar. Halsom had not been home in three days. Kissing Colin on the top of his head, and clamping my teeth tightly, I limped back to the company store.

Chapter 12

It was on a Saturday morning in winter that I heard a knock on the door that changed my life yet again. I had learned to open it only a crack, for many reasons, but most of all because it was so cold in that hollow; I had counted out my coal very carefully for the fire to last. But on this winter morning, it was not some miner collecting a gambling debt, a random woman looking for Halsom, or his foreman dragging him to work. A detective and two officers were standing on the rickety porch.

"Yes?" I said as if I were addressing Bible salesmen.

"Are you Mary Jenkins?" What have I done? I thought frantically, and I turned to look back at Halsom who was tying on his boots to go to work. Halsom stood up and went to the door, and I retreated to the back of the house scared out of my mind. I thought the law had shown up to finally take him away, so you can imagine my surprise when Halsom said, "There she is. Take her."

I held my son, Colin, close. I held onto him for dear life. "Halsom!" I yelled, "Halsom! Do something! Why are they taking me? Am I going to jail?"

"We are taking you back home, Miss Jenkins." Home? What home? I have a home?

Halsom just shrugged at them. "Take her," he said again. Then in a second beat he said, "but you can't take the boy."

The agents gently moved their coats to reveal their guns. "Miss, you go pack your and your youngin's things. This will just take a minute."

"Please, please, please, don't do this, I can't bear it, don't let them take me and the baby." I sobbed in Halsom's direction.

"Miss Jenkins, we have orders to bring both you and your child," the deputy said calmly.

Whatever love Halsom had for me he left up in the woods back on Weaver Hollow in Elkton. From the moment I left with him at the Shenandoah River, the only feelings he ever showed me was contempt. What I could not understand was my own heart in this matter. How could I love a man who treated me with disdain no matter how much I tried to please him? And I did. I tried hard to please him.

It didn't take me too much time to pack, as I had less now than what I came to this mining camp. I wrapped my head in a scarf to hide my face so that all those woman and men of the row wouldn't see me bawling my eyes out. I had hidden some of my washing money in an old shoe that had a hole in it, and when I looked for the three dollars I had saved, it was not there. "Halsom, my money? Where is it?"

"Are you accusing me or something?" I registered this as one completely dumbfounded, the deputies, Halsom's indifference.

Since I was standing, as if I were made of stone, one of the deputies took me by my elbow and guided me to the wagon waiting outside. The other stayed behind in the little coal-fired room with Halsom. As I was walking out, I could hear the deputy say, "Redding? Or should I refer to you as Clarke or Davis or perhaps Mr. Clayton?" That deputy came out directly, and when he slammed the front door, the whole house shook.

With a slap of the reins on those two mules' rumps, the wagon rolled forward, and I just kept my head down buried into my sleeping son's hair. My tears fell like rain rolling down a window and baptizing my son's head. Of course, the people of the row come out to gawk at me as if I was a sideshow in a carnival. Maybe I was a sideshow in a carnival. My man didn't want me.

Going back to Elkton felt agonizingly slower than coming to that coal camp. The unhurried mountainous ride gave me a lot of time to think about what my fate was going to be. Girls just didn't up and run away unless they were a scandal like me. My reputation was ruined, and I was ruined. I was stained beyond redemption. Johnathan Abel wouldn't have me now. No man would. I couldn't go to the teacher's college like my parents planned. Even I didn't want me.

I half hoped, and feared, that Halsom would come after Colin and me, and I got exhausted listening for the fall of a horse's hoofbeats behind us. He always told me he would kill me if I tried to leave. My mind was racing, and my brain had gotten so jumbled by living with him that I wasn't sure what he would do if he came after us. Kill me maybe, and take our boy? Halsom would somehow blame me for this. I knew him. He blamed me for everything, such as running out of food and coal when he had drunk or gambled the money away. That fear of him kept gnawing at me throughout that entire long, long ride back to Virginia.

By and by, the Shenandoah River loomed in the distance as we crossed the Alleghenies. At the very least, it was not as cold on this side of the valley. My heart finally lifted. I was home, whatever that meant to me at the moment. The sight of that river was the most beautiful thing I had seen in over a year. I had forgotten about woods, and mountains not cut up and carved by big machines, and that flowing and churning clear river of all life in my own backyard. For a moment, I was hopeful.

"Where are we going?" I asked as we passed the turnoff to my parents' home.

The deputies looked at each other. Finally, one of them cleared his throat. "We're taking you to your father."

"Oh." I just assumed we were going to my daddy's tannery. I didn't think to question anything else because I was so road-weary from traveling, nursing the baby, and my crying the whole trip missing Halsom, yet relieved to not be with him all at the same time. But we didn't turn towards the road for the tannery either. My shoulders slumped forward. My heart began to beat wildly in my chest as I was looking all around, and we began the climb up Spotswood Trail, past Lam Mill. The men didn't make eye contact with me. Where were they taking me? Had I been indentured to some job somewhere? Where was my daddy? Fresh tears gathered in the corners of my eyes again.

I swear I cannot figure out how women have so much water in our bodies to cry as much as we do. I have come to figure that every time we cry, we cry all the tears for all the women who have walked in our shoes. This thought gave me some comfort at that terrible moment. I wasn't the first, nor would I be the last woman to find myself in this type of trouble.

When we got to top of the ridge, I steeled myself against the thought that I would never ever be going home, and I'd better face whatever came with some courage. Yet, much to my surprise and joy, I saw Daddy standing beside his car once we crested the hill. He was waiting there for me. I didn't take in anything else at that moment. I scrambled off the wagon with my little boy and ran to him. He opened his arms wide, hugging me to him, kissing me on the top of the head, and crying too. How I needed his love.

"Oh, Daddy, I'm so sorry. Please believe me. I'm so sorry. Oh, Daddy, I've missed you so much."

"Shhh," he said, rocking me, and he rocked me in his arms for a long while. He smelled like aftershave. He smelled clean. "My little girl, you're skin and bones. Oh, Mary..." His voice cracked. "Let me take a look at my grandson." He smiled at me, his eyes wet with tears. "Look at that fine head of dark hair...what a handsome little man."

"Why am I not going home? I promise I'll be good, and I won't leave the house so no one can see me and—"

"Well, I'm not sure that would be such a good thing right now, but don't you worry. I've made arrangements for you. You're going to be just fine and provided for. Your mother had, well, it's what the doctors' call a nervous collapse after you left. Took to her room for a while. She is getting better, but the doctor says she can't handle any upsets to her nerves right now. I felt it was best to get you back home and close by and get you settled, then we can see how things go. Don't you fret. Her heart will soften, and she will come back into her right mind. I'm sure of it. In any event, you're back home and safe." He hugged me so tight.

I nodded mutely, and in that instant, I realized what I had done to my parents so many months ago. I had just been thinking of myself. I stood up straighter and looked at daddy and the worst heartbreak I had ever given anyone.

"Come on. Get your things," he said to me. I did what I was told. I looked at Colin and resolved I would do whatever it took to get through this next chapter in my life. Daddy took my arm. It was then that I noticed him in the shadows of the wood line, mounted on his dark horse, his hat pulled so low over his face that all I could see was his red beard. "Mary, you're going to live with Tom Dodson and his people over on Hightop Mountain." Daddy followed my gaze.

The man dismounted from his horse, and I noticed he didn't even have to tie that animal up. It just stood there as Tom Dodson walked over to us and shook my father's hand, nodding at me. "Go on and get your belongings," he said to me. "I'm glad to see that you made it back from Granny's in that snowstorm." The corner of his mouth lifted in a smile, but he didn't look at me. I gave him my small bundle. I watched as he lifted up the rifle on the left side of the saddle and put my things in a saddle bag on the horse's rump. "Come on. We best get going," he said.

He led me over to a little chestnut pack horse. Daddy motioned for me to hand him my baby as I mounted up. There was a lambskin covering on the saddle that was warm and soft. He kissed Colin on his forehead and handed him to me, giving my knee a squeeze and smiling a funny kind of smile. He nodded at Tom, who tied my horse to his with a long lead line. Throwing the reins over his horse's neck, he mounted, tipped his hat to my father, and his horse and mine moved forward. I took one last look at Daddy standing there in his town clothes, looking so refined and respectable, but his face had changed. He looked tired and old. He was still a handsome man, and living in those coal camps, I had forgotten how civilized men dressed. I was leaving civilization again for the second time. I had relinquished my right to it. I had brought shame and disgrace on myself, my family, and my hardworking ancestors.

If I had not been so exhausted, I might have been less disoriented, distressed, and emotionless, but the coal camps, Halsom, and what it took for me and Colin to survive there had so traumatized me that I numbly looked up the mountain trail. There was no one to blame for my choices but myself. This I knew as I knew my name, but I also knew that I was riding into the mountains, which were familiar to me. I knew where the trilliums bloomed, and this thought provided some comfort.

Chapter 13
Hightop Mountain, Late February 1920

The ride was smooth and slow and the horses sure-footed. As we crested the Blue Ridge, into Greene County, I thought to myself that I had never been this far east. Perhaps I could keep heading east to the ocean. Perhaps I should just go back to where my people had come from so long ago. Both sides of my family had come over with just the clothes on their backs, and my daddy's Scotch-Irish family had come over as indentured servants. I tried to imagine how desperate, and also adventurous, they must have been to leave behind everything they had ever known, their people, land, country, and sell their soul, trading seven years of hard work just to finally be able to own their own land.

I thought of that and of my mother, from a hard-working hardscrabble German family that had to eek their living out from between the stumps of trees they had felled, and there she was today with fine China and pretty little figurines and velvet couches in her parlor and her smooth white hands. After all my family had amounted to in this world, I had managed to put us back a century. My horror and humiliation were a pit with no bottom. It sat on the top of my head like a big ancestral weight. Yet, I had no choice but to hang on to the present, to the horse, to my child. I was resigned and ruined, and there was not much place to go from there.

At least I had the mountain. I began looking around and noticing the first hints of Eastertide, as it was just past St. Brigid's Day, Irish Spring. The ground was spongy in places even though icicles held to the rocks, and the earth was issuing forth flowing rivulets where underground springs were running. As I looked closely, buds on the trees were beginning to swell ever so slightly, and maples were dripping sap from cracks in their bark. But the real evidence of spring for me, what I have noticed in all of my long days, was the change in the singing of the birds.

They knew winter was receding with the darkness. All animals feel the light. The bird carols sounded like snippets of an orchestra tune that I had heard in my mother's parlor, their voices trilling and leaping and warbling the second coming. Even with a gloom in my heart, I could not help but be uplifted by their happy, hopeful, and joyous little melodies. Listening to the birds and nursing my son, along with the sweet rhythm of that horse, I was free from myself for a moment.

When we stopped to rest, Tom tied up his horse and reached into his saddle bags. "You hungry?" I nodded, yes.

Motioning me to walk over to him, he handed me some venison jerky and a wedge of cheese. I grabbed at them like one starved, and quickly shoved the jerky into my mouth, the meat going down my throat in scratchy lumps. He didn't ask but handed me some more, watching me. It was only after we had remounted that I realized he had given me what he was going to eat. Before remounting, we both knelt by the stream, cupping our hands to take drafts of that sweet, ice-cold water. My little Colin started to fuss a bit, and I changed his didy, but all that traveling, and me not being able to keep up with his messes had taken a toll on his little bottom. It was as red as a tomato and speckled with a rash. I hated to leave his little bottom exposed while I blew on it, but I knew it had to be hurting him. The cold air did give him a fit, as did the rash, which, I'm sure, burned. Nothing can make a woman more frantic than wanting to help her baby and not having the tools or means to make things better. I rinsed out one cloth and applied my last dry cloth to his bottom. Wrapping him up tightly in his blanket, like a little Indian papoose, helped to quiet him, as did giving him a bit of a suck. I began shivering from the cold and exhaustion. The shivers came on me like big uncontrollable shakes. Watching this, Tom handed me his canteen.

The sweet and sharp liquid made my eyes bulge out, but in a good way as it tasted like cinnamon candy with a kick. It went down like liquid glass. He laughed. "Apple pie."

"Huh?" I said to him still blinking.

"Here, take another sip." I did, and I felt the life return to my body and spirit. "I think I can see better," I told him.

Everything seemed so crystal clear and with shaper edges as I looked around the woods at being in the forest. I followed his lead as he began tightening our horses' cinches and repacking to mount up. A bit restored, I said, "I know how to ride. I don't need to be led." He looked at me as he walked over and undid the lead that connected my horse to his, saying, almost under his breath, "You sure?" I looked at him, trying to read him because I had a feeling, he was making fun of me, but he turned to his horse.

We traveled mutely on until we finally headed right back up and into another mountain. When I looked at where we were going, as the crow flies, I was probably just a handful of miles from home, clear on the other side of the Blue Ridge, south of Saddleback mountain. Up we went again, but this time the sun was on my back. I believe we were on Snow Drift Road, which leads on up to Hightop Mountain, one of the tallest mountains in the Blue Ridge at 3,400 feet. "Are we headed up there?" I asked.

"Not today."

It relieved me to see that we were coming into the small community of Dyke where I could spy a church and general store and a few houses. I kept looking straight ahead, as I could see window curtains moving. A fellow or two called out to him. "Hey there, Tom." He swung his horse around to stop. "What you got there?" I thought to myself, *what does it look like he's got there?*

"He's got me and my baby, that's what he's got here," I said before Tom could answer. I wasn't going to be talked about like I wasn't breathing ever again. Tom Dodson looked at me with what I later learned was half amusement and half annoyance because, quite simply, women were not like that in those days, outspoken and brash. As much as I didn't agree with my mother, she was just holding the course for how women were supposed to behave. Maybe in big cities women were different but not here in small towns and definitely not in the South.

Little did I know on that day, that falling off the railroad tracks would eventually lead me to Belle, who was like no other woman, praise God. I wondered if it was because Belle was raised in these mountains and she followed her own rules and more importantly, she followed her gut instincts. *The mountains don't hold to the same type of rules as other places, she would say.* Even today the sheriff won't go into Sandy Bottom.

Maybe it is because of the elevation and the hollows, the darkness, mysteries, and the admission of light on those bald-face craggy peaks. It can strip you down, and reveal you, and the code of conduct becomes different, but it wasn't like the coal camps. Mountain living was a primitive type of living, but it was polite, honest, real, and true, and it held to a celebration of personal independence. If my mother was a stuffy Victorian parlor, Belle was a Blue Ridge woodland in summer.

"Ya got a live one there, don't you, Tom?"

"I reckon," was Tom's only response.

"Did you notice if the Lam Mill was busy? I've got to bring over some corn I got stored in my barn before the first of the week."

"I didn't notice." I came to find out that it was Tom's way of not giving his opinion on matters outside his control, especially to strangers, and he counted strangers as anyone who wasn't family. "Well, we'd best be headin' on," Tom said, as he looked back from where we had come. I could tell the man was curious as to who I was and what was going on, but everyone would know soon enough; they just had to wait.

At the base of the mountain, past Simmons Gap and along the road to Hightop, we turned off onto a road that opened onto a clearing. A small farmhouse stood nestled into the foothills surrounded by fields and a handful of grazing shorthorn cattle. The house sat on a rock foundation with solid stone masonry and a chimney which was, thankfully, spewing a strong stream of woodsmoke. Laundry was strung on the front porch. Chickens ran to and fro, and it was here where we stopped and finally dismounted. I followed Tom as we climbed the steps to the porch, my legs feeling all wiggly from the riding while clutching my baby close and hanging onto the porch rail with exhaustion.

He flung the door open and a waft of heat and close smells of cooking and people hit my nose. Perhaps it had been so long since I had been inside that I had forgotten these smells, but I must admit it was off-putting. The scene inside did little to comfort me, for I was surrounded by wide-eyed strangers who looked at me as the stranger I was. As my eyes adjusted to the dim light, my baby started crying.

"Glad you're home, Tom," said a woman, looking up from her sewing.

He turned to me. "This is my mother, Ruth."

She nodded at me. "Here, give me the baby, and take off your coat. Warm yourself by the fire. Tom, get her a glass of milk." I did what I was told, and so did he.

"Bettie," she called to one of her girls, "go get those dry linens on the porch. Let's change this baby."

The girl, who was about my age, I guessed, did what she was asked, and returned keeping her eyes fixed on me. I watched the mother and the four children and the girl and this man, Tom. I was trying to make sense of them. I had heard so many stories of the mountain folks that made them out to be as magical as leprechauns, as dangerous as dragons, and more primitive than Indians, yet, to me, they looked just like regular people.

As this family began bustling about us, I realized this was the first time I was not caring for Colin and there was a sense of nakedness without my baby to hold onto. I had not realized until then what a comfort he was to me and how alone I was without him, with no man, no friends, no family. Ruth administered to my baby, who had stopped crying as he pinched together his cute little brows, trying to figure out who these strangers were. I studied my situation. There appeared to be a staircase over the main floor of the house as well as two rooms off of the main room that were the kitchen and sitting area. A bed rested in one corner, and twin children, a boy and girl about twelve, sat on it. They were vacant-eyed and seemed to act younger than their years.

Tom caught me looking at them. "That there is my sister, Susan, and her twin, Bobby. They got Scarlet fever when they were little, so they ain't right."

My gaze shifted to the girl that I figured was close to my age and had the prettiest long red hair I had ever seen. She was playing with a younger child I thought had to be about two years old. The young girl's dress was stretched out and faded from too many washings. Of course, mine was too. On her feet were brogans, and her stockings had fallen down around her ankles. She was grasping the little boy's fingers, and he would pull up and stagger around, his face filled with glee. A small smock covered him just below his bottom, no shoes, or socks on his feet. She didn't look at me.

"That is my older brother's son." Tom continued. "He got killed on Thornton Gap. His wagon went over the mountain. Luanne is my oldest sister. Ellen, my twin, died last year."

Good God, I thought. All this catastrophe. I now looked at his mother, a big woman who walked with a pronounced limp, holding my baby on her hip while taking out foodstuffs and placing them on the table. How did this woman survive all this? Tom motioned to a photo of a couple over the mantel. "My mother and father when they were first married. My father has been dead for a long time now."

I walked on over to the photo and looked at this woman who bore little resemblance to Ruth, the woman I saw before me. The woman in the photo looked like a Gibson girl. She was beautiful. Her hair was done up in long curling ringlets, there was a smile at the corner of her mouth, and she was wearing a fine high-necked lace dress. The man she stood beside was in a uniform.

"My dad was in the Spanish-American War, and his father fought for the Union and believed in the Union."

"Must not have made him too popular," I said.

"No, it didn't, but he was not the type of man to care." I turned to his mother, who was putting a plate down in front of me as Tom said, "My father was considerably older than my mother. How old were you, Ma?"

"I was just thirteen when your father and I got married. He was twenty-six."

Good God, I thought again. But then I remembered my situation. As a ruined woman, whom a man had discarded, whose own father had to debase himself to rescue, *I* had no right to judge *anyone*. By then, the plate of food had been put in front of me, and Tom motioned for me to sit down and eat. Side meat, green beans, or leather britches as they were called in the mountains, cornbread, and the best applesauce I have ever tasted before or since. I ate like a man, washing it down with two glasses of milk.

"This baby has a nasty rash on his bottom," Ruth said. "We've got to do something about that. Luanne, go get that jar over by the cupboard."

"I've been traveling a long while and haven't been able to change his diaper as much as he needed since..." I was as ashamed as a mother and then ashamed of my life and where I had been. I wondered how much they knew about me.

"There, there now, sweet baby boy," Ruth said, as my Colin, placed on the bed, kicked his little feet all over the place, completely naked and happy as a jay bird. She unscrewed a jar and began putting some thick yellow goop on his red rashy bottom.

"What's that stuff?" I asked. No one answered me. I turned to Tom. "What *is* it?"

"Bear grease with pine turpentine."

I walked over and picked up my baby from the bed. "I suggest you let that little bottom air out," said Tom's mother, "and he'll be fine." I knew she was probably right, but I also didn't know what right was any more. Bear grease and turpentine? I didn't grow up with such things. Everything that I had known about life, past, present, and staring into my future, made me feel like I had been placed in a foreign country, and it seemed as if I kept moving from one foreign country to another and I couldn't speak the language. I had made such a foul and life changing error that I'd been banished, from what I knew, as civilization forever. What was I doing among these people? Was I to live here?

"I'm going to feed and put up the horses." Tom, who had still not taken off his coat, put his hat back on and walked to the door.

Wait a minute. I handed my Colin to the Luanne girl and ran outside after him. "What's going on here? Am I supposed to live here? There's no room for me. How am I supposed to live here?"

He kept on untacking the horses. "We're just staying the night here. We're headed up the mountain tomorrow to the home place."

"This isn't the home place?"

"No, my mama moved down here right before my father died and her legs started giving out."

"Who lives up on there?" I pointed to the mountain shrouded in clouds.

"I do."

This took me back with a bit of relief as well as trepidation. I didn't want to have to live my life in that crowded house with all those bodies and the two odd children, but I wasn't sure what this news meant either.

"How do you know my daddy?"

"I've known him a long time."

"How does Granny Hite know him?"

He laughed but didn't answer me. "I would think you'd want to rest after all the traveling you've done, and we still have some to do at daybreak."

"Don't I have a right to know where I'm going and what's going to happen to me, or have I lost all power over myself?" In my sorry state of affairs, it had come to my attention that I *had* lost all power of myself and had to turn it over to men once again.

He ignored me, but by and by, I would come to learn that he heard every word. "I've got a load of tan bark I need cut and hauled by the end of the week. I need some help up there. Can you milk?"

"No."

"Well, it looks like you're not going to be much help, are you?"

I studied him silhouetted against the mountains which were all turning that bluish purple as the sun set tangerine. The peepers began sounding off, and as I looked to the distance, the west was turning indigo, and stars were filling the sky. Spring was tugging at winter, thank God. I watched as the last few chickens pecked and hemmed and hawed their way into the chicken coop. For one fleeting moment, the anxiety that I had been carrying for over a year dissipated again. I had a sense that whatever it was, it was going to be all right. I walked over to the chicken coop and closed their door. He was watching me as he put up the horses. Looking at the mountains, I took a big breath of fresh air before making my way back to the house of these mountain people.

Chapter 14

I slept like the dead on that little pallet, made up of old quilts on the floor with my beautiful baby curled up beside my breast. I woke to Colin staring and smiling at me. "What are you laughing at?" I asked him.

"He's probably laughing at all that snoring you did," said one of the young girls, but I couldn't make out who it was, so I could not shoot her a dirty look. The family all laughed. I began undressing Colin to change him, half afraid to look at his little bottom. It was still red, but it was no longer weeping. "It's better," I said to no one in particular. "Here, put some more on him." Ruth hobbled over with the liniment jar. I took it willingly.

The family was busy going about their morning, someone toting water, the odd children holding hands, another bringing in eggs, another carrying a milk pail. I have to admit I felt a bit funny sitting on my fanny nursing Colin and not helping.

"Where's Tom?" I asked the mother. I half thought he might have left me there, not wanting to deal with me and my inability to milk a cow. The odd children came up to me and stood in front of me, staring. "Get on away from her," said the mother, and they did, giggling and jumping backwards.

Retarded people scare me probably because I had only seen one other special person like those twins. People like them were kept at home or sent off, just like they did to the mountain folks and me. When the government came to take the mountains, all the newspapers were writing about what the government people said about the mountain people, inbred, illiterate, feeble minded, violent, but in reality, that was just some of them. There were feeble minded people even in downtown Elkton. It wasn't like the mountain people had a monopoly on human frailties. I'm ashamed to say that I held the same views as many lowlanders and government people. But one thing is for sure, by the end of things, in the early 1930s, when the federal government came to take the homes, I wasn't afraid of anybody any longer, especially men. I stood up for myself, my family, and all of the mountain folk, calling out those in power for doing wrong. Yes, I did. Still, those who were called feeble minded, to include unmarried women with babies, were sent to the Virginia Colony.

Just as I was thinking Tom had discarded me, a satisfying spring breeze blew through the door as Tom came in and he pulled a chair for himself over to the breakfast table. His mother commenced putting food down, and the rest of the family joined him.

"You'd best come on if you want to get anything," he said to me. I buttoned my shirtdress, and they pulled another chair over for me. There were bowls of fried potatoes and cornbread, more sliced side meat, milk, and coffee, which Tom and his mother were drinking.

"Tom always makes sure we got us coffee and sugar, but I still prefer honey and butter in my coffee," said his mother.

"Go on, get you some," Tom said to me. I noticed he was not eating, and to be certain, my appetite had gone somewhere far away. It seemed I could go days living off nothing. Then once in a while, I would get famished and want to eat everything, and it was like I could not get full enough, even when food was plentiful. In the coal camp, it often was not. Once, I ate limestone chalk in the coal camps I was so hungry. I'm not sure if it was the sadness or doing without food, hit and miss, for so long that got me that way, but food would stick in my throat for that first little bit when I got back to the Blue Ridge. I took a glass of milk and crumbled a bit of cornbread in it. I didn't want to gag and make them think it was their fault when it was mine. Tom and his mother shared a look.

"You best not be bashful. In this family, those who linger get left behind," said Ruth. "Well, good then, there is more for me," said Betty, as she took more meat and gave herself another helping of potatoes while shooting me a dirty look. "Really, Betty," Ruth said in a tone that reminded me of my mother. Thinking of my mother filled me with sadness again with the memory of home. Colin, on the other hand, started getting excited as he saw the bowl of potatoes pass by, swinging his hand and arms around like a wild man.

"Go on, give that boy some. He can't be on his mama's milk forever," Ruth said.

I took a small spoonful and placed it on the plate in front of me. No sooner had I done that than Colin reached out his little hand and grabbed a mouthful and stuck his whole fist in his mouth, making himself gag. The whole family thought that was pretty funny as I got frantic, patting him on the back.

"Go on and feed him a little piece at a time," Ruth said.

That worked. Colin gummed it around, his little eyes lighting up and his hands slapping the table for more, and so began Colin's first food at this family's table. Everyone, including me, ate their fill.

"We best be going," said Tom as he pushed himself away from the table. "Luanne, you coming with us?"

She jumped up as if it were Christmas. The table rocked. "Really? Ma, I can go?"

"Yes, you get your things packed. You can help, too." Ruth replied. Luanne scurried around so fast I could barely see what she was grabbing as she stuffed items into a yellow rucksack. She grabbed her little poke saying, "I'm going to help Tom and this girl. See ya," and flew out the door without a look back.

"Luanne!" her mother called after her as the door stood swinging wide open, letting in the morning light. "I swear, she's a mess."

Though we were only a few years in age apart, Luanne being about fifteen and my now going on eighteen, we were separated by a huge chasm in how we were both raised, and I don't mean it was because I grew up in town with Victorian furniture. Luanne was loved as an integral part of her family. I gathered my satchel. Tom's mother handed me the liniment as I walked across the porch. I was glad to be outside where the yellow light and bird chatter greeted me. The horses were tacked, and Tom was waiting. Once I was situated on the horse and holding my son in the sling I had made for him, Tom mounted up with

Luanne sitting behind him on his horse's rump. Colin was quite revived from his potato experience and was bright-eyed and looking all around. I repositioned him in the sling so he was facing outwards and could see where we were going instead of pressed into me and my breast.

I have to admit I was looking forward to getting wherever we were going. I was very tired of being a gypsy, and my boney bottom was hurting and sore from all the riding. There was not much cushion on it in those days. Not like there is now. But it's funny the way a woman ebbs and flows. I was skinny for a while, then, as life got smoother, I would fluff out a bit, and then I went through the change, and the shape of what had always been a beautiful body, if I do say so myself, went to Hell in a hand basket until I ended up an old skinny woman with my face drawn as if I'd never eaten a good meal or laughed. Yet, I had eaten good meals and I did eat good meals and now, after a long while without them, I was getting ready to eat well again.

Chapter 15
Hightop Mountain, the Home Place

We rode our horses in silence up to Hightop Mountain where the elevation made it so that it was still the edge of winter, and we were up in the clouds. I was not looking up at the clouds but straight into them. I knew I was high up when I was taller than circling vultures. Have you ever watched a vulture soar? They soar as if it is the last and only thing they have to do, slowly and gracefully, in circles, they ride the rising hot air. They float, waiting for death, because death has all the time in the world.

There was no coming down off this mountain for a wee visit anytime soon. Even though it was not so far in traveling time, there was something about being up on a mountain that made me feel cut off from the rest of the world. I felt like I was on another planet. I thought of Halsom, Ethel, my mother, Johnathan Abel and even Luanne with her pleasant, hopeful, and sunny disposition, and I was filled with a hate, jealousy and resentment that turned my blood to ice, and I hated this man and his homeplace. My lips tightened and shoulders tensed, and I could taste stomach acid in my mouth. Oh, how I did hate myself most of all.

The house stood in a bit of a clearing. It was a two-story house with, I was surprised to see, both front and back porches. Even though the house was a big size, the barn was bigger, and there were numerous outbuildings placed around the house. A springhouse sat close to the back door. The lumber and cobblestones all looked secure. Nothing was leaning. And there were two chimneys, one on each side of the house. That was a good sign, at least Colin would not freeze to death.

But there were no lights on. Gray weatherboard, cold stone chimney with no smoke, the gray and brown fields, and not a sign of life on the trees made the place seem almost abandoned. As if reading my mind,

Luanne said, "Don't you worry, Mary, we'll get the place warm soon enough, won't we, Tom? And Tom's water is the sweetest spring water in the whole wide world. Isn't it, Tom? And remember, you're closer to God being this high up. That's what Tom says to the preacher when the preacher gets after him about not going to church."

Luanne had jumped down before Tom had even brought his horse to a complete stop. She ran over to me, lifting her hands for Colin, whom I gave to her so I could dismount. Even though I was a young girl at the time, I was extremely stiff. It was if my joints had locked up from all that riding. Granny Hite had once said the reason I was so stiff and achy in my joints was because I was holding onto things and was not letting them go.

"Don't worry. I'll get a fire started soon enough, and we'll have us some corn bread and milk and Tom's always got meat. And you know, sooner than you think, the fiddleheads and greens will be pushing through, and we'll gather us buckets of them." She was so very busy holding Colin on one hip, loosening saddles bags full of supplies with the other hand and running her mouth all at the same time.

"Here, come get your things." Tom handed me my little bag. I didn't move. I didn't want to be here. He looked me in the eye as he continued to offload the horses, holding my bag out to me, and waiting as I gingerly reached my fingers towards him. As our hands touched, I pulled back violently as if shocked.

"I'm a going take her to the house, Tom, and get us settled."

"You do that."

I followed Luanne to the house. While there was not much in the way of furniture or knickknacks, the house was as neat and clean as a pin, and that gave me such a sense of relief. A big pine table sat near the fire with four cane chairs around it. There were clean ceramic crocks lined up on the floor and dried goods hanging from nails as well as kerosene lamps on that table and a sideboard with smaller crocks and cutlery. A large kitchen cupboard, almost as big as the wall, held plates and tin cups. There was a bucket with a gourd dipper on the dry sink by the door. I saw a crib, a churn, and a rocker, too. Luanne motioned me to follow her to the other room, which must have been a living room, and it had a bedroom off of it. There was a pretty clock on the mantel and two pewter candlesticks with bay candles in them. There was a fiddle case sitting on a lattice laced chair beside another table though, this table looked to be made of walnut.

"Ain't this nice, Mary? Tom, he sure has a nice place, don't he? It's just 'cause he ain't had a family for a while that it's gotten a bit bare, but we're here now, ain't we. Here," she said handing Colin back to me, "let's get a fire going and some cornbread cooking."

Which she did. I watched silently as she twirled around the kitchen, out the back door for wood, grabbing a mixing bowl. She was a whirlwind of action, and as the heat came off the stove, I moved closer to it and tears started running down my face because I was so tired and scared and unsure of these strangers and my role with them. I wiped them away quickly. "I think I'm going to make us a treat with some stewed apples. Here, you take down two strings and put them in this here bowl." Being addressed and told to do something brought me out of myself, and I blindly followed her orders. I balanced Colin on my hip and located the dried apples among the dried beans, pattypan squash, and pumpkin. It felt good to cook. I placed Colin on a quilt on the floor where he rolled around and tried to put his toes in his mouth. It hit me at this moment, that I was safe here. Even among this moment of peace, suddenly, a feeling of terror rose up my spine and landed in my heart, which I could feel constrict. But who *is* Tom? What manner of a man is he? I thought I knew Halsom. Now, I really felt like I was going to die or fall off the face of the earth. I wanted to run out of the kitchen to I know not where. *Lord, help me help me, help me, though I'm not deserving.* A sweat broke out on my lip and forehead as I struggled to stay calm. My hands were shaking.

Tom came in with a bucket of milk in each hand. Luanne showed me how to strain it and put the fresh milk into crocks, placing two pitchers on the back porch for drinking while we brought the rest down to the spring house. "As soon as we get enough cream, maybe by

Friday, we'll make butter," announced Luanne. Tom made another appearance with eggs and a slab of side meat.

By midafternoon, I was dizzy. Perhaps I was not used to the constant flow of work or the traveling or everything, but I felt like I was going to pass out. "I need some air, Luanne. I need some air." I stumbled out onto the porch, and for the first time, looked around me as the drafts of cold pierced my lungs and revived me. The air was so cold yet fragrant. I cannot explain high elevation mountain air well enough to do it justice. It was clean, lightsome, and pure smelling. Through a gap in the mountains, I could make out a sliver of the valley far, far, far below. Up here, there were still patches of snow on Hightop as we were nestled into the darks and dales of the hollows and mountain blinds. A fog was settling into the hollows, or was that clouds? I was in another world; I had landed in another world. Where was the rest of the world? Not here. In this new world there was just me, Luanne, and my baby, perhaps not even Tom. Maybe he was just a ghost. There was certainly no sound of him in the silence of the mountain.

And it was a bone-crushing silence. I had to listen to appreciate the quiet. If I strained, I could hear a creek. Occasionally, I could hear a cow bellow far off in the field. I startled as I heard the unmistakable and piercing call of a hawk, and I looked above and saw him. That hawk had some wing feathers missing from his left wing. Unexpectedly, I watched as a wing feather dropped from him and danced slowly to the earth in front of me. Picking it up, I placed it in my hair. I felt less alone, and my head cleared. The hawk circled and then disappeared over the ridge line. I remembered the wild, and things that were untamed and beautiful just the way they were.

Halsom? Where was he? Was he looking for me? Or was he long gone? And there was a pang for Halsom, which was immediately followed by fear. *He cannot find me here,* I reminded myself. I feared him yet loved him with a child-like need. How could he let me go? How could he not love me? When did he stop even liking me? I'm old now, and I still cannot make sense of how you could love someone with all your heart, and you would lay down your own life for them, and they can hate you completely. What had I done to make him hate me? Halsom spit on me once.

Yet, I knew that I was safe on the mountain of HighTop and finally at home surrounded and held in the bosom of the Blue Ridge.

I was nursing my baby that evening when Tom came in, carrying buckets of water. Luanne was busy with the kettles on the fire. "I thought you might could use a bath. Luanne, help me. I have water heated outside." Blushing until my cheeks were as red as apples, I wondered if he thought I smelled, which I probably did. Luanne dragged in the bathtub from the back porch, and Tom brought it close to the fire. He began filling it with water and placing kettles on the stove with more water. He hung a towel by the fire too. I watched in fascination and awe and with a bit of concern too. "You don't have to do that for me." Tom ignored my comment.

When he and Luanne had gotten all the water poured, he turned to Luanne. "Take her clothes, and we'll wash tomorrow for all of us. Do you have something you can put on once you're clean?" I looked at him, ashamed. "Luanne, there should be some things in that trunk in the bedroom."

Off Luanne went, just happy to make things right. I eyed Tom. I decided not to say anything which does not happen too often with me. I was beginning to learn to let things unfold. Sometimes asking does no good.

"Good night," he nodded to me, and left the room.

Luanne took Colin from me again. "Just leave all those clothes on the floor. I'll get them. I'll take care of it," Luanne said absent mindedly as she played with Colin.

I did, for once, what I was told. I stepped into the bath, and the water was hot. The lye soap did sting my skin, but I sank down as if I were a mermaid who had been kept from the sea way too long. I had forgotten what bathing was like and at the thought of this I started to cry. I splashed water on may face over and over again. I wanted to wash parts of my life away. Luanne helped me wash my hair and then she covered me and patted me dry with a towel, lowering a clean white chemise over my head. I felt like a child, and I realized this was an experience I had rarely had, to be touched with kindness. I knew I would never be able to repay her for what she had done for me this day. "Thank you." She grinned as if I had thanked her for the sunshine.

"I'll take care of all this in the morning," she replied. "Go and rest. Here, let me take Colin to rock him. He's old enough to not be needing his mama's tittie every five minutes."

"Where should I sleep?" I was so tired.

"In the bed. I've got me a bed upstairs in the bedroom, but since we didn't get a chance to start a fire up there, I'll either lay down in the kitchen or sleep in the rocker."

I slowly went over to the next room noticing the air change from cool to warm. A fire was burning in the fireplace on that side of the house too, and little pictures of the flames were dancing on the walls and ceilings. The alcove of the bedroom was dark. It was really a side room off of the living room. My eyes tried to adjust to the dark as I made my way over to the bedroom. I saw him lying there.

"Where am I supposed to sleep?" I asked him. "You get a side of the bed, or you can sleep on the floor; suit yourself," he replied.

So, *this is how it was going to be.* Slowly, I walked to the bed and made out the dark outline of him, understanding that who I was now was who I was, and I was free because I was a ruined, but free. There was no longer any worrying about what was proper. I pulled the covers back and got underneath the warm layers of handmade quilts that smelled clean and had been washed in lavender, which I had spied growing in the garden. I scooted to the far corner of the bed and turned my back to him, my breath coming quick and shallow.

"I'm not sleeping with you," I whispered.

"I think you already are."

"You know what I mean."

"What makes you think I want to sleep with you?"

I was so taken aback by this I didn't know what to say. I settled my head into the down pillow. A down pillow. Though my mind was tense and racing, my body was loving the comfort. A man that kept a house that had goose down pillows and warm, clean comforters had to be all right. Exhaustion was giving me the shakes as I tried to slow my breath and wait. Turning on my left side, as is my way, I pulled the pillow under my head and when the rooster crowed, I finally slept. And so began my days on Hightop Mountain.

Chapter 16

Spring came to Hightop slowly and late and with much anticipation because winter held on long that year. We could see it getting greener and trees leafing out down in the valley. We were without color until April. The buds stayed tight, but the animals knew. The lambs were coming. Luanne and I, carrying Colin, would hike out to find the herd grazing on a hillside, and we would count the ewes where we would find a ewe off to herself, staring at us proud and watchful, with a lamb sitting up in the yellow grasses. Also, the chickens were laying a lot as they responded to the light, and we put back many eggs in the springhouse for Tom to take to town and sell.

The first time he came home with the egg money and turned it over to us, I looked at him like he had just handed us a rotten chestnut. When slowly dawned on me that he wasn't keeping anything for himself, and that was our money, I took a completely different approach to managing the chickens. I kept a closer eye on them than the hawk that circled us daily.

My mother had always told me that a woman should have some money that her husband didn't know about. Many years later, when she died, I looked for but never found this hidden stash. I agree with her on that, keeping some money for yourself. I don't care how good a man is, but I finally did learn that a woman has got to keep something back.

"Luanne, there are seven roosters."

"They are noisy things ain't they?"

"They are noisy, and a few of them are plain ugly, and they are worrying the hens, and that is extra mouths to feed that are doing nothing. It only takes two roosters to take care of that many hens. Women don't need that many men around, that's for sure. Where's Tom?"

"Shoeing a horse."

"I'll be right back." I got set to pick up Colin, who was grabbing our house cat by the tail, when Luanne said, "You don't have to carry him with you all the time. I can watch him." I nodded at her, wiping my hands on my apron, and grabbing a coat.

As I got closer to the barn, I could hear the anvil ringing. His big black horse sleepily twitched an ear at me as he stood in the crossties. Tom was bent over a back leg hammering a shoe on. I looked around the barn as I waited for him to acknowledge me. Everything was so neat and tidy, for a man I mean. His workhorse harnesses were polished and hanging up. Tools were hung up too, and the barn was raked out. Even the manure from his horse, who was standing in the crossties, was shoveled into a corner.

"Well, that about gets it." He stood up.

"Doesn't that hurt your back bent over like that?" I asked him.

"Would make no matter if it did." He began putting away his tools. "Get me that set of nails over there."

I handed the nails and the lead line to him. He placed a lead line on his horse and led him out of the barn. I followed him. He handed me the line as he unhooked the pasture gate. His horse wandered out, turned around, and around, and laid down, giving himself a good roll. Standing up and shaking himself off with a grunt, he went bucking over to the herd.

"You see the chickens over there?" I said. The chickens were scratching around on the south side of the barn.

"What about them?"

"Have you noticed that there are seven roosters?" He studied me.

"I wonder if we could butcher them."

"You going to do it?"

"No, but I can help."

He sort of smiled. "When do you want to do this?"

"You tell me."

"Which one you going to keep back?"

"I'm not sure yet, but I'll let you know. We can give half of the meat to your mother." He just looked at me.

I walked back to the house with his eyes on my back, feeling like I had accomplished a big step and feeling more like myself than I had in over a year. I had made a decision and was not afraid to tell a man what was what. I had addressed Tom like I was a part of his household and not just some wayfaring stranger. As the time away from the coal camp and Halsom increased, I occasionally had more and more days that I did feel like my old self, but I also had days of horror. Memories from the coal camp, and what I did there with men so that I and Colin could eat, would find me in the darkest hours of the night. And, I had chosen Halsom, who had led me into that entire dire predicament. I was thankful for Luanne's company because it kept me from my own thoughts. I was also thankful that we were busy from sunup to sundown, but I could not be busy all the time, and that was when I thought about the choices I had made.

We had a full day on April 5th, planting onions and potatoes and butchering the roosters. Colin had been fussy the previous night because more teeth were coming in, and I was tired, tired, tired, bone weary. He cried, and he cried, and he cried. Cooing and clucking at him, I bounced him up and down trying to soothe him. His little face was scrunched up, and his eyes were tight as tears streaked his face like rain on a leaf. Balling up a fist, he shoved it in his mouth, and we tried rubbing whiskey on his gums and a tincture of willow bark that Granny Hite gave us, but still he cried on. When Luanne said she would stay with him that night so I could get some rest, I said *Hallelujah,* and for the first time, I gladly handed my son over to her.

Going out on the porch by myself as she took Colin upstairs, it was the dark of the moon, and I could not see a thing, like being in a cave. Drawing my shawl around myself, I looked out into the night. I had been on Hightop two months. The stars were coming out in the sky, as faint as a light on a flickering candle nub, and it was clear and cold; Was real spring ever going to come to the top of the mountain?

A warm light glowed across the field, and it was Tom down in the barn. He had picked up his fiddle and was playing the most mournful tune I had ever heard. Listening as the veiled sounds floated around the pastures and through the mountain, I stood on that porch with hot tears running down my face and covering my face in my hands. Then, I sobbed. I thought how I had always been alone, and now I was fated to live alone and unloved and completely disconnected from anything familiar. I deserved it all, especially after what I had to do in the coal camps, and what I had done to my parents. Why had they not protected me from all this? I wished they had locked me in my room, said *no,* and run Halsom off.

As I thought on this, the cat came up and circled my legs, purring. The little house wren suddenly appeared and began flitting about on the porch. Why are you not in bed? I asked it. The wren cocked its head and looked at me and then it hopped into the house through the open door. I followed it to find some breadcrumbs, drying my tears on my apron. The cat curled up by the stove, which I banked. The wren decided to hop back out onto the porch and flew off into the darkness and as I looked at the already dark valley bellow, I prayed for peace in my heart and mind.

Chapter 17

May came, and it brought with it the swelling of the purple redbuds and the white and pink of the dogwood. I had heard in Bible class that the dogwood was what Jesus's cross was made out of and that after his crucifixion it never grew tall. My grandmother would gather the redbuds because they are full of vitamin C, and we would eat them, and it was like eating spring itself.

I do believe this was the first morning that the air felt warm on Hightop Mountain, and I didn't need a coat to go outside. Luanne opened the door, and the sun and warm air came pouring in. As we sat around the table finishing breakfast, the sun blessed us, and even Colin started clapping his hands and laughing as it fell on his face like divine grace.

"We should go gathering today." Luanne looked at me with a broad-rimmed smile on her perfectly oval face. "I think that would be a fine idea," Tom said, as he pushed himself away from the table. "Take the red mare, Mary. I'll watch the boy today. I've got to finish up some leather work to take to town tomorrow. It won't be no problem."

Luanne looked at me, trying to gauge what I would say. I was not so sure about this. Tom was a man, and what did they know about babies? Luanne must have been reading my thoughts.

"It will be fine, Mary. Tom helped take care of all of us growing up. We'll be able to cover a lot of ground this way." For a moment I wavered between the mother I was and the girl I remembered. Guess who won out?

We started off right after we cleaned up the breakfast table, heading southeast with Luanne out in front and me leading the pony. Luanne was a tracker, that one. I told her if I was ever lost in the woods, I was confident that she could find me. She pointed out every bird's nest, and chipmunk hole nodding to where bears had been breaking apart stumps and spring gobblers had been scratching. As she broke off pieces of spice bark twigs for us to chew, we dug sassafras root, while I breathed deep of the sweet loamy soil and the faint spice of the trees and leaves. We pulled fiddleheads, yellow dock, and along the creeks, watercress. Suddenly, she stopped and looked around.

"They're here. I can feel it."

"What's here?" I asked, petting the velvet nose of my little horse.

"*Mushrooms.*" My head shot up and I was on fire now, as I love mushrooms more than anything, well most things. "Let's tie up the pony here and spread out heading down," Luanne suggested.

I needed no prompting to untie my basket. Do you know why you need to use a basket for mushrooms? Pure and simple, you got to let the spores out. I got educated by my Irish grandma; she was a wise one, and I followed her around the woods as soon as I could walk, at least that's what Daddy told me. Back then, the finding and learning of wild things got in my blood. Some things are just magic, and morels and ginseng are the most magic of all. And the Fairies move them so you can't find them, at least that's what my grandmother used to tell me.

I was once fairy-led in the mountains when I was about twelve years old. I was so intent on looking for mushrooms that I was not paying attention to where I was going, so when I finally looked up, I had no idea where I was. All I could remember, I had been going up the south side of Jollett Hollow, following a deer trail that was hugging a creek. Ferns dotted the mountainside in incandescent lime green. Solomon's seal, wild yam, and the early starts of black and blue cohosh were emerging from the leaf-packed soil. I headed up by a boulder slide that looked as if giants had thrown those boulders down in a beautiful jigsaw mess. I took off my shoes and rolled up my stockings, and with my toes grabbing the stone, I began climbing on top of them. I could see everything, like God, from the top of the boulder slag.

Then, everything looked strange. The trees and rocks looked unfamiliar, and I was unsure if I was looking north, south, east, or west. I shot my glance upwards towards the sun, but it provided me no compass, weak and vague behind the sudden presence of gray clouds. I was lost. A cold sweat broke out on my body that immediately gave me a chill, and my head began to swirl so that I was dizzy. Then I was overcome with such sleepiness that I had to lie myself down and rest a minute. My eyelids were so heavy. About that time, I was hit in the head with an acorn. Frantically, I looked around, for there were no oak trees around me. Sitting nestled up to that lichen covered boulder, I closed my eyes and took a deep breath. In what could have been a minute or an hour, I didn't know, I slept. Waking with a start, I felt I had come back to my senses, and I began walking downhill and followed a creek home, but I was far from where I had started.

With Luanne ahead of me this day, leading our direction, I could concentrate on looking for mushrooms, and I knew she was too practical to be led astray. The whole woods felt like it was screaming at me, because I was too anxious about finding them, but as I calmed down, I spotted one, then another, and another, and I walked some more, and saw another, and soon my basket was filled with the earth colors of blond, light brown, gray and dark brown cone shaped beauties of morels.

By the time I looked up, I was not sure where I was or the direction I had just come from. I had been fairy-led again. That is what happens when you go messing with magical things. Lady Gregory, who was the first woman to write these things down, and my Irish grandma, both agree on that one. My Grandma had a wee little book that Lady Gregory had written. Gregory was a grand Irish lady that went into the small Irish villages and talked to the old ones about fairy stories and charms. My grandmother spoke very highly of her, because she had met her in her own small village in Ireland. I have Lady Gregory's book to this day.

Yet, this time, I was not afraid. Finding myself drawn to a pine grove, one of my favorite places in a forest, I breathed in deeply as the squirrels chattered and the blue jays called. Sitting down on the dried pine needles and watching the sun slant through the tall hemlocks, pitch pine and chestnut oak, I felt such peace and, calm, and maybe it was joy, that I melded into the forest and felt like I was a part of what was, what is and what was to be. Very soon, however, this trance was broken, and I came back into my body. A squirrel barked at me. I spied its nest and realized it probably had young in there. I looked to see where the sun was and started walking in the direction away from it and down the mountain looking for one of the creeks Luanne and I had crossed. By the time I made it back to our pony, I was ready to sit, and I did. I laid myself back and closed my eyes, trying to recapture that magical feeling, only jumping up when I realized Luanne was standing right over me.

"We got ourselves a mess of them," she said. We surveyed our bounty, pretty pleased with ourselves. "Let's get on home and surprise Tom."

The sunshine was on my head, and for the first time in a long while I was caught in the moment of my life. I was at peace. Yet, as afternoon was wearing on, I was anxious to get back home to Colin who had been eating more and nursing less, and my breasts were achy and starting to leak as I thought of him. I was anticipating seeing my son and having a mushroom feast. I couldn't remember the last time I felt so light; this is what happiness feels like.

We could hear Tom before we got back to the house. The music was soft, sweet, and merry, dancing over the field to us. He was playing a fine tune called "Down by the Salley Gardens." I remember this as if it happened to me yesterday, so fine, bright, and clear it was. Tom was leaning back in his chair on the porch, and little Colin was dancing around him. We led the horse right up to the porch, proudly showing Tom our haul.

"Looks like we'll have a time of it tonight," he said.

I wish I could have bottled that day right on up. Luanne was chattered a mile a minute as we unloaded our satchels and placed them on the porch. I swooped up Colin who was delighted to see me, and I covered his face with kisses. Tom laid down his fiddle and untied the horse to untack her and let her lose in the pasture. Luanne and I went to the kitchen and busied ourselves soaking the mushrooms in big bowls of salted water. Carrying Colin on my hip, I got the fire up. We both hauled water for the cleaning and rinsing of the greens too. Tom had gotten the eggs for us and brought in a pitcher of milk. I used yesterday's milk to make the cornbread and gave the extra to our cat. I snuck out to the back porch, and Tom's Plott hound was wagging his tail and circling me. I looked around to make sure no one was watching, and I gave the hound some milk. I always felt when times were good, everyone in the household should share in the bounty. And it pays off, too. That hound, many years later, jumped the hog pen to help me when I got attacked by the sow, and she was an old dog then.

I raised some pretty pigs once. Red ones they were, and I had a sow for about six years or so. Someone was coming to buy two of the piglets, and I had gone down to the pen to get them. The sow came running to me for the food. I fed her from the pig bucket that held all the house food scraps and corn while I went to the other side of the pen to grab two of the piglets. By then that old hound was constantly at my heels, as we were each other's only companions.

Of course, when you grab pigs, they make a sound like you are killing them. It is a hair- raising squeal, but I got two of the piglets by the legs, and next thing I knew, that sow had come up behind me and flipped me ass over teakettle. I actually spun in the air. Good God, but pigs are powerful, and the old hound cleared the fence and started barking and nipping at her while I was crawling away as fast as I could, watching that 500-pound sow twist and bite and foam at the mouth, she was so mad. I decided right then and there I would not raise any more hogs by myself, and I didn't.

The night of our mushroom party, we had a beautifully set springtime table. Luanne even got out the lace tablecloth. We had a fresh watercress and poke salet with wild onions, cooked wild greens with bacon grease and bits of bacon, fiddleheads sautéed in butter and plate after plate of fried morels. Tom came in the door and put two bottles down on the table.

"Persimmon and blackberry wine from last fall," Luanne said. "This *is* a party!"

The only alcohol I ever saw my mother sipping was some blackberry cordial when her lady friends came over for bridge. She would serve it in these tiny, intricately designed colored crystal glasses with long stems. Luanne got out our glasses, and they were not long-stemmed and intricate. They were jelly jars.

"Tom, open up the persimmon," she said. He poured and held up his glass. "To your feast, ladies." We all clunked them in unison and took a nice long draught and that was my first sip of wine and I liked it. And I had another, and another, and another sip, until I was smiling from ear to ear, and so full up with mushrooms I thought I would burst.

After we had cleaned up and I had Colin laid down, I went out to the front porch. Tom was leaning back in his chair smoking with his fiddle in his lap. The valley below was almost dark. The green of the new life had finally shown itself on Hightop along with bursts of pink, white, yellow, and fuchsia on the redbuds, dogwood, and tangerine orange on the tulip polar trees. They seemed to be sparkling. The birds were still singing here and there along with the trill of a flicker.

"Not long before we will be hearing the whippoorwills," he said.

"Yes." I let out a sigh. I was more than content.

"Here, take you a seat. Try a sip of this." His blackberry wine was sweeter, and it coated my tongue. We looked at each other awhile, then I got nervous and turned my gaze.

"Who taught you to play?"

"Well, when I was younger, I used to go on over to Bacon Hollow on the other side of Brown's Cove. There is quite a group of music makers over there, and I would listen to John Shifflett and Birdy. One day, Birdy told me she was going to teach me how to play. I could not have been more than five or six, but I was willing, and she saw it. She had made herself a banjo because her brother would not let her borrow his. So, I learnt the songs and how to play from her on her homemade banjo. By and by, I finally persuaded my daddy to get me a fiddle, and I taught myself how to play that too. I just took to it, I guess. And every time we traveled over to Bacon Hollow, I would bring my fiddle and learn me some more songs. They're definitely some fine music makers. I don't hold a candle to them."

"Play me something, but not too sad."

He studied on me a long while. Finally, he put the fiddle to his chin and leaned forward in his chair. And he played, long, soft, sweet, and slow. When he finished, I asked him if that song had a name, because the music rose and fell into my heart, and it had silenced me.

"It's called 'Gypsie Laddie.'"

"I know it."

"Then, sing it."

"Well, all right. I'll try." I cleared my throat and began the sorrowful love song of a woman, a lady, who runs off with her lover and her husband, the lord, overtakes them and kills them both.

"What are we doing singing about lords and ladies in the Blue Ridge?" I said when I finished.

"From what I know, all the music came from over the oceans from the old ones, when they were peasants sleeping with their cows." I closed my eyes to better remember and send my soul to travel back in time, rocking in my chair back and forth, back, and forth until I found Ireland.

"I better be going to shut up those chickens." Tom stood up. "Did you smell that skunk last night?"

I picked up my skirts and went down the porch stairs and nearly fell. I was a bit tipsy. I turned to him. I smiled my first genuine smile at him then I started giggling as I tried to walk ahead of him, but I felt his presence behind me, and I was glad and unnerved at the same time.

"Well, that's that," I said closing the door to the coop tripping over my skirts and falling to the ground in a tangled mess.

He gave me is hand, and when he lifted me to a standing position, he brought me straight into his arms. He kissed me, and he smelled of the Sweet Annie he had been clearing from the fields, and it smells like fruit. I had never kissed a man with a beard before. I kissed him back because I was feeling pretty confident with all that wine. I laid my hand on his chest, feeling the beats underneath the palm of my hand, but confused and not as sure of myself. Pulling back, I turned my face towards the house and the kerosene lantern that Luanne had lit and put on the porch.

"It's all your choices, Mary. I come to you honestly." I shook myself free of him because I felt sober and sad.

He looked at me steadily. I turned, gathered my skirts in my clenched hands, and ran to the house. I regretted it the moment I did it, but it came down to not wanting to mess up whatever place I had with this family. And, of course, my addled tipsy mind was going everywhere. Did he think I was easy because I was a fallen woman? If I slept with him, would he not know me in the morning? Was there something wrong with me because my body was on fire, again? I had already made too many mistakes. What if this was another mistake? Obviously, I could not trust my own judgment.

What if I got pregnant? How would it be with us? Have I ruined all my chances at a decent life? Do they all want to sleep with me and not marry me? What is wrong with me?

These thoughts ricocheted through my head like a crochet game. I thought all of this over and over again, when all I wanted to do was lie with him, even though the other night I had elbowed him hard in his ribs because he was snoring. We slept with our backs towards each other wrapped in our own quilts.

After checking on my sleeping child, I settled myself in bed with body and mind racing. My woozy brain finally drifted into sleep, and when I woke up to the first rays of morning coming in the east-facing window, I realized Tom had not come in that night. I don't know where he slept, or if he slept at all. Maybe he went back to his spirit self, but he was definitely human again when he came through the kitchen door when breakfast was cooked. Perhaps spirits like coffee. I wondered if I had imagined our encounter the night before.

"Mary, I'm headed to the Hites this morning. Why don't you come with me and pay your respects to Granny?"

This was the first thing he said to me after our encounter the previous night, like nothing had happened at all. Had I imagined it? Even though I was nursing a bit of a headache, I decided I would go along. "Yes. I'll bring Colin, too."

"Luanne, are you going to be fine here till we get back?"

"I plan to be." She didn't even look up at us, but I could see her grinning.

"Well, that settles it. I'll meet you down in the barn. Go get ready."

Chapter 18

The road over Hightop was steep and rocky and dotted with twiggy blueberry bushes and scraggly pines bent by the wind that blew across the ridge line. I followed him, staring at his ramrod-straight back for mile after mountain mile. *Would I end up following him like this forever?* We were sitting higher than the buzzards who were below us riding the thermals. Behind me was the flats of the Piedmont that led to the ocean, and in front of me was the Shenandoah Valley and the Alleghenies. I may never have gotten to Paris, but that view caught my breath and held it there in completely union. He paused on the top of the ridge to give the horses a breather. Their sides were heaving.

"I wonder how many women have crossed this mountain," I asked him because that thought had just jumped into my head.

He turned around to look at me and laughed. "Not many."

He dismounted and motioned for me to give him Colin, who was sleeping. He was tender and considerate with my son, so different from Halsom, and neither Tom nor Halsom had any natural reason to be that way. I thought of this as Tom kissed Colin on the top of his head.

It felt good to stretch my legs. We stood while eating some cheese and a biscuit we had packed, washing it down with a canteen of water, for there was no water up there.

How did my roads lead me to being a woman on the top of a mountain? *Maybe all roads,* and as I thought this I felt, for the first time, a glimmer of satisfaction. *All roads, all roads, all roads.* And it made my head spin to think how many lives I had lived to be here, in this moment in time, where maybe I should have been born all along.

"How much longer till we get to Granny's house from here?" I took a nice long draught of that cold water as I admired the granite and slate rock formations, some laid together side by side like homemade paper stacked in layers.

"Not much longer, a lot shorter than the time that you walked it from town." I wished he had not brought up that despair filled walk in the snow. Did Tom know what I went to her for? I held Colin fast to me.

Our descent down the mountain to Granny Hite was a bit harder, as downhill always is, and we had to lean back in the saddle. I had the weight of Colin to keep balanced, too. Though my sweet red mare was sure-footed, she still had to scramble over rocks, and I felt every jar of her occasional uneven footing as her hoof slipped on the cliff edges with nothing but air on one side and mountain on the other. Tom had to periodically get off of his horse and move downed trees. Sometimes he would have to pull out his hand saw that he brought with him, and we would have to wait till he sawed through it before we could keep on with our journey.

We came to a small graveyard that had stone markers and little grave houses over the plots. It made me think that we had to be close to a homeplace, and we were. Tom swung his horse parallel to the Shenandoah River, which I had seen below us, before we descended again onto a dirt road that was, thankfully, clear, and wide. By and by, we came to the mountain bald of the fields above Granny's house. Smoke spiraled out of her chimney, and Tom dismounted, tying up the horses to the fence posts. His horses had manners. They didn't pull back; they didn't try to eat grass; they stood there quietly just resting a foot.

I set back my shoulders because that was one thing I remembered from my mother's advice. When I was scared or didn't want to do something or just felt unsure, she said, *"Lift your chin and throw back your shoulders and take in a breath of air that completely fills your lungs."* I could hear my mother saying that to me as she pushed me through the church door to apologize to the preacher for drawing a funny picture of him in the back of the Bible.

The door swung open, and Granny Hite was silhouetted against the dark of the house.

"Ain't you a sight?" I heard her call to Tom, who was unpacking the horse's saddlebags. He had brought Granny many parcels. "You're in luck today," she said. "I have John, and his wife Florence, visiting. This nice weather is bringing out everyone."

"Tom, it's good to see you," said a man coming out onto the porch.

"How have you been?" said Tom.

"Oh, can't complain, I reckon, but here, let me ask my wife, she knows everything. Flo, how have I been doing?"

"Ornery and hard to live with as always," said a woman, coming out to join John on the front porch.

"See? What did I tell you, Tom?" They shook hands, and John patted Tom on the shoulder, looking for all the world as if he had swallowed a canary at the sight of Tom.

"Flo, John, this here is Mary." Tom motioned as he made the introductions.

I nodded and smiled at them, because I had not seen another living soul but Tom and Luanne in almost three months.

"Nice to meet you, and what do you have there? Why look at that young boy," said John.

"Why don't you get out of the way and let them into the house. They've been riding all morning," said his wife.

"I'm letting them into the house. I'm just inquiring about this here good-looking young boy. And what is his name?"

"It's Colin," I said smiling because this man was the warmest, silliest, smiling and talking man I had ever met in my life.

"Well, now that you know his name, help Tom with his parcels so we can visit," said his wife.

John did what he was told, and I followed them all into the house, Granny holding the door for us all. I was the last one in, and that old woman and my eyes met. Her eyes were palest blue I had ever seen. She followed behind me, closing the door.

"I just want to know what you brought me," John said, as he watched Tom put all his parcels on the table.

"You know, Granny, I don't know why I married this fool of a man," Flo said.

Granny cackled saying, "Honey, I don't know why you women go on a marrying any of them."

I kind of sat there a bit dumbfounded, as I had never heard anyone talk like this in my life.

"You married me, Flo, because I make the best love on this side of Brown's Cove." John was grinning at his wife. They all laughed, and I tried not to look too shocked.

"Here, let me see that smart-looking boy." Flo held out her hands for Colin who reached for her, and he was swooped up into the air then bounced in her lap as if he was a jack in the box.

"Watch out, wife of mine, or you might catch yourself another baby," John said.

"That would do both of you right at your age," Granny replied.

The group settled in to talking and cutting up among themselves, speculating and ribbing Granny about her age, talking about people I didn't know. I watched them, fairly mesmerized by their good-natured banter, and enjoying myself immensely. Finally, as the afternoon light started to slant, Tom made like he was ready to leave.

"Well, Tom, what all did you bless me with this time? I swear you have never come empty handed anywhere," Granny said.

"Let's see." Tom rifled among the packages and untied the twine holding then together. "There is a side of bacon from this past fall. This here are some mushrooms that Mary and Luanne got us yesterday. I also dug you some sassafras and picked fiddleheads. And I don't need to tell you what this is." The last one was a jar of clear liquid.

"Hey, Tom, did you hear how much Adams is paying now that the Peterson boys got in trouble?" John said.

"I heard."

"You could make a pretty penny at that Skyland Resort."

"I have no truck with those Petersons; that's their county. Plus, that is a lot of miles to haul, a good four days there and back with a wagon, or loaded down with a string of horses, and I don't want to mess with those Madison County boys. You Greene County men are a lot easier to bargain with."

"But they say Adams can't buy enough of it. It takes a lot of liquor to run a fancy resort for city folk, and those people from Washington come by the truckload to play up on that Stony Man Mountain. He's got those parties going all summer long. Why, they dress up in costumes and have masquerade balls. I hear they got women running around half naked up there." John winked at his wife.

"I haven't quite seen the likes of Skyland since I was out West and those mining boys would come into town with half a year's wages, or those river rats on the Shenandoah when they would roll into town in Front Royal. It's just a bunch of people drinking like there will be no tomorrow, and no one to tell tales back home." Tom spoke in a kind of weary-like way. Halsom was a river rat and I wondered if that was what he was implying.

"That Ole Harry better mind what he's doing bringing all those rich people up there to dance around and act like crazy people. I'm surprised the whole lot of them haven't gotten into more trouble than I ever heard of," Granny said.

"He does pay good money for lumber, firewood, huckleberries. I hear those people from Washington even buy up the quilts and the baskets the Caves make." Flo chimed in, "and their land is not good for nothing, so I know that helps."

"There's just something that doesn't sit right with me. I can't quite put my finger on it," Granny said. "He's got big ideas, that Adams."

"He just wants to make money," John replied.

"He wants to make money all right, at the expense of the people living around him. Those Caves have forgotten their ways and have taken to peddling to those people, like beggars. It's shameful. Adams's got bigger plans than Skyland. He knows what he's sitting on up there on Stony Man. He thinks he's God, and he goes orchestrating all those people. He's going to orchestrate all of us off our land one of these days, mark my words." Granny stood up.

No one had much to say after that till finally John said, "I tell you something that doesn't sit right with me is having to say goodbye to our Tom here. Don't make yourself a stranger. As soon as you get your planting in, you come down our way."

"Yes, and you bring Mary, too. You're such a quiet girl." Flo regarded me.

"I'm really not that quiet. I just wasn't able to get in a word edgewise." They all laughed, but I had not meant it to be funny. When I was a girl and had the world by the tail, I had the luxury to be full of myself, but not now. Halsom had choked my voice out of me. Tom noticed and stared at me. I think he understood.

Chapter 19

I lived with Tom and Luanne in our own world up there on Hightop through the spring and summer. Being young, I had always kept thinking my life was ahead of me. Instead, I was living it now. There was no future for me, and if I thought about what was going to happen next week or next month or next year, I would just start chewing on my fingers.

One evening, as we were sitting down to dinner outside at a table Luanne and I had put under the cool of the apple trees, Colin was crawling along the grass; time, and my thoughts, were suspended as I watched Tom washing his hands and face at the outdoor spigot as fireflies danced all around us, for Tom always came to the house for the evening meal. My head felt light as I realized all we ever have are our breaths, just like each moment, and just like I couldn't hold onto my breath, peace would only come to me with just being. With the fireflies twinkling, Luanne laughing at Colin clapping his hands, Tom rolling down his shirt sleeves, I came to realize that not having a future wasn't such a bad thing, until my friend Ethel reminded me otherwise.

My second trip down the mountain was with Tom, Luanne, and a load of tanbark in mid-July, but this time, he had hitched up his team and we were going in the wagon. I had started cleaning myself and Colin up the day before, because I knew I was going to see Daddy too, and I was hoping that maybe he would take me home my having spent enough time in purgatory. Luanne and I were doing the wash, and I was worrying about what I could wear to go to town. I had been wearing the same three dresses for the better part of a year.

"I know," said Luanne when I mentioned this, and she boldly went into Tom's room and began rifling through a large mahogany hope chest that was on Tom's side of the bed.

"Should you be doing that?" I asked her.

She looked at me like I was foolish and kept pulling out clothing and placing them on the bed. First came a beautiful hat with peacock feathers and flowers, then tiny leather gloves with pearl buttons, then lace handkerchiefs. This was followed by chemises, pantaloons, stockings, and dresses that were simply the most beautiful things that I had ever seen.

"This is from Tom's first wife." Luanne handed me a picture of her that was in the chest. First *wife?* I studied the picture, not quite sure what to make of this news and her. Staring at the picture, I regarded what looked like silk curtains in the background with an ornate vanity that seemed inlaid in a floral pattern of mother-of-pearl. This wife was sitting cross-legged on a rug that was the actual hide of a tiger, head included. A glass tray of small, dainty bottles sat in front of her, and she held something that looked like a very long pipe. Statues of a large grinning Oriental fat man dotted the table, and there was a full-size white statue of Aphrodite shell, and all, behind her. The woman in the photo had hair that was dark and very straight and fell around her shoulders and body like a waterfall. Dressed in white with beads around her neck, interesting rings on her fingers and more beads around her wrist, she glanced at the camera from under the lids of her dark and large almond-shaped eyes, inviting the viewer into her lair, the corner of her upper red lip slightly upturned.

"Who was she an actress, a painter? a gypsy?"

"I don't know. She may have been all of that, but she was a cultured lady, though dreamy. She seemed to float. How about this one?" Luanne asked holding up a pale blue chiffon dress with ruffles.

I was now so curious about this woman I wasn't even looking at the dress, but I have to admit I did like clothes. I was so spoiled by having had brand new pretty clothes that I didn't realize I was a clotheshorse until I went without. My mind was torn between this wife, and this treasure laid out before me of gossamer, finery, ribbons, and lace. That trunk and that woman's clothes was God throwing me a bone. I told Luanne how my mother instilled in me that a woman must keep going to town clothes that she does not wear unless she was going to town to do business. Luanne was listening to me, her eyes scrunched up as if she couldn't fathom a woman doing business. I did my best to sound like my mother, and I put my hands on my hips as if I were acting in a play. *"Mary, I don't care if you go to town once a year, or once every two years, but you need one set of well-made clothes that you can wear and hold your head up in. You never know when you might have to talk to lawyers or judges or superintendents or people who you need to stand on equal terms with. There isn't anything worse than for people to look down their noses at you because of your clothes. They will not listen to you if they think you are trash, so you cannot dress like it. So, mind my words and keep yourself something nice and tailored to go to town. Now, get out of my hair and find yourself something to do."*

Luanne smiled. "How does that work for you?"

I shot her a look. "I don't know yet. Now, what's this that Tom was married?"

"Yep, and she was a fine, fine, lady. Nothing like you."

"What does that mean?"

"She could not do for herself. I lived with them, too, and I did it all, well, me and Tom. She didn't cook or wash or nothing."

"What did she do besides float around?"

"She read and painted and fanned herself, pressed flowers, and wrote in her journals, but Tom loved her and would have done anything for her. She loved Tom, right back, as far as I could see. They was always kissing and hugging." Luanne giggled.

I was startled by this information, and I slowly approached the beautiful items laid out on the quilt, running my fingers through the fine material.

"Here's all her stuff. She left it all." Luanne opened up her arms as if to take it all in.

"What happened to her?"

"She got up one morning, and sweet as pie, told Tom she was walking off the mountain and never coming back, and she did just that."

I rolled that around in my head as Luanne commenced to pulling out the soft watercolors this woman had painted and a leather-bound journal. There were also slim volumes of poetry I was delighted to see. There were books like Richard Burton's *Thousand and One Arabian Nights*, Shakespeare's *A Midsummer Night's Dream*, Mary Shelley's *Frankenstein*, and Poetry by Yeats, Shelley, and Keats. The stories of Edgar Allen Poe and *The House of Seven Gables* and *the Scarlett Letter* were also tucked into the chest. I was so excited. I forgot about the clothes.

"Maybe we'd best ask Tom," I said.

"Suit yourself, but here it all is, getting moldy and moth eaten if not used, and it will solve your problem."

We repacked the items. I kept thinking about this woman throughout the day as I stirred our dirty clothes around and around the kettle later that morning. Lifting those wet hot clothes out was such a chore because they were so heavy. Luanne and I took turns stirring and switching off with the lifting and the scrubbing and the rinsing. My favorite part was when we were hanging the clothes out on the line. Sometimes, if we were doing sheets, we would hang them on the trees. Anyway, I was so caught up with the work and wondering about this woman that I didn't hear Tom come up behind me.

"Do you need more wood?" he shouted at me. I jumped and looked at him, annoyed and startled, and then curious as I tried to reconcile this man with my new knowledge. "What?" I replied as if broken from a trance. Now, he was a different kind of stranger.

"Hey, Tom, Mary wants to know if she can use one of those dresses to go to town with tomorrow," said Luanne.

"She might as well. They ain't doing any good sitting in a trunk." He turned on his heels and started walking towards the house.

"See, I told you," Luanne said.

Well, at least that was that.

Later, much later, when I fell into bed after getting Colin down, I was almost so tired I couldn't fall asleep. I heard Tom come in and begin undressing on his side of the bed, the laces of his boots tapping the wood floor, and the bed creaked with his weight. He sighed as he pulled out his shirt and I knew he was unbuttoning it. I could hear him reach over and lay his pants on the rocker. Just as he laid his head on the pillow, I said, "Tom?"

"Yup."

"Did that woman break your heart? Is that why you left the farm and went out West? He took a long deep breath in and let it out so slow I thought he might never breath again. "Where did you go out West?"

"Well, let's see... I went to Montana and up through the Dakotas. I went up to Alaska then down to San Francisco then Nevada."

"What were you doing?"

"Kicking around."

"Why did you come back?"

"This is my home."

"Why did you go there in the first place?"

"I told people I needed to see something different." He was laying on his back talking to the ceiling, but I had rolled over to look at him. "I suppose that was true," he continued. "I just knew if I stayed in this house another minute without her, I would shoot myself or drink myself to death. You got any more questions?"

"No."

"Good."

He turned over with his back to me. That's how we slept, back-to-back like two turtles, as if that night he kissed me had never happened, and maybe it hadn't. Maybe it was just the actions of two desperate people. I might have imagined it all in my loneliness.

Chapter 20

The next morning dawned warm and humid. We were up early. Tom had the wagon loaded the night before, so we all went about our business silently, getting ready for town. I was nervous about going back home and so excited to see my Daddy, but I was not so sure about seeing anyone else. Getting dressed in another woman's clothes, wondering about how she was and who she was, and what had happened to her, I was grateful to her, nonetheless. Eventually, I would come to know her more intimately from her things, and her journal, than she probably knew herself, but right at that moment she was a blue dress of soft fabric.

Colin and I were the last to get in the wagon. I handed the baby up to Luanne so I could get in. "Aren't you a pretty sight? You clean up good." Luanne grinned approvingly at me. Tom gave me his hand and hauled me up with a jerk. Thankfully, it was still a bit cool so early in the summer morning. The golden sun was stretching out its rays across the light blue sky like a satisfied woman. The mountains and forest glowed shades of a million colors of cerulean and lime with the clear white water entering into the Springhouse and splashing down the slate stones as if someone were spilling a glass of milk. Fresh was the air across my skin like an invisible benevolent ghost. The bluebirds, wrens and mourning doves cooed and twittered, soared and slid in harmony with their melodies. Our enormous garden stood like a royal palace with big buzzing bumble bees lifting and settling like courtiers greeting the flowers.

The morning seemed so calm and the farm and mountain so safe that I wondered what I was thinking even wanting to go to town. My cathedral is here, I thought with a pang of foreboding.

Luanne was trying to decide what she was going to buy herself. Candy was on the top of the list. She was crazy about rock candy and lemon drops. I wanted to buy myself a start over card and I wondered where I would be if we had not passed each other on court day. I would probably be going to the State Normal School for Women in Harrisonburg and joining a sorority and maybe studying to be a teacher. I had a foot in two worlds, the town I had left, and the mountain I loved.

Luanne and I passed the time talking and handing the baby back and forth. Remembering we were young; we were plainly excited about being dressed up and away from our chores. When we had traveled for a few hours, Tom pulled the horses to a stop at the foot of Tabletop Mountain. After stretching out our legs, Luanne grabbed my hand and yanked me into Stepp's store for a soda.

"I'm ordering an ice cream soda," she hollered. The soda fountain boasted gleaming white counters and silver and red stools. Luanne and I sat down, smoothing our skirts, and looking over the menu as if we were the finest of ladies.

"Mr. Dodson, what can I get for you?" asked the soda jerk, his outfit so clean and white it must have been dipped in limewater.

"You get these girls whatever they want. I'm not needing a thing," Tom told him.

We lingered over our ice cream sodas till we were slurping the bottom of the glass like saloon women. But we didn't linger long, as we had the climb up and over Swift Run Gap to still travel. By the time we remounted the wagon, the sun was high overhead, and the cicadas were buzzing. As the horses pulled up the mountain and into Swift Run, the temperature dropped, the cool of the forest shading the road.

It was past midday when we approached Daddy's tannery, and for half a moment, I worried. What if he was doing something else today and was not in the store? My heart started to clench up, but then I saw his automobile and I started to smile. Colin, sensing my excitement, started jumping up and down in my lap. Daddy came out and watched us approach. He was grinning from ear to ear. I practically jumped off the moving wagon as he came over, stretching up his hands for Colin, whom I handed to him while Tom was putting on the brake. Giving me his hand, I had forgotten it was so smooth and soft. He hugged me tight, and he smelled of his spiced rum aftershave and the clean starch of his shirt.

"Look at how much this boy has grown. And look at my girl. You look like the mountain air is agreeing with you, my Mary. And Tom, that is quite a load of bark you brought me. Come on in; Russ will take care of you."

We followed him into the tannery office, and Russ came out from behind his desk. I had gone to school with him. He nodded at me and looked away quickly. A fallen woman makes people nervous, ask Mr. Hawthorne, who wrote *The Scarlett Letter*; he was *a man,* and *he knew.*

"How would you like to go down to the house and see your mother?" My heart leapt. "Oh, yes, Daddy!" I looked at Tom. He knew what I was thinking even though his hat shaded his eyes. "Luanne and I'll be headed into Elkton." He said. "We'll be there when you're done."

I smiled and waved to Luanne who enthusiastically waved and smiled back at me. "You have yourself a nice visit, Mary, and Colin, you be a good boy," she called.

Daddy took off his apron and ushered me around to the passenger side of his car. "Look, Colin, you are riding in a car." I told him. I was so happy to be going home. As we lurched forward, I could see that his driving had not improved as we went whizzing down the mountain and into town. People turned to wave, and then they would startle as they caught sight of me. I smiled at them none the less.

The house looked so fine as we flew into the driveway, Daddy honking his horn as if it were the Second Coming. It was almost as if I were seeing that house for the first time, the Victorian latticework, the shiny leaves of the two magnolias with their sweet white lotus-like flowers, the red geraniums on the porch with my mother's white wicker summer furniture. It all felt so odd and so familiar at the same time. I half expected my younger self to walk out the door carrying a glass of my mother's iced tea.

Then the door did open, and it was my mother, wiping her hands on her apron and looking thinner than I remembered her. Her eyes grew wide, and she put a hand to her mouth, and suddenly, I didn't feel so happy. Daddy put his hand on my knee. "It will be fine." He smiled at me.

As I approached the house, she didn't move off the porch. Then, she slowly came down the stairs towards me. She was crying. "Oh, Mary." She was shaking her head back and forth. "Mom, I'm so sorry... I'm so sorry." I was crying now, too.

"Let's go into the house," said Daddy.

The parlor was just like it had been. Nothing had changed, and I was thankful for that. My mother stood looking at me and my baby as if we were strangers. I wasn't sure what to do. "Here, sit down," my father motioned to me.

She sat on the edge of the settee. "He looks like his father," she said. I realized I was home.

"Would you like a glass of your mother's iced tea?" Daddy asked. That lifted my spirits, because my mother made the best iced tea in the whole wide world. I remembered that when he would get back home from work in the summer evening, my mother would bring him a tall glass with a jigger of bourbon in it, and he would sit on the porch with his newspaper and his tea.

"Yes, that would be nice. You make the best iced tea, Mama. I've missed it."

Daddy left us alone and my mother regarded me once more. "Well, you have the dress of a lady, but your hands and skin color tell the truth." I had nothing to say to this, and I wanted to leave. "Mary, Mary, Mary..." she said shaking her head, "what were you thinking? How could you? He has ruined your life now. Was he worth it, throwing away your whole life? Obviously, he didn't think *you* were worth it."

"I loved him body and soul and I thought everything he told me was true." Her last comment stung me and pierced my soul.

"That was your first mistake, of many."

My father returned with the tea and with ice. I had forgotten about ice. I gave Colin a sip first and he put his chubby hands around that glass and would have drunk it all if I had let him.

"Humph," was my mother's comment, and I know it was a commentary on ill breeding and commonness.

"What a handsome son you have," said Daddy with a laugh, "and what a head of dark hair. He is a good-looking boy, regardless." I took a long sip of my mother's tea, and it tasted fine but didn't feel as good to me.

"How have you been doing, Daddy?"

"Well, we are finishing up the tanbark and will be getting ready for logging and firewood here soon. You know we got those mineral companies coming through, too. I hired Russ and another young man, Stan Peterson, to help. You went to school with Russ; do you remember him?"

"Yes." I smiled politely.

"Good workers, especially that Peterson boy. They breed them strong, hardworking, and honest as the day is long in Free State Hollow, I'll tell you that. He has been staying at the Elkton Inn and goes home on the weekends. How about you? How are you getting along? It sure is God's country up your way."

My way? "I'm getting by fine. Knock on wood, Colin is growing well, and Luanne has been a help and a good friend."

"You know," my mother said, "your friend Ethel got married this June to Johnathan Abel. They had such a beautiful wedding. Her mother got her dress in Richmond, and Preacher Dean built them a fine house on the river. You know that John loved to fish. I hear she has decorated her house in blue and peach. She's hosting a luncheon over there next week, so I'm looking forward to seeing what she has done. I'm planning on bringing my lemon cake, the one I always make for Easter."

A wave of panic with nausea rode up my spine. This was a life I would have had, but it was not my life, and there were no lemon cake parties going to be held for me. I was wearing another woman's clothes and living with people who took me in. *What if my father paid Tom to take me?* Not outright, of course, but more dollar for the tanbark in some gentleman's agreement. Then my mind discarded that idea and grabbed hold of Tom just needing a body, anybody, to hold a woman's space for his house. It all came to the same end, I thought, in despair and defeat. No lemon cake or decorating a house in my future or a man who wanted to marry me.

"I'd best be getting back. I don't want to keep them waiting."

"Yes, you have a long road back, don't you? I expect that wagon is quite a bumpy, dusty, and uncomfortable ride." My mother looked at me hard.

I felt I could not breathe, and I had to control myself to not bolt straight out the door. I stood up, holding my son. My mother walked us to the door. She grabbed my arm. "Take care of yourself," she said with clenched lips. I nodded and briefly glanced into her eyes, and the pain was palpable. I so longed to turn the clock back, way back.

As Daddy and I zoomed into town, we spotted the wagon right on the side street next to the theater and Conrad's Store. The horses had their heads low, and one leg cocked at rest. Next to the automobile, the wagon looked so old timey I wanted to die. I could see Tom had got a lot of supplies. There was coffee, sugar, white flour, beans, cornmeal, nails, tools, horseshoes, fabric, kerosene, oil, sacks, and sacks of things we would need for house, farm, and kitchen. I knew he was buying for his mother, too, and he would stop off on the way back. Tom supported two households, but his shoulders were big enough.

"You can leave me here. I will find them."

"It did my heart good to see you. I hope you take the opportunity to come back when you can. Don't mind your mother. At least she is out of her bed. Here," he said, handing me a twenty-dollar bill, "buy something for yourself and the boy." He didn't look me in the eye like my mother did but kissed me on my forehead. If he could have given me every twenty-dollar bill he made to make things right, he would have. I looked down at the bill in the palm of my hand, and I looked at my daddy who was giving me a sad smile. I felt very empty inside as I put the bill into my little purse. It was all he could do, since he had not protected me as he should have.

I got out of the car, and blew him a kiss, and watched as he drove down the street. It was hot and humid in town, reminding me how cool it was up on the mountain. I went into the mercantile store first to see if Tom and Luanne were there. As I looked around, I got an idea. I purchased a small toy horse and cherry stick for Colin and then I eyed the English tea. I chose the orange pekoe. Then I bought some candied almonds and a sack of lemons. Mr. Cubbage rang me up, saying, "Why Mary, what a pleasant surprise. Nice to see you in town."

Sometimes I wished I didn't live in a small town in the South and that I lived in a big city so that when I didn't want to, I wouldn't have to talk to anybody. "Hello, Mr. Cubbage, nice to see you, too." I smiled my Southern lady smile, that smile that is not with your eyes.

"You know, we just got in some nice rose skin cream. Do you want to take a look at it? It is over by the women's hair products."

"No, thank you," I said icily. I carefully counted out my egg money and paid, removing my purchases from the counter. I didn't use the money Daddy gave me. Outside in the heat once again, I gave Colin his cherry stick which he happily sucked on, and I tried to decide if I should sit in the wagon until they came back, but the thought of being out in plain view of everyone was more than I could bear for this day. Luckily, I saw Luanne walking towards me.

"Hey, Mary," she shouted. People on the street turned. I hurried towards her. "Tom's waiting for us at the Elkton Inn. Come on."

Being the end of the day, the restaurant was filling up with people, men getting off of work and families whose fathers could afford to take them out to eat. Luanne led the way to Tom who was seated at a table. It was not lost on me that Tom could do likewise. "I found her." Now we can eat."

"They're serving trout," Tom said, as a waiter put a plate down in front of him. "Bring us another plate." I wanted to get out of there. I wanted to get out of town. I wanted... I don't know what I wanted, as I felt so out of sorts, but my energy was all used up.

"Mary?" with dread I turned towards a familiar voice.

"It *is* Mary. I told you, John, it was her. Why look at you. I never would have believed I would see you in town again. This is something, isn't it, John, sitting there large as life."

"Hi, Ethel, congratulations on your marriage." I wished God would strike me dead, but he didn't. He is not merciful.

"Oh, you heard? I didn't think you would have heard, since you're living up there with those mountain people that took you in."

"My mother mentioned your marriage to me."

"She did? Your mother agreed to see you? My, my, will wonders never cease. Did she mention my luncheon I'm hosting? You know you are invited, but I don't expect you'll come. All of our friends from school will be there, along with their mothers. I have two ladies helping with the cooking, and I finally finished decorating our new house. You really should try and rent a mule or whatever you do to get back on over here and come. Shouldn't she, John?"

Johnathan Abel looked at me smugly. "Yes, she should. Come now, Ethel, we have to be going." He placed his hand on her arm and began leading her away.

"See you, Mary," Ethel said over her shoulder.

I looked over Tom's head and far off though the walls of the restaurant and farther off past the trees of the forest and over the river, past the blue clouds and out into the sky. I'm flying far away from here; I tightened my jaw and began grinding my teeth together as I felt the tears coming up.

"Don't do it," Tom said, calmly eating his trout.

I pinched my arm as hard as I could, twisting and twisting the skin and willing the tears to stay put. I could feel one on the edge of my cheek, and I used Colin's cap to wipe it off.

"Here, take a sip." Tom slid his drink over too me. I took a giant swallow of the cold beer, leaving foam on my lip, and I hoped everyone saw. I ate the rest of dinner in silence while Luanne and Tom chatted easily.

Walking to the wagon in the cool of the evening, Tom was whistling, and Luanne was swinging her pocketbook. I walked the streets of home wishing for peace yet looking east to the mountains and wishing we were there. We got settled in the wagon. Tom clucked to the horses and so began the long slow ride home. But whose home? Their home. Where was my home? I realized, alarmingly, I didn't fit in anywhere. Even my parent's home, the only home I had known, was foreign to me now. I don't have a country, I thought. I have one foot with these people, one foot where I was raised, and I don't belong anywhere. There was no man to put his arm around my waist and take me home. This filled me with such a horrible sense of myself, my plight, and my future I didn't know what to do. Empty. I felt empty inside, and I looked at my child, my sin, like a stranger.

By the time we got to Tom's place, the moon was high over the mountain waxing to full. Luanne, Colin and I had actually hunkered down in the back of the wagon, dozing on and off, with Tom's old wedding quilt covering us. That felt safe with Tom humming and whistling, the lone cry of the whippoorwill, the careful plod and snort of the horses and Colin and Luanne snuggled beside me. I'm safe, I thought, as I dozed to the rocking of the wagon. When we got home, Tom covered the supplies with a tarp. "I'll unload all this tomorrow."

He began unhitching the horses as Luanne and I stumbled in weariness to the house. The fill moon made it easy to see. The world was blue. Luanne began lighting the oil lamps, and I carried Colin over to his crib. He was gone, sleeping deeply, his hands in little fists and his little legs splayed wide. I ran my hand over his sweet head and wisps of hair. I loved him so. *You're all I have in this world.*

Luanne passed me in the kitchen, saying goodnight as she headed upstairs carrying her glass of water. I left a lamp on for Tom in the kitchen and sat myself in the rocking chair on the front porch. Tom came in and washed his hands and face at the sink, stripping off his shirt. "Ain't you going to bed?" he asked me.

"I'm tired, but I don't feel sleepy." He looked at me a moment and I him. There he was, standing half naked before me, this stranger who took me in. I looked at this handsome spectacle of a man. Was I drawn to him merely out of loneliness? I had not saved myself for a proper husband. I would never have a proper husband because I had given myself freely and without marriage. There was Ethel decorating her house, having teas, going to church with a husband on her arm, and having a man who wanted her as his wife. She got to be a wife. Someone wanted her.

"Well, morning's going to come soon, but suit yourself."

What I heard was, *you better get to sleep because there's a mess of chores to do tomorrow, but I don't give a damn what you do.* And why should he? He was burdened with me and took me on for whatever arrangement Daddy had worked out.

The bed creaked as he got in. I rocked and rocked and rocked until I could not take the closeness of the house. I thought how I could walk out the door and no one would care. I thought how I could hang myself and no one would mourn. I thought dark, horrid thoughts until overtiredness came over me and I began to weep, running from the house so no one would hear me. The grass was wet with dew, and as I kneeled holding myself and rocking back and forth, I tried to understand why Halsom and my mother didn't love me. And no one would ever love me. Yet, Daddy did, even though I was so flawed and ruined, he loved me in spite of the shame I caused him, in spite of the way I had turned out; he loved me even though I was so different from my mother and many women. But no one loved me now, and if no one loved me, could I exist at all?

I cried for my overall pathetic self. When that got old, I finally crawled into bed, yanked the quilt over to my side of the bed, and listened to the rest of the house sleep; I realized how alone we are with our pain. Hot tears ran from my eyes, but I bore them with clenched fists. I decided that every time I thought of Halsom, I would pinch myself hard. I thought that my mother or Halsom may not have loved me, but God still suffered me to live, and Tom and Luanne put up with me, so that could be enough. As Daddy often said, *Life is not some romantic dime store novel.*

That next day, I made my mother's iced tea and lemon cake for Tom and Luanne with the lemons I had bought in Conrad's store. I thanked them both for being so kind to me and taking me in. The only realization I had was that I'd better be grateful for these people, or I might be walking the streets of Richmond, or worse.

Chapter 21
Late August

My malaise passed, thankfully, with my fingernails digging into my palms every time I thought a destructive thought. I did my best to replace it with a thought of thanks, because what cannot be changed must be endured, and at least I was far away from people and living in the mountains, where I was meant to live, I now knew. It was sort of like a time out of time up there on Hightop Mountain. We were removed from the rest of the world to a certain degree. I mean, we got the paper, and went to town, and could get Sears and Roebuck deliveries at Nethers, but if I didn't want to know about the rest of the world; I could choose not to know. And what did I need or want to know about the rest of the world? There was unrest in Europe, despite the war, and Versailles, influenza pandemic, Lenin, workers on strike, mail bombings, prohibition, and the awful Ku Klux Klan right in Magheysville. Then, I just had to add in how I was perceived as the whore of Elkton. Why would I trade reality when I could be my outlaw self in the wild and wonderful woods?

The work it took to keep the garden up, and get it all dried, salted or canned for winter during the summer months kept Luanne and me busy, blistered, and sore. We worked from early morning to around the heat of the day, then busied ourselves with work inside the house. After dinner we were back outside until it was too dark to see. Tom was not home much. He was moving a lot of horses or headed to Adams's place over at Skyland, doing carpentry and selling him what he needed of his reserves to keep those parties going. Adams paid Tom well. I know, because he would come home feeling very proud of himself and with a wad of cash that he would put up on the mantle in a Waterford vase that came from over the ocean.

But one day, it all changed between me and Tom just like that.

It was the dog days, which came late that year, and there was not even a breeze on the mountain. We had gotten a bit of a tease of autumn coming with the air getting dry and a bit of a cold chill in the morning and evening, and then it hit. They were the hottest days in Virginia history, and some of the smaller creeks started drying up and the ground was hard packed and turning a brown not usually seen except in winter. Luanne and I hauled water to the garden, buckets, and buckets, having to water every morning and evening now, then pick, can and dry all day. It was draining work. It was so hot that Tom stopped hauling and splitting wood or working horses until evening. He said it was too hot for the horses to pull. Luanne sought refuge from the work with a boy who had come to take her to the Ruckersville Fair. She had asked to take Colin, saying the boy would not mess with her if she was toting a baby. I let Colin go with some reluctance and forbearing, but I knew what she was saying.

Plus, I didn't want Colin growing up being afraid of people because he lived in banishment with me. It would not be fair to have Colin suffer because of my choices. He had a right and deserved to make his own way, but I wasn't sure how I was going to accomplish this for him. Watching Luanne, her beau and Colin head down the mountain and to the fair, I had a funny feeling when I watched my Colin go away from me, and especially as Luanne and that boy laughed and played family. I was happy for Colin but a bit envious that it was not me with a beau on my arm and I was jealous I was not the one taking Colin to the fair. No one asked me, and I had no agency to get there. I watched Luanne and her beau head down the mountain until they went around a bend and were out of sight headed into the world of candy apples. Tom came around the side of the house where I, in a sticky sweat, was stringing beans and feeling out of sorts and just plain cranky from the constant unrelenting heat. "I'm going to go down to the swimming hole and see if it has any water," he announced, as he wiped his face and turned to leave.

"Can I go, too?" He regarded me.

He shrugged. "Suit yourself."

It was late afternoon, and the cicadas were buzzing so loud my ears were ringing, their fever pitch matching the heat of the day. Sweat ran down between my breasts and legs and down the sides of my face. We walked for what seemed like a long time, crossing many spongy muddy creeks that should have been running full with water. It was hot and dry in the forest. I was thankful for having no sun on my head. Watching him in front of me, his shoulders and the back of his head, his slim muscular legs striding forward and his gun over his arm, I thought that in some lifetime, I have followed him all my days. It was all too familiar. I was in a heat trance.

Then, I heard it and smelled it. Water. Moving water. The rushing sound lifted my spirits.

"We're here all right," Tom said, moving through a stand of spice bush and revealing the waterfall splashing over the ledge and into a small pool.

There really is water. God has not taken it away. I took off my brogans and rolled down my socks and stepped into the pool. Ice cold and delicious. It was so cold that it took my breath away, but then I wanted more. I quickly bent over and splashed some on my face and arms. I was in heaven. When I stood up, I saw that Tom was in the process of stripping off his clothes and neatly laying them over on tree branches.

"Oh." I felt the flush rise up in my checks, and I turned my back on him.

I felt silly. I have seen a naked man, though not this one, and for once, I didn't think of Halsom in my heart. I reflected on how Halsom's body was soft and that was not something I could see under his clothes, but maybe who he was physically was also who he was in personality. He had to show everyone he was boss because deep down, he was weak and soft. Tom was rock solid all over, and I knew that without his being naked. I have laid beside him these last few months, though we stayed as far apart as if we were fire and ice, yet I knew him. Diving in from the ledge, Tom emerged from the dark blue green pool with a yell.

The light was drawing sunshine onto the rocks and making all the splashes sparkle like crystals. The ferns were throwing off their fresh green smell in the cool spray, sweet, light, and effervescent. The moss that clung to the rocks glistened. The water beckoned, crystal clear near the surface and then fading to fine shaded layers of transparent green below. My body was so hot and sticky. Inspired by Tom's boldness, I pulled my dress over my head and flung it. I untied my chemise and pantaloons and flung them. Naked, I climbed the rocks to the ledge about fifteen feet above the pool. He watched me. I stood on the ledge in all my naked glory and jumped from the rocks. Down, down, down I traveled to the dark blue pool. My toe touched the sandy bottom and I kicked off and sailed up and broke through the water my hair floating around me. I swam to the other side of the pool. I was so cold; I was on fire from it.

"Feels good, don't it," said Tom.

"Yes," I said, spitting water.

I clambered over the slippery rocks and dove in again.

And again.

And again.

And I was so happy, and I felt completely like my true self; this is my soul, pure, free, and home.

Tom floated in the pool like a lily pad and then submerged like a catfish blowing bubbles with just his eyes peeking out at me. "What are you doing?" I asked him as he dove under the water and emerged next to me.

"What should we do now?" He kissed me. He pulled back and waited to see my reaction. "Kiss me again so I can see if I like it."

He kissed me again waiting, trying to gauge my reaction. He kissed me like this until I started kissing him back, which I did.

I looked directly into his eyes, unwavering. I was not afraid or pressured or doing what was expected. I'm here in this moment. *He kisses real good* was all I could think about. There was no roughness, or haste and he waited for me.

He played with my lips and let his tongue flick off my teeth, and his hands pressed into the small of my back as we treaded water. Then he kissed my face, and throat and breasts and smiled at me. We were treading water all the while. Leading him, I swam to the edge of the pool, and he followed close behind me to the ferns and grass.

He and I looked at each other for a while, and I gingerly touched his shoulders. The muscles were so solid, hard, and sculpted. I laid my hand on his heart and the curly golden red chest hair swallowed my hand up. Then he took over. He grabbed up my hand, and kissed the palm, and he kissed my lips, and he kissed my feet, and he kissed my toes, and this went on for a while till the cicadas and heat and tumbling water made me lightheaded. As tears stung my eyes, I realized I was being worshiped.

I pulled away from him and laid back down in the ferns. Tom was a very smart man. And he had a lot of patience. He waited until I reached for him, and he would have waited until the end of times too. But he didn't have to because I could not stop running my hands down his body, from his torso to his legs, and checking out how he was put together. Yet, he finally grabbed up my hands, and held them tight, and he did things that made me giggle, gasp, and moan-all in that order.

Praise Jesus.

I was born again, and all my sins erased.

That night we slept arms, body and legs wrapped up around each other like puppies, and we slept like that for the remainder of our days. Sometimes I would fall asleep holding his hand, and I liked, and was amazed, at having him always reach for me no matter how tired he was when he got into bed. Once I relaxed into knowing he was not going anywhere, or changing his mind about me, or treating me different, I slept on his chest because it was the best place in the world.

The next morning my ankles were very itchy and my waist, were the pantaloons gathered, was itchy too, and the more I scratched the more I itched. When Tom came in from morning chores, he lifted up his shirt and showed me his waist. The bites were up his back.

"What's happened to us?"

"Seems we got into a patch of chiggers. Punishment for our sins?" he said grinning at me. I blushed.

Luanne came in carrying the butter and eggs from the spring house.

"What did you two get into yesterday?" she said innocently.

"How do we get rid of them?" I asked, scratching my body frantically.

"Come here." Tom went over to the cupboard and removed a medicine jar. It was a mixture of moonshine, witch hazel and tee tree oil that we used for cuts. There was also a bottle of straight shine. You know, moonshine is good to use when the world has gone dark, and you need your eyesight to clear. Like years later when I was riding to Skyland and the temperature was in the teens, and I thought I would freeze to death and die, unable to feel my fingers or toes, I opened a jar and took a few sips until I felt life come back to me. And the potion, as we took to calling the moonshine, witch hazel and tee tree oil concoction, would heal up a cut overnight. Once, when I got a snake bite from a black snake, I was trying to get out of the chicken coop, I put the medicine on and it closed the wound right up, but the wound festered.

"Here, lift up your shirt," he said. Slowly and with great care, he dipped a rag into the medicine and then onto the bites. Luanne watched us and she looked to me, and to Tom and then back to me and I saw the slow dawn of realization on her face.

Chapter 22

The chigger bites healed up. Our hot and dry summer gave way to autumn, and October came to the mountains in all its rainbow glory. Colin was walking and calling me Mama, Luanne, "Looloo" and Tom, "Ta." As Colin got older and could walk more easily, Tom seemed more comfortable taking him to the barn, and he even rigged up a little saddle that held Colin firmly in place and he would put it on the plow horse for Colin to ride when he was working the soil. We had a good crop of grapes and made juice, and Tom put up his wine, and, of course, we ate those grapes fresh. We put up a few pints of grape jelly but not too much, because no one in the household was a big fan of it. There had been a good crop of beans, too, and there were rows of beans drying in the attic and canned in the root cellar. I had never worked so hard in my life. Let's see, we also put up pattypan squash and pumpkin, tomatoes, and cabbage some of which we made into sauerkraut, putting the rest into what Tom and Luanne called bings. This is where you dig a pit, in a dry place, place your cabbages in there, and cover them with hay. They will be perfect when you pull them out, well, mostly perfect. Now, in October, the garden held turnip greens, fall crops of spinach and kale, and winter radishes. This was how October and the fall equinox of the year found us. I had been with Tom and Luanne for eight months now.

I never minded the work of putting up food or cooking. I never forgot going almost three full days without eating when I was in the coal camp. Once, in the camp, out of desperation, and before I knew about *Esau,* I had started scouring the stringy hills behind the camp houses looking for food. One of the families, seeing me, left me some cornbread, and they didn't have anything to spare, having five children. I'd hide to hide it from Halsom.

On Hightop, a few weeks past the fall equinox, it was apple time, and while we had, of course, put up and dried and stored in the root cellar the Milam apples on Tom's place, we were all excited that Tom was taking us to Bacon Hollow to the apple butter boiling. We were going to stay overnight and take his mom and family, too. We had organized most of our traveling needs on Friday, and the wagon held what we needed. Luanne and I had washed our hair and cleaned our nice dresses that Tom had bought us with some of his money from Adams. Tom had fed the stock well Saturday morning because we would not be home till late Sunday, and I had put up the chickens with extra water and feed. The team was ready by daybreak, and we started off in the chilly early hours. It was quite the job to go away back then, but I was so excited.

When we picked up Tom's family, the wagon was alive with chatter. As an only child, I really was enjoying being with a big family. Considering I was an outsider, and a fallen woman, they were good to me. They rarely judged when it came to life circumstances. I heard Tom say many times, *it is what it is*, which I have decided is one of the better life philosophies. Everyone on the wagon was talking, sounding like a murder of crows.

"Now, how many tomatoes did you put up, Luanne?" asked Darlene, a first cousin.

"About fifty quarts, but we got to move the squash next year because we got a vine borer."

"Beatrice Shifflet told me they got vine borers this year, but they was so busy with her daddy's grippe, and did you hear about her husband? He got so afflicted with some headaches that he could hardly get to the mill, and her with those young children to manage."

"I read that they are putting streetlamps in Stanardsville."

"Well, Susan got her a job down there at the hotel, and she is making good money."

"Did Johnny get engaged to that girl he was courting?"

"Well, he better have because she was seen talking to Nathan Dove, and his horse was hitched at her place on Sunday."

And they talked like this for hours, never letting up for a minute. Colin got passed around and played with by everyone, and he added his squeals of delight to the chorus. Coming into Brown's Cove, we saw a big black bear. It ran right in front of us, crossing the road. Tom was always one for seeing bears. Whenever he was doing something in the woods, he would tell how he saw a bear, or two bears, or a sow with her cubs. I clapped my hands in joy and elbowed Tom, as I was sitting up front with him on the wagon. "Did you see that?" I asked.

"She was a big one."

"What do you think the Indians would make of that?"

"When I was out west, I had an encounter with an Indian healer. I think the Indians call them a shaman. We were sitting at a bar in some dive town in the Badlands. Good God, he had to be about the oldest person I had ever seen or met."

"What's an old Indian holy man doing in a bar?"

"Same thing I was. You know, we got to talking, and we started talking about animals and hunting, and he was asking me about the mountains where I lived, and somehow, I must of mentioned seeing a lot of bears. He pulled out a necklace from under his shirt. It was strung with bear claws. He took it off and held it high up in the air. I will never forget him looking at it and tears started to form in his eyes. He told me the spirit of the bear is strong in times of difficulty. It is a creature of courage and stability and patience, for they can sleep in the womb of the earth. He then said when the bear spirit shows up, it's perhaps time to stand for your beliefs or your truth and take action without fear."

With that, he pulled the horses to a stop and applied the brakes. As the bear stood on its hind legs, I swear it looked to be six feet tall and 400 pounds.

"They'll be hunting them sure enough," said Tom with a sigh.

"I can't abide that, running a bear to death with hounds."

"No need to eat a bear with all the other game in the woods. When I was younger, I used to hunt coons. There was good money in that. Remember, Mom, when there would be 30 hides drying on the side of the barn?"

"Yes, I do. You and your daddy were a fine team."

"How come you don't hunt them now?" I asked.

"Takes time to mess with them, and I got other stuff I need to fool with." He winked at me as the bear ambled off into the forest as if it had never been there.

By afternoon, it was warm, and we could smell the wood smoke from a hollow away. People had already been hauling and cutting apples for days, and the men had gotten up early to build the fires under those copper pots. The home place of the Hendrickson's was buzzing with families as we pulled up their road. The horses, as if knowing their own and their master's mind, walked into a shaded knoll where Tom pulled the brake and jumped off the wagon first. I spotted Florence and John coming over to us.

"What a good looking and fine pair you are. Summer has agreed with you," John shouted.

I looked around at the people all about, the children running and screaming, women coming in and out of this big two-story farmhouse carrying plates, and men standing around the copper pots watching the young people stirring the apples. All the Dodson family flew off the wagon leaving Tom, his mother, me, and Colin.

"Young'uns, you help us here bring this food into the house," his mother called. Luanne and Darlene came back to the wagon.

Because we were traveling, it was quite a decision to choose what food to bring that would travel well. We had spent the better part of the week shelling black walnuts and chestnuts. Luanne had made a jam cake which she guarded on her lap the entire trip. Tom's mother brought her vanilla gem muffins, I brought elderberry cordial, which I had figured out how to make from a cookbook I found in the chest, and I don't need to tell anyone what Tom brought. I helped Tom make his wine this year, and as soon as the persimmons got ripe, he was talking about making persimmon wine. He kept the jugs and funnels and tubes and such all down in the root cellar where the bottles were lined up on nice wood shelving along with all the other preserves. But the other, I didn't know, and for once in my life, I didn't want to know. Shine is a good cash liquor business.

I followed Luanne into the house with my cordials. We placed our food on the heavily laden tables that were filled with food of all sorts. It was so nice to see so much food laid out and know that you wouldn't have to listen to Preacher Dean's ten-minute blessings to it eat it. There was chess pie, biscuits, venison, string beans with ham hocks, pearled onions, cobblers, cornbread, chutneys, coleslaw, chow chow, stewed tomatoes, apple stack cake, and a cured Ham the size of Texas. Tom's family had scattered far and wide, so I found a group of women with small children and sat with them, and they made me feel right at home chatting with me. If they knew I was a fallen woman, they didn't seem to care, and Colin was delighted to have little friends to run after.

By early evening, the decision was made that the apple butter was cooked and it was time to pour off. Now, that was a job, too. Crates of the jars and lids were hauled to two sawhorses with planks across and the woman lined up. There were women doing the pouring, women doing the lids, and women lining up the jars. And you had to be careful because that butter could scald you. When the last of the butter had been scraped out, the men hauled the kettles off the fire and began the process of scrubbing them as other men hauled the water for the scrubbing. Others began building up the fires again for evening.

This house had gas lights just like my parents' home, and the lights were lit in every room of the house, making it look like Cinderella's castle; the women began bringing out more cooked foods and laying them on the tables. As twilight slowly cloaked the mountain in orange and violet, we began to fill our plates again. I ate and ate. I was so hungry. Tom spied me and came walking on over, smiling at me.

"Did you get yourself enough?" Before I could answer, as I had my mouth full, a bold and pretty woman came up behind Tom, covering his eyes with her hands. Her face was tawny, her nose long and she had bright blue eyes upturned and black hair. She was tall and lean. Her eyes were too merry.

"Guess who?" she whispered into his ear.

"Hmmm, let me see. You know, I need to feel more than your hands to know who this is." She threw her head back and laughed loud. She spun him around, and his face lit up in recognition. "Ain't you a sight," he said, wrapping his arms around her.

I wasn't sure what I was feeling as I watched all this. I had no right to be jealous. They looked at each other, smiling for what seemed like a long time. Colin squealed, and that made them both look at me. I patted down my hair.

"Now, who's this?" she asked, "your new wife?" Before Tom could answer, I quickly stood up and answered. "I live up on the mountain with Luanne and Tom."

"I see." She regarded me with no emotion, but with a slow, steady gaze never taking her eyes off me. I could feel her eyes boring into me, into my core; I regarded her, too, with that long black Indian braid to the bottom of her back, her tan skin and sky eyes. She stood with her shoulders back, as if daring anyone to take her on.

"What brings you back to these parts, Belle?"

Turning her gaze back to Tom, her face softened.

"Mama has been ailing, and I wanted to come up and see her. Brought my son with me. I haven't seen him all day. I hope he isn't getting himself into trouble." She looked now past Tom to where some young men were standing at the edge of the fire.

"That's what young boys are supposed to do."

"Well, I remember the trouble you used to get into, so I know enough to keep my eye on him. Now, do you still play?"

Tom nodded.

"Good. I'm going to have a song and a dance with you before this night is over." And with that she tossed her long black braid behind her, kissed Tom squarely on the mouth and walked off. Tom laughed out loud as he watched her saunter away. As if remembering me, he said, "Did you get yourself enough to eat?"

"Yes, I did." I stood up. "I think I might go back to the wagon and get a shawl."

"If you don't mind, I might walk with you."

We walked in silence through the groups of young boys, young girls, children chasing each other, men talking, women sitting and talking to their friends and neighbors, men at the dark of the fire light passing whiskey while the rich sweet smell of cooking apples, cinnamon, cloves, allspice, nutmeg, and pungent wood smoke permeated the air.

"Here, I'll get your wrap for you." He climbed into the wagon and yanked for my shawl, and also carefully retrieved his fiddle from under the driving seat. As I placed the shawl around my shoulders, we walked over to the blaze and heat of the bonfire where people had gathered, and instruments were being tuned.

"I guess, if Tom's here, we can start," said someone.

Tom motioned me to sit by him with a cock of his head. Holding Colin in my lap, I sat on one of the hay bales that had been dragged from the barn. After some discussion over what to start playing first, Birdy McAllister took up her banjo and began playing "Po' Ole' Tucky-hoe." She was the only woman playing an instrument. After Po' Ole' Tucky-hoe, the musicians followed with "Who Killed Cock Robin," "Georgie," "Two Brothers," and "Matty Groves" in rapid succession.

Belle, with the black braid stood, up and said, "Anyone remember 'The Wind and the Rain'?"

"I do," said Tom, as others chimed in agreement.

"What woman here can sing it with me?"

"I can," I said.

Everyone turned to me, and I blushed as I faced all these strangers' stares. I rapidly looked from one face to another, but my panic turned to determination as I stood up, looking Miss Belle square in the face. I balanced my Colin on my hip. "My father's mother sang that to me many a night. I know that song as I know myself," I assured her.

"All right, then," said a man's voice from the crowd. Belle nodded to me, and we started with no music and just our voices in the cool autumn night.

There were two sisters of County Clair
Oh, the wind and rain

One was dark and the other was fair
Oh, the dreadful wind and rain
And they both had a love of the miller's son
Oh, the wind and rain
but he was fond of the fairer one
Oh, the dreadful wind and rain...

Tom's fiddle playing began to swell around us as we continued the song of the two sisters who were in love with the same man, and the sister with the dark hair drowned her fair sister. Their lover strung his fiddle bow with the fair sister's yellow hair, but the fiddle was then doomed to only play a lament. Our voices drifted off into the night and I stood there in front of all those people feeling more than tolerable. There was a moment of silence as we finished.

"You're all right," Belle said to me, smiling and she put a hand on my shoulder, squeezing hard, winking at me, and drawing me into a bear hug.

"And she's pretty easy on the eyes, too," said one gentleman in the crowd. I looked at Tom who was looking directly at both Belle and me.

"Let's have us a dancing tune," someone cried out, and the music swelled once more as people cheered and started flat footing to a Virginia reel.

The music played long into the night, but by midnight I was feeling tired. Colin was sleeping in my arms as I carried him over to the wagon. Tom had rigged up a bed covering for us though I know his mother was sleeping in the house. No one was at the wagon but me, so I just laid my body down on the pallet and pulled all the blankets and quilts over me so that just my nose was sticking out. Colin's soft breaths were rhythmic, and I listened to them as I tried to quiet myself down. I could hear the music and laughter and the occasional large snap of the fire; I didn't fall asleep. I heard the crunch of footsteps, like a deer in the leaves, approaching the wagon. I listened as he placed his fiddle back under the driver's seat. He hoisted himself into the wagon bed. He laid down beside me and pressed his body into my back, put his arm around me and buried his head in my hair. This was new.

"Tom?"

"Ain't you asleep?"

"No, I can't seem to settle down."

His hand ran over my dress, across my hip, sliding over my belly as he pulled me to him.

"Mmm."

"Tom, can I ask you something?"

"Mmm."

"The woman you married, what happened between the two of you?"

There was quiet for a long while, and I thought he had fallen asleep. "Well, I think she liked the idea of me better than the truth of living with me."

I thought on this a bit but then peppered him with questions and Tom patiently relayed meeting her up at Skyland, watching her dance at the fancy dress parties like her people from Washington, and how she had a smile and a mystery that drew folks to her like moths to a flame.

"Tell me about Adams," I asked.

Tom described Adams like a tiny banty rooster, dressed up in ruffled shirts and high boots with holsters and guns at his side, putting on fancy dress parties for his Washington tourists. Adams sounded like he could give Barnum a run for his money. Also, the arts and craft movement was popular and why the city folk were so hot to buy baskets and quilts from the Caves to display in their living rooms back in the city. But it was the rich women he described that I lingered on and his description of her fair skin and smooth white hands, which got me thinking on that photo of his wife.

"How long were you married?"

"About a year I guess." He turned over and away from me.

"Did you love her?"

"Yes, very much."

"And what about this woman Belle?"

"That's enough for now."

A great horned owl was calling. I stared into the darkness for a long while.

Chapter 23

We butchered at Thanksgiving, supplementing the bounty of the mountain as Hightop's woods and fields were filled with grouse, quail, and pheasants along with rabbits and deer. We were butchering a hog my first November with them; Tom guessed the hog weighed in at about 500 pounds. We had been feeding weanlings since late spring and turned them out at the first frost. This pig had roamed the mountain, getting fat on acorns, hickories, walnuts and grubs all autumn.

Thanksgiving morning up on the mountain, Tom got up at four a.m. to get the fires going. *Oh Lordy.* We were always up early, but when we were doing something like that, we were up extra early. I tell you, Tom was funny. If Luanne and I had not gotten up for some reason, he never would have gotten us. He would have just done it all himself. Slowly, I roused myself in the pitch dark, lit the gas lamp, slipped my old dress over my head, walked to the kitchen, tied my apron around my middle and stoked the fire Tom had already got going. The coffee that he also had started was warming on the back of the stove. I looked out the front window, and I could see him as a shadow moving down at the barn as he was setting up his hanging poles and kettles and laying out his set of butchering knives that were wrapped up in a leather jerkin when they were not needed. Many people would have friends and family over to help with butchering but not him. Yet, he helped neighbors butcher all winter. Seems like at least once a week he was going to someone's place to help out because he was asked. Sometimes, for helping out, they would give him something, like sausage, meat, tools, or a sack of flour. I remember that he paid the doctor with a ham one year.

Tom did a bit of everything to get by. For instance, he broke horses. I remember his coming home with two horses tied to the wagon when we went to Bacon Hollow. He also shoed horses, bred mares to his

Percheron stallion, made leather harnesses and bridles, and repaired leather; he even shod horses if they would stand. He cut, sawed, and hauled logs, some for tanned bark, sold cattle, picked any fruit that could be sold like apples, blueberries, wineberries, mulberries, or persimmons; he also hunted ginseng, performed carpentry work when he could get it, tanned hides and sold the skins, and made and sold liquor, moonshine, wine, and brandy.

That morning of the butchering, I stared out at the cold wet and drizzly day. The rain came down in misty gray sheets. It made you want to crawl back in bed. Reaching for a cup of coffee, I took a sip, but it tasted bitter and like poison on my tongue. I could not finish it. I always knew if I could not drink my coffee in the morning, I was coming down with something. I put on my coat, and Luanne, who had come downstairs, was staring out silently at the rainy day. Wrapping our shawls around our heads, we hardened ourselves against the rain as it hit our face like bullets. I wrapped Colin, who was still in dreamland, inside my coat.

Tom had hung the dead, headless hog under the overhang of the barn, and he had set the kettles right at the edge of the entrance of the barn. The smoke from the wood and the steam off the kettles was settling around us. I felt like I was choking. I glanced at the decapitated hog's head staring at me from the makeshift worktable Tom had rigged up with a plank and sawhorses. Placing Colin inside the barn on an old quilt, I put hay around him to keep him warm.

"Mary, go grab those buckets and put them under the hog. Luanne, start working on that head," Tom told us.

Luanne and I scurried to follow Tom's orders. I watched with fascination as Tom ran his long butchering knife up and down the sharpener, fast and quick, the metal on metal sending chills up my spine. Swiftly, he cut around the pig's anus and then with a thrust, drove the knife into the sternum and sawed his way down the animal's gut. The innards peaked out, and Tom placed his hands on both sides of the hog's rib cage and pulled that animal clean apart. Like a waterfall, the guts and intestines spilled into the waiting buckets as steam escaped from the carcass, and the rise of blood and everything else we, and that hog, have inside us, filled my nose. I wrapped my scarf around my nose trying not to gag.

"Take that bucket of clean water and the cup and start washing this hog out," Tom ordered. He placed the buckets of guts on his sled. "I'll run this up to woods later along with everything else. Here, get me that pan," he said motioning with his knife.

Expertly, taking a smaller, finer blade, he removed the kidneys, liver and heart and slid them into the waiting kettle to make ponhaus. With all three of us straining, we lowered the carcass into the waiting barrel of steaming water and began scraping the hair off the sides. "Luanne, start working on those jowls; Mary, when I pass you the meat, use that knife to cut away the fat. Put the fat into that kettle and you and Luanne keep that kettle stirring. Got it?" I nodded.

I watched him saw into that hog with a mixture of revulsion and interest. I can't remember how I ended up with the lard and crackling job, but I did. Tom and Luanne threw in the fat, and I kept stirring and stirring and stirring and lifting off the cracklings, and feeding the fire, and stirring. The smell of the fat and the smoke was strong, overpowering and suffocating. Tom was cutting the meat, separating it, and salting it, wrapping it, and putting some aside for us, his mother, and Granny Hite.

Luanne and I took turns with Colin. Thank goodness he was such an easy and happy baby. The only time that child ever cried was when he was cold, not even when he was hungry. He had such a good appetite and teeth now. Clapping his hands, he tried to pull the orange barn cat's tail as it tried to curl up with him on the quilt. I watched him study the cat and the cat study him. Colin lunged for the cat's tail again and the cat gave a swat at his chubby little hand. I held my breath expecting Colin to cry, but he stood still a moment, then attempted to crawl after the cat who had bounded into the loft.

The cold rain gave way to an Irish mist as the day wore on and on in butchering monotony, and it was early evening by the time we got everything put away and the lard poured off. Because of the fog, not even the light had changed. It could have been 10 a.m. or 4 p.m.; it was hard to tell. The meat went to the smoke house. The cracklings were cooling, and the ponhaus was steaming; I had not eaten all day. I picked up Colin and held him close to me, smelling the top of his sweet round head, the only thing that didn't smell of smoke and grease.

We all got to the house as dark descended, and I was so thankful to be inside. Although I reeked of lard, smoke, and death, I sat down at the kitchen table too tired to clean or change, holding Colin on my lap. This was the first time I had sat down all day. Luanne placed the ponhaus on the table and began stoking the embers in the fire. Tom had rolled up his bloody sleeves to scrub his red stained hands in the sink, and I watched the white sink fill with streaks of blood like a kaleidoscope. I was just sitting there in a stupor, watching the red colored swirls, thinking I would never get away from this smell, and would smell like this the rest of my life.

Luanne cut into that ponhaus and turned to me. "You want a slice?" My hand went to my mouth, I placed Colin on the floor, and I ran from the kitchen and out the back door.

Dry heaving is not a pleasant business. My whole body convulsed as wave after wave of nausea rose within me. My stomach hardened, cramped, and tightened with every heave wracking me deeply and forcing me to my knees. The back door opened with a squeak. "You all right, Mary?" Tom asked. He came over to me where I was praying in the grass and tried to lift me up. I pushed him away.

"I'm sick."

"I can see that."

"I think it has passed."

Right then, I was afflicted with another horrible retch, and I wished he were not there to see this. He gave me his hand and I grabbed it, helping me to my feet. I took in some deep breaths of the cold air, wiping the spittle off my face with my sleeve.

"We work you too hard today?" Tom patted my back. I shot him a glance as he opened the back door, and I sat down at the kitchen table again.

"You all right?" Luanne studied me; her eyes knit together in concern. I nodded and tried to smile.

Tom brought me a glass of water which I sipped. I was trying not to look at the ponhaus. Colin toddled over to me, and I ran my fingers over his hair as he hugged my legs. I swung him up into my lap and gave him kisses. He giggled.

"Why don't you lie down? I've got the boy," Tom told me reaching for Colin and swinging him high in the air as Colin squealed in delight.

I was afraid to talk, so I nodded and went to the bedroom where I stripped off those stinky clothes, but I could smell it on my skin and in my hair. I tried to take long deep breaths, hugging a towel to me in case I got sick again. Tom came in carrying Colin, who was sucking on his fist. "Here, put this cool rag on your head. Luanne has it filled with peppermint."

The cool, sweet smell of peppermint was a godsend. I tried to reach for my baby.

"Shhh, just relax, we have you safe and Colin and I are having some man-time." Tom didn't give me my baby who was perched on his shoulders.

I looked at him, embarrassed. "Thank you." I was ashamed for anyone to see me so...vulnerable.

"No need to thank me." He ran his hand over my forehead. "You are the most stubborn woman I know. Just rest, damn it." I smiled weakly, but gratefully, and thanked God a million times for Tom and Luanne. Who would I have been if I had been raised by them? I fell into a dreamless dead sleep. I didn't even hear Tom come to bed, but I woke to both him and Colin lying beside me like two pieces of bread and me the peanut butter and jam.

The next morning was even colder, but sunny, and I woke as the light filled the eastern windows, feeling hungry, and I felt like I had never been sick. Tom was still sleeping, and Colin was fast asleep curled up with his lips in an o. I was the first one up. Stirring up the embers in the stove, I went and put some corn husks and kindling in to get the fire going. I put cornbread in the Dutch oven and fried up some apples with brown sugar, some of the pork, and I even fried up some eggs. Tom eventually came in, fastening his overalls. He reached for a cup as I pulled the coffee from the stove.

"I'm glad you're feeling better." He kissed me on the cheek quickly. It was one of the few times Tom and I were completely alone at the table. It happened so rarely that I can remember it. I poured him his coffee and put the plates on the table, and I have to say I ate four pieces of pork and two slices of cornbread with butter. I guess I wasn't embarrassed by how much I was eating even though I can still remember my mother telling me ladies do not eat like farmhands. Tom ate a piece of cornbread with jam, a slice of pork and a few spoonfuls of apples. I ate more than Tom.

"What are you planning on doing today?" I asked him.

"I have to put up the butchering kettles. I need to finish salting some of that meat. I might work that horse for a bit. Taylor said they were coming for that horse before Christmas."

"You need any help?"

"No, it's all right."

We sat a spell, sipping our coffee as the stove threw off a nice, sweet heat into the kitchen before he slid his chair out, grabbed his hat, and out the door he went.

It was later that morning when I was washing and stirring clothes in the front yard that a realization spread over me that caused me to stop in mid-stir. I tried to remember the days and weeks and tried to convince myself otherwise, counting days, months, and full moons on my fingers. I went back and forth all day about time and summer and swimming and Tom and me.

Once, I asked my mother outright if she used birth control when I was really thinking that she and my father must have never had any relations at all. She just looked at me with those thin pursed lips and that glare and told me, *we took care.*

We took care, I thought. What in the world does that really mean? But I knew better than to ask. We just didn't talk about those things then. Now, they talk about them while waiting in line at the grocery store. I'm not so sure that's progress.

When I had hung the clothes on the line, and the heavier pieces in the house by the stove, I stored up the courage to walk down to the barn to see Tom. "Tom, where are you?"

"Here, I'm over here." A long black harness was spread out on his work bench, and he held a long chisel for working in the metal clamps to the leather. He had reading glasses on the table so he could see the close work, the stiches. He was 18 years older than I, the best I could figure.

Now that I was right in front of him, I wasn't quite sure what to say. I watched him a while.

"Hand me that hames." He didn't look up from his work. As I handed him the hames, I said, "Tom, I think I'm going to have another baby." There, I said it; He looked at me.

"Now what?" I asked him.

"Now what?" he said.

"Yes, now what happens?"

"Well," he was laughing, "you ought to know better than I do."

Chapter 24

The news of the baby made Tom very happy even if he never said so. In a show of attention, when he walked in the door at the end of the day, or at dinner, he would smile and run his hand around my waist. Luanne would turn red and look away as if nothing in the world was going on. I was, as usual, trying to pretend that all of this was not happening, yet feeling panicked at the prospect of a second child out of wedlock. I had heard and knew the whispers, and my mother and her friends talking around the bridge table. They took women like me away to places, like the Virginia Colony down in Lynchburg where they kept crazy people and the feeble minded. Once they had you at the Colony, the doctors did something so you could have no more babies because women with no morals were *deviant.* I was, once again, in despair because I didn't check myself *and followed my fancy instead.* Everything my mother ever said to me, and about me, was echoing in my ears.

Tom, Luanne, and I were soon making plans preparing for the dark of winter when the nights were long, and we would spend more time in the house and more time telling tales. I had already listened to stories about Stonewall Jackson coming over Swift Run to outwit the Union, or gossip and silly stories of friends, family and loved ones in Bacon Hollow like the man that shot his wife's lover. Well, that was not so funny, but her kin wrote a ballad.

For Christmas that first year, Tom came home with a radio. Luanne and I screamed like schoolchildren, and Tom told us if we weren't quiet, he would take it back. The world came to Hightop Mountain through the crackle and grainy sound of technology. Even we, at the end of the world, could hear Woodrow Wilson talking on the radio. It was scary, exciting, and sad at the same time.

Christmas night, Tom and I climbed into bed, talking about all we had.

"You know, we need to get married now."

His words, which I had so wanted to hear in a man, fell flat on my ears. "I suppose."

"What's wrong?"

"Nothing."

"There ain't a man alive in the universe that doesn't know that when a woman tells him it's nothing, it's something. Don't you like me, Mary?"

My eyes shot wide open, and I sat up in bed to look at him. "Oh, Tom, oh, Tom, oh, Tom, you are the most decent and honorable man I know. I'm so sorry that this happened. I'm so sorry that you ended up with me."

"What's wrong with you?"

"I didn't want it to be like this. I wanted a man to fall in love with me naturally and love me because he wanted to not because he had to."

"More important than loving you, I like you. From the moment I saw you walking up that mountain to Granny Hite in your cold, wet stockings. A woman like that was something. Plus, you ain't moody like some. You always seem to have a light about you. You always try. In a horse, we call it heart."

Tears ran down my face.

"And you're sort of easy on the eyes." He continued pulling me to him.

I turned to him. He was grinning at me. "And I like the shape of your bottom." I pinched his arm hard. "We partner each other well." I thought about this. "Yes, you're right, we do."

"It'll be fine, dear. Breathe."

"How can I breathe getting married with my belly sticking out?"

"Ain't going to make any bit of difference. You're a hard-working, steady woman; a baby doesn't change any of that. Maybe you just don't like me?"

"I don't have a choice now."

"You didn't have to lie with me."

"Well, it was kind of nice."

"Kind of?"

"Very." I felt a blush rise in my cheeks. His hand ran across my hip. Propping himself up on his elbow, he looked down at me. I'll have Mom get the preacher in spring. You want to get married up here or down there?" He tickled my hip and I squirmed away from him. "Down "in town." I answered. I thought about that for a moment longer. "No, let's get married up here."

"Okay, then, that's settled."

He kissed my neck, nuzzling me till I giggled at his scratchy whiskers, but I liked his whiskers on my neck all the same.

Our wedding took place on an April morning when the redbuds were swelling, and the daffodils were waving their golden trumpets. It was April 23, 1921. Tom's mother had come up two nights before with his sisters and cousins, and we had spent two days cleaning and cooking. Tom had gone down to Granny's homeplace, John and Flo's house in Whitehall by Bacon Hollow, where they were throwing him some type of bachelor party that Tom assured me would be mostly playing music and drinking. Even with all those women in our house, when I watched him ride down the mountain away from me, a feeling of panic that I would never see him again rose up and rattled me to my core. I felt like a little girl again, remembering the time I got separated from my parents for over six hours in Charlestown, and I wondered, and was convinced, my mother would not come back for me. As Tom waved and turned, I felt like I was losing footing on this solid earth.

"Come on, Mary, we got to iron your dress." Luanne followed my gaze. "He's coming back, don't you worry. You just got yourself a case of wedding nerves. Hey, Mom, Mary's got herself a case of wedding nerves."

I looked at Luanne who was grinning at me like a fox.

"Ain't going to do no good now. We've already baked the cake," answered Ruth.

"Let's see what we should do with your hair. I already got the curling iron in the fire. Here give me a piece." With that, Luanne took the hot curling iron and wrapped a length of my hair around it. The smell of burning hair filled the room as I screamed and pulled away from her. My screaming continued as I suddenly realized I was now physically separated from a chunk of hair that had once been connected to my head.

"Oh, my." Luanne looked at the iron with a length of my burning smoking hair hanging from it.

Ruth came through the doorway and regarded us. "Well, I guess you will need to wear it up. Luanne throw that stinking hair outside."

I felt for the spot where my hair was missing.

"I hear pregnant women's hair grows fast." Luanne looked at me hopefully.

"It won't be grown in by *tomorrow.*" I glared at her.

"Don't worry, Tom won't notice. Men don't notice nothing. Let's go polish your shoes."

I was up early on my wedding day, and I watched the sunrise in the eastern sky and the new moon hang like an icicle with Venus there beside it. Slowly, the house came to life, and I was joined by Tom's sisters, Luanne, and my little Colin, who had also woken up feeling the excitement of the day. He was walking steadily now, and he would talk a mile a minute in a language of his own making, but I answered him like as if he was speaking English. Why, even Tom got in the habit of talking to him. "You don't say? Is that your opinion? Or where you headed to now?" This is how we engaged with him. That morning, Colin toddled into the kitchen waving his hands in the air like a hysterical woman.

Suddenly, we heard a cowbell ringing and men shouting. Ruth went to the door first and flung it wide open letting in the sunshine and morning air. "I'll be damned." Ruth wiped her hands on her apron as she went in direction of the shouts.

Luanne, the sisters, and I crowded around Ruth as a wagon crossed the field scattering the cattle in a million directions. Tom's horse had even stopped eating and was standing erect as a statue, his ears pricked forward intently, watching the wagon get closer to the house.

"Who are they?" I asked as I watched the men clanging cowbells, shooting off guns, and hollering war cries.

"My, my, my," said Ruth. I looked at Luanne who shrugged her shoulders. "It's that bunch from Bacon Hollow bringing our Tom home for his wedding." Ruth smiled. "Luanne make sure there's enough coffee. Goodness gracious, it's a shivaree," Ruth threw her head back with a laugh.

"Tom? I don't see Tom," I said as I squinted into the morning light at these men coming from the east of the mountain. With the morning sun at their backs, they were all cast into shadows.

"It's bad luck for the groom to see the bride before the wedding. Why don't you get yourself ready upstairs?" Luanne said.

Slowly, I walked down the porch steps, not regarding at all that I was in my chemise, barefoot, and my hair in pin curls tied with Ruth's quilting squares. My eyes went from face to face of the men, and then my hand covered my mouth. "Oh, oh." The wagon pulled up right in front of me with the men grinning, clanging cowbells, and hollering at the top of their lungs, except one man was just smiling from ear to ear and not making a noise.

"If you Bacon Hollow boys don't stop clanging that bell, I'm going to hit you all upside the head. Mary, you get in here. Don't you know its bad luck for Tom to see you before the wedding?" said Ruth.

I was frozen as I watched a clean-shaven man, his beard all gone and in a crisp white shirt, tie, and form-fitting black suit, get off the wagon. "What happened to your hair?" Tom pointed at my head grinning.

I looked at this young man's face, at the blue eyes and coifed hair and smooth skin and burst into tears, running into the house. Tom looked at his mother as the men all laughed. "Don't mind her. It's a case of nerves," said Ruth.

"All women are high strung," a man said from the back of the wagon. "I should know; I have me five daughters."

I sat on our bed trembling and watched as the man who was Tom slowly walked towards me. I knew, but didn't know, this stranger who looked nothing like the man I had been living with for over a year. Clasping a hand to my mouth, I regarded him. Tears ran down my face. "It's me, Mary." Tom grinned at me.

"It doesn't look like you."

"Well, it is."

"What did you do?"

"Don't you like it?" He reached for my hand and laid it on his baby smooth face. I shook my head no. "It doesn't look like you."

Between his clothes and his clean-shaven face, he looked like a man from a magazine, very handsome, but not my familiar Tom. I simply didn't recognize him. "You look a lot younger." I finally said.

"Is that a good thing?"

"It's a thing. Keep talking to me so I can hear your voice."

"Well, it is going to be a sweet day for us. The sun is shining, and we are with family and friends, and I know my Mama made you those vanilla gem cakes you like." Tom gathered me up in his arms.

I gave him a kiss. "Well, you kiss like you," I said.

"We can pretend it's not me. Would you like that?" he said with a mischievous grin.

"I swear, Tom."

"Oh, my, Mary, what a woman you are."

"Tom. Have you got her calmed down yet? Cause we need you and the men to move those tables and help outside," hollered his mother.

"I'm coming." He shouted towards the kitchen.

"Oh, Mary, don't you weep no more. It's going to be a fine day. Besides, you're marrying me. Doesn't get much better than that, my dear girl."

I watched him walk away, and I stood up with a deep breath. Looking in the mirror, I started taking the pin curls out of my hair, and my hair began to fall in loose ringlets around my face, which I patted with cold water, but it didn't cool the flush of my cheeks. My dress lay on the bed where Luanne had placed a lace handkerchief beside it along with my stockings and garters. Tom had gotten me some violet water which I sprayed on my hair, neck, wrists, and private place and slid into my pink chiffon tea length dress. I removed the flowers I had gathered that morning from their vase. I arranged the fern fronds, daffodils, grape hyacinths, and dog tooth violets and tied them with a purple ribbon. "Luanne, I'm ready."

She ran into the bedroom with her boar's hairbrush. "Not till I comb out that hair. Let's get it fluffed and get that missing piece hid."

Outside on the farm and inside in the dining room, I heard voices and laughter from men, women, and children. Along with Tom's family, neighbors had been arriving all morning in wagons and cars that made it to the foot of the farm lane, and some walking. Why even Granny Hite and the Browns Gap clan had made the trip. Tom was well loved.

The preacher from the Mt. Zion Church at the bottom of HighTop Mountain arrived last. Preacher Lam and Tom's family went way back, and this was the church of Tom's mother who held considerable influence. I would have liked to have been the fly on the wall for the conversation between Ruth and Preacher Lam with Tom divorced, not believing in the church at all, not attending church, and me so far along, again. But there was the preacher, chatting with everyone as if he were marrying the King and Queen of England. This is not what would have happened down in Elkton at my mother's church with Preacher Dean; there would have been stones.

Ruth beamed like a spring sunrise. "Come on now, Mary. They're ready for you."

As I looked across the garden, Tom was a handsome sight with his dark wedding suit, and freshly washed hair falling over his forehead. With a sweep of his hand, he would push it back as he laughed at a comment one of his friends said. He had his father's gold pocket watch on a chain that crossed the vest of his suit. When he saw me, he clasped his hands in front of him, rocking back and forth on his heels and staring me down.

I surveyed the crowd of neighbors, all beaming smiles at me as I walked towards Tom and the preacher. I slowed and looked to my right into my father's eyes. And next to him was my mother! Daddy held his hat in his hands and smiled at me with such love and joy. I was astonished. How could he have that much love for me here and now?

"Oh, Daddy."

"Look at my beautiful girl." My daddy kissed and hugged me tight while my mother, in her beautiful hat, matching dress and forced smile, air-kissed my cheek saying, "I swear, Mary, must you always put the cart before the horse?"

"Yes, it appears that I do, Mother, yes." I then turned and focused on Tom who was staring into me as if he had waited for me though many lifetimes; his gaze was steady, true, and unwavering, and in that moment, I was no longer afraid. It was at that moment I knew, without any doubt, that I was supposed to be here on this mountain with him. And I felt, through his and my father's love, that maybe God loved me, too.

The preacher, Bible in his hand, cleared his throat, looked at me and Tom, then out at the congregation. "We are here today to give glory to God through the union of God's children in holy matrimony. And God is watching over us here today. He is watching us and walking beside us whether you have recognized it or not. Because here, today, is proof. God so loved man that he gave us his only son. And God so loved Adam that he sent him woman, to walk beside him all his days, to offer him hope, salvation and the way to divinity because if God left it up to us men, well brothers, we would have never found the way."

"But some of us do find a way. We open our heart to God, and in doing so we open our hearts in the ability to give and receive love. Because marriage is a sacred union and should not be entered into lightly. But we do. We do enter into marriage lightly in the same way that some of us might call ourselves Christians without ever doing the spiritual work of Christ. And we enter into love just as lightly."

"So, here we are with our two sinners, yet he, who is without sin, can cast the first stone for God has regarded them and all of us. And God loves us just like we love Tom and Mary, despite their sins and ours. Now, if we know our true Lord's love, how it is unwavering, steadfast, and constant, then we may not ever question love or need to look outside of ourselves for our true love's mate. But as mortals, we forget. And our pains get the best of us. We make mistakes. We make them again, and we question God and his love."

I stared at the preacher, sweat beading at my brow, who was paying no mind to me but was on a roll filled with the holy spirit. Is this his standard marriage sermon? Or is this especially for me? But Tom is in this with me; he is a sinner too, *he has been divorced*, and that made me so happy that I squeezed his hand and almost giggled. Tom regarded me, and I knew he'd read my mind.

"Then we find a mate. And we are lucky, when we *do not* think with our body, but with our heart and mind, when we know at the core of our being, that this is the person that not only completes us but honors us as the divine, as we honored God's son here on earth. For when we do this with another, we raise ourselves up; we raise our partners up and then the chore that they didn't do becomes a small thing in this lifetime. For God so loved the world that he sent his only son. God so loved you he sent you a helpmate. Recognize, honor, and exalt your helpmate. When you see fault within them, look to yourself. When you lose patience, look to the stars. When you are frightened, reach out your hand, for God will move through you. And have wisdom to not enter into this union with God, or a spouse lightly for this is your divine union on earth."

"Now, Mary and Tom have taken the approach of many of our ancestors, for they have lived together a year and a day, and their union has been blessed, and their families, friends and community look on their marriage with joy. So, I'm pleased today to join these two people, the daughter and son of God, in holy matrimony."

I grabbed Tom's arm digging my fingers into his flesh. I was getting ready to faint. The world was drawing down to a pinpoint and my knees were buckling.

"I'm here, Mary."

I glanced frantically at the preacher who motioned for a chair. "Bring her a glass of water," he shouted.

Luanne came to me. "What's wrong? You not feeling good?"

I shook my head no, but I meant yes. From somewhere a glass of water was handed to me, and I drank down the pure cool spring water. I grabbed hold onto Tom's arm and I looked at his calm face. "I love you," I whispered to him. It was the first time I had said those words.

"Preacher, give me that ring," said Tom. The preacher took the ring out of his vest pocket and handed it to Tom who now had his arm around my waist as he lifted me to my feet, since my knees continued to buckle. "Mary, I give you my promise that from this day forward, I will give you all my love, and you shall not walk alone. I have no greater gift to give, as your love is my anchor, and your trust is my strength."

Tom looked right into my eyes as he put the gold band on my finger.

"With the power of the Father, the Son and the Holy Ghost, I pronounce this couple man and wife."

And that was it. The crowd erupted into joyous shouts. I blinked. Tom smiled. "Let's get you up to the house to do the receiving." And with his arm encircling my waist we made our way through our friends and well-wishers.

Luanne carried Colin, who I grabbed up and kissed, and the sea of faces blurred before me, but their kindness was something I had never experienced before. Face after face of Tom's friends, kinfolks, and neighbors rose up before me with their eyes smiling. People were pumping Tom's hands, genuinely hugging me, greeting their friends, calling after children and grandchildren. There were women calling to their men to bring their covered dishes, men ignoring them but slapping their good friends on the back, children knocking over the pulpit, and, finally my parents staring, sitting apart from everyone else.

Ruth had taken off her hat before we'd said, "I do," and was putting her apron on as she began serving the wedding meal. She pulled off the white linen cloth that were covering the two hams, and women started uncovering the plated side dishes. It was not for me or Tom to help this day, for as Tom got me seated, women surrounded me while Tom was dragged off by the men. The women's chatter overwhelmed me with their talk about deliveries, carrying low, leaving your hair unbound so you didn't tie up the birth, making sure to put an axe under the bed to cut the pain, walking the floor, squatting on all fours, midwives reaching deep inside to pull out breach births, and so on. The voices seemed to be coming to me from everywhere, and the faces were of woman I didn't know. Someone handed a cordial to me, and it was sweet, cloyingly so. I could not recognize the flavors but felt an odd heat in my body.

A shadow came in front of me, and I looked up unaware that I was grinning like a fool.

"Well, now, you must have some magic in you to get Tom to marry. He swore to me he would never head down that road again." I looked at the black-haired woman, recognizing her from the apple butter boiling so many months ago. Belle regarded me with her hands on her hips. I was astonished to see she was wearing pants. "What's wrong with you?" she asked as she looked me up and down.

I thought about this for a minute. "I don't think I've had anything to eat proper since yesterday."

She looked at me, half frowning. "Let's, get on up then. Come on." She grabbed my arm and yanked me to my feet as the woman around me gave each other sidelong glances. She pushed her way over to the wedding table. "What you want? I'll make you a plate."

I had no appetite. She regarded me. "You're going to eat this here meat, and this bread. You want some of these apples? Yep, you do. Let's get some sugar into you."

As I was standing there, my mother suddenly appeared beside me. "Well, Mary, at least I have lived to see this day."

"Who are *you*?" Belle asked belligerently.

My mother regarded this woman as if she had been accosted by a handmaiden of the devil. "I'm Mary's mother."

"I didn't think she had no mother."

"Well, really!"

"Mama, I'm so glad you and Daddy came on up here. Did Daddy's car make it all right? Did it bottom out on the potholes?"

"I suppose we did fine, though I expect that undercarriage might never be the same, and I'm sure he will use it for an excuse to get a newer model, which he has been talking about endlessly for the last three months."

Belle nudged me. "Mary, eat your food before you faint."

"Who *is* this woman, Mary?

I put a piece of ham in my mouth. "I'm not quite sure. I think she is one of Tom's old girlfriends or maybe current girlfriend." I looked at Belle who was staring at us, looking almost bored.

"Oh, my God." My mother's hand went to her brow as if she had been struck.

"There you are. Missy, a woman in your condition must rest." My father kissed me on the top of my head as he appeared beside us. At that moment, Tom came into the mix.

"You devil," remarked Belle as she swung Tom around and they wrapped their arms around each other like holly and ivy.

"Who *is* this woman?" My mother grabbed my ear, I squirmed away from her, and my father beamed at my husband.

"Congratulations, Tom. I have been hearing that you have got yourself well set up over at Adams's place these days."

"Well, I'm not so sure about that. The Petersons and Caves have had him in their back pocket for a while."

"But you've got other expertise that the Petersons, and, for sure, those Caves do not have. Adams has got more money, or other people's money, than he knows what to do with, I hear."

Tom laughed. "He knows how to spend it, and now he's got himself a woman that can bankroll him, so he's spending it as fast as she gives it to him."

"Every man's got a woman who can bankroll them; they just don't realize it," Belle said deadpan.

"Belle speaks like a true philosopher; it must be her Indian blood." Tom looked at Belle, admiring her.

"Hmm, Indian? Why, that's worse than a nigger." My mother's words silenced the gathering.

Belle wheeled around so she was toe to toe with my mother. "I may be Indian, and I may be a nigger, but that is way better than being a bitch."

My mother looked as if she had been shot. All color drained from her face, and her eyes grew wide. Belle didn't smile or frown but stared pitchforks at her.

I put down my plate. "Daddy, why don't you get yourself some of that custard cornbread that you like? Mama, the woman folks have this elixir that I think you need a sip of."

"No, thank you," she said curtly.

"Alma, let's pay our respects to Preacher Lam before we cross the mountain." Daddy tried to usher her away.

My mother spun around and turned to me. "I can see you are where you belong."

My father turned back and winked at me as he led my mother away. I plopped down in my seat like a ton of bricks. I wasn't sure if I should be mad at Belle for disrespecting my mother or pleased.

Belle didn't miss a beat. "You got yourself enough to eat? Tom, when is this baby due?"

"The doctor says June, but Granny says July."

"Who you going to use?"

"The doctor, I reckon. Why, he's from UVA."

"You want to tell me what a doctor knows about a woman?"

"Belle, I'm not going to debate with you right now. Mary, how are you feeling?"

"I'm doing fine." I stood up. "I'm going to get me some fresh air." With that, I left them both and walked out to the front porch as a married woman, and as the people smiled and congratulated me and gushed about the food, I watched my parents motor down the mountain and felt a sigh of relief and a bit of triumph.

I felt a hand at my arm, and I turned to see Ruth's friend, Theresa, holding me. "Mary, if you are feeling up to it, we are planning a get together at Rose's the first week of May. You come on. Get Tom to bring you."

"I'll ask him."

"And bring Luanne. I'm going to find her, too, and let her know. Why I think I see her there with Asa Dean." I nodded. "What should I bring?" I shouted after her.

"Yourself."

I thought about this. I had not had friends in a long while. I regarded my surroundings and the clan of these strangers. Tom came up beside me. "You get yourself invited to a hen party?"

"A what?"

"A hen party. If you have those women on your side, I might as well leave home." He kissed me on the check and leapt off the front porch, strolling to the men who were waiting for him at the barn and slapping his friends on the back as he walked past them. Belle came out on the porch, and I regarded her as the men hollered at her to join them. Belle regarded them as she ate a ham biscuit.

She turned to me. "I'll see you around, little Mary. Mark my words." She winked at me as she bounded off the front porch, her hair bouncing behind her like a half broke horse.

"Who *is* she?" I asked no one in particular. Ruth was coming on the front porch drying her hands on her apron and squinting in Belle's direction. "She's a woman who has always called her own shots."

Chapter 25

The wedding came and went, and Luanne and I put my wedding gown to rest nestled with cedar chips, pennyroyal, and lavender in the bedroom trunk. May came and went with its mayapples, bloodroot, trillium, sweet warm air, and greening and growing of the pastures, wild and lush. Tom always said the April grass had no strength, but the May grass grew the livestock. Then came June with a bit more heat, the garden needing weeding and the fireflies circling the night air like so many fairies. By July, the heat came on more heavily, the flies were a nuisance, and I was big, round, and the baby pressed on my pelvis and bladder. I felt as if I might be pregnant forever. False contractions came and went, and came and went, and went.

The doctor came to call with his snake like stethoscope, listening and pronouncing me a picture of health.

"Mary," said the doctor, "I think it is now time to see what is going on. If you don't mind, I would like to see if you are dilated. Let's get you to your bed."

I had never had a doctor looking at my lady parts before, having had Colin with the midwife at the coal camp. Tom hung back, not sure what I wanted him to do, or what he should do. "Tom, can you help me?" the doctor motioned for him.

As Tom came into our bedroom, I pleaded with my husband. "Can't you delivery this baby? Haven't you delivered horses and cows? Why do I have to have this man poking me?" Tom looked panicked. The doctor attempted a good-hearted chuckle. "Up here it may come to that, so don't go wishing it."

Tom looked at me without a hint of a smile. The doctor rolled up his sleeves and washed his hands in our dry sink. "Now, why don't you stand up there by her head and talk to your dear wife? Yes, that's it. Hold her hand. Now, Mary, let's see you raise up your knees, that's it.

Okay now, I'm going to raise up your skirt, and let's see what is going on here."

I forced a smile at Tom who continued to look at me helplessly.

"My, my, it appears that you might be getting ready to have a baby here soon."

"What does that mean?" asked Tom.

"Well, the way her perineum feels and her uterus and cervix, why it gives every indication that it won't be long now."

"See, Mary?" said Tom, trying to rouse my spirit.

"By my recollections, Doctor, I have been going on pregnant for ten months." He chuckled. "Well, maybe you'll be one for the record books. In any case, let me just stir the pot a bit."

I screamed and jumped as I felt a poke way up inside me.

"What the hell?" yelled Tom.

"Just helping things along; you'll thank me." The doctor rolled down his sleeves. Now, where can I wash up properly?"

Tom lead the doctor to the kitchen spigot.

"Watch and see, it won't be long now. You might want to bring her down to your mother's and send word if that water breaks." He waved as he crossed the door and into the light of the summer evening.

I laid in the bed feeling sore and finally I pulled down my skirt and pulled up my panties. Slowly, I swung my legs over the side of the bed, wishing I were not a woman. "How much did he charge for *that*?" I asked Tom after he escorted the doctor out.

"Why are you asking such things?" he looked at me, not really expecting an answer.

That night, when we had turned in, I struggled to find a comfortable spot in the bed. The heat in the house and my bulk kept me, and by default, Tom restless. "How about I open the doors wide? Will that help?"

"Yes, that would be good." I watched Tom's slender body walk across the room and open the door. He stood silhouetted against the ever-dark night and open door. "Oh, Tom, hear the whippoorwill?"

He turned and smiled back at me. "Yes, I love that summer sound. Looky there! A shooting star."

"Maybe it means the baby will come. Your mama and Granny told me it was going to come last full moon."

"The baby will come when it's ready."

"I know." Tears rolled down the side of my face. This in between, this stuck on the edge of something, was making me feel like I had spiders in my head.

He climbed into bed beside me and laid a hand on my giant belly. "Want me to read to you?" I nodded. Tom picked up the volume of William Butler Yeats.

"Read me about Innisfree."

Putting on his reading glasses, and in his slow, sweet way, he read the tale of faraway.

I will arise and go now, and go to Innisfree,
And a small cabin build there, of clay and wattles made;
Nine bean-rows will I have there, a hive for the honey-bee,
And live alone in the bee-loud glade.

And I shall have some peace there, for peace comes dropping slow,
Dropping from the veils of the morning to where the cricket sings;
There midnight's all a glimmer, and noon a purple glow,
And evening full of the linnet's wings.

I will arise and go now, for always night and day
I hear lake water lapping with low sounds by the shore;
While I stand on the roadway, or on the pavements gray,
I hear it in the deep heart's core.

"Shall I keep going?"

"Yes."

And so, Tom read softly, quietly, slowly, pausing after each poem, and turning the page until he found another and until he was sure I was asleep.

Later that night, when all was dark and quiet, I woke with a start. I steadied myself against Tom's deep breathing when I heard and felt a faint *pop*. Water leaked between my legs. "Tom," I whispered as I shook him awake. "Tom!"

He mumbled and his eyes remained closed.

"Tom, my water has broken." He was suddenly awake. "You sure?"

"Yes, I need a towel for the bed." I raised myself to a seated position.

Tom swung himself out of the bed and found some clean towels in the kitchen pantry. I placed them underneath me. "Now, what do we do?" I said.

"Don't you *know*?" he looked at me, panicked.

I thought a minute, remembering Colin's birth and how it took a day and a half to bring him into this world. "I think we should just sit tight. That UVA doctor you insisted on might charge us double if we wake him in the middle of the night. I'm not feeling anything yet. And this might take a while. It's going to do no good you leaving me and riding down the mountain in the dark and risking your neck. We'll go for him in the morning. Here. Just put the light on low. That will give me some comfort."

Tom lowered our gas lamp and slid his fingers into my hand as we both lay on our backs breathing hard and deep. He turned over on his side, propping himself on his elbow. "It's happening now, isn't it? Our baby is coming into this world. What a beautiful day, Mary."

I placed one hand over my heart and one on my belly. "Yes. Tell me it's going to be all right?"

"It's going to be a dream." Brushing the hair away from my eyes, he looked at me. "You are going to give birth to a beautiful strong baby, and if I'm right I'm going to have to tell you to keep to your bed and rest. Enjoy your confinement with this one. You have me, Luanne, my mother. Lie in this bed and love your child and rest and get strong. You will be fine, my girl." He brought the palm of my hand up to his mouth and kissed it and then closed my fingers around his kiss so I could hold onto it.

The hoot owl called, who always called late in the summer night. We both dozed off, but we woke to my thrashing the covers off and the contractions bearing down hard and low and hateful. Tom sat up and was staring at me. "I think you best go for the doctor now and wake Luanne."

He slid out of bed like a phantom and silently drew on his clothes faster than I had ever seen before in my life.

"I'm going for the doctor and will wake Luanne on my way out. Can I get you anything?"

"A cool glass of water."

"You wait to have that girl until I get home." He smiled at me slyly.

"How do you know it's going to be a girl?"

"Oh, those women haven't told you the tales yet?"

I smiled, shaking my head.

"When a woman is given pleasure by a man, when she conceives, it will be a girl." Laughing, he grabbed his hat and ran out the door.

As soon as Tom left, I swung myself up and out of the bed, but I couldn't stand up straight because of the pain racking my body. In my billowing white nightgown, I looked like a fat old man. Hunched over, I grabbed the corner of the brass bed, and held on for dear life as a contraction took me. When it passed, I crept over to the kitchen. Picking up Tom's pocket watch on the mantle, I looked at the time, 6:12 in the morning. I kissed the watch and I placed it where he had left it the night before. Reaching for the kitchen door handle, which stuck, I yanked it back with such force the door hit the wall, yet swinging wide open to the August morning. There was no heat yet, but cool comfortable air greeted my face and my body. I seized the porch railing as another contraction wave grabbed me straight on like a flash flood on Naked Creek. "Holy Mother of God," I said to our barn cat.

Creeping down the porch steps and holding onto the railing, I made my way across the yard, noticing the fall flowers getting ready to come on. Along with the passion vine, the goldenrod and tansy had just started blooming, as well as the first flush of asters. The tomatoes were splitting in half on the vine, and it looked as if the cucumbers had doubled in size from the day before. *I can get to them before all this comes on.*

In what seemed liked very slow motion, I made my way to the chicken coop and opened the door to let them out into the morning. I thought about the chickens, the horses, the sheep, the cows, Tom's hound dog, all of which gave birth while chewing their cud, or laying peacefully in the grass, except for when the time comes, when that newborn descends into the channel and the pain gets so fierce like you're cracking in two, both human and mammal fall silent and glassy-eyed.

"My God." Another contraction hit me. I closed my eyes and tried to ride it like you ride a horse over a rock crag, and you're up and grabbing that saddle horn, and there's a moment of panic, and then whoosh, you are safe, and can draw breath, and you don't realize you haven't been breathing until you get to the other side.

As my head cleared, I cooed at my sweet chickens flinging them laying mash and cracked corn and seethed at the rooster, who strutted around his hens, dancing them into submission when they stepped too far away from him. But he also gave his hens the best of the barnyard finds. Whether it was a worm or grub or some such tasty morsel that he had come upon, he would begin a loud staccato clucking, and they would run from far and near, and he would rise above them proud of himself as they grappled for the tidbit. I watched them peck about my bare feet, and turning, admired the morning mist rising around the horses and cows grazing in the haze that circled the mountains. Clouds were gathering in the east. Richmond might be getting rain, I thought. Another contraction hit, and I tried to remind myself that all this was natural and good. Waddling, I made my way towards the house, but it seemed like hours, and it felt like hours had passed before I got there.

"What are you doing?" Luanne emerged from the front door as I gripped the stair rail.

"I've no idea." I looked at her blankly. Luanne made a motion to come get me.

"Leave me be." This stopped her dead in her tracks. "Where's my son?"

"Sleeping."

I pulled myself up the stairs, motioning her away. "Tom's gone for the doctor. Get more towels and the clean dish rags."

"I know. He told me. Let me freshen the sheets on the bed."

"No, it does not matter now. Just help me untie my hair."

As I clutched the railing, Luanne undid my braid. "Don't you want your hair off your face?"

I shook my head no. "Granny says it binds up the birth."

"Oh, that's so old-timey. Your hair is just going to get all sweaty."

"No." I glared at her like a crazy woman as another contraction gripped me. I waved her away as I made it back to the bed. Sitting on the side, I stripped off my undergarments and changed my nightgown.

"You're stark naked," Luanne shrieked. With that Colin woke up with a yowl. "I'll go get him." Luanne darted upstairs.

Drawing a clean nightgown over my head, I smoothed out the towels underneath me as the next wave hit. "Faith and begorrah," I whispered, hearing my Irish grandmother's voice in my ears. "Luanne, what time is it?"

I heard her foot falls pounding down the stairs and travel to the kitchen. "9:10." She ran back to me holding Colin who reached for me anxiously.

Instinctively, I grabbed him up in my arms and held him, covering him with kisses. "Your baby sister is coming into the world today my sweet boy. You be a good boy today for Luanne."

"Mama, Mama, Mama," he shouted, clapping his hands. I looked into his eyes which were as brown as walnuts and knew he would always be my first, yet also realizing the heart expands to love more and more and more.

"Tom has gone for the doctor and will be home soon and play with you. Would you like Luanne to get you some milk?" Colin nodded jumping up and down on his chubby baby legs as Luanne reached for him and he circled his legs around her waist clinging to her.

"What are we going to do?" Luanne looked at me pleadingly.

"I'm going to be fine. Tom will be home soon with the doctor. Women have been having babies for a long time, Luanne."

"I'm going to go for my mother."

"You don't have to go for Ruth. I'll be fine. Take Colin to the kitchen and feed him please." Luanne put Colin down, who ran after the cat and into the kitchen, with Luanne following at his heels. Yet, she looked at me from across her shoulder, and for a moment I felt worse for her than me as she was completely unknowing being a virgin and having never born a child through the same channel that was getting ready to crack open like the very earth itself.

Another contraction hit that was so severe that I didn't know if more water was leaking from my uterus, or I was passing water. I closed my eyes, and the pain receded away from me as I felt like I went floating upwards, and before I knew it, I was flying above the farm way up in the air. I could see the cows and horses grazing and the chickens scratching in the wood pile and the roof above the house. I'm so free, I thought. I'm flying like a bird through the blue sky. With my God-like view, it seemed like I was looking into the east, searching for Tom who was nowhere to be seen. In the next moment, like a magic trick, I was back in my body, feeling horrible pressure down my spine, into my gut and at the bottom of my being. The heat and pressure on my female places were too much to bear. Just when I was thinking I might die, a flood of relief came over me, and again I seemed to float way above the house and over the mountains. Was I on the back of the hawk?

"Tom's coming," called Luanne.

"What time is it?"

"Just past noon."

"Is the doctor with him?"

"No, he's alone."

I heard his heavy footsteps bounding up the porch stairs, and suddenly he was in our bedroom. "I'm so glad you're here." I grabbed his shirt collar.

"It's going to be fine; the doctor's on his way."

"How long's it going to be?"

"Not long at all, I'm sure. He'll be here very soon."

"You got to check for me."

"What do you mean?"

"The pain is so bad that I'm flying. I'm flying over the house. I'm flying over the mountain. I need to know something's not wrong. Shouldn't it be easier the second time?" He looked at me helplessly. "You've got to see if that baby's head is what's pressing or if it's the feet. You've got to tell me. I feel like I'm tearing in two."

A moment passed as he looked at me. He jumped up and made for the kitchen. "Luanne! You got hot water on?" When he came back to the bed, he was drying his hands with a towel and had his shirt sleeves rolled up. He was also carrying a bowl. Luanne, holding Colin, followed.

"Get on that porch and keep an eye out for the doctor. You hear?" I had never heard him raise his voice before. When she had left, he turned his attention to me. He pulled the covers down.

"It's going to be fine, Mary," and he grinned. He was my old Tom, and I was just Mary, and I smiled for the first time all morning. I turned my head away. "This is so embarrassing. I'm sorry. I'm just scared." I was so filled with embarrassment that I hid my face with my hands.

"What do you have to be sorry about? You think I haven't seen my share of..." he looked around for the word, "female places before? I swear, Mary."

"I just don't want you remembering me like this."

"I've been to war; I'm good at forgetting."

Rubbing lard on his right hand, he closed his eyes and took a deep breath. I closed my eyes and took long slow breaths like the midwife in West Virginia had told me so long ago. First one finger, so slowly, then a second, then a third with his steadfast patience he felt his way into me.

"I feel her head. It's okay." I thought he was going to cry. "It's the end of things now. She's ready." He cleaned his hand on the towel and kissed me full on the lips. "It's all good now. It's all you."

Reassured, I felt calm. I closed my eyes.

"Rest a bit now. You're at the end of things." Tom held my face in his hands. "Luanne, Is there any coffee?" He called towards the porch. He then turned back to me. "You holler for me when you need me. I'm getting some coffee."

"You need me to turn that horse out?" asked Luanne." He's still tied to the springhouse gate."

As Tom walked on towards her, I heard him say. "Best to leave him tied. I may need to ride out before this is all over." He means nothing by that, I thought, as tiredness overtook me.

Chapter 26

It was early evening when I was roused by Luanne staring down at me and Colin, whom she was holding, reaching for me as if I were an island in the vast sea. Pulling myself up, I held my arms out for my son; he smiled the only smile of a child for his mother. I drew in a long breath of him.

"You all right?

"Yes." I took stock of my body. Nothing hurt and everything was calm; "Where's that doctor?"

"I don't know. Tom went out after him a little while ago." I nodded as I hugged my son.

"Luanne?"

"Yes?"

"You promise me you'll always keep an eye on my Colin. No matter what.'

"Stop this. It's going to be fine, mark my words."

With clenched teeth I told her, "If there is one thing I know, it's that we don't know if it's going to be fine. I just need to know that if it isn't, Colin will be cared for and loved. Don't you let my mother take him away. You hear me? I mean I don't know that she would, but if you and Tom don't want him..."

"*Mary.*" Luanne looked pleadingly at me.

"You've got to make sure that he knows someone loves him." I grabbed her by her dress shirt. Her eyes opened wide as if she were staring into the face of a lunatic.

"I promise, and besides, everything's going to be peaches and cream. Why, I've seen women lie in bed for three days before their babies come."

"And I've seen women in the coal camps bleed out, or, worse yet, lie in a bed for days with that baby stuck inside them till they die like they are in hell," I said through clenched teeth.

"You're not well, Mary. You're talking out of your mind. I'm going to make you up some tea to settle your nerves."

"Who's that?" I called. We both turned upon hearing footsteps dragging on the porch.

"There ain't no tea being made unless I'm making it." There was no mistaking the outline of Granny Hite, and Tom's figure coming in behind her.

I began crying at once and clasped my hand to my mouth so that I wouldn't shout out my joy and relief. "Granny, I think I'm dying," I told her.

"Well, you may be, but I will be here beside you. Luanne, put this here raspberry leaf to boil and make it strong. Why don't you sweeten it with a bit of honey if you got it?"

"Tom, I'm sorry," I whispered in his direction.

"Shh...what in hell are you sorry for?"

Granny Hite sat down by my bedside, smoothing out the covers. "Tom? Is this here coverlet from your mama's mother? I don't recognize it."

I could not believe my ears. I was dying and they were talking about the quilt.

"No, this came from my daddy's first wife. You remember her? She died," and he retold the story of how she had died from complications of childbirth back in 1885. Then he realized what he was saying and stopped abruptly. Granny felt my forehead.

"You're nice and cool. You know it took three days to bring my son into this world. Here, let's get up and get some fresh air." She motioned towards Tom. "Go get under her and help her up. Lying flat on your back never helped a birth."

Feeling like an elephant, I slowly raised myself with their help till I was standing by my bedside. Heavily, slowly, and stiffly, I diligently placed one foot in front of the other as my bare feet shuffled along.

"Where you want to walk to? asked Tom.

"To the Promised Land, but I think I can only get as far as the garden."

"That's a good idea," Granny Hite replied. "Why don't you tell me what you all got planted."

The sun still shone down hot and thick, and it made it difficult to breathe as I looked ahead to the garden shimmering in the heat.

"Tom has us planting salsify, but I've never tasted it," I told Granny.

"I like it. Why, it tastes just like oysters. Of course, it's has been a long, long time since I had any oysters, and I love them, too."

"I will get us some oysters this Christmas, Granny," Tom said.

"My Daddy would get them every year. They would come on the train from Richmond, and he would come home with a bushel of them, shouting, '*Alma. Get my shucking knife ready!*' I smiled as I remembered my father and a moment touched with joy.

"I will come home with a bushel of oysters this Christmas." Tom looked kindly at me as he said this.

"Well, you better invite me," Granny said.

And with that I doubled over and fell to my knees.

"What's happening?" Tom looked pleadingly at me.

"I got the tea ready," called Luanne from the back porch.

"Good. Let's get things rolling along. Come on, child, let's make our way to the shade."

With cramps gripping at my gut, I crept to the shade of the back porch. String beans lay in heaps, ready to be strung. I thought about picking up my needle and thread and making a dent in the work, but I sat on our bench just staring at the beans.

"Luanne? What you going to do with these leather britches? Bring us out some needles and lets string some so we can make ourselves useful. Tom, you go about your business. We'll call for you."

Luanne shot Granny a look as she handed me a cup of steaming raspberry leaf tea. It was sweet and bitter at the same time and made my lips pucker, but I drank it with conviction because it was going to make things better. Luanne then returned to the kitchen for the sewing basket and came back, handing each of us needles and thread. As if I were in a dream, I slowly threaded my needle with dark black thread and pierced the top of each green bean, sliding it down to the knotted end, continuing until the strand was full. Too fatigued to stand up and hang it from the eave of the porch, I tossed it to Luanne who hung it like Christmas garland from the eave of the house.

By my third cup of tea and third garland, I was bone tired and so sleepy I felt I might swoon. Carefully standing up, I reached for my son who was tossing bean tops at the chickens scratching around under the porch. "Let's take a nap, Colin."

Ignoring their abominations to *not hold my boy*, I carried him to the clean sheets that Luanne had placed on the bed. They smelled like summer. We dropped into the down mattress, displacing goose feathers as we lay into the cloud-like bed. Colin wrestled about as I tried to get him settled. I sang him my old grandmother's tune.

Where Lagan streams Sweet lullaby
there grows a lily fair.
The twilight gleam is in his eyes
The night is on his hair
And like a lovesick lennan-shee
He has my heart enthralled.
No love have I
Nor liberty
And God is lord of all.
There on the cricket's singing stone
He lays
A bog wood fire.
And comes and goes,
In sweet undertones,
The song of heart's desire.

I smiled at my son who sucked his thumb and I prayed to God to forgive my sins and not to punish me now and leave him an orphan.

It was dark when I woke again, and Colin was gone. The gas light glowed on the bedside table, and Luanne had placed a jar of purple asters, yellow tansy, and orange and speckled marigolds by my bedside. The cat was curled up at the foot of the bed. I looked around, wondering where everybody was, when I heard laughter coming from the kitchen. I was still pregnant, and it felt as if my giant belly had gotten rounder and harder and my breasts felt hard and heavy, too. Swinging my feet over the bed again, I shuffled over to the kitchen doorway. Fried tenderloin sat in a platter and Luanne, Granny and Tom were playing kings in the corner, one of my favorite card games. "Is the doctor coming?" I asked.

"I don't know. I was expecting him by afternoon." Tom stared at his cards.

"How many babies have you delivered, Granny?" I asked.

"Not too many, but I have been present at whole bunch of them." I took this information in as I felt the excruciating pain of the baby's head pressing down on me. "Where's Colin?"

"Asleep. I tell you, he was a time today. He had to be into everything and overturned the milk bucket and then looked so pitiful when he did that, I didn't have the heart to fuss at him," Luanne said.

I smiled, thinking about my sweet boy, and then I gasped.

"Mary, relax and just let that baby out," Granny advised while looking at her cards.

Tom put his cards down and stood up. "Luanne, I know you are cheating, but I have not quite figured out how. Don't be messing with my cards until I get back. Come on, Mary."

He motioned for me to follow him, and he held the front door open for me. I seemed to be in and out of my body now. He held his hand out for me and led me slowly out into the front field. We scared up some finches that flew out from under our feet. The old red mare, who had carried me up to Hightop Mountain, raised her head and regarded us. Ambling over, she lowered her head to my belly as I stroked the top of her head and mane. Tom cooed softly in my ear telling me how much he was going to love being in a house with three women and that he and Colin would be outnumbered.

He gently turned me around, my back pressed against his chest. As he held me tight, his hands lifted my nightgown, and he stroked my swollen belly as if it were a chalice in the Ark of the Covenant. His hands cupped my throbbing breasts, and I relaxed on into him. With his breath on my hair, he whispered into my ear. "There's no good in being scared, especially when we've no hope but to trust what's coming, because it's coming, for better or worse, and it will be what it will be. I realized this when I was on a battlefield, frozen in place and a hair's breadth from running for my life but freezing in place like a bullseye. The sergeant, dripping blood from his forehead, grabbed me by my shirt and, pulling me up till we were eye to eye, said, 'Boy, your *fuck you* better be stronger than being scared.' He then tossed me down, and this country boy said to himself, '*I'm going to live, even if it kills me.*'" Tom laughed at this. "You know I'm your loyal dog, and as long as I draw breath, I'll be standing here. I got you." He rocked me slowly back and forth, and it felt dreamy, and I felt as if I were drifting into the stars and surrounded by the sparkling lights of the heavens and the waves of the Milky Way. I rode this dream till the moon had shifted over the mountain.

The next thing I knew, Tom was bracing me from behind as I squatted with the force of myself pushing and grunting and pushing as the pain caused fireworks in front of my eyes. "Hold me up. Hold me up. Now! Now! *Oh, my God*!" I bore down with the force of a sledgehammer, and I split right down the middle.

"Lay me down, Tom, catch the baby!"

The rip and the tear and the whoosh of what was inside coming out was followed by the relief and with one hand, Tom reached out for the child and with the other, he pulled off his shirt. I laid in the grass, panting and grunting, as the waves of the contractions slowed. Our child's calls filled the air, and Tom was laughing like a crazy man, holding our child in his shirt. I started laughing and crying in the dew filled pasture and it seemed as if God's time stood still. He handed me my daughter. Her eyes opened big and dark, and I saw the cosmos reflected in those midnight eyes without pupils. Then suddenly, her pupils were given birth too, and I watched them form in the dark orb of her eye, and she blinked, and her arms moved like whirligigs and her legs kicked like a frog. "I swear, Mary, this beats all," said Tom, like a man out of breath.

"Tom." Granny was silhouetted against the front door, a faint yellow light behind her.

"Don't you go anywhere. I've got to figure out how to get you two back to the house."

Laying the baby to my breast, I began to tell her that she was Queen of the Universe. As the life force pumped from me to her and the umbilical cord turned from red to pink to white, I whispered, "You shall be Queen." Then I laid back on the grass and tears rolled down my face.

When I opened my eyes again, I could hear the commotion of them all coming back for me. The three of them surrounded me lying in the field, staring, and not talking. Granny moved first. "Let's get this cord tied off proper. Luanne, you tie that thread where I tell you. Now, you see where I'm pointing to?" Luanne nodded, frightened, but then she looked at me and attempted a reassuring smile.

"Tom, you pour that shine over those scissors. Yes, now cut about an inch above that thread. That's right. Luanne wrap that baby in the blanket. We can clean her up at the house. Tom, help Mary sit up a bit. Wrap that blanket around your wife; she's got the shakes. Mary, I'm going to push down on that stomach until we get that afterbirth delivered, do you hear me?"

I nodded, and as she commenced kneading my belly, I screamed like a banshee, and the warm gush of baby jelly flowed out as the spams subsided. "Is it done?"

"Let me take a look. Luanne, shine that light for me. Yes. Now, let's get you up to the house, cleaned up and in your bed."

"It seems wrong to leave all this here in the field." Tom looked troubled.

"Well, come first light, you can bury it," Granny answered.

As Tom and Granny got on either side of me, I struggled to walk, as my body had the shakes. "Why does it still hurt so?" I winced and struggled to draw breath.

"Because you just gave birth to the biggest baby ever born in Greene County," laughed Tom.

"If you ever do this again, don't eat so much," Luanne said, half seriously.

Dawn was turning the sky a pale orange with indigo streaks swimming through the clouds and into the dark heavens. I rested my hands on our kitchen table as Granny commenced to bathing me in warm soapy water. Tom held his baby, smiling down to her, and running his finger around her face and examining her tiny fairy-like fingers. The warm water felt good on my bottom and legs. Granny brushed out my hair and leaves and bits of grass fell to the floor. Drying me off as if I were a baby myself, she pulled a clean chemise over my head, and we fitted my panties with a thick rag.

"You go pass water before you get into that bed," she told me. I remembered the women making me do this at the coal camp, too, so I meekly tried to, but I could not feel anything. Granny looked into the pan. "Good. Let's get you to bed, and I'm going to clean up this little girl. Tom?"

Reluctantly, Tom handed over the baby and swooped me up into his arms, carrying me to our bed. He laid me down, grinning at me like a fool. "You're a fine woman, Mary. Do you know that?"

"I'm something, that's for sure." At that moment, we heard the hound barking. "Maybe that's the doctor?" I said. "If so, don't pay him."

He stood up as Granny came in, holding my baby and placing her in my arms. "Seems it's the doctor. Ain't that special. Good thing we didn't need him. Fine lot of good that would have done." Granny was frowning.

As his footsteps crossed the porch, I heard the doctor say to no one in particular, "How's our girl doing?"

"She's doing fine and delivered of a girl this very morning," replied Granny.

"That's wonderful. Let me go check on her. I wish I could have gotten here sooner, but I had business over in Charlottesville and didn't get word till I arrived home yesterday evening," he said as he approached the bed, carrying his giant black doctor bag. I eyed him, annoyed, as I half-heartedly handed him my girl.

As I was handing her to him, I heard Colin's little footsteps coming down the stairs. He pushed past the doctor, who was blocking him from me, and scampered onto the bed. My eyes went wide as he clambered over my stomach.

"Be gentle, Colin," said Tom, reaching for him as Colin shifted from me to Tom happily.

"It looks like you have yourself a beautiful addition to your family, Mr. Dodson, two healthy children and a contented wife. I tell you, Mrs. Dodson, to look at you now, no one would suspect you just gave birth." I regarded the doctor without enthusiasm.

"Well, we did the best we could. Thankfully, the Lord graced us with no complications," Granny said, bringing the doctor a cup of coffee.

"Why, thank you. Now, I would like to see the afterbirth before I check the mother. We don't want any complications in case it was not completely delivered."

"You'll have to come with me then," Tom said. "Luanne, get my shovel from the shed." The doctor looked around at us questioningly.

"It's outside, in the fields." Granny motioned her head towards the door.

"Oh, I see," said the doctor, his lips in a straight line. "I guess you'd better take me to it. This is one for the University of Virginia Medical Journal. I'll have quite the story at the next meeting." I shot Tom a look who winked at me in return. "Come on, Doctor," he said, taking his elbow.

Our child was trying to nurse by the time the doctor and Tom came back. Luanne sat by my bedside holding my hand. "You know, we all thought that baby was stuck, and you weren't going to make it. Well, I did. Granny was worried that cord was around the baby's neck. Tom thought the shoulders were too big. But here you are, baby and all. What are you going to name her?"

"Evelyn, the morning star," I replied to Luanne.

"Beautiful name," said the doctor, approaching us. "Now, before I go on my way and leave you all to your business, I would like to check you."

"No."

Tom forced a smile and tried to placate me.

"Mary, the doctor's come all this way. It makes sense for him to make sure you're all right."

"You did give birth under less than sanitary conditions Mrs. Dodson and with lay people," the doctor said.

"You best let him check you," Luanne said. "Lord knows if there's a complication, you could be dead five days before he gets back here."

"Well, in my defense, you mountain people live way on up here. Hightop Mountain is *not* Main Street in Ruckersville. Why, you're a good twenty miles from Swift Run. And that's mountain miles, I might add."

"Here, I'll hold the baby. Come on, everyone, let's give Mary some privacy," said Tom.

"I don't need to tell you, to keep yourself clean and change that padding. It looks like you've got help, so if you can, stay in bed for at least three weeks."

"Three weeks? I was up after one day with my son."

"I forget you mountain people are hardier than most, but you don't want to bring on any heavy bleeding. Why, a woman last week in Dyke bled right out after giving birth to a healthy baby."

"She's not me."

"I suppose not."

Tom came back into the room with Evelyn whose kitten-like mews were filling the house.

"I think she's hungry. Here you go, Mama." And he called me Mama for the rest of our days. I was glad of it, too, for he had claimed me, and since he never called me Mama at night, I became both maiden to him and mother to his children while he was alive.

Chapter 27
Hightop Mountain, September 1926

Married five years now, the days, weeks, and months were going by in a blur. Evie was five, Colin was going on eight, and I was a woman of twenty-five years of age. Old women are right, once you have babies, time starts exploding forward like geese leaving a lake. It's always a never-ending cycle of diapers, crying, coughs, cleaning, cooking, gardening, canning, washing, drying, mending, day in and day out without a break.

This early autumn morning, Luanne and I were gathering our cordials and apple stack cake for a neighbor woman's hen party. This is what the *men* called a group of women getting together. We just called them gatherings and this one was for working on a wedding quilt. I was happy to be away from the farm and taking a break from chores. Also, my children would have other children to play with, and they were looking forward to the visit as much as Luanne and I were. Tom was not as happy, as it meant he had to hitch the team and take us and stop the million things that he was doing, but he was a kind man. What I wanted and needed mattered to him.

Luanne and I were welcomed with open arms by the women folks, and my children scattered into the gaggle of youngsters. We were caught up on the concerns and joys of the holler and mountains, and we shared ours as well.

"So, Mary, how are you keeping up?" asked Theresa Dovel as she watched Colin chase Evie around the room.

"Fine, but a bit out of sorts." I threaded my needle. All the woman clucked and nodded.

"You just got the mama blues," Theresa opined.

I didn't know what that meant, but I did know how this out of sorts feeling reminded me a little bit when I first saw the coal camps, or when my mother wanted me to court Johnathan Abel, and I was filled with a response of something not being right, like a rock on my shoulder. I had nothing to complain about. My children were healthy, good food was on the table, I had a hard-working husband, but there were nights I would not want to close my eyes because I knew if I fell asleep morning would come too quickly.

An older woman, who was laying out quilt squares and pinning them because her eyesight was too poor to sew, piped up. "I had six children and two were Irish twins, and it was not the work that wore me down, but it was waking up in the morning and thinking, this is my life?"

"Ain't that the truth," said another woman, "and men don't understand. They come home and want a meal, and they don't give a lick what you have been doing or thinking all day. Then, they turn to you in bed at night with a grin."

Another woman around the circle said, I came closest to just wanting to kill my husband on those nights and he had the nerve to ask *if I liked it.*" All the woman chortled.

I wondered if my mother ever thought these things, and now I would never know. Maybe if I had married the preacher's son, my mother would have talked to me, but I didn't think so. I sat in a trance, looking at all these women gathered around the large kitchen table, which was covered with a wedding ring quilt, batting, quilt squares, plates of cookies, iced tea and, of course, cordials. For a moment, I was inside their circle and felt ease. But, my sense of belonging, anywhere, was always fleeting. It was like I was born with this sensation of always being the red headed stepchild. I suppose it was because that was how my mother made me feel as I was not the child she wanted but the child she got. This feeling abated at times like when Tom and I were making love, I was reading bedtime stories to my children, or Luanne and I were laughing, but the sense of being cast out always lurked. It was when I was surrounded by no one but trees and the forest, so that I melted into every rock, fern, and bird song, losing myself in it, well that was home, and it was safe because no one could take it from me or change their mind about me and I was part and particle of everything. This was all I knew of God and myself.

So, where's Tom at these days?" asked a younger woman who reminded me of my long-lost friend, Ethel. I waited a minute before I answered. I always hated nosiness.

"He's busy breaking some horses for Adams up at Skyland, and, of course he is hauling wood. He cut three hundred loads, fall and winter." I was boasting on my husband. What I didn't say was that he was headed way back in the mountains to conduct his other business. Coming like a specter through the house at odd hours, grabbing a bite to eat, kissing Evie and patting Colin on his head before being gone again, before I could say a word, was how it now was between us. Sometimes, this would give me my gnawing anxiety, and I would spin my mind round and round the idea that he had gotten saddled with me, just like the horses he was breaking, and he had to take them whether they were honest or rank.

"We've been hearing that Adams's got lots of government types up there now, maybe for making a park up in our mountains or over on the Massanutten ridge. Does Tom know anything?" a woman asked.

I shot a look at Luanne, as I didn't want to admit that we weren't up on any news, and if Tom knew, he hadn't told.

"Well," said Luanne." if they are going to build a park, there better be a carousel and Ferris wheel or I'm not going. Someone pass me more gingersnap cookies," and that seemed to satisfy the women.

The gathering broke up around 3:00 in the afternoon. Tom picked us up and we drove home with me yelling at my children most of the time to quit rolling around in the back of the wagon. "One of you is going to get hurt." They ignored me.

Luanne turned to me. "You ever notice, how women count on getting married and having children and then they complain about it for the rest of their lives?" We looked at each other and laughed as Tom made a sour face. Catching my breath, I said, "Belle doesn't."

"Ain't *that* the example," Luanne shouted as we both looked at Tom whose face revealed nothing.

Sometimes when you talk or think of someone, my Irish grandmother, who had the sight, told me, you can *call that person in*. Little did I know that I *had* called Belle in by thinking of her and mentioning her and, she arrived the next day. We had not seen her since the wedding. Well, at least Luanne and I had not seen her.

We had just finished cleaning up from breakfast, and I had swept the kitchen for a second time that morning when we heard, "Anyone stirring?" Evie ran towards the door as Belle walked through it like she belonged in Tom's house.

"My, my, my, seems that girl is a go getter like me." She picked Evie up and swinging her around. My child squealed with delight and beamed at Belle. "I'm looking for Tom. Where might he be at?" She didn't pay a bit of mind to me. As I took in Belle's presence and sense of herself, I found myself bristling with anger and envy. Yet, I was drawn to her, but not like a moth to a flame because even though she was the flame, I knew there was more to learn from her than what could harm me.

"Belle, to what do we owe the pleasure?" Luanne asked, as if it were usual for people to drop by way up here.

"I've come to check in with Tom about our usual business matters. Plus, I got some news from the Shiffletts, Cubbages, Comers, Deans and Doves, *and* the U. S Government that I need to relate to him." She looked around as if Tom might be hiding in the crack of the stove.

"What news?" I was looking at her hard, my heart beating fast.

"I ain't going to repeat myself twice, so let's wait till we can round up Tom. Now, where's he at?"

"He's putting some miles on one of Adams's horses," I said.

Belle snorted in what seemed like indignation. "Adams! I figure he is at the heart of this matter, that damn banty rooster. I have a notion that when Tom and I go to Skyland, Adams will be talking to us like nothing is stirring, when he is getting ready to *stab us in the back*. Him and all those son-of-a-bitchen Washington folk." Belle sat herself down in a chair, though she had not been asked. She looked at us with world-weary woe on her face, and then looked at me as if I were feeble minded. I handed Evie a glass of milk, making faces at her to make her laugh, hating and liking Belle with every molecule in my body.

"How many more of them are you planning on spitting out?" She looked to me, nodding at Evie.

I was so surprised, I just stared at Belle with her assuredness, confidence, moving through the world as if she were a man, her relationship with Tom. I wanted to punch her and fall at her feet in awe all at the same time. My emotions were so confusing I couldn't sort them out, ever it seemed.

"Where do you figure he might have gone with that horse?" I was anxious for Belle to do her business and leave yet wanting to stay close to her and see if some of whatever she got would magically jump off onto Evie. It was too late for me.

"It's hard to tell. He might be home in an hour, or he might be home at dark," Luanne said. This was the truth. The day was early, and the day was going to be long.

"I'm glad I'm done with my child rearing," Belle continued, "I only had one and I never planned on having any more. There ain't no freedom for a woman who chooses to tie herself to babies, child rearing and the kitchen." Belle looked me straight in the eye. Damn it, she knew; she knew me. Somehow, she was a conjurer and could see into my soul.

"That might be better than being an outlaw," Luanne told her as she set flour, sugar, and the lard on the kitchen table.

Belle laughed. "I rather be an outlaw than a wife."

As I was thinking about this comment, Colin came in with a cut hand. I jumped up to see how bad it was when Evie, trying to beat me to it, ran to her brother, but hit the side of the table with her head and she commenced to howling. Scooping Evie up and kissing her forehead, I simultaneously reached for Colin's hand with a wet washcloth.

"I could say you got your hands full, but you know that already." Belle got up from the table. She then opened the door and stood in the doorway, pulling out a cigarette from her trousers and lighting it. She took a long draw and blew the smoke out toward the mountain.

"When did you start smoking? Are you adding another vice to your growing list?" Tom chuckled as he walked in through the back-porch door. Belle spun around, putting the cigarette out on the heel of her boot; Tom walked right past me even though I had Evie on my hip whimpering and a washcloth stained with blood cleaning Colin's hand. Belle and Tom embraced and kissed on the lips, and he was grinning from ear to ear.

"Now, to what do we owe the pleasure of this visit?" Tom released his embrace of Belle to wash his hands in the sink. He dried them on the kitchen towel that was covering the fruit bowl even though I was holding out a towel for him.

"Like I was telling these ladies, I'm here on business and to pass on some news."

"Good, you saved me a time tracking you down. I've been needing to talk with you. Mary, can you bring me a glass? What happened, Colin?"

"Knife slipped as I was sharpening it." Colin whimpered as I bandaged his cut.

"You won't die. It's a long way from your heart," Belle said as she punched him in the arm.

"Here, talk to your sister and keep her occupied so she quits whining. Hold this cold cloth to her little goose egg on her forehead." I looked at my son. Colin regarded his sister who smiled and let out a giggle as Colin put his nose to her nose. I swept by my husband and Belle and slammed a glass down on the kitchen table for Tom. Luanne wasn't even looking up from cutting the lard, water, and flour into dough. I was so mad, but if I'd had to tell someone why, I would have had no words.

Tom went into the little shed by the back door and came in with a yellow-colored jar. Taking two glasses from the cupboard, he poured a splash of the liquid into each glass and motioned for Belle to take it. She held it up to the light, swirled the liquid and smelled it, and then took a sip rolling it around in her mouth.

"My, my, this is fine."

"I know, my feelings exactly." Tom and Belle regarded each other.

Luanne, ignoring them, motioned for me, with a knife she was holding, to start on the fruit for the pies. Watching Belle and Tom, though pretending I wasn't, I began washing and drying the small mixed fruit we had collected in a bowl, putting the ones that were too bruised into the pig bucket. I took out of the cupboard honey, that our neighbor harvested, then cinnamon, allspice, and nutmeg because I like nutmeg.

"You bringing this all up to Adams?" asked Belle downing her jigger of moonshine and twirling the jar filled with another amber liquid as if she was a juggler.

"Most of it. I'm fixing to bring him a sample when I take the horses. It whets his appetite."

"You won't have any trouble moving that golden liquid, and that cash will be needed before the end of things. Pour me another jigger." Tom poured one for himself and one for Belle, and they raised the glasses to each other and swigged it down.

"You here with some news, or are you and Tom just planning on getting lit up?" Luanne said, sounding annoyed.

"Don't you women like female company?"

"Belle, maybe we aren't sure if you're a woman with that hair so pulled back and wearing pants *and* smoking."

"They're trousers. Amelia Earhart wears them and so does Clara Bow, so I'm in good company. You mark my words; the days of skirts and dresses are coming to a close."

"I think you look right smart in them, Belle."

"Why, thank you, Tom."

I wondered if they would hang a woman for murder. Heat was raising in me.

"This filling is mixed." I walked out of the room.

"So, now, what's your news?" said Tom, pulling out seats for Belle and himself. I heard the chairs scrapping across the floor as I leaned into the wall to eavesdrop.

"You heard of the Shenandoah Valley Corporation, or something called the Shenandoah National Park Association?" Belle's voice had gotten flat.

"Can't say that I have," said Tom, and I knew, *because I was his wife*, that his voice held a tone of trepidation.

"Well, I bet Adams's got a hand in it, so maybe you can find out when you head there. It seems they're talking about putting in a big park, like they got out west, here in the mountains."

"So?"

"So? What do you expect they're going to do with us when they put in a big road down the spine of our mountain from Washington to Waynesboro so city people can take in the scenery?"

"I own this land. I've got a title free and clear. It's been in my family since the 1700s. This land was part of the original Big Survey. Besides, the Dodson's didn't switch sides in the Revolutionary War to fight for the Feds so that the same government could take the land back."

"The government might be offering us money for this land and some people say if they get cash money, they might be willing to move. Some of the Deans and Shiffletts are already cutting deals. *And* the government is planning on building what they call resettlement homes for some of the mountain families down in Ida, Grottos, Port Republic, and Elkton."

"Resettlement?"

"It's these little houses with electric and running water, and the houses are all placed close together, but you got to prove you can pay for them before they put you in one."

"Sounds like a military camp to me. How do you know all this?"

"Ha. You know I run with the big boys."

"Is that what you call it, Belle?" piped in Luanne.

"And I *read the papers*," Belle replied.

"I don't plan on selling, so they can build their park around me."

"I'm not sure that's how it's going to work."

"What do you mean?"

"It's called eminent domain, a federal law, and you know how it goes when government and men with money, when they get ideas."

"Well, isn't that a fancy ten-dollar word. They can't get rid of over fine hundred families with this eminent domain. It makes no sense. They just can't take our home places or buy our farms up like that." I heard Tom snap his fingers.

"It's the sign of the times, Tom. More and more people, especially city people, have cars that they want to motor around in, and there're motion pictures, and this year will be the first talkies. Times are changing, thank God. Hear that, Mary? *Times are changing* and that means for women, too!"

I stiffened. She knew I was listening. How did she know this?

"From what I hear, these government men want to preserve what's left of the mountains on the East Coast and then people can have a relaxing Sunday drive in their motor cars. And have you looked around recently? Many families are struggling now that the chestnut trees have the blight. Plus, at one dinner party I went to, the rich government folks weren't talking so nice about us."

"How do you get invited to fancy parties?" I shouted from the back room. She was a mystery to me.

Belle shouted back to me. "I'm keeping company with a federal land surveyor from Northern Virginia."

"I'm not concerned with your latest beau, Belle," Tom said with annoyance. "What are these government men saying?" Belle hesitated.

"Let's just say the stories they are spinning, well, it isn't good. Flatlanders never have had nice words to say about Highlanders. There have even been articles written in the *New York Times* and *Washington Post.*" Belle let out a deep sigh before she continued. "They are painting all of us as primitives; that is what they call the mountaineers in the papers. They say that mountaineers are behind the times and holding the United States back from progress. No schooling, wild, violent, crazy, destitute, and feeble minded, like they would be doing us a favor to bring us down to civilization."

I heard Tom's chair creak as he leaned back. After a moment, he said, "Nah, I just can't believe that'll happen. The government can't just take our land. We aren't Indians. I'll talk to Adams when I'm up there and see what he knows."

"You think he will shoot straight?"

"I can read him pretty good."

I wanted to think everything Belle was saying was a bunch of nonsense, but I knew better. I had seen enough of life at the coal camps to know how people with money operated and where the real power was. I walked back into the kitchen, ignoring Tom and Belle, and turned my attention to making another of what Luanne and I called a mountain pie.

"You work on more of the filling and I'll get the crust." Luanne motioned to the bowl of fruit.

"What you girls making?" Belle asked peering into the filling bowl. We didn't answer her, but I started to gather more of the fruit we had placed on the back porch the night before. We had some ripe and soft peaches, rhubarb, grapes, and, of course, apples. Luanne, her eyes on Belle, began pouring out the flour, cutting in the lard, and salt and sprinkling it with cold water, as she slowly, and with expert feel, worked another pie crust. Belle sat back in a chair, watching, and lighting another cigarette. With that cigarette smoke circling her head, she examined Colin's .22 rifle that he brought over to show her. He was proud of that gun Tom bought for him.

"Miss Belle," Colin said, "what do ya think? Daddy got it for me." Belle made a show of looking it over and slowly handed it back to my boy as if she were handing back the Hope diamond.

"You're going to get a pile of squirrels with this Colin, that is, if your Mama will let you." She shot me a look straight on and steady, and my body trembled because I wanted to tackle her. The kitchen was quiet for a long while, but just as Luanne placed the pie in the oven, Belle broke the silence, again.

"I have decided I'm going with you." She directed this to Tom.

Luanne almost dropped the pie as she opened the oven with her free hand.

"That sounds like a good idea. You can ride one of Adams's horses and break it for me on the way."

"Then you're paying me for that service, Tom Dodson." Belle laughed.

"We'll work it out in trade," Tom said, as they both shared a laugh.

"Who's minding your son, Belle?" asked Luanne.

"He's minding himself these days. He got a notion to go up the country and work. He's almost 17, and fancies himself a man. He don't need no minding by me anymore. Lord knows I have had my hands full trying to mind him, haven't I?" She looked towards my husband.

"Yep. Remember when I first took him squirrel hunting, and he shot my hat clear off my head? I swore I would never take him again, but I did."

"You were the only person he would mind and that was true from day one."

Before I knew what I was doing, I slammed my hand down on the table, and stormed out of the house. I was so mad it was like I'd been stung by a thousand bees. I felt both foolish and vindicated all at the same time. Then I just felt mad, and like with any strong passion, it made sense and a whole lot of nonsense.

No one came after me. I stood in the hot sunlight and wished I could go far away from this mountain. I wanted to go back home to my mother's house, and that was a scary, desperate thought. What do I do or feel about Tom and Belle? Was her child his son? I wondered. I just knew Belle made me mad as hell. Now, my husband was going away with her. He was not taking me. I was trapped. *You have no way of making your way in this world with two children,* I thought as Colin came outside. "You all right, Mom?"

"Yes, I just needed some air away from that hot stove." I took Colin by the hand, who still held my hand, and we went walking to the hayfield. I felt the earth that I was standing on, which felt so secure and steady under my feet. That gold hay field was now filled with dead black-eyed Susan seed pods hanging from stubborn stamens, with the occasional mullein plant and the sturdy white yarrow sprinkled through the fescue. Though the earth lay firm beneath my feet, I felt I was being swallowed into a cave, and falling through a deep tunnel. Would I fall like this forever? My whole body trembled with this thought. *He has something with Belle that he doesn't have with me.*

After some time, I came back to myself and looked at Colin investigating a gopher hole. His skin shone as if a thousand pearls had been rubbed into his cheek.

"Why don't you like her, Mom?"

"Who said I don't like her?"

"You think she is sweet on Dad? And Dad is sweet on her? Is that why?"

I looked at my son who was grinning at me.

"Don't be silly. Why aren't you squirrel hunting on such a nice day? Come on, let's go back." I felt the security of his hand as we walked back up to the house to see Belle and Tom fastening gear to two horses who were tied up and stomping at the last summer flies. Belle was leading the other two trail horses.

"Wondered where you'd got at," said Tom absent-mindedly, tying onto his leather straps a hatchet and handsaw.

"So, you're going?" He nodded. "We'll probably be back by the 28th."

I quickly counted it up.

"Why, that's almost a week and a half from today." No one answered me. "You're not taking any horses to ride back?"

"I figured after I'm done, Belle and I would head into Luray, spend some money and then catch a ride home."

"Well, that's fine then." But it wasn't fine, and I turned on my heel and marched way up the stone path to the house.

I came inside to the sweet smell of our pie baking and found Luanne leaning back in a chair on the rear porch. The front chair legs were off the ground, and she was leaning against the wall like a man and smoking one of Belle's cigarettes. "Luanne?" I looked at her astonished.

Startled, she slammed the front legs down on the floor with a thundering blow and was getting ready to hide the butt behind the potato basket when she stopped in mid motion and said, "I have worked all morning, and I'm taking a much-needed break in any way I see fit." She looked me square on in the face.

I paused for a moment, studying her. "I see." I said with my lips tight as I pivoted on my heel and went with determination into the kitchen. I stood on my tiptoes to get to the top shelf of the breakfront cabinet, and I pulled down a jar of Tom's mother's Nerve Elixir. Then, I took out a demitasse cup left over from Tom's first wife and poured the elixir full in the glass. I sauntered out to the back porch, and I leaned against the porch rail and lifted my glass to Luanne. "Here's to a much-needed rest." I took a generous sip of the elixir while Luanne leaned back against the rear legs of the chair and took a long draw of her cigarette.

"I can toast to that."

We looked out past the back of the house and up the mountain to the forest with the cool eyes of detachment. I liked how the elixir made my head feel, a part of everything and not a part of anything at all. Our moment was disturbed by heavy footfalls falling on the floor like lone kettle bell strikes in an empty opera house. Belle came to the back porch and looked from me to Luanne and back again. "We're off, ladies."

We received her with silence. I spun my back to Belle and Luanne commenced to rocking in the spindle chair. The creaks of the chair legs on the old pine porch echoed the discomfort we were feeling. Seeing this, Belle walked to where she could be in both Luanne's and my line of vision, and putting both hands on her hips, said, "I get it. You two are something else. I haven't done a damn thing wrong, but you are damning me, nonetheless. We all make our choices, ladies. I made mine, and you two have made yours, and I made the choice to not be beholding to any man, ever, because I value my freedom. I think you both are jealous since I can do what I please."

She let this sink in before continuing. "And the world is changing, even if it doesn't change much around here, but our time on this mountain is coming to an end." She paused and expectation hung dramatically in the air. Then she said nothing. She took a big intake of breath, and let it out with a whoosh, and then she stopped making any noise at all. Luanne and I strained our ears, waiting to see what she was going to say next.

"You," she said pointing to me. "You with the two children still hanging off of your titties, *come with me.*" Belle spun around with her braid bouncing on her back as she walked to the kitchen table. Hesitatingly, I followed through the door, casting a glance at Luanne who raised her eyebrows at me. Belle regarded Evelyn, who was drawing with her pencils and tablet on her little desk that Tom had made for her. Belle's eyes softened, but her smile held like a taught kite string. She moved till she was inches from my face.

"*I know you.*" She looked into my eyes like a snake charmer holding my gaze. "I know you want to swing your leg over that horse's saddle and be the one going with Tom. But you can't and I can, and that is making you crazy, heart of my heart. You're going to stay home and mind your children and sing to them when they are sick and play with them when they are happy, and they will go off and maybe never look back because that is how life works, doesn't it, Mary? All you got, listen to me—all you got is your choice of what you're going to do about it in this moment 'cause you can't get out from under those children as easy as you got out from that man you run off with. But you got *yourself* and how you are going to face your load. Face it."

I felt like I had been slapped.

"And Tom..." Belle nodded in the direction where Tom's frame was outlined by the shade of the springhouse, holding the horses, waiting for Belle, "he may do the same, but not with me. Not with me. Big things are stirring, which will make your worries seem like trifles." She motioned to her and me. "The government is coming, and they plan on taking the lands, and there will not be a damn thing we can do about it, and your," she paused, regarding me, "*insecurities,* will make no...never mind."

"You don't know what you're talking about," I yelled, hurt by the comment she made about my children and Halsom. She has no idea, I thought. I didn't get out of that easily, not at all, but of course, she knew that, but she suffered no victims.

She smiled and nodded as she got ready to leave through the front door. Her shoulders relaxed as she looked back at me her face suddenly fallen and sad. Holding my chin in both her hands she said, "Sweet Mary, my beloved girl who has walked many dark, lonely roads, when you realize that you have no control, not over anything except one thing, yourself, and how you are going to feel about it, that is when you will find grace; that is when you will find the sweet spot, and no man can take it from you."

She planted a kiss on my lips and her lips were so soft and gentle; I was stunned as I watched her back recede from me as she sauntered into the daylight and towards Tom. She grabbed the reins of her horse out of Tom's hands. They said something to each other. Belle waited as Tom mounted his horse. Grabbing the pommel and holding the reins with her hand on the saddle horn she swung her leg, *with those man britches*, up over the horse's rump. Tom gave me one last wave as he and the packhorse rode out first and Belle, settling herself in the saddle, followed behind. She never looked back.

Chapter 28

I drank the entire bottle of nerve tonic the week Tom was gone with Belle. *Heart of my heart, she had said.* I felt a shift that I could not name taking over everything that I held dear. As if the world felt it, too, in the space of a week, autumn came on full, and we had hard frosts at night that blighted the few remaining tomatoes on the vine and left the tomatoes looking like an old woman's breasts. The mountain erupted in color so full and so fast it was if God had thrown his painter's palate at the trees while we were all were sleeping. I always liked autumn because it reminded me of going back to school. My mother would take me shopping for new dresses and undergarments, stockings, and shoes before every school year. Where are my new clothes now? I tried to be present as my childhood days were far behind me. It wasn't new clothes I was longing for I slowly realized. It took having children that I adored to recognize the longing I had felt since I was a child was a sense of a lack of love, and it had left me with a hollowness as well as a yearning. Looking at this beautiful farm way up in the mountains, I reminded myself that I had a steadfast husband, a delightful sister-in-law, two healthy and mostly happy children. Could I have peace knowing I would never be anything like Belle? Or that Tom probably loved her, or worse?

Towards the end of the month, when I was sure Tom would never be back and that he was living the life with Belle in Luray, Luanne and I chose what would likely be one of the last warm afternoons to go gleaning. We were gathering hickory nuts, acorns, chestnuts, if we could find them, and sassafras root for tea, since we had not dug them properly in the spring like we should have. Luanne watched Evie as I took Colin to the barn to ready the chestnut mare. Colin got a currycomb, rubbing it over the horse's leg who stood there patiently, her eyes drowsy. I put on the blanket and saddle and adjusted packs on the saddle and saddle horn. Colin mounted and rode the mare to the house. Watching my son as he rode away from me, I could never imagine this child, who would crawl out of his own bed at night to come and sleep with me, would ever stop loving me. Unlike my own mother, I hoped I would never give him reason to.

Luanne was waiting with a basket of food and two jars filled with spring water. As I placed Evie in the front of the saddle, Evie commenced to arguing that she wanted to hold the reins. She was so headstrong; I wonder where she got that from?

"Forget this," Colin said. "I'll walk." He glanced at his sister, shaking his head. I ignored them both.

Luanne packed our lunch into the saddlebags. I was feeling hopeful and excited and not so putting one foot in front of the other to simply get through my day but orchestrating my day as if I were the conductor. It was good to be going away from the house for a bit and having an adventure in the woods like I used to do.

Luanne led the way, and I followed behind her. We went down the stone path from the house. It had been built by Tom's great-grandfather, made from the flat rocks off the mountains and washed smooth by the springs. We strode out towards the fields, which were holding onto the last of their green. *He that goeth forth and weepeth, bearing precious seed, shall doubtless come again with rejoicing, bringing his sheaves with him.* The cows raised their heads, and Tom's big Angus bull sat regally in the sunshine, a king surrounded by all his heifers. Tom still had two heifers yet to calve, and their bellies were low and swollen. All the horses were out to graze, since he knew he would not be needing them, and I always was in awe at the sight of his two gray Percherons. Each of their feet was bigger than my head, and they looked like ancient stone monuments. They observed us as we silently passed them by, heading south as we vanished into the edge of the woods like elves. During lunch, we stopped by a creek sparkling with jewelweed. The beads of water were glistening prism spectrums in the midday sun. Luanne summoned the courage to talk to me.

"I hate to make you sore, but you should stop ailing about Tom. In his own way, he loves you, I'm sure, and it's in a different way than he feels for his first wife or Belle. I mean, he does like Belle a lot. Most men do."

"*Loves me in his own way?* What does that mean? Is that supposed to make me feel better?"

"See, there you go getting sore. I mean, there are different ways of loving people. You and Tom give each other good days, and when he comes in the door, he always looks to you and smiles, even when you don't smile back, like lately."

I thought on that. *I'm turning into my mother.* A weight sat on my chest, and I looked around the forest. My gaze fell on Colin dozing on the horse blanket. Evie had taken off her shoes and was playing in the creek. The chestnut horse was sleeping with its foot cocked, and Luanne squinted at me as she looked into the sun. The last of the summer birds were calling.

"Besides," she continued, "you don't want to be like Belle no way, at least, not on an everyday basis."

"Why is that? She does what she pleases, charts her own way in this world, is not beholding to anyone. And like you said, the menfolk like her."

"Yes, she sure does, but she doesn't fit in. Can you picture her chatting at Theresa's gatherings? I don't even think she can even sew. I don't think she likes women company ether, never has. As long as I've known her, she never wanted to be with girls, only boys. I guess she can't help herself being so bold. It's almost a curse; comes down her family line. All the women in the Doyle family have strong wills and don't keep a full-time man around for long." Luanne said the last part real quiet. "Plus, she is haughty. You can't go on living like you don't need anyone *and* have lace curtains in your window. I don't know if I want to live my life alone like that, without a full-time man and a house of my own."

I looked at her, trying to decide if I wanted lace curtains or men's britches. I wanted both. The quiet of the woods and comfort of Luanne made me feel safe and calm enough to think about my life and future. Slowly, like a glowing ember in a morning dead fire, I realized I might be able to find a middle ground. I was a mother now, first and foremost, but Tom and Hightop also gave me the freedom to breathe and be as close to my wild self as I could be. *Maybe my mother's ways were not so important. But could I live with Tom's loving and liking Belle more than me? And what if it was not a contest? There was a lot of love to go around. Why, I could love more than one child. And on Hightop, I'm free.* I rested my head on a carpet of multicolored leaves that smelled of the sharp and clear earth. The sun warmed my face like summer, but the cool of the air was thoroughly autumn. Winter would be on our doorstep soon, but I was still planting iris bulbs for spring and covering my parsley so it would be snug and winter over. My body relaxed into the moment as I thought of myself and Evie and then Belle. I almost loved Belle like I loved and held true to my true part of myself.

Turning to Luanne I said, "Belle has traveled all over just like Amelia Earhart. Look at that coffee-colored woman we read about in that women's magazine...What's her name? That soft, beautiful black woman Josephine Baker. I read, in that magazine, that in a Paris night club, she said hello to the writer Ernest Hemingway by letting the fur coat she was wearing drop to her feet, *and she was stark naked underneath.* There are women who have the world by the tail these days, just like Belle. And Belle doesn't *need* a full-time man. Belle's right. Our world won't be Evie's world."

"Humph. Well, you can't be Josephine Baker in Powell Gap, Virginia. And maybe Belle's got no full-time man because no man wants her full time. She's got no one who calls her his own for long. And she's turned good ones away. And Amelia Earhart doesn't have to live in Bacon Hollow, and I don't, nor will I ever, have a fur coat, and if I did, I wouldn't be dropping it at any man's feet; that's for sure. The world ain't going to be changing that much, at least not until God makes men birth babies."

"Well, maybe a time will be coming that a woman doesn't have to be yoked to a man to live her life, and she won't be judged badly by it.

Maybe there'll be a time when a woman doesn't think of love first." I sat looking at Evie while wishing it had not been so with me. *I had thrown myself away and given it to Halsom, because he pursued me and made me feel wanted and special, something I should have known was my birthright to begin with.* This was what Amelia Earhart, Josephine Baker and Belle knew from the start.

"I hadn't thought about it quite like that, but then what? I don't want to go to work like a man. I don't want to fight in a war. But I tell you something, you know what I *would* do?" Luanne looked at me.

"What?"

"I would bob my hair. I sure would. Now, that would be freedom."

We finished the pork, crackers and farmer's cheese Luanne had laid out as the sun smiled down on us, too.

Chapter 29

The crescent moon hung like an icicle off the porch eave as Luanne and I, and my children, traveled our path back to Hightop Mountain. Evie was tired, which made her less bossy, so Colin was able to ride the mare as Evie sat behind him, content to lean against him and rest. We had traveled long and far to find our bounty of herbs, nuts and roots as the deer, squirrel, and bear, had been feasting on them too.

"I think we walked the whole length of Greene County today. At least that is what my feet are telling me," I told Luanne.

"Well, we walked a right bit. If we'd turned west, we might have ended up at Roach Gap, but we didn't. We're headed home and will be there directly." Luanne could walk mountain miles forever and never seem to be tired.

As we crossed the hayfield on our homeplace, the little mare whined at the sight of home. And whose outline did I see, but the silhouette of Tom on the porch tuning his fiddle. He was home. As we approached the barn, I gave the reins to Luanne and started to hurriedly unpack our belongings from the saddlebags. Luanne, feeling my haste, said, "I got it. You go to the house."

"I can do it," Colin said.

I grabbed Evie off the horse and made my way to the house, hoping it was not too dark for Tom to see that I was smiling from ear to ear. Tom laid down his fiddle as I approached, and I threw my arms around him, covering his face with kisses.

"I guess you're proud to see me."

Evelyn, who had her arms crossed and appeared to be getting jealous, pushed me out of the way and crawled into her father's lap. He ran his fingers over her cupid bow lips. Her fingers opened and closed at his touch. "Evie, have you changed since I have been gone? How could that be?"

"Oh, no, Daddy, not me, but you have." Tom regarded her, then gave her a kiss on her forehead and said, "You go get to bed. It's late now."

"You will blink and before you know it, you'll be marrying her off." I turned to him.

"My, my, I'm not sure I want to live to see that day."

Evie, satisfied, scrambled out of her father's lap, and took off into the house. I went after her. When I caught her, I washed her hands and face, put on her nightgown, and placed her in bed, covering her good with the warm store-bought coverlet, but underneath there was another coverlet made by the women in Tom's family, made before I was even born.

I came back out to the porch just as Luanne and Colin were throwing the saddlebags down. "I'm glad to be home. It's been a long day but a good day. If the fire is going, I'm going to roast some of these nuts." Luanne climbed the porch.

"Can I stay up, Mom?" Colin looked at me. I thought a minute, and being ever easy, I told him, "Yes."

I sat in the chair beside Tom. Looking down into the valley. We could see the twinkling of electric lights down by Routes 29 and 33. They looked like foxfire glowing and flickering in the damp evening air. I wondered if we were coming to a time when the electric lights would drown out the foxfire and the stars.

"Did more lights come on, too, while I was gone? Is everything changing?" He looked at me, but he was not smiling.

"I don't think so."

We sat in the silence, only broken by the last crickets, a screech owl, and a cow mooing in the far field. Tom reached for my hand and held it. After a while, Luanne came out with the pan of nuts and the lantern. Colin helped himself, blowing on them as he cupped them in his hands, and then gave the plate to Tom and me.

"Let's start cracking and getting at the sweet meat, and Tom can tell us what's going on at Skyland. What type of dress up parties did they have this time?" Luanne directed this to her brother.

Tom forced a smile and rocked back and forth on his chair. "Oh, Adams has got him a powerful group of people up there, and he's running around like a rooster that sees an ax. He went all out this time with one of his annual cakewalks and carnivals on the tennis courts at night. Why, he had the bonfires so high I thought he'd raise the fire alarms in five counties. Here, I brought you all back a program and a menu."

Luanne and I held the lantern up to see it.

Programmed!

Stony Man Camp Cake Walk and Carnival.

September 25, 1926

Master of Ceremonies and Drum Major,

Henry Adams.

Judges,

Mr. A. D. Heaton, Mrs. Mefeleff, Mr. G. K Gilbert

PART I- Entrance of the Wood Sprites. Misses Uilia and Welleska Adams, Mr. H. G Dyer and Mr. C. W. Blackstone

Part II- The Young Orientals Misses Dorothy and Zenida Merriam

Part III- Spanish Toreadors and Lady of Seville. Mr. P Jaminson and Miss Ada Townsend

Part IV- Grand Negro Cake Walk. Mr. Sam Washington, Miss Eboneza Johnson, Mr. Blount Mason, and Mr. Eli Bannon

Part V the Butterfly and the Fairy- Mrs. E. S Sprague and Miss Eleanor Simms

Part VI- Robinson Crusoe and Man Friday Robert Black and Piccaninny Assistants

Part VII- The Carnation and the Bumblebee- Miss Mary Pennington and Mr. Harry Nichols

Part IX Blue Beard and Tatum's- Miss Ethel Martin and Mrs. Cragin

Part X The Prince and Princess- Miss Mary Jamison and Mr. Henry Adams

Finale.

Grand March and Judges Decision.

Cake Walk Reel.

As Luanne and I looked over the program, I kept thinking to myself what a sight this must have been to witness.

"What's wrong with these people that they do this type of make-believe?" Luanne finally asked.

"There ain't nothing wrong with these people, Luanne, except they got lots of money and time on their hands and Adams's got to keep them busy and entertained up on Stony Man and, believe me, he's a master at it. He's the P. T Barnum of the Blue Ridge."

"Well, I want to hear about this from start to finish, Dad." Colin looked up admiringly to Tom.

"You mind pouring me another cup of coffee?" Tom said, as he laid a gentle hand on Colin's shoulder. Luanne raised herself from her seat to do her brother's bidding, and I took the opportunity to look at Tom's face, which looked old and haggard in the lantern light. Tom took a sip of his black coffee but remained silent.

"Well?" said Luanne. "I don't want to sit here all night."

"Let's see, Belle and I came into Stony Man camp around dark on the 14th, but the main cabins were lit, as Ole Harry had put in gas lamps a few years ago, so it was a welcome sight for both to us. She was feeling her age after three twelve-hour days in the saddle, though she would never admit it. Adams's main Negro, Will Grigsby, greeted us. About that time, I heard the bugle blowing and knew Adams must be close at hand." Tom started laughing. "Why, Belle turned around to me, and said, 'If he blows that damn bugle next to me, I'm going to shove it up his ass.' You know you can't say nothing to her, so I didn't even try, but in the next few minutes, I saw Adams coming towards us with that quick step that he does, dressed in his Teddy Roosevelt outfit."

"What do you mean, Dad? What was he wearing?" asked Colin.

"Oh, high-top button boots that went to his knees and this leather long sleeve jerkin that came to his mid thighs and leather pants with fringe running down the legs. He had this big silk tie wrapped around his neck and a hat bigger than himself, and of course, that 45 Colt strapped to his waist. I think he calls it Ole Fletcher or something. I could hear Belle muttering under her breath as she saw his get-up."

"'Tom, my man! So glad that you could make it!' Adams told me. 'I have been keeping a keen eye for you these past few days. And, Miss Belle, what a pleasant surprise. I have me a sweet new bird rifle I'll show you in the morning that I know you'll be interested in. Are you still the best shot in Bacon Hollow? But first, let me get Will to lead you two to your cabin. My guests and I are sitting around the big fireplace at the dining hall, and you are welcome to join us. In fact, I insist on it.'"

"He gave a big bow, sweeping his hand in front of him and catching the hand of Belle, which he raised to his lips and gave a kiss."

"What did Belle do?" asked Luanne.

Tom laughed. "Why, she just gave him a world- weary gaze and said, 'Really Henry?' But I caught the twinkle in Adams's eye, and he gave her a wink and a smile before he darted off.

"Well, I cleaned up and went down to the Skyland Hall where Belle was already holding court with the men. She had her back to me and was facing the roaring fire, which had been built up in that floor to ceiling fireplace with what must have been a half-cord of wood. She had cleaned up, too, and was wearing a fresh set of pants, of course, and a crisp white blouse that was open daringly low, and her hair was brushed out and draping down her back like a waterfall. She held a glass of whiskey in her hand and said, 'Well boys, I tell you what happened next. I fed that bear apples till he followed me back to the cabin. Then I smeared honey around the doors and windows and sat back to watch,' All the men hooted over that."

"What was she talking about?" I asked, my hackles getting up by the way he had described Belle, *hair like a waterfall.*

Tom laughed, rubbing his face. "Because Belle's boyfriend was lying in bed with another woman. Of course, the men were all leaning into her, smiling, and wishing they were her beau, and the woman were all sitting there wide-eyed, pretending to be shocked. About that time, Belle turned around, flashing me a smile, and hollering at me to join the party. Adams, who hasn't taken his attention from Belle for the last ten years, waved me over without glancing my way. It was good to sit at the fire, and I gladly accepted the whiskey, and I did eat two plates of food."

"Tell me about the food," Luanne said.

"He keeps Negro cooks he brings in from Washington, D. C., and, of course, he's entertaining all the up-country folks, so the menus were over the top. Let's see, he had oysters and Hawksbill clams, duckling and goose with some orange sauce, potatoes, boiled bass from the Shenandoah River, this apple cabbage slaw with cress, ginger ale, champagne, a really good chocolate-ice box cake, and the men were smoking their cigars and drinking their whiskey while the women were sipping what Henry called Mountain Dew cocktails."

"I would like to see Skyland sometime," I said.

"Well, I wouldn't," said Luanne. "Did many of the women have their hair bobbed?"

Tom thought a moment. "Why, yes, the younger ones did, but many of the matrons still kept their hair up in that Gibson fashion."

"What are the people like?" I asked.

"They all have money and status and are from cities as far away as New York and Philadelphia. Some, of course, have permanent cabins up there like the Byrd and Evan families. Aside from the regulars, like Senator Byrd, there was some author whose name I can't remember, and a filmmaker who was scouting out a mountain setting for his latest film, and an army colonel and his wife who had just gotten married. Adams's wife had conveniently returned to Washington, leaving Adams to flirt with all of the women. Oh, and there was a Dr. Mitchell and his patient, Mr. Blake, who was taking in the fresh mountain air for his aliments. There was a lot of excitement around Blake during my visit, as he suddenly had a full recuperation and shot Matt Cave's pigs because they were rooting around his cabin all night, keeping him awake."

"I'm sure that didn't sit well with the Caves," Luanne said.

"No, it didn't. In fact, along with the order Adams put in for my shine and horses, the Cave pig incident was the highlight of the trip."

"I'll get you another cup of coffee if you tell us the pig story." Luanne went for the coffee pot warming on the stove.

"All right, then," said Tom handing her his cup. "We were about getting ready to turn in for the night when Blake turned to Adams saying, 'Henry, I just cannot take another night of those damn pigs grunting and squealing around my cabin.'

'Well, Mr. Blake, I told you that those pigs belong to Matt Cave and our mountaineers are in the habit of letting their livestock free range. I've talked to him about it. He's my neighbor, and he's a rustic, with all the sentiments that would imply.'"

"The next day, Blake took one of the horses and rode down to Luray and came back with a rifle. That following night, we could all hear the gunshots followed by pigs squealing. It seemed Blake was a very good shot and not wanting to kill them, was just nicking them in the ear. Matt Cave showed up the next morning, as expected, saying, 'Mr. Adams, I ain't going to stand for you shooting my pigs and you need to pay up now,' to which Henry replied, 'I had nothing to do with shooting those pigs Matt.'

About this time Matt saw me and said, 'Tom, who in this mess is responsible for the holes in my pigs' ears?!' Adams looked at me with alarm as I told Cave, 'Why, Matt, I rightly don't know.' I was sleeping, which was the truth."

"'Come on, Tom, I know you are in thick with this bunch, but you got to stand by your people,' Cave said.

"Now, that got me mad and I strode over to Matt and, looking at him square in the face, I told him, 'I'm not in any thicker than you or the rest of us up here are, and if those pigs had been rooting around my bed keeping me from my rightful sleep night after night, they would have more than holes in their ears.'"

"Then Blake came striding into the conversation, grabbed Cave by the nose, drug him the full length of the porch and shoved him into the arms of the Cave posse. 'I'm the one shooting those damn pigs and will kill every one of them tonight', yelled Blake, who didn't look to be suffering from any ailment that I could see. Cave then said something about getting the Sheriff as he beat a hasty retreat back to Cave Hollow."

"Everyone at Skyland had a good laugh over the matter, but I knew this wouldn't be the end of it. In fact, right after we all ate breakfast, Adams came up to me. asking me what he should do. 'You know Tom, I try to do right by these people because I have to live among them most part of the year but my guests, on the other hand, are in and out.'"

"'I know, Henry.'"

"'What do you think I should do?'"

"'It's quite simple. Instead of leading the hike today to White Oak Canyon, put Belle in charge of the hike. She'll tell the guests enough off-colored stories to keep them all amused, and you ride the five miles to Cave's cabin and pay for those pigs.'"

"Henry thought this over. 'You're right Tom, I will do just that.'"

"So, all's well that ends well." Tom drained the last bit of his coffee. "Oh, before I forget, I brought these for you from Adams's library. He said he has finished them and hopes you'd enjoy them. I told him you're a reader."

Tom handed me *The Sun Also Rises* and *The Castle*. I took them eagerly, starving as I was for something to read, yet wondering why Adams chose a story about doing silly things like running with bulls and a story of a person struggling against blind power.

"Ladies, I'm going to bed. Come on, Mary." He held out his hand to me. Hesitating, I gave him my hand, but I was keenly aware that he had said nothing about all of Belle's dire predictions about the mountains being sold. I also remembered my mother's advice. *You have to pick the right time to talk to a man and not when he's tired.* I vowed to question him in the morning. I chose, for now, not to question him about Belle as well, though my curiosity was burning like a flame on dry dead fall. It was hard for me to hold my tongue while Tom and I lay in bed the next day after getting reacquainted, but by the time he sat down to breakfast, and before he lifted the first forkful of food to his lips, I could stand it no longer.

"Was there any talk about the government taking the mountains like Belle said?" I sat down next to him with my coffee. Not missing a beat, Tom put a forkful of food into his mouth, and wiping his lips with a napkin, said, "I have known Ole Henry for almost twenty years now, and, he's always been looking for ways to make money, especially since he seems to run through it so fast, but, he and I did get a chance to sit and talk for a while, away from Belle, and he showed me a piece from the *Winchester Star* about a group of men calling themselves the Shenandoah Land Corporation. They're planning to build a park, or something like that, on Massanutten Peak. Henry was pretty honest and said he thought Skyland was a better opportunity for them, and he said he had met them all in Washington, to convince them of that." Tom took a few more bites of food.

"And?"

"He's going to have them up to Skyland in the spring and show them around. He wants some fine smooth-gaited horses for them, so I expect I will meet these men and size the whole thing up for myself. Selling Adams ten horses will bring in some nice money for us."

"Good. Could we put some money aside for Colin and Evie to go to college if they want to?"

"I suppose we might be able to do just that." He looked straight at me.

"What's wrong, Tom?"

"You know, you can read people just like horses, if you're quiet, watch their body language, listen real intently, and sometimes, what they are *not* doing or saying is more important than what they are doing or saying."

"So, what does that mean?" Luanne asked, coming in with the milk pail.

"It means, my sister, that I know you want to go down to Mom's this weekend so that you can go out with Asa Dean *and* that Adams is not telling me the whole story. But in any case, even if they put in a park, Skyland is miles away from Hightop Mountain, so I wouldn't be worried."

"I haven't made up my mind about Asa Dean, either." Luanne strained the milk.

"I'll help you with the horses, Dad," Colin piped up. He had gotten himself a plate of food and slipped quietly into the seat beside Tom.

Tom nodded at him. "I'll be spending the winter gathering and breaking a good group for Harry. While I hate to carry so many animals over the winter, it will have a worthwhile pay off in the end." Tom pushed himself away from the table, grabbed his hat and put it firmly on his head.

"I'll see you ladies later. Colin, get ready to come with me. Luanne, you tell Asa to come get you up here. I won't bite him."

"It's a long way up this mountain for courting."

"*Make* him climb the mountain, Luanne," Tom said to his sister.

"I know I'm not climbing a mountain for any man," Luanne replied.

"Precisely." He winked at both of us and went out the door.

"I swear, he's spent too much time with Belle." Luanne shook her finger at me.

I nodded at her, but I thought about what he had said the rest of the afternoon. *Make them climb the mountain, make them climb the mountain, make them climb the mountain.* Was Tom climbing the mountain for me? I had to admit that having Evie, his child, gave me a sense of security with him, since I knew he would not turn me out now, but I had not any good understanding of men, though I seemed to be getting a better understanding of myself with each passing day and I had the growing and unsettling feeling that all along, it had nothing to do with men, but with me.

When I was younger, this was because of my inherent recklessness, according to my mother, and after Halsom and the coal camp, I knew circumstances could turn on a dime, and for no apparent reason, which kept me anxious and always anticipating, so I couldn't help but worry about what the new year would bring to me, my family and Hightop Mountain.

Chapter 30

Horses came in all colors throughout the winter and there was not a day, even in the snow, that Tom didn't work them to get them bomb proof for Adams and his people. He let Colin help, which seemed to make my son grow a little taller. Seeing all the horses grazing on the mountain top bald, outlined against the pale blue sky with the wind wiping their manes and tails, and the tall yellow grasses bowing, put me in mind of something grand out West like I had seen in books. It was a pretty and tranquil sight. But it was cold, and that fierce wind whipped all winter. Towards the end of February, when the evening light finally made its switch after February 1, there was hope in the wheel of the year actually turning and we got a week of balmy spring-like weather.

Colin, Evie, Luanne, and I were walking down to the barn to see the last group of horses that the horse trader was delivering. J. B Stickler was an anomaly among horse traders. He was honest and I'm not surprised that Tom had a long-standing relationship with him. JB would often take a horse back from him without question, knowing that if Tom could or would not break that horse, he best not sell it and the animal was best destined for glue. This was a beautifully colored group of horses-chestnut, copper as a new penny, blood bay, black, storm cloud dappled gray, which was rare and looked like a quarter horse cross, a strawberry roan with some draft, my favorite color because they sometimes looked pink, one pale winter yellow and one butterscotch palomino, and a tall long-legged coal black giant who towered among the trail ponies like Samson among the Philistines. All the horses milled around the paddock nervously.

"JB, now what am I supposed to do with him?" Tom motioned to the black horse. "He's got to be 17 hands."

"You can use him to pick apples and mend roofs." JB smiled good-naturedly.

Tom went into the paddock and the horses moved around him. The good-natured ones turned towards him, and the ranker ones swung their butts in his direction, and others just glanced quickly and looked away. The giant horse pricked his long well shaped fox ears towards Tom and looked at him square on as he approached him. Running his hands down the horse's back and over his rump, Tom pressed into an indentation in the horse's left buttock.

"What's this?"

"Don't know but it does not hinder his movements. He's sound, and from what I gather, a very easy keeper especially for his type. That one doesn't need grain."

Tom lifted up the giant's lip.

"When was the last time he raced?"

"It's really been a few years. I picked him up from a man in Orange whose been using him for foxhunting and some gentleman's steeple chasing. I thought Adams might like himself a profiling Thoroughbred."

"JB, Adams's about five feet tall. How in the hell is he supposed to get on him?"

"That's what God made tree stumps for. I don't know, maybe he can get one of his hired men to lift him up and down off the horse."

"I'm not taking this one, JB."

"Look, I've got a deal for you. Just take him and see what you think, if he doesn't work out, I will consider selling you that spotted riding horse of mine that you've long admired—the one that rides and drives."

I could see Tom consider this.

"Tom, why don't you men come to the house for some pie and coffee?"

"Now, that sounds like the best deal I have gotten in a long while," JB replied.

Evie ran under the fence to Tom before I could grab her. She darted under the horse's legs and Tom swung her up on his shoulders. Colin, who had been sitting on a fence rail slid off and followed behind Tom. JB opened up the gate as they came out and we all walked up towards the house. I pulled on Tom's jacket and motioned him to hang back behind the others.

"Tom?" I was nervous asking him this.

"Hmmm?"

"Can we keep that horse for a bit and see?" I was not thinking of anything except this is my chance. That horse, that horse's predicament, my life, and everything I had wanted for myself were suddenly tied up with that horse; I felt, and I know this was silly, like I *knew* that horse. He was my own.

"And see what? That he'll be strong and pulling on the bit and want to be so forward that he'll scare most of his riders and be prancing instead of standing?"

"These mountain trails might humble him a bit. I'll ride him. I *want* to ride him."

Tom breathed in and let out a sigh. Feeling his hesitation, losing all my impulse control, and just wanting something I could not name I said, "I'll give you all my egg money for him."

I looked back at the horse who was watching us as we climbed the steps into the house. He turned to me. "Mary, the kind, dependable and sure-footed horses are worth their weight in gold. I can sell them, for a good price, as the day is long." He grabbed me by the shoulders. "You can have this horse, if that's what you are after, and I hope he'll please you, but being on the edge of a knife gets you nothing but exhausted—in man or animal." He pushed open the door and left me on the porch feeling like he had given me something yet had taken it away.

Tom took the whole bunch of horses from JD and the giant horse did pull on the bit until I thought my arms would be yanked out of my sockets. But I could ride him and when I rode him, *I was alive.* He jigged constantly, bouncing up and down if I would not let him run forwards, and it felt like all my teeth and brains were rattling loose when I rode him. But he plowed through sticker bushes, creeks, over log piles, down ravines, up rock ledges, galloped up a mile trail and was still jigging when he got to the top. He didn't spook at anything to include gunshots. And every tree branch smacked me in the head and face because of his height but he was doing remarkably better than the chestnut that Tom had gotten on. The moment Tom swung his leg over the saddle, the chestnut lurched sideways, crashed into a tree, and then collapsed on all fours.

"Son of a bitch!" Tom yanked the horse's head up and with his spurs gunned the horse on all sides as it wildly jumped up and crashed into my horse who stood like a brick wall.

"Tom, get off him before you get hurt!"

He ignored me. Slowly, Tom reached down beside his saddle and began to untie a lead rope. Keeping his eye on his horse's ears and bending his horse's head to his boot he clipped the line to the bit. The horse stood silently, and I held my breath.

"Come on over here and take the lead rope," he told me.

I slowly moved my horse around so that I could bend over as Tom leaned towards me and handed off the rope so that we were connected like an umbilical cord.

"OK, now move on."

I turned the Giant, as I called him, up the trail and we walked off, but Tom's horse planted his feet firmly in the ground. The pulling of the rope on his bridle unnerved the chestnut, but not my horse, and Tom's horse leapt up in the air, his front hooves almost striking my head as it pawed wildly. Finally, the horse crashed into my horse's rump. I nudged my horse forward and the chestnut, in fits and starts, walked reluctantly behind. My heart was beating frantically, and I kept glancing back to make sure Tom was all right.

Because my horse was so long strided we had to stop periodically for the bad behavior horse to catch up, but by the time we made it to the old Indian trail on the top of the mountain, Tom told me to unhook the rope. He looked at me and laughed. I didn't find this predicament funny. What would I do if Tom got hurt way up here? I watched his horse nervously as we moved off again. Eventually, Tom moved his horse into the lead and the horse went obediently forward. It didn't even spook when he disturbed a covey of grouse, which exploded like firecrackers. Eventually, we came to a stream with a clearing and Tom halted his horse.

"Let's take a break here."

As Tom swung his leg over the horse, he kept one eye on the horse's ears and head. As he tied it's lead rope to a tree the horse's muscles rippled as if he was going to balk back, but Tom growled at him and smacked him on the rump.

"Get up." Tom yelled directly to him.

The horse's ears flipped back, and it made a move forward and Tom yanked down on the lead line.

"Stand."

With its eyes nervously darting around, the horse did just that as Tom unpacked our food from the saddlebags. Before he turned to sit, he ran his hand over the horse's neck as the horse stood quietly. Tom patted him gently.

"Good boy."

I helped unpack our lunch. We had some pork tenderloin that I had fried up for breakfast, which was sandwiched between an egg bread that Luanne had made, and I had found two apples from the root cellar that looked to be in fairly good shape. Tom and I ate in silence, and I remembered how I had first followed behind him up these mountains in what felt like a lifetime ago. I wondered if I was dreaming now or back then. Sometimes I had to pinch myself because it felt like I was dreaming. I was so far away from my life in Elkton and the life my parents had imagined I would have. Watching my horse rubbing his head on a pine tree and proceeding to destroy it with his big fat head, I felt very lucky to be here. I knew, with certainty, that I loved that animal with a sureness of which I have only loved my children, but never the sureness of loving a man. I looked at Tom, who was staring at me. My very fragile heart softened.

"Come here." He motioned.

With his hands, all callused, the knuckles red and swollen, he gently wiped the side of my cheek.

"Mustard." His big smile warmed me, and his eyes lit up as I blushed a little.

"Oh, my Mary."

I planted a big kiss on his lips and hugged him through all the layers of our warm clothes letting my head rest on his shoulder. My eyes rested on the ice encrusted creek and the sun dancing through the patches of snow. I loved Tom too. These were the days when I walked in the sun.

We rested awhile and I laid back on Tom's legs eating my late winter apple and watching the patterns of the clouds in the pale blue sky as if this was the only moment in my entire life.

"You ready to head back?" He looked down at me.

"Yep." I sat up.

I lead my horse around to an old log so that I could reach the stirrup and the Giant swung his head to my face where I could kiss his velvety muzzle. As I swung my leg over the saddle and got myself comfortable and ready, I pointed my horse in Tom's direction and with apprehension, I looked towards Tom. I didn't trust that chestnut horse.

Tom was making a big show of tightening girths and snapping down straps to see what the horse would do. The horse's eyes and ears rolled back towards him, but the horse stood quietly. Leaving the lead rope tied to the tree, and without hesitation, he put his left foot in the stirrup and swung his weight until he was standing on his left leg in the saddle. The horse went to move, and Tom yelled. "Stand," and the horse stood frozen. Tom continued to swing his leg over the saddle and place both feet in the stirrups. He rocked in the saddle side to side placing his weight in first one stirrup than the other and picked up the reins.

"Do you want me to untie your horse?" I asked.

He shook his head no, and with slow movements, he leaned forward across the horse's neck, and like Houdini, undid the knot with one hand.

"Do you want me to go in front?"

He didn't answer me but turned the horse's head in the direction of the trail and put his spurs into the horse's side. The horse lurched but moved forward without incident, splashing through the creek like an old trail horse. I turned to follow, and my horse lowered his head as if to drink then proceeded to play and paw in the water, causing waves to rise up all around us and getting my legs wet. He made the water sparkle like crystals. I smiled, inwardly delighted with my horse, but when I looked up and saw that Tom had moved up the trail without us, I pulled up the Giant's head and we jigged and cantered and jigged our way to Tom where I pulled my horse up with a jolt, so we didn't run into him. Tom was causally smoking a cigarette and he turned to me laughing. "Pity your horse is not as well behaved as mine." As another tree branch smacked me in the head, I thought that maybe it was true, but this horse was me and mine. We got home without incident.

The Ides of March came and went when Adams sent word to Tom that he was back at Skyland and Tom could bring the horses at any time. For one week, the wind blew the moisture of the spring rains for the fields and gardens, and a respite from the winter came with almost mild, sunny weather that released tiny no see-ums floating in the air, earthworms up from the ground, and crocuses, snow drops and grape hyacinths blooming around the house. Tom stood on the porch looking into the distance.

"I best be getting organized to go before the weather shifts." Tom turned to look at me. Luanne and I were on the front porch separating potatoes to plant. Evie was drawing pictures with her Crayola crayons, and Colin had gone off after trout. "I'm going to need all hands-on deck to clean those horses up." His tone was flat, and Luanne and I exchanged a look.

"What's eating at you?" asked his sister as she threw another potato on our planting pile.

"I sent word to Belle, and I have not heard a thing."

"Where's our cousin Lucas at? He'll ride with you." Luanne looked at her brother.

"He and Jay took jobs up the country."

"I'll go," I said.

Both their heads swung around to look at me. "Are you out of your mind, sister?" Luanne punctuated this by throwing a potato at me that bounced off the porch and onto the grass where Tom's hound proceeded to pick up and toss in the air.

"No."

Tom looked at me steadily. "You can't ride that knucklehead of yours," he said, calmly contemplating my offer.

"Tom? Have *you* lost your mind?" Luanne said.

"Who can I ride?" I asked calmly trying to hide my excitement.

"I'm thinking on that. In the meantime, I'm headed down to the barn." He put his hat on his head, threw the remainder of his coffee off the side of the porch, handed his cup to me, and strode off. I had a smile from ear to ear.

"This is just the most ridiculous thing I have ever heard of. If there's an accident or God knows what else, there will be no one to blame but *you and my stupid brother.*" Luanne threw down her paring knife and stormed into the house, slamming the door behind her. Evie looked at me and rolled her eyes. I knew better than to go to talk to Luanne, so I continued on weeding through the potatoes until I had finished the pile. It took three trips to the garden to set myself up for planting because I was moving hoes, spades, and potato baskets.

Tom had plowed and turned over the garden earlier in the week and Luanne and I had cleared the potato patch of rocks and dirt clumps. We had also cleared the sections of the garden where the salsify, horehound, lemon balm, bergamot, feverfew, comfrey, and purple irises were growing. A patch of parsley, that I had strawed in the fall and uncovered when we began working the garden, was greening up and had new leaves emerging. With my basket beside me, I got down on my hands and knees, and I carefully placed potatoes in the soft brown earth. Whether it was the planting and weather of spring or the upcoming adventure, my heart felt light as a feather. I had gotten about half of the potatoes planted when Luanne stepped out onto the back porch. "Evie is crying and throwing crayons," she said.

Wiping my hands on my apron, I walked to the house. Luanne had her back to me and was ironing. Evie was mad. She was not so much as crying as yelling at me. "Maaaaaaaaa... My picture is ruined. The dog walked on it." I scooped her up and told her it wasn't ruined despite the paw marks. Evie scrambled out of my arms and, with her hands on her hips, threw down the crayons still in her hand, and stormed off.

"Evelyn! Don't you climb those stairs. Don't make me climb those stairs after you." I went after her. Luanne walked past me. She grabbed Evie off the stairs and set her down firmly saying, "Evelyn, if you don't listen, I'll spank your bottom and you won't get a candy after dinner. Do you hear me?"

Her face was sour, but she stopped fussing and stood with her little arms crossed in front of her chest as Luanne came over to me and grabbed the hand towel out of my hands. Tentatively, I followed Luanne back into the kitchen as Tom came through the front door. Colin also walked in with a string of brook trout that we all admired.

"I'll fry these up for dinner," I said. Colin was proud and looked to Tom for approval.

"I've never seen someone so canny with mountain trout, Colin. I appreciate your bringing us home our supper." Tom gave Colin's shoulders a squeeze, and as I watched this, I was thankful that Halsom was not raising his boy. Tom was always quick to take Colin with him and quick with affection, and Colin responded by always wanting to be with Tom to the point where he wouldn't want to go to school.

"Well," said Luanne, "I was planning on going with Mary and Evie wild harvesting tomorrow for cress, dock, and dandelions. I saw the new shoots coming up, but now I don't know what you've got in mind with this trip and getting her to go along with you." She gestured in my direction.

Tom had his back turned to Luanne, but I could see him crack a smile at her comment. "Now, you know this wasn't my first nor my second choice, and I'm completely aware of the possible challenges. I can't take Colin because he can't miss any more school." Colin started to protest, but Tom shot him a look, and Colin cast his eyes down kicking the toe of his shoe into the floorboards.

"You also know if the going gets too rough we have relations and friends along that route that I can settle Mary with. Finally, I don't have to explain anything to you or ask your permission." Tom shot a look at his sister.

"But, you know word will get out, and everyone will know that you'll be coming home with a pile of cash money. What about that?" Luanne looked worried.

My ears perked up. I had not thought about this. Now I was not so sure of the trip.

"I reckon I'll just cross that bridge when I come to it."

"She won't be able to ride fast."

"I won't be able to ride fast with a string of fifteen horses."

"But what about coming home when you are loaded down with cash money? You know the people I'm talking about. They would steal from their own mothers."

"Enough, Luanne. It won't be the first time I've headed home loaded down with cash, and hopefully, it won't be the last. I'm not going to talk about it again. And don't you go running your mouth about this either, you hear me?"

Luanne glared at him.

"Now, where are those shucky beans and corn bread? Let me eat something in peace so I can go back to the barn and finish laying out gear."

I fixed my husband a plate in silence, and no one talked as Tom sat at the table with his reading glasses and his account books, eating his midday meal. Colin silently began fileting his trout over the dry sink. Tom went over to Colin. "Now, son, there's no better man that I would want with me than you, but you have gotten yourself into a pile of trouble in school. Now, get those grades up to a C and I'll take you to town for that new coonhound you're after. Get those grades up to a B, and I'll take you on my next trip to Skyland." Colin spun around and hugged his father hard.

Tom went back down to the barn, telling Colin to follow him when he was finished with the trout. I settled into the rocking chair to do Evie's reading lesson and watched as Luanne went up and down the stairs to the kitchen attic, bringing down onion and garlic bulbs we had saved. We were also planting Deer Tongue lettuce, Bloomsdale spinach, Georgia collards and Dutch cabbage from seeds that Tom had bought on his last trip to town. The clock struck 4 p.m., and Luanne hadn't talked to me in over four hours. In silence, she put the basket with the garden bulbs and seeds on her hip and left. As I put Evie down, we headed out to the garden with trepidation.

We all worked in silence for a long time. Luanne would make gestures to me when she wanted some item like the hoe or more bulbs. She may have been mad at me, but we got along so well together. We really didn't need to communicate; we knew each other's wants and needs. Finally, as we got the last of the cabbage seeds in the ground, she leaned on her hoe and turned to me. "You know I can't stay mad at you long, but there seems so much at stake, and for the first time in my life, I would breathe a sigh of relief if Belle would saunter up the walk."

"It'll be fine. I traveled long, cold miles when Colin was a baby. Remember what that preacher said last time we went to church? 'I have walked through the desert without water, and I didn't die of thirst.'"

Luanne leaned on her garden hoe with her face set. Slowly, a smile lifted a corner of her mouth. "Well, I don't know about the desert, but I suppose you can consider this your honeymoon."

"It's about the type of honeymoon I deserve."

"I plan on honeymooning at the Massanutten Resort and hot springs, and if my man can't afford to take me, I ain't marrying him,"

"I think you should think bigger, Luanne. Go for the Homestead."

"Ya know, you're right. He can drive me there in his new car."

The spell was broken. Luanne continued, "My Daddy once took Mama to the Massanutten Resort. They traveled all the way there, and it was not till he was checking in he found out they served no alcohol. He was going to leave, but when he saw the disappointment on my mama's face, he couldn't bear to do it. But according to Mama he did make rude comments about Bible thumpers all weekend."

Grabbing the garden tools, Luanne and I walked back to the house holding each other's hands, while Evie ran circles around us. That evening, the family sat around the kitchen table in strained silence, because now we were all nervous about this trip. Luanne was reading me the pencil graphs from the *Luray News and Courier* while I darned Colin's pants, because he had ripped another hole in the knee. She added a lot of her own comments to the news.

"*Luray News and Courier,* March 1927 Pencil graphs: Keep your ice houses full; an early spring thaw is called for." *Well, not up here.* "The town hotels predict a boom this season." *Good, then I'm going.* "Mr. B. F Deford was in town this week and marveled at how modern and cheerful our town looked." *Oh please.* "A good deal of crooked whiskey and mean apple jack have been getting in its work for the last week."

Luanne looked at me with a sly smile and kept reading. She told us about the scarcity of turkey and quail because of the mountain lions, Miss Sours falling off her horse, the telegraph office in Berryville becoming a telephone company, a scientist from the Smithsonian Institute at Washington D. C. digging on Indian graves and finding skeletons and Indian relics, and a storm that blew the roof off of the Female Institute. With a flourish, she folded the paper and put it on the kindling pile by the stove.

Tom said, "I've got the gear packed and about six of the horses cleaned up. When Colin comes in tell him, I'm going to need him to come down to the barn at daylight and help me finish cleaning and loading the horses. Mary, you're riding in my old trousers, but you pack yourself one day dress if you want and one fine dress from the trunk along with whatever else you'll need for your toiletries. Make sure you pack one of my old union suits for warmth. I have already packed an oil slicker and gloves for you. Luanne, before you turn in, help her get what she will need for enough food for five to six days. We leave tomorrow morning." He stood up from the table, pushed his chair out and looked down at the both of us.

"I'm sending word to Ma to send Sissy and John to come up here and keep you company and help. They'll give you a hand till we get back." He motioned to grab his hat, but Luanne jumped up and grabbed his arm.

"Oh, no, you don't, Tom. I'm *not* putting up with being bossed around by them the entire time you're gone. There will be nothing going on around here that I can't handle myself. Besides, I'm sure if I ask Asa Dean, he will call on me and help."

Tom regarded his sister silently, and then he walked around the table and looked hard at her. "That's funny, Luanne. Very slick. So, you and Asa going to play house while I'm gone?"

Luanne's face reddened. "I'm not saying that. All I'm saying—"

"*All I'm* saying is you don't know everything about this world even though you think you do. You do what you want, but I'm not having any more children in this house that are not...." He stopped short and walked out slamming the front door.

I was so stung and shocked by what he had almost said, I could not draw breath. I could tell Luanne felt the same, as her eyes were boring holes in the closed door. She came over to me and put her arms around my shoulders. Evie looked at us both. "Don't you mind him. He's just worried about things, though, I suppose, that's no excuse."

"I don't want to go with him now." Looking at Luanne square in the face, I said, "I don't want to be stuck with him now all alone. It has all been a lie."

"No, it hasn't. He's just acting mean and ornery because he's worried. He'll think on what he said and apologize, I hope, and if he doesn't, so be it, 'cause you always have me and that's forever."

Luanne started to clear up the dishes and I rose to help her. "You know," she said, "I'm going to have Asa come up here, and what better way to know if I can get along with him than to have to do work together. I want to see how he partners me and if he can take some bossing. Tom don't know everything either, obviously." She rolled her eyes in a dramatic gesture.

"Really?"

Luanne nodded and I remembered advice from my mother that I had not heeded. "Not that I listened to this advice, of course," I said, "but my mother used to say, 'a man won't buy a cow if he can get the milk for free.'"

"Well, that never seemed to stop men from wanting to marry Belle."

I stopped in my tracks. Luanne was right, I thought, pondering this. "Just be careful... You don't want to end up like me; that's not a good road to travel. I'm telling you."

"I don't want a baby, because then I know Asa will insist on marrying me, and I'm not sure yet if I want him. Besides, you know what Granny used to tell all us girls once we got our courses?"

I shook my head no.

"If you don't want butter, you better pull out the churn." It took me a minute, but then I looked at her, and we doubled over in a fit of laughing just as Tom came back in the house, looking at us warily.

"Glad to see you all are working hard getting ready."

We stopped laughing but were still giggling as he strode to the other side of the house, and we could hear his heavy foot falls as he went to the bedroom and opened and slammed the bedroom door. As soon as the door slammed, we started laughing again, making faces in his direction. I loved Luanne more than anyone on earth, and I went to bed that night thinking how I wished I were leaving in the morning with her.

Chapter 31

Morning came quickly, and in the faint light of dawn with the oil lamps glowing, we all moved about the house silently getting ready and placing parcels and packs by the kitchen door to take to the barn. Luanne and I walked the loads to the barn where Tom and Colin had already tied all the horses to the fenceposts. Seeing the string of horses, the reality of what we were doing finally sank in, and I was filled with such dread. I whispered to Luanne, "I don't want to go."

"Too late for that."

"What do you want us to do?" shouted Luanne to her brother, breaking the still of the morning silence. The horses pricked their ears in her direction as Tom came out of his shop carrying two shotguns.

"Start packing the food on the palomino with the blaze. Mary, put your things on your horse."

"Which one is that?" I looked around for the old chestnut mare.

"Your horse; he's in the barn."

I walked into the barn with curiosity and trepidation, wondering which nag was going to carry me on this long and dangerous trip. In the dim light, a horse's head poked out of the stall when it heard me enter. It was my boy. Surprised, I stroked his velvet head. I jumped as Tom entered the barn. "I thought... I mean you think it will be all right?"

"Get him saddled and packed."

I wondered if he was punishing me for something, though it put my heart at ease to have my horse as a companion, especially considering Tom was currently no companion to me because I almost hated him. Men were fine and all, but it was Luanne and even Belle, and of course, my children, and my horse, who had my heart. My spirit was kindred to theirs. With women and animals, I was safe, and even though Tom was good and mostly kind, he had his vices. And his comment yesterday left me with the inability to forget. I'm not sure this is what my mother meant when she said, *the secret to a good marriage is the ability to be stone deaf when needed.* Not that I ever could, really, but I didn't want any reminders about my past from him.

Quickly, I got the Giant ready, and when I led him out of the barn, Luanne's eyes widened when she saw him. "Tom? Why don't you let Mary ride your horse? Prince is so rock steady."

"Because I'm not fighting with her horse for four days," he said, motioning to the Giant. "The red mare is too old to go that far, and *that* is the horse she has chosen to partner with."

Luanne and I shared another look as we finished tying down the parcels to every inch of my horse's saddle. Tom came over and strapped a hunting knife to the horn and a rifle to the saddle. "We are about ready. Colin let's start the string. Go get that roan and bring him to me."

I walked back to the house, which now was being hit with the first rays of dawn light as Mars faded in redness to the west, and the sky grew in blue brilliance to the east with Venus giving her last glow in the light of the crescent moon. I looked down at my sleeping Evelyn with her beautiful dark hair and resting so sweetly that the corner of her mouth was turned up in a smile. I had tried to tell her that we were going on a trip, and she wouldn't see me in the morning, and I would be back with a toy and a candy bar for her. I hoped she would be a good girl. Luanne had promised Colin that they were going to go on hunting adventures in the woods and that Asa was going to show him how to use a bow. Evie was told she could bring her bow and arrow with the rubber ends that she got for Christmas. We only let Evie play with it under strict supervision, since she tended to shoot, with very good accuracy, the chickens, the dog, the barn cats, or anything else she fancied, which included her brother's behind.

How I didn't want to leave. I thought of telling Tom I couldn't go and had made a mistake, but I also knew that would have been wrong, wrong, wrong. Being an adventurer seems like a good idea when you are thinking about it from inside your cozy house.

I walked out the door and saw the horses lined up and ready to go, and the sight didn't comfort me. I brought the Giant over to the fence so I could climb up and mount him as Colin held his bridle to make sure he stayed steady. It was no mean feat to get on a horse that tall, but once I was in the saddle, I was centered and fine and took the reins.

"Luanne, make sure you don't give Evie too much chocolate."

"I'm going to do what I have to do to keep her happy till you get back. Don't worry. It's looking like a nice day today, so we 'll go on an exploration in the forest, and that will distract everyone. Plus, they both like Asa." She whispered this last part looking around for Tom who, as it turned out, was already mounted with the string of horses tied to him. "Well, you got your escapade. You'll be fine but good luck with him." She gestured in Tom's direction.

"I'm ready," I shouted at Tom. He kicked his horse and slowly the team of horses began walking forward. Luanne blew me a kiss. "Love you," she called.

"Love you, too."

My horse grew impatient with being in the back of the line and started jigging, which distracted me from my heart. I prayed that a few mountains would take the edge off both him and me. I watched Tom disappear into the darkness of the wooded trail as each horse followed and the shadows closed in behind them.

It was two and a half miles to the top of the peak when we turned north, and the sun moved from my back to my right shoulder. In some spots, the trail was blocked by fallen trees that Tom had to saw through. All around us was undeveloped wilderness, and the rocky trail was narrow and the mountain desolate. Snow clung to the western slope, but to the southeast, spring was rising. We were so high up, the only things clinging to life on the spine of the mountain were scrub pines, blueberry bushes and the occasional elbow bent tree. If it hadn't been for the deer trails, I would have thought we were on Mount Horeb. As I waited for Tom to saw through a tree, I wondered what wisdom God would bestow on me with all this silence. Finally, he, Tom, not God, pushed the tree up and over the side of the trail, tied his hand saw back on his horse and mounted without even looking back to see if I was still with him. But, I thought, that is how it is with God too. Was my hopefulness indifference or blind faith?

We traveled another six miles and by now, the sun was riding high in the sky, and we had crossed back over to what was called the South River trail that overlooked Wolftown. I thought Tom was never going to stop, as by now I had to relieve myself. But on about noon, Tom tied up his horse in a clearing, and he finally glanced back to the end of the trail and me. I didn't want to ask him for help as I turned my horse off the trail to a place where I could try to dismount. I sure liked just being able to drop my trousers instead of hiking up skirts, I thought, as I squatted behind my horse. Walking over to him, I saw he had put out some food. I reached for a tenderloin sandwich in silence.

"I want to see how close we can get to Lewis Mountain before dark." I nodded, not sure what he wanted me to say to that. "Can you handle that?"

"Yep."

He nodded contemplating this. He lit a cigarette as I reached for an apple. "Before we leave here, fill your water up at the creek."

I was already planning to do that, but I nodded as I stood up, grabbing my canteen. I bent before the creek and splashed some water on my face and neck, and though it was cold, it felt good. Filling my bottle, I also cupped my hand and drank some water, as the canteen always seemed to give the water a metal-like taste that I didn't fancy. By then, my hands were ice cold and numb. Opening and closing them tightly to get some circulation flowing, I was thankful to stretch my legs though the walking on the rocky ground was rough. As Tom got the pack line of horses ready, I remounted.

We passed an east-going road a few miles further down the trail, but even though it connected us to civilization down below, we saw not a soul. It was not so much a road as another trail since it was not wide enough for a wagon. As the woodland bore witness, I thought on the aloneness of it all. I wondered if that is what Moses felt crossing the desert. Did he wonder if God was still with him? Yet, the oneness I felt being with my horse and the solitude of the forest was more God-like than I had ever felt, and it gave me more comfort than I had ever felt from praying, which seemed to do a whole lot of nothing. Looking down along the eastward road, I wondered who lived down by the hollow of Kirby Mountain and what type of people they were. Would the woman have worked their gardens earlier than us? Should I leave and find out? By now, the sun had moved to my left shoulder, and I could feel the temperature dropping. I figured families were probably thinking about dinner.

Tom continued on until he found another south facing clearing a bit lower off the ridge that was gently sloping but with flat places to pitch a tent. This time, I found my own flat place and led my horse to it. I swung my leg over the saddle and, facing my horse's head, moved my body completely to his left so I could dismount at a right angle. As I landed squarely on my feet, I smiled. I undid the cinch and breastplate of my saddle and laid it in some dry leaves with all the packs still attached. It was heavy. My horse's back was dark with sweat, and I flipped the saddle pad and let it lay loosely on his back so he would not get a chill. He cocked his back foot and I grinned to myself that I had finally worn him out. I patted and loved on him and didn't hear Tom approach.

"You love on that horse more than me." He laughed, and I could tell he was relieved that we had had a trouble-free first day. I ignored him. He had sacked out the trail horses in a mildly grassy area having let them drink their fill at the last creek we had passed on the trail. "Do you want to set up the tent or get a fire going?"

"I'll do the fire," I told him.

I immediately began exploring, noticing overturned rocks and broken tree stumps. Keeping an eye and ear out for bears, I placed some rocks for a fire circle and began to look for kindling. I could find no pine needles since we were mostly in an oaken area, but I found enough bark, old, dried grasses, and twigs to start a fire, which I promptly did. By the time I had circled back to camp with more wood, Tom had his old Army tent set up and was unpacking our bedding. I set up the crane and spit over the fire so we could heat some coffee and cook the two chickens we had butchered back home.

By now it was dark and cold. Never had coffee tasted so good. And even though we dropped one chicken directly in the fire, which caused Tom to laugh and tell me he would eat that one, we went to bed as soon as we finished. I laid under the covers with my back to Tom.

"Here, why don't you get comfortable and lie on my chest?"

It was a good thing it was dark because my face screwed up in disbelief. "I'm more comfortable this way."

"Suit yourself."

And soon I was gifted with the sound of his gentle snoring.

I woke to Tom stirring, but I pretended to be asleep. Hearing him making coffee, though, worked on my guilt, and I slowly rose up on one elbow, blinking my eyes and gearing myself up for another long day. I pulled up on my trousers, and then left the tent barefoot to see if my socks had dried where I had left them by the fire. It felt good to have my feet on the cold earth, and I wiggled my toes around and stretched my stiff back.

The fire was going enough to heat up our coffee. I looked around the clearing and remembered I had seen some snow on the west bank, which I began walking towards. With my bare feet, I stood on the snow, and I felt the cold travel up from my feet and through my veins to every inch of my body and finally up through the back of my neck, into and out the top of my head. I breathed long and deep and would have stood in the snow longer, but I knew I had to get back and start some breakfast. Feeling renewed, I walked back to camp where Tom already had the side meat frying. He looked up when he saw me.

"If Granny Hite had not told me that what you were doing was true, I would have sworn I married a crazy woman."

"What do you mean?" I began to make cornpones to fry in the bacon grease.

"I've never seen anyone stand in mountain streams or snow to pull out pain until I met you."

"I used to have some mean headaches when I was growing up, and I found, quite by accident, if I stood in the snow or a mountain stream, I felt better."

"You know, I've never had a headache in my life.

"That's because nothing troubles you; you're lucky."

"That's because I see things for how they really are." He took the side meat out of the pan, and I moved beside him and placed four pones to frying in the grease. I gave him a sideways glance. He poured some coffee and handed it to me.

I placed two pones on his tin plate and two on mine and took the pan off the fire. I looked at the long streaks of clouds in the pale morning sky and Tom, as if reading my thoughts, said, "Weather is changing. A front is moving in. I wonder how long it will give us?"

"It is what it is," I said. Tom nodded.

"I'll start getting the horses ready then come back and help you break down camp," I told him.

Tom stood up, and looking down at me, said, "What's eating at you?"

I looked up at him and, innocently and inauthentically, said with a smile, "Nothing."

"Suit yourself." He looked at me a moment and walked off.

We kept to the south side of the mountain, and the trail dropped in elevation as we traveled to Bootens Gap. Day two had found the horses all sound. My spirits rose, though the day was not as sunny as the first. It was a sight to see so many horses traveling along the trail, and it made me think of all the people who had traveled not just for a few days but who had traveled for months and months on the Oregon Trail. Then, here we were, still going by horses when many companies were turning out automobiles.

By late morning, the trail began climbing again. It was winter up here. Even at the high elevation, there were still last year's withered grapes clinging to vines; perhaps the birds and bears didn't want to venture up this high. Perhaps they knew better than people. After an hour, the trail was still headed up, and I patted my horse, but I was thankful that this ride had worn down his jigging. He was moving like an old steady trail horse now. In the distance, I could see a bit of a clearing and what looked to be a turnoff heading east down the mountain. Suddenly, the horses all stopped, and as was my horse's way, he banged into the horse in front of him and began rubbing his head on that horse's rump. I tried to pull his head up as I saw Tom walking down the trail towards me. He placed his hand on my leg.

"We have one last pull till we get to the top of Hazeltop, but we're coming to the wagon road that leads down to Jones Mountain and the Deans. My mother is a Dean and that's my kinfolk, so now is the time to tell me if you want off the trail."

"No, I'm fine." Tom stared at me.

"This first bit has been a cakewalk. Tomorrow will be on the west side of the mountain, and that's where we'll stay until we get to Skyland. It'll be tough going, too." He thought about this. "I'm thinking maybe it might be a good idea for you not to do this."

"I'm not a quitter."

"There's nothing wrong in throwing in the towel. In fact, it's a wise man who knows when to do so."

"And I'm not going to show up on strangers' doorsteps."

"They ain't strangers; there're my family."

"They're your family, not my family."

"Mary, damn it, you met some of them at our wedding."

"Oh." I considered this. "Well, I'm still not going."

"I swear you are the most stubborn and headstrong woman I have ever met," he said walking away from me but then he turned around and looked back at me. "But that's one of the reasons I like you."

I watched him walk back up the trail. It would have been my nature to say I don't like you back to Tom, especially after what he said back at the farm, but riding in silence with my own thoughts for so many hours, I realized he was just stating the facts. It *is* what it *is,* and there was only my own doing if I chose to get worked up about it. Realizing this made me less sore at him. If I had realized these pearls of wisdom sooner in my life, I would not have created stories around love and Halsom, and if I had seen him for what he was, I might have turned tail and run. Might have.

The horses moved forward again, and the trail dipped south and down the mountain and then opened up to a giant meadow where a few cows were grazing. The horses' ears pricked up at the sight of the grass. I watched Tom get off his horse, and he motioned me to come up. His horse was so well behaved that it would not drop his head to eat, though Tom left the reins loose on the saddle horn, unlike my horse who was already pulling at the reins and grabbing clumps of grass. Tom yanked my horse's head back up. "We're going to make camp here and let the horses graze. Don't let him graze until he's turned out or you'll make him rank."

"But it is only midafternoon. Why are we stopping so soon?"

"The next two days will be rougher going, and they have had a long pull today. I thought you would be happy to rest here."

"Is it okay? I mean whoever owns this will be fine with our being here?"

"It's owned by Tom Stump down in the valley, and the Joneses have been farming this land for four generations, maybe five. I know all the parties, and I have permission to be here, unlike others. They shot and killed a Cranson for poaching up here a few years back. They did warn him first."

"That's reassuring."

"Before we set up camp, let's hobble the horses. I'm trying to decide what to do with yours. I don't need him breaking a leg up here, and I'm not so sure he has ever been hobbled. Until I figure it out just tie him to a tree."

I put on my horse's halter and draped his bridle over the saddle horn so I could tie him low enough to let him graze a bit. I walked up to Tom to help with the trail horses. The few cows lifted their heads to watch us. I set to placing the hobbles on each horse's back legs and turning them loose.

"I thought they moved the cows back down the valley for winter. Isn't it too early for them to be up here? The grass has not come in yet," I said to Tom while we worked.

"Stump leaves a few steers here but brings his heifers back down. He usually runs them back up in May."

The horses attacked the grass pulling and chewing nosily as we set up the tent, and I was happy to see some mountain blue birds flitting across the meadow along with flocks of robins. I had noticed the bird song changing, but had not seen either a bluebird or a robin at Hightop even though we were farther south, but I supposed it was the elevation that kept them from settling in by us until early April. Tom got a nice fire going as I shook out and set our bedding inside the tent.

"What are we going to do with my horse? We can't leave him tied with nothing to eat all night."

"I've thought of a solution," and with that, Tom went and got him. Taking off the breastplate and saddle, Tom turned him loose with his halter and lead rope dragging. I watched as my horse immediately started eating but would jump up surprised with a jerk when he stood on his rope and tried to go forward. It was quite a sight to see the horses all grazing quietly and my Samson-like horse, hands above them. His chest alone seemed to be the size of the roan horse's whole body.

Tom used his saddle as a back rest and let out a long deep sigh as he settled down to rest. He reached over to untie my brogans and take off my socks. I wiggled my toes and was glad my feet had been set free. His tenderness softened my heart. Tom handed me the flask, and I took a long warming draught of the Apple Pie. Tom's recipe was the very best I ever tasted, and I think it was because he didn't over do the cinnamon.

He went to get more firewood. The faint and pale rays of the sun settled upon us. I watched my horse graze. He lifted his black head up, and that white star on his forehead shone like a beacon as he looked around as if he were surveying his entire kingdom. Slowly, and with what seemed like careful deliberation, he seemed to be working his way towards the far circle of the horses and the south side of the meadow. By now, twilight was upon us, and I had a steaming pot of chicken, carrots, and potatoes on the crane. Tom had come back carrying an armful of wood when he suddenly said, "You son of a bitch."

I looked up to see my horse heading down the trail back towards home carrying his head slightly cocked so as not to step on his rope. With dread, I stood up and watched as Tom dropped the wood at his feet and began to stride off after him his eyes flashing fire. As I watched Tom disappear into the dark woods, I looked up to the cloud filled sky; I closed my eyes and prayed to my horse to stop. Time slowed, and I waited and waited and was torn in wanting to follow. When I couldn't stand it any longer, I moved the chicken off the fire and began walking across the meadow just as I saw Tom's black hat and the rest of him emerge from the woods leading my sheepish horse behind him. It was my turn to let out a deep sigh. I met him in the middle of the field. "I'm sorry."

"It's not your fault. He's gotten away with shit all his life, and he knows he can. Plus, he's too damn smart." Tom looked straight at me. "You don't want too smart a horse, remember that." I was relieved Tom was not sore, and I went to take the lead rope from him, but he shook his head no. Tom led my horse to a tree behind the tent and tied him so tight his muzzle was kissing the tree bark.

"You're not going to leave him like that all night?"

"Don't you worry about him. Let's eat some of that stew. Something warm will be good."

I cast an eye at my horse. His brow was wrinkled in concern, and I felt sorry for him, mad at him and kind of proud of him, too. That night, after I heard Tom snoring, I snuck out of the tent and looked at my horse. Trying to decide what to do, I made up my mind and untied him from the tree. I took the last set of hobbles and placed them around his back legs. I left the lead line dragging too and prayed he would not kill himself or take off again. He immediately set about eating and walked over to his favorite mare and placidly grazed beside her. I stayed up awhile and watched him. Perhaps he was smart after all, for in the morning, he was still there.

The wind was gusting, and we both worked quickly to break down camp and gather horses. Tom didn't mention my horse being untied, but his mind was preoccupied with the weather as he pulled his collar around his throat, glancing at the sky. The sky was gray, and it seemed as if all color had been sucked from the meadow, the horses' coats, and the day. The temperature had also dropped, or maybe it was the wind that made it feel so. In either case, the horses' heads were erect, and their ears swiveled forward and back, as if listening to a hidden message.

We didn't talk much, and soon we were mounted and heading over to the west side of the mountain, which offered no protection from the wind as we rode across the rocky spine, revealing the knob of Massanutten standing out against the Alleghenies. The air on the peak was white and swirling with ice flakes, and with alarm, I realized it was raining snow. I couldn't take my eyes off the western sky so that when my horse occasionally tripped over a rock or limb, I was jarred awake, as if out of a bad dream. The swirling mass of white blew ever closer and churned around us.

By noon, we halted by Tanner's Ridge, and I dismounted as Tom approached me. I was stomping my feet and banging my hands together to get the circulation moving as my toes and fingers were cracking with pain. Tom's breath came out in little clouds. "We're only going to stop for a short while till I can think of what I want to do next. We've got a major front burying us."

"I've been watching it all morning."

He nodded, drawing a deep breath, and letting out a sigh. We were both thinking the same thing.

"As soon as I see a deer trail heading back east over the mountain, I'm going to take it and we are going to head to the Meadows farm. Let's just keep our fingers crossed we don't break up the line trying to get over the mountain. Grab some food and whatever else you need. I'm going to head back to the front of the line, and then we are moving out."

"The wind is so bad, and I need to change. My courses have come on."

He considered this, starring at the ground. Looking up he said, "All right then."

Tom moved fast pulling leather ties off my saddle and a blanket. Using the stunted blueberry bushes, laurels, and ghost pines for stakes, he fashioned a tent of sorts and began rolling boulders onto the blanket ends to hold it to the earth. It billowed like a sail and the horses at the end of the line looked back nervously. The wind began to howl as the cold air hit my skin, and I worked frantically to clean myself up and adjust my clean rags. As I backed out of the tent, I was greeted by the swirl of snow and ice that hit my face like daggers.

I was frightened for myself, my husband, and the horses. I could not get over how things can change so quickly; one minute it was spring, the next winter. Quickly, pulling, yanking, and cursing, I broke down the makeshift tent. I heard Tom's wolf whistle before it got carried away on the wind, and I knew we were headed out. Just as I was about to retie the blanket to the saddle, I changed my mind. Draping it over my horse's butt, I tightened the girth, and with my muscles taught and not wanting to stretch, I barely got myself into the saddle without bumping into the saddle horn. I began tucking the blanket under and around my legs and over my head like a hood. Even so, by the time we began weaving our way east on a deer trail, my body was shivering violently, and my teeth were chattering. I had always thought that chattering teeth was just an exaggeration.

We rode for hours, days, what felt like a lifetime. I don't know how long as the sky was flat gray and dead-looking, and the faint light of day offered no solace. The wind seemed maniacal as it whipped around us, first at our backs, then blasting us in the face, and finally swirling like a vortex till I felt it would lift me up and carry me away. Hell is not fire, I thought.

I had let my reins fall loose, barely able to tighten a grip around them, and my face was buried down in my coat so that I had stopped looking out ahead of me miles ago. The only way I knew that I was still alive was because of the cramps in my pelvis and a slight nausea. Finally, the light changed as we emerged from the dense woods, and I squinted in wonder as Big Meadows laid in front of us in a beautiful blanket of snow, appearing as if an oasis among the barren trees and boulders of the mountain. Dried grasses hung with ice poked out of the snow and deer tracks crisscrossed the field. I remembered my teacher, Miss Halfyard, telling us about Big Meadows and how it had been a meadow for thousands upon thousands, of years because of the glaciers and mountain magic that always kept it clear. She brought in arrowheads to school the day she talked about it. Zebadiah Baugher had spoken up that day in class and said it had nothing to do with magic, but the Indians and the mountain farmers would set it to burn every few years. Miss Halfyard didn't even answer him but kept right on with her lesson.

With Dark Hollow to the left of us, Tom snaked his way back into the woods, but by then, I was so numb that thought, care, and worry had left me. I had even stopped shivering. Icicles now hung from the horses' coats where sweat and snow had frozen. Faintly, a thought rose up in my numb brain that I was going to die. *You will not die,* I said to myself three times as tears began to form, and for some reason, I began to think of my friend Ethel who was probably, at this very moment, sipping tea in her yellow kitchen that she probably made on her gas stove Johnathan Abel had bought her. For all I knew, she could have been having my mother over.

Suddenly, I became aware of a stone wall, then we passed a cemetery with a mound of fresh dirt among the headstones that had resisted the snow. I saw a spring house. As we made our way, the deer trail opened up to a cleared lane, and in the distance, I could see a large two-story cantilevered barn, and I smelled wood smoke. Then, coming around a turn in the path, there in my sight, was a two-story frame house, a porch lined with cut wood, and the most beautiful sight of my life, smoke curling up from the chimney, piercing the falling snow which greeted us like an oasis in a parched desert. A lamp glowed in the window, and I knew this was a vision I would never forget. A dog emerged from under the porch and began barking furiously, and a curtain moved in the window. Immediately, a man, pulling on his coat, emerged from the front door. The man sprinted towards us, his pipe in his mouth.

Tom stopped the line and dismounted, and I saw the man place his hand on Tom's shoulder. The man looked down the line and nodded as he motioned for Tom to follow. Tom looked back at me, motioning with his hand. Then the line moved off as we headed towards the barn. The chestnut barn provided immediate shelter, and the men worked quickly placing the horses in stalls and throwing them hay. The horses were shivering violently, and their bodies were steaming. Two Guernsey milk cows looked up from their byre with their spring calves bedded down beside them, and they let out a disgruntled moo at having been disturbed by the circus that had disrupted the peace and plenty of their kingdom. I sat hunched over in the saddle in a daze but thankful to be out of the wind and ice which I could hear pelting on the tin roof. The barn was so huge it felt like a great Viking hall, and the entire second story was filled with mounds and mounds of sweet-smelling hay.

"Let's give these boys some corn and oats, and that will get their blood flowing," I heard the man say.

One by one, the horses were moved to rest, warmth and safety till the man came to the end of the line and looked up at me in surprise. He turned his head to Tom at the other end of the barn and shouted with the pipe still in his mouth, "Your man here is half froze. Come on, boy, get off that horse and we'll get you to a fire."

I tried to pull off my wet gloves, but my fingers would not work I had to pull them off with my teeth and they dropped silently to the floor. The man looked at me alarmed. "You all right, boy?"

I nodded and, with a grunt, swung my leg over the horse, but as I dismounted and my feet touched the floor, my legs gave out and I fell to my knees. By now, Tom was with me, lifting me up and shaking me. "Come on now," Tom said, alarmed. "Here." He held the flask up to my lips, and sputtering and coughing, I managed to get three good swallows. Tom put his arm underneath me, and we followed the man to his house as I tried to walk. I climbed the stairs of the porch like a drunken man.

"Let's get that boy to the fire. Get us two cups of coffee," the man called to his wife.

Interestingly, the warmth of the fire got me shaking again, and the pins and needles sensation in my hands and feet were unbearable.

"Well, that's a good sign. I think he'll live," said the man. "Come on now and take off that coat of yours." I was handed hot black coffee that was so sweet it made my teeth tingle, but it was good. Tom pulled the blanket off my head and removed my hat.

"I'll be damned," said the man as my tangled hair fell around my shoulders.

When Tom peeled off the coat, I heard the woman say, "Goodness!" as she rushed over to me. She looked at me and back at Tom and to me again. The woman rushed to get the coat and began hanging our clothes by the cook stove. "My, my, my in all my days," she kept saying.

"You're just full of surprises," said the man pulling out a chair for Tom to sit on. "I didn't hear that you had gotten yourself a woman. But then, we have been so preoccupied with Joanna's illness, we haven't been paying too much attention to the outside world, have we, mother?"

"She passed two weeks ago."

"I'm sorry for your loss, Louise, Benjamin," Tom said.

"She had a time of it all right," said Benjamin.

I threw a glance at Tom, trying to catch his eye, but he was looking down into his coffee.

The room was quiet except for the crackling of the fire. Finally, I said, "What happened?"

Tom shuffled, and I could tell he was uncomfortable, as he rushed to fill the silence. "When I saw her in the fall, she looked a picture of health. Wasn't she headed to Sweet Briar to see her sister?" said Tom, rescuing me.

Benjamin nodded.

Louise said, "It was a terrible thing. She came home from her trip so excited and happy. She had even met a young doctor on her visit who worked at the Virginia Colony and was writing to her real regular."

"Then, one day, she woke up and told us she didn't feel so good. Could not hold down any food at all. Her brothers went for the physician who gave her some tonic, but that did her no good," Benjamin added.

"She just faded away before our very eyes," said Louise, looking at me.

Tom and I didn't say anything. What could you say? It was another reminder to me that life seemed to be filled with calamity.

"Are you warmed up, little lady?" Benjamin smiled at me, shaking himself lose from his sadness.

"Yes. Thank you."

"Is that lamb stew ready?"

"Let me see about that."

Tom and I now exchanged glances, and Tom attempted a palliative smile at me.

Benjamin said, "So, I ain't feeding you until you tell me what you're doing bringing Adams all those horses." He then turned to me and winked. "I'm just kidding. I'll feed *you*," he looked at me, "but maybe not Tom." And of course, Tom was slow to answer, weighing his words and thoughts.

"Benjamin, I don't ask Adams what he wants with any of my goods and services. I just deliver and pray the check clears." They both laughed.

"Ain't that the truth. He's had a hell of a time up there recently. More so than usual. I'm not one to spread ill will, but I hear his wife moved into her own cabin up there, then hightailed it back to Washington. He's hurting for cash. But I have also heard that he has been bringing some Washington types up and down Stony Man." By now, Louise had placed four steaming bowls of stew around the kitchen table along with bread, butter, cheese, and jam. She motioned me to come join her at the table.

"Papa, come on."

The men joined us, and they motioned for us to join hands. "Dear heavenly Father, you who gives all and takes all. Watch over our travelers and watch over our dear Joanna and hold her and keep her in your arms until we can join her. And keep an eye on our sons and lead them not into temptation and bring them home safe and sound. Through you is the power, the glory, and the wisdom. Amen."

Food was passed to us first, and I cut myself a big slice of the bread and loaded it with butter and jam. I cut myself a healthy slice of the cheese, too, but I found, after the first bite, that the cows must have been eating new spring onions. I swallowed it without chewing and dove into my stew.

"Jake and Jed butchered this lamb before they left. Would you believe he was born on the first of the year? In all my years of raising sheep I have never had one come that early."

"How are your boys?" asked Tom.

"They are making themselves a good bit of money working up the country these days. As soon as those chestnuts started failing, they got a lead about a job up North when they were at Cisnor's store and went straight away right up there. They come back home on some weekends."

It's a funny thing to have your house empty after all those years of raising children. Ain't it, Papa?"

Benjamin nodded, drawing on his pipe.

"Louise still cooks for an army, so it's a good thing you all dropped by."

"Well, that's good," said Tom, "because my wife can eat as if she was in the army." I didn't mind the laugh at my expense, and I used the opportunity to ask for another bowl of stew. Tom, looking at my plate, rescued me again. "You going to eat the rest of that cheese?" I smiled at him, pushing it in his direction. "Here, you get your fill."

"I swear, girl, where do you put it?" asked Benjamin as I finished my second bowl of stew and another slice of bread.

"Leave her alone. Thank God for a healthy appetite," Louise said, bringing me another steaming bowl. "Did you all get a lot of grapes last year? I swear the mountains were full of them, and we have vines over by the clothesline too."

"Yes, but my jam is not as flavorful as yours."

"I put a pinch or cardamom and cinnamon in mine," said Louise.

"So, now that you got yourself a woman, how many children do you have?" asked Benjamin.

I held my breath.

"We have two. Colin is just over ten and Evie is going over six years. Colin is kind, helpful and eager to please and Evie...why...Evie is whiskey in a teacup."

"Jake and Jed were only twelve months apart and got into enough trouble for twelve boys, but Joanna didn't come to us till many years later." Benjamin looked at his wife and patted her hand.

"We're blessed," Louise smiled at her husband.

"I feel blessed that you have offered us such bounty and hospitality. Thank you," I said.

"You're quite welcome," replied Benjamin. "We're happy for the company. Now, I know you're not a pipe smoking man, but you have got to try this tobacco that the boys brought back last visit."

"I'm not going to send you out into the weather with your pipes, but I would be grateful if you went into the sitting room to smoke," said Louise. The men excused themselves.

"Now, you take your time and finish up eating," Louise said. "I'm just going to clear up the dishes and then we can visit."

I was only too happy to accommodate her. While Louise cleaned up the dishes and table, I asked for her receipts for the stew and bread. Louise was Irish, and I had not had lamb stew and soda bread since I had been at my grandmother's house.

As evening enveloped the farm, the snow stopped but the wind kept blowing, and the tin roof rattled like an old woman's bones. Louise moved about the house, lighting her gas lamps.

"I just cannot abide a dark house," she said to me.

The men's voices rose and fell from the next room with the occasional peel of laughter. As Louise sat down next to me with her crocheting she said, "You're a brave girl to accompany your husband on such a trip. You know, my grandfather came here from Galway when he was fourteen years old, and he landed in New York City not knowing a soul. I just can't imagine leaving your whole world behind and starting again."

I can, I thought.

"And now, there is talk that the government wants to make a park and maybe kick us off our own land. Have you heard anything down your way?"

"Yes, we have heard some rumors about that. It's one of the reasons I wanted to go with Tom, to see what I could find out from the people of Skyland."

"Lord knows the men won't tell us anything. If you find out then, you stop back here and tell me. I have half a mind to go there myself, but Benjamin of course, won't hear of it. I get most of my news on Sundays. Some of the congregation live that way, and they have been telling a tale or two. I've heard the government people will let us all stay, then I have heard they will pay for the land, then I have heard that they are just planning to kick us off. You know that John Ciser, down in Madison County, is getting ready for Armageddon and is stockpiling his guns. He says no one is going to make him leave his land. They are going to have to take him out feet first, I can tell you that. My family didn't build a life here in America to have this happen." She rested a while with that thought and then said, "Knowing men, they probably have not even figured it out what they are planning to do and are just running their mouths with ever cockamamie idea that comes into their brains."

"That's the truth."

"Well, woman, you didn't think it was a cockamamie idea to get you a new stove," said Benjamin.

"I do believe we have been maligned while we have been out of the room," said my Tom, "but we probably deserve it."

"Speaking of running our mouths, let's get these good people bedded down. I know they're tired."

Louise stood up and placed her crocheting on the table. I noticed a spinning wheel and carders in the corner. "Is that your wheel?"

"Yes. My husband gives me heck about still spinning, but that is my great-grandmother's wheel that she brought over, and it just sooths my nerves to spin."

"Lord knows the wool prices ain't worth a damn. She might as well spin what we shear."

"You don't have to make any fuss on our account. We're fine in the barn," said Tom.

"I won't hear of it. Why, you can have our Joanna's room with the nice down mattress."

Oh God, I thought.

Tom said, "I can't let my woman get soft, Benjamin. If I let her sleep on a new down mattress, she's going to start demanding electricity and a telephone next."

"I'm going to stay with my husband, and our place is with our horses. We've been sleeping out this whole journey, and your barn will be like a castle," I said.

"Well, suit yourself. Louise, you get them some quilts."

Tom motioned for me to stay quiet, and we bundled back up to walk to the barn with the men carrying lanterns. I was relieved to see the wind had stopped and the clouds were breaking up to reveal the stars in the dark blue-black sky. The snow crunched under our feet, and the stillness and silence of the snow-covered forest was beautiful. With my belly full and my limbs mostly working, I felt renewed, though I never told Tom that I had chilblains in some of my toes for the rest of my life.

He left us with the quilts and lanterns and made us promise to join them for breakfast the following morning. When he had exited the barn, Tom drew me up in his arms and held me, placing his check against mine. It felt good to be pressed to him. We stood that way a long time, and I was the first to draw back.

"Thank you for getting us here and getting us to the barn."

"Don't touch the blankets," he said, eyeing them warily. "Who knows if it is another strain of the Spanish flu?"

"I won't." I looked at them warily.

"Come on." He took me by the hand and bade me sit on a sawhorse while I watched him fix up our resting spot. I looked over the horses who were munching hay. Their coats had dried, leaving lines in their coats, but they had survived. Tom led me over to a hay filled corner of the barn, and we nestled in like two mice, Tom pulling his wool army blankets over us. Tom spooned me wrapping his arms around me. "Well, it looks like you survived another one, my dear."

"Another what?"

"Trial by fire.

"I think I may leave the next adventure to Belle."

"I never thought I would hear you say that."

"Neither did I."

Tom's snoring soon filled my ear and blended with the chewing, snorting and other life noises while I stared for a while into the dark, wondering what tomorrow would bring, and drawing deep breaths of the sweet-smelling hay.

Chapter 32

The blessed sun cast rays on our face by 6:30. I looked around and saw Tom was up and running his hands over the horses, looking each one over. Rising on my elbows, I took a long swig of water from the canteen that Tom had left by my side. "How are they all doing?" I asked.

"At the moment, they appear fine. Getting them moving will work out any stiffness. And the weather has shifted again. The sun is warming the world back up and chasing away winter."

I stood up and stretched, and I could not believe my body could hurt all over so badly. I thought only old people should hurt this way. Walking like an old woman, unable to stand straight and with my knees locked, I lurched over to my horse who looked at me dully.

"So, you're finally wore out my boy," I whispered to him, rubbing his face. He smelled like green hay, baby powder and rich earth, a smell so comforting and pleasant I drank it in.

"Mary, when your finished making over that horse, you can meet me at the house 'cause I need some coffee. Feeling a bit stiff, are you?" said Tom as I wobbled his way.

"I'm fine," I said, but I thought to myself, how is he not stiff? He's an old man. He's pushing 40.

The family had installed an indoor toilet that I happily utilized, and I marveled at all the white porcelain and copper piping. Tom's house was nice, big, warm, and comfortable, but their house was as luxurious as my parents' house. This made me think on my Mom and Dad, and I suddenly missed them. Even my mother. I was so far away from them.

The table was laden with biscuits, pork gravy, side meat and apple butter, but it was the delicious smell of roasting coffee that made my mouth water. Louise told me she put eggshells in her grounds. It's supposed to do something to improve the flavor, but I can't remember what it is.

"Too bad you didn't stop by on Sunday. The boys have been catching a mess of trout that we have been frying up with spring onions."

"I never was much of a fisherman, Benjamin, but my wife can catch a trout with her bare hands."

I blushed from ear to ear, and I kicked Tom under the table. He ignored me.

"My, my," said Benjamin. "I've heard about bee charming, but a fish charmer? You part Indian?"

Louise looked at me.

Trying to distract everyone, I said, "Now, this apple butter is some of the best I have ever tasted. Which apples did you use?" I then realized I had not even eaten any and quickly put some on my biscuit and took a bite, crumbs falling all around me.

"Mostly Milam's," Louise said. "My granddaddy planted a nice orchard the first year he settled here. Before I forget, let me get you a jar of grape jam and apple butter for your travels." She continued, pushing her chair back from the table.

"Benjamin, I know you are not a drinking man, but I would like you to have some fine peach brandy and a bottle of dandelion wine, for medicinal purposes." Tom placed them both on the table.

"We'll take them all right," said Louise, reaching for them with a smile. Nothing warms the bones better, revives the spirit and soothes a cough."

"Louise, make sure you hide them well, because if the boys find it, that will be the end of that."

"Finish your breakfast and I'll meet you at the barn." Tom put on his hat and coat, and Benjamin did the same, leaving Louise and me at the table.

Drinking my coffee, caramel colored with cream and sugar, I watched Louise rustle through her sideboard as if she were looking for something. Finally, she turned around and pulled her chair up close to me till our knees were practically touching. She looked intently into my face, and I felt my heart begin to race. She reached for my hand and opened it up and then she placed a folded white lace handkerchief in my palm. "Open it."

Delicately, I folded back the corners to reveal a green shamrock.

"Keep this with you always. May it protect you from all the storms and evil that will approach you." I nodded.

"Fold it back up and keep it safe, and I know I don't need to tell you to never show it to anyone, otherwise, you'll lose its magic." I did as I was told, and I placed it against my left breast in my brassiere where it remained all the rest of my days.

I stood to leave. "Thank you for everything," I said to Louise, who smiled at me and watched me as I bundled back up and opened the door into the bright morning sunshine. Striding to the barn, I could see that all the horses were lined up, and even my horse was saddled and ready to go.

"You be careful young lady," Benjamin said, "and stop back by on your way home. Louise and I would welcome the company."

"Thank you, Benjamin, and say hello to your sons for me. I hope I get an opportunity to see them before long," Tom replied.

Tom held my horse as I mounted. Tom waved one last time to Benjamin and we moved off, following the Rose River northwest across the Blue Ridge as we began our way to Skyland.

The trees dripped as the sun melted the snow, and the horses' hooves shot ice cannon balls as they walked. As we rode, I could see the river running fast with the melt off. It was hard to believe that it was winter yesterday and back again to spring today, but I was thankful for it. I thought if I really was magic, I could make the weather change or something practical, instead of charming fish and birds. But I wasted no time telling Tom my thoughts when we stopped for a break. I had over four hours to stew about it as we rode. We had reached Spitler Knoll, and Tom had not even finished tying off his horse as I came flying up the trail to him. He spun around, surprised.

"Don't you ever tell people about me again. Ever." He knew exactly what I was talking about.

He nodded. "Now, don't you go getting sore at me. It is too pretty a day."

"*Ever.*" I had so few things about me to myself.

"All right, now. You have my word."

Satisfied, I relaxed. Thankfully, we by passed Hawksbill, the highest peak in this section of mountain, and by late afternoon, we bore left at Betty's Rock and followed the Robinson River. Within an hour, we turned south again. Coltsfoot, violets, and little beauties were blooming and carpeting the woodland, and we passed through a hemlock grove that smelled like lemons and felt like a cathedral. When the hemlocks opened up to reveal the sky and we began traveling a well cleared trail, I knew we were getting closer, and my excitement started to build to see the famous Skyland I had heard so much of. And then I saw the buildings through the trees and across an open expanse of mowed lawn.

As we approached, I could see how the cabins were laid out like bunkhouses. Some were attached and others stood apart, but they all looked to be of dressed-up rustic fashion with cedar shingles and fancy arbors and some with names on signs like Kramer Lodge or Highland Cabin. We then got on a nice road that had signposts pointing the way to the tennis courts, dining hall, pastime hall and even had arrows stating, "North, Washington D. C 104 miles; East, Istanbul;5,072 miles; West, San Francisco 3,945 miles." This camp road took us through the northwest section of Skyland, and I was surprised to see that there were some people there. They came out of their cabins and smiled and looked at us with amazement. Riding to an open field, I could see a stable and corrals and one large white horse that I assumed must be Adams. Our horses came to a stop; we had made it. Tom tied up his horse and approached me.

"I'm going to find Adams and Grimsby. If you feel like it, untie each horse and put them in the paddock. Need help getting off?"

"Maybe."

Tom held my horse's reins as I swung my leg over the saddle, and he grabbed hold of the back of my coat, so I didn't hit the ground like a ton of bricks. "Hang in there, darling. We'll be sleeping in a warm cabin with down pillows, central heat, and indoor plumbing tonight." His relief that we had survived this trip was palpable.

I untied each horse, opened the gate to the paddock and turned them out. Before they even looked around to see where they were, each horse found a piece of ground and started rolling on the ground and kicking its feet in the air. Finally, all that was left was my horse and Tom's. Tom was funny about his things, so I didn't want to touch his tack, or his horse and I didn't want to carry my tack all the way to the barn across the field. Just then, I saw two Negro men loping towards me.

"We got it, we got it," they were saying as they approached. "Now, you tell us where your personal belongings are and we will get you set up, yes, we will."

I started to undo the leathers of my pack, but they jumped in and finished the job for me, one man throwing the leather saddle bags over his shoulder.

"Now, where are Mr. Dodson's things?" One of the men took the reins of my horse as I pointed to Tom's pack. "You follow Johnson here, and I'll be getting your horses bedded down in the stable."

And with that, he undid the reins of Tom's horse from the gatepost and walked off while the other man smiled at me and motioned for me to follow.

With some trepidation, surprise, and a bit of awe, I followed the man. We walked past another section of cabins and finally stopped at the Trout Cabin. I thought that was a funny coincidence. Johnson opened the door for me, and I walked past him into the main room to see a large brass bed with white linen sheets and comforters and a large buffalo plaid blanket in black and red at the foot of the bed. Two floral chintz armchairs sat beside a table with a large reading lamp. In front of a huge window was a walnut table and chairs, and beyond that, a door leading to the bathroom. There was even a closet with hangers. An intricately carved pine dresser was positioned near the bed.

"You can adjust the heat with the thermostat over here. I can start the bath water for you," said Johnson.

"No, no, that's quite all right. I'm fine. Thank you."

"Dinner is at the dining hall at 7."

I smiled and nodded and could not believe my eyes or ears or that I was at Skyland. No wonder Belle and Tom come up here. For a moment I wondered if they stayed in the same cabin, but I let that thought fade as I investigated the bathroom. Soap from France. And bathing salts too. There were big beautiful white towels and two bathrobes hanging on wrought iron hooks. While the deep claw foot tub dominated the room, the toilet sat behind the door and the sink was positioned near a shuttered window. I wasted no time in starting the bath water which came out so hot it was steaming.

As the water ran, I stripped off my clothes, and I was as naked as jay bird in the warm cabin. I walked around the room putting my clean clothes up in the closet. Just then, the door swung open. I turned around to see Tom, and Henry Adams. I stood frozen.

"What a pleasure to finally meet your lovely wife. Seems she's a bit of free spirit like me." Adams tipped his hat and smiled at me then turned to Tom clasping him on the shoulder.

"I'll look forward to seeing you both at dinner." And with that he backed out of the cabin and closed the door behind him, grinning like the Cheshire Cat. I was so shocked and flabbergasted that I was still standing there without moving.

"I suppose we should have knocked," said Tom, grinning. He took off his hat and threw it on the table. "You're mighty fine, my Mary." He began stripping off his clothes and placed them in a hamper that was by the door. He picked up my clothes from the floor and did the same. "You know they will launder them for us. Put whatever you need cleaned in there tonight. It will be back tomorrow afternoon washed, dried, ironed, and folded."

I tried to take in this information as I was still standing naked in the room. Tom came over to me and slid his hands around my backside. Initially, I wanted to push his hands away, but his caresses were making every muscle and sinew in my body relax and melt. "You've got the sweetest bottom I have ever laid eyes on." He kissed me on the neck.

"I'm going to get in that bath."

I walked to the bathroom, which was just as warm as the rest of the cabin and poured a big helping of the lavender bath salts into the water. Bubbles and foam filled the tub, and I was so happy. The next thing I knew, Tom was in the bathroom. I turned to look at him as he came in. My eyes looked over his biceps and the dark hair on his chest, and his belly was as flat as a young man's. He was fine. Without a word he got in the tub. I slid in the tub opposite him, and we looked at each other and both of us let out a deep sigh as the bubbles rose around us.

I cannot describe to you how good clean clothes feel and how good a bath feels when you have been dirty. Tom and I put on those robes, and we felt, well, I know I felt like a queen. What a luxury to not be cold and be able to walk naked and yet be warm in a house.

"Don't get too spoiled, but I'm glad you are enjoying this. Wait till you see what he serves at dinner." Tom pulled on a clean shirt and pants.

I decided to wear my nylons and a dress and the heels that I had packed but the only coat I had was my hand-me-down farm oilskin. My hair was clean and brushed and I even had a bit of rouge that Luanne had given me that I put on my cheeks and lips. How I hated putting on that oilskin to walk to the dining hall, and in a moment of impulse, I decided to leave it behind. Tom gave me his arm, and we ventured out into the spring night like a couple who owned a cabin at Skyland.

The dining hall glowed warm and amber from all the electric lights and candelabra. We could see the guests down the camp lane and hear the laughing and dishes clinking like wind chimes. I fluffed up my hair, pinched my checks and walked into that dining hall like the daughter I was raised to be. We strode through the door with Tom opening it for me and whispering, "You clean up real well."

I took a deep breath and looked past the sea of people until I saw Adams, and I flashed him a confident grin. Adams strode toward us, and I couldn't fathom how a man so small had so much presence, but he did. Talking, gesturing, and laughing and with a glass in his hand, he shouted, "Here is the man of the hour. Crossing mountain and dale to bring us a string of fine ponies and fine spirits. Raise your glass to Tom Dodson, a prince of men, and his fine and beautiful consort, Mary."

People clapped, cheered, and raised their glasses. Now I knew why Belle wanted to shoot Adams. In any case, I looked Adams straight in the eye and extended my hand. "Perhaps we don't need a formal introduction after our afternoon acquaintance, but I don't hold much count by Biblical law. Pleased to meet you, Mr. Adams. I'm Mary." Adams threw his head back and whooped.

"My, my, my, Tom. You've got yourself a live one." Clapping Tom on the back, he leaned in closer to Tom whispering, "I'm jealous." As if by magic, a Negro servant appeared, and handed us a drink. I glanced around and realized that all the help were Negroes. I suddenly felt ill at ease as I looked around at the high dollar white people from Washington, D. C. I took two big swigs of my drink.

"Go slow." Tom whispered in my ear as he took a glass.

I immediately drank it down in two more large gulps. I looked around as if we were on a National Geographic expedition. There were more men than women, but all were dressed stylishly and put together with care. The men wore coats and ties, and the women had bobs or left their hair long down their backs, pinned to the side with jeweled clips, and the older women had up-dos. Necklaces and bracelets and pins and baubles adorned them. Adams introduced us to so many people, I could not even begin to remember their names. I smiled and hoped that whatever I was drinking would ease my nervousness and help with my charm.

We were seated at Adams' main table, and the china was bone with gold piping and the flatware gleamed silver. More black waiters appeared from the kitchens, bringing steaming plates of food. First came a crab bisque that was so rich and creamy I wanted to lick the bowl. Along with the soup came darling little crescent rolls, all light and flaky, with honey butter. Next, we were served a heart of lettuce salad and some type of blue cheese with little crackers. I had another drink, too. I was so busy eating and drinking that I barely paid attention to the conversation, which was mostly led by the men. Conversation then turned to a colonial ball that Adams had held the summer previous and was thinking of hosting again.

Adams said, "You know, I practiced the minuet every day for a week and had shipped in a colonial costume with brocade velvet, lace around the collar, colored knee breeches and a white wig."

"Was that your intention? To dress like our founding father, Henry *Washington*? asked one of the ladies sipping her cocktail.

"It was my intention to get a kiss from the prettiest girl at the ball and that summer there was a slew of them. Do you remember the Hardings, Mr. Heaton's guests that summer? Well, Mrs. Harding brought with her two very pretty nineteen-year-old nieces. And on that fateful night, the orchestra was playing, of course, led by my man Grimsby. I gallantly opened the ball with a toast and stated that I would like to be permitted to get a kiss from the girl I chose as my partner. As there were no 'nays' but a unanimous chorus of 'hurrahs,' I chose one of those nieces and thoroughly enjoyed my kiss."

"Henry, you really are just an old reprobate," said another matron.

"Well, I almost ended up at the end of a dueling pistol. You see, Mr. Harding, as the night went on and his inebriation swelled, decided I had taken undue liberties. 'Mr. Adams', he cried loudly, 'you have insulted my niece, and I demand a duel at dawn for your outrageous conduct.'" Adams pretended to be drunk as he said this and accentuated the last bit of the sentence with a burp.

"I'm sure you would not let a little something like a duel dampen your mood," said a gentleman next to Tom.

"Indeed, not. We danced until the moon was up over the mountain. The next morning, at dawn, when I was not sure if I was hung over or still lit, a fair group of my guests had gathered on the far lawn to witness the duel. Well, the sight of my 45, ole Fletch insured respect, and as I stepped onto the dueling field, I was right. Harding was looking a bit recalcitrant and a bit green around the gills as the dawn light rose. I proceeded to make quite a show of taking out my gun, examining it, sighting it in and so on and out of the corner of my eye, I could see Harding growing nervous and shuffling about. Suddenly, a dear friend and longtime guest of mine, Bishop Heaton, jumped into the mix. 'Mr. Adams, Mr. Harding, I do believe this has gone far enough. Mr. Harding, I understand that you believe it was an improper act to kiss the niece in question. Adams, sir, would you agree to go to the lady's tent and apologize so we can put this matter to rest and get on with the tennis tournament today?' I, of course, bowed low, and with my best and most sincere tone, agreed. Harding looked relieved and we shook hands."

"Did you go and apologize to the young lady?" I asked. Adams turned slowly to look at me and a sweet and mischievous smile spread across his lips.

"Come on, Henry," said another gentleman, "how did the young lady take it?"

"My dear Mr. Evans, she took it like a champ, the entire afternoon while her chaperones were playing tennis." The table erupted with laughter, and I blushed like a schoolgirl which made Tom laugh as he looked at me.

"So, tell us, Mrs. Dodson, fair of face and fair of form, since your husband always heads back home to you with books from my library, did you enjoy Hemingway? Kafka? Or the poems of Millay? And tell us, darling girl, how do you have the time to read, rustle horses *and* raise babies?"

All eyes turned to me, and time seemed to pass slowly.

"I think you have shocked her, Harry, with that ribald story," said a matron. "Don't pay him any mind, dearie, his bark is worse than his bite."

"That's quite all right, ma'am," I finally said, because my good manners required I say something though my head was swimming. I didn't want to be part of the show. I had hoped I could just watch and take a break from doing and thinking. Taking a deep breath, I looked directly at Adams who was knocking back a glass of port.

"I'll try to put into words why I don't care for Hemingway. Perhaps it is his short sentences. They make me feel like I'm chewing on day-old bread. It is not that I don't like modernism, for I love the poems of Ezra Pound and Millay. I'm a bit old-fashioned when it comes to literature, because my heart lies with Hawthorne and Emerson and *Margaret Fuller.*" I said this loudly and I looked around the table. I didn't want them to think Tom had married an imbecile or that all mountain people were unlearned and backward. The table erupted in laughter again.

"Well, Adams, you have been dealing with the Caves too long," said Tom, and I could hear the pride in his voice.

"Hmm, you have yourself a horse rustling suffragist, who is also fine on the eyes. I'm going to have to encourage you to leave your mistress home and bring your wife, and you know I never recommend that to any man."

The table erupted in laughter again and with this, the main course was served. I had beads of sweat on my brow, and I wanted to be home and with my children. I had heard what Adams had said clearly.

Yet, the next morning I awoke refreshed, well rested, and I laid in that bed thinking I was a lucky girl. Tom was, of course, already up and had gone to check the horses. I relaxed in bed like a lady and was in no rush to move. I snuggled back into the covers with the joy of knowing we were here, in paradise, for another day; I didn't have to do a damn thing.

At breakfast, plans were made for the day's outings. I agreed to go on a hike to Limberlost with some of the guests. Some of the older matrons, whose days were well past tramping in the woods, planned on watercolor painting. A few of the men were going riding with Tom and Adams to try the new horses and look for spring gobblers. By mid-morning the sun and air had warmed the mountain to a balmy 45 degrees, but that didn't dampen the enthusiasm of the hiking or shooting parties. Adams's guests seemed always primed for adventure and conversation, which ranged from politics, people they knew in Washington, plans for the summer, articles in the *Washington Post* or *Atlantic Magazine,* and I listened to every word, so starved was I for conversation that went beyond house and farm chores.

The Negro servants had packed each of us box lunches and drinks, and the hike was a pleasant loop around the swamps, which was a terrain I had not encountered before. Strange rock monoliths dotted the trail and were surrounded by mountain laurel, and I thought how pretty it would look by May. We used these Stonehenge-like rocks as our lunch area, and I enjoyed my sandwich of roast beef with some type of sweet dressing that had horseradish in it.

"So, tell me, Mary, how you and your mountain man got together?" said a woman not much older than myself. I wasn't sure if I was imagining it, but I thought I saw some mischief around her eyes. For a moment, my mind went blank, and the weight of my life returned to my chest, pressing down on it like a thing I could never escape. Finally, smiling sweetly, I said, "My father introduced us." Comments of how quaint and charming followed.

"Now, where are your people from?" asked another woman.

"We're from Elkton, Virginia, which is south of here. My people fought in the War." I added that, I think, as a stab at some proof of Southern respectability. But I didn't tell them which side, as I wasn't so sure anymore which was the right side to be on. I knew for myself how hateful the South was, but I didn't know these people, and Washington was still the South. "My daddy owns the tannery there in Elkton."

"God Bless the Confederacy!" shouted one man lifting his glass.

"Now, Cecil, really," said a thin and well-coiffed woman with a sapphire hair comb holding back one side of her hair so that the remaining side curled alluringly in front of her face. "What I want to know is, are they proposing that this new park will go down that far?" She looked at the men steadily and unwaveringly holding her head tilted in midair, waiting for them to reply.

"They are proposing, my dear madam, that this park is going to extend from Front Royal to Waynesboro," said one gentleman.

"I see. And what will be done with these mountaineers?" she added, looking around the group.

"That's not really a worry. Right now, we have a delegation coming up to Skyland headed by Mr. Ferdinand Zerkle of the Shenandoah Land Improvement Company that will be inspecting the area and making recommendations. You know, they had been considering that Massanutten range, but I believe Old Harry has swayed them to seriously consider Skyland," he said.

"And what of Skyland?" she asked.

"Why Skyland will be the center of it all," said Cecil. Content with this, the woman nodded and examined her cucumber sandwich before taking another bite. The oatmeal cookie that had been in my lunch box stuck in my throat. The sunshine seemed to go out of the day.

Uncharacteristically, I didn't mention this information to Tom when he walked into the cabin later that afternoon. Both he and Adams had bagged two turkeys that the cooks were preparing for dinner that night. I was reading a book from Adams's library, *The Land of Mist*. Our room was warm and gently lit by the lamps, and I wanted time to stand still. I wanted, for once, not to worry.

"Good day in the woods. Horses behaved, Henry shot a turkey, and the gentlemen had a fine time being rugged woodsmen." said Tom, peeling off his coat. "How about you?

"We circled Limberlost, and it was a nice walk." I smiled at him.

"Are you going to be in good shape to ride home tomorrow?"

I nodded with enthusiasm.

"I'm going to enjoy that bath," he said.

As I listened to the water running, I couldn't shake the heaviness that hung on me. I tried to continue to read but my mind would not focus, and, with relief, I remembered that at least there would be drinks at dinner, and someone would be cooking for me and, even better, washing the dishes.

Dinner in the dining hall was again started promptly at 7. Tom and I walked into the dining hall and took our seats at Adams's table, and I noticed that Adams had placed me next to him. He held out my chair as I sat down, and I thought I felt his hand pat my bottom, but it could have been my dress bunching up behind the back of the chair. In any event, I turned my face to him and looked at him square on like a viper preternaturally stares down its target. We were being served the cooling mint sherbet when I struck.

"So, Mr. Adams, Cecil was telling us today about your plans for Skyland. I have so enjoyed your hospitality and the oasis that Skyland is that I'm anxious to hear." Adams slowly lifted his head and dabbed at his lips with a napkin.

"Why, I was discussing that very thing today as my mind was busy flitting over delightful adventures and masquerades for my guests. I'm thinking of hosting The Wedding of Wetona in June which was well received two summers ago. I have a fancy to dust off my buffalo horn headdress and handmade Indian blankets. Lucinda, do you remember how beautiful Miss Lorraine Sikel was as our Indian maid?"

"Why, of course, I do. Every girl was vying for the honor," said Lucinda.

I smiled. "How delightful, but I believe, if I understood correctly, that you will be hosting important visitors here next month to maybe expand Skyland?"

Adams shifted in his seat. Cecil Woodhouse spoke up.

"Why yes, Harry, during our luncheon reprieve, I was telling our hiking group about the plans for a park, and I was giving you all the credit for steering that committee away from Massanutten to our beloved Skyland."

Tom put his spoon down and sat back in his chair, staring past the food. Adams let out a giggle and a cough and, with a big beaming smile, looking around at his table of guests. "That is correct, Cecil. We just cannot keep this gem to ourselves forever. Why, with the automobile, these mountains will be a refuge for all. We cannot let Yosemite be the only National Park." As he spoke, he wagged his finger in the air.

"I do hope you will be able to manage it all, Harry. As it is, you run yourself ragged keeping up with all your guests and activities," said Lucinda dabbing the corner of her mouth with her linen napkin.

"I thank you, Madam, for your sincere concern over my health, but I have been tramping these mountains and running our beloved Skyland since 1890. The world is getting bigger and so must we." He held up his glass for a toast, and his guests raised their glasses, clinking them together, but to me, the sound was not like little bells but like a resonate dull clang. Tom and I didn't lift our glasses.

"Well, that will be a big world with this park going all the way to Waynesboro," I said.

Adams turned to me slowly, and his lips were in a tight grin. "My dear, you need only to worry your lady brain with your husband and home and let us men figure out the rest. Grimsby! It's time for some music and dancing. Bring our desserts to the main hall. Now, Tom, I wanted to ask you about the swelling on my horse's left fetlock." As he leaned over my plate to engage with Tom, I was forced to back up in my seat to make room for him. Then, on my ankle, I felt his foot running up and down my leg; I moved my leg away and kicked him.

That night, as Tom and I settled in bed, I turned to him. "Did you hear what they were saying about the park?'

"Yep."

"It's true, then, what the people have been saying?"

"They aren't going to turn people out of their houses and farms for a park. We've got a long day tomorrow. Get some rest." And with that he turned over on his side.

I wanted to believe him, but I wasn't so sure. The very air around me felt like it was hanging and waiting.

Chapter 33

We rose as the cool light of dawn struck our room because both of us were anxious to be home. My mind was now on Hightop, and I ached to see our mountain and was almost frantic to feel my children's bodies and know all was well and safe and normal. We packed silently and left the cabin. For a moment, I was conflicted as I wanted to just stay in that cabin protected, isolated, and cocooned forever. As we were carrying our bags across the Skyland compound, one of the servants spied us and sprinted across the greenway to help us. Tom knew it was fruitless to argue, as the servants were primed to assist everyone with even the most menial tasks.

"I appreciate it, but you can assist my wife. I've got these packs well balanced."

I felt guilty and decadent to be having someone carrying my load, and that would not have mattered if they were black or white servants.

Tom culled our two personal horses from the pack of grazing horses, and I wondered how much he had made from the training and sale of the horses and his other transactions, but it was not my place to ask. I also had my mind on breakfast and hoped that he would let us eat before we started our journey home.

Silently strapping our belongings to our horses, Tom lifted the saddle for me and placed it on the Giant's back. We led our horses back to the dining hall where I could see guests assembling for breakfast. I was not so sure I wanted breakfast dressed as I was in my traveling clothes, but I followed Tom into the dining hall just the same as my stomach was getting the better of me.

"My man, you must join us for breakfast before your long road home. At the very least you must let Miss Mary get some refreshment before her journey back to the confines of Hightop Mountain." Adams wiped his mouth and gestured to two seats at the table.

"We've a long day ahead of us and I'm inclined to head out," Tom replied.

"Well, I can see that you are in no mood to be dissuaded and never have it be said that Ole Harry stands in the way of a man's home and hearth. Grimsby!"

At the shout of his name, Adams's long-standing Negro servant rushed out from the kitchens carrying a towel and wiping his hands. "Yes, sir, Mr. Adams?"

"Get these two fine travelers a packed lunch and refreshments and keep my breakfast warm as I escort them to the boundaries of Skyland."

"Yes, sir. I'll send Johnson to the stables right quick." And with that he bowed and went back to the kitchen.

Tom shifted away as Adams put his hand on his back, but Tom cordially tipped his hat to the many guests we had met that were seated around the table and I smiled and told them how much I enjoyed meeting them, which was the truth. Adams led us first to his cabin and Tom and I waited outside. When Adams came out, he was carrying a canvas saddlebag. We continued walking to the stables with Adams chattering and prancing the entire way.

"Now, Tom, in this here bag is our agreed upon sum for your services. I know after that last incident that you will not take any checks and I encourage you to find a quiet spot, if you are so obliged, to count it thoroughly."

"That won't be necessary, Henry. I know where you live." Adams smiled nervously at this comment and turned his attention to me.

"For you dear girl, I have taken the liberty, and Tom hear me out on this, and I dearly hope you will not feel I'm being too bold, but this comes from a genuine concern for your safety, I would like Miss Mary to have this." He placed in my hand the tiniest little gun I have ever seen. It laid in my palm like a toy. I looked at Tom and back at Adams.

"That is an ivory handled Colt pin and as fine and dainty example of a lady's firearm as I have ever seen. I hope you do not have to use it, but I can tell you I have found the presence of my Ole Fletch very reassuring when traveling in these mountains."

"Thank you."

"You do know how to shoot? I just assumed a lady of your character would."

Tom cut him off. "She knows how to shoot, and that will be a nice compliment to her Smith and Wesson revolver, which is not as pretty, but it will also do the job."

"Wonderful. I also have included two books from my library that I believe you will enjoy, and I hope we can discuss them on your next visit as I'm going to insist that Tom bring you back so that your wit, wisdom, and beauty can grace my table." Adams handed me two books that were wrapped in a brocade cloth and tied with a velvet ribbon. I smiled at him and put them in my saddlebags.

"You ready?" Tom looked at me and I knew he was ready to leave and be done with the whole business of Adams and Skyland.

We mounted and were just about to head out when a servant ran up with another canvas bag that was filled with food. Adams motioned him to give it to Tom who placed it over his saddle horn. As we pointed our horses south, Adams called, "Remember to watch your back, Tom."

Tom gestured that he had heard him but didn't turn around and I put my jigging horse in behind him and watched my husband's back for the next eleven hours; we rode straight through to Lewis Mountain, camped, and made it home the next day.

It was twilight when we reached the open meadow of home. Had the pasture grown since we had been gone? The crocuses, colt's foot and violets were blooming. How long had we been gone? It was only a week by a Christian calendar, but I felt we had been gone for far longer than that. The farm looked the same but different, and I wondered if this was how Rip Van Winkle felt. I brushed aside my anxieties, attributing them to exhaustion.

"Feels good to be home," said Tom, and with that, he put his horse into a fast rack, something he never does, and we were soon galloping the last ¼ mile over the field, scattering nesting birds and rabbits as we went through.

"I'll put the horses up. You head to the house."

I ignored the stiffness of my body, and I left my packs on the horse telling Tom to leave them and I would retrieve them from my saddle in the morning. I never walked so fast in my life. As if by premonition, Luanne came out on the porch, and her eyes got as wide as half dollars at the sight of me. Colin came out behind her smiling from ear to ear. Evie followed with her hands on her hips. I grabbed up Evie and kissed Colin hugging him with all my might. Evie squirmed but Colin held on tight. This, my flesh of my flesh, this is the only true thing. Then I kissed Luanne's soft cheek and hugged her hard.

"Was everything okay?" I asked pulling back from her and looking her in the eyes.

"Of course, it was."

I tried to gauge the truth, yet as I glanced around the kitchen, the house was still standing, my children had all fingers and toes, and then I noticed her hair.

"Luanne, where's your hair?

"Why, it's on the floor of Ellen's Beauty Parlor. Do you like it?" She tilted her head like the women do in the advertisements and let me consider her. She batted her eyelashes at me.

The bob made her look older, but there were still soft strawberry blond curls around her ears. It showed off her long, elegant neck. I reached for her hair and touched it gingerly. It was so soft. I nodded at her. I hugged her and gave her a kiss on the cheek again. "You're beautiful."

"Looks like you're glad to be home." Before I could reply, Asa emerged from the back porch carrying wood. For the second time in the fifteen minutes I had been home, I was disoriented. My mind was racing at the sight of him coming through Tom's home as if he lived there.

"Stop staring as if you have seen a stranger. I want to introduce you to my husband." I looked at Luanne and back at Asa who was grinning like a cat. I finally blurted out, "What?"

"My husband. We got married the day before yesterday in Stanardsville."

"It was so much fun," said Evie. "I got to go to town and eat ice cream and carry the flowers."

"It wasn't fun for me. I had to wear a suit," said Colin. "I was the best man."

I sat down slowly in my rocker and looked down the mountain as the last glow of day left the sky.

"Well, aren't you going to congratulate us?" asked Asa.

I looked at him, dumbfounded. "Were you planning this all along?" I said to both of them.

Luanne sat down beside me. "Actually, no. You see, Asa came up to help me like I told you he would, and we had some small disasters like the heifer having to have her calf pulled, a horse coming up lame, and he just stayed and kept helping. He takes direction real good." She regarded her husband as she said this. Asa rocked back and forth on the balls of his feet, and it made his lanky frame look as if he were blowing in the wind. Evie climbed into my lap and began to tell me about the wedding day, and I could not take in a word as I scrutinized Luanne in continuing disbelief.

"It's fine. I like being with him." She whispered in my ear, patting my shoulder. Tears started at the corners of my eyes.

"You going to live here?" I asked hesitantly and hoping with all my might. Luanne patted my knee next.

"I don't think Tom would like that much. Plus, I think you have everything under control now. Asa just inherited his granddaddy's farm down on the Rapidan River. Its 200 acres of nice river bottom land."

I wiped the tears as they fell from my face.

"You know, all you have to do is holler for me and I will be here as fast as my legs can carry me." Luanne then leaned in close to my face and I could feel her lips brush my ear. "Besides," she whispered as soft as a call of a dove, "you know I will always love you best." With that, she stood up. "Here comes Tom."

I stood up, too, and watched with trepidation as Tom, unaware, made his way to the house, carrying all our bags over his shoulders. Just then, Asa leapt off the porch. "Tom, let me help you."

Tom slowly raised his head and looked squarely at Asa, stopping dead in his tracks.

"What's he doing here?" Tom demanded of Luanne as he walked past Asa and right into the house, and he dropped all our bags on the kitchen floor with a loud thump. He wheeled around, and I jumped in between Tom and Luanne.

"Now, Tom, we are all tired. Let's take a minute here and catch our breath and talk about this."

"Talk? Talk about what?" He looked back and forth from me to Luanne.

"Oh, Daddy!" Evie piped in excitedly and I grabbed her and covered her mouth. "Shhh!" I told her, but she squirmed away just as Asa stepped into the house.

"I don't understand what all the fuss is about. I like Asa. We went squirrel hunting almost every day you were gone and..." Colin looked at his father, his words falling silent as Tom swung around towards Asa with menace. I grabbed Tom's arm.

"Tom, Luanne has...." I began timidly, but Luanne cut me off.

"Don't be telling my news. Asa and I *got married*! There, it's out in the open."

I watched Tom's face grow dark. It was like watching a wild thunderstorm come up from the valley, and he looked like a demon in the half-light of the porch lantern. Suddenly, he spun on his heels out of the kitchen, took one step off the porch, and headed in the direction of the barn.

"Tom," I shouted, but I knew it was no good to follow him. I turned to Luanne. "Do you think he will shoot Asa?" Luanne looked at me incredulously. "Hell, no. He's just mad is all. He'll have to get over it. Won't he, Asa?"

"That's right. You're my woman now."

I looked at Luanne who shrugged nonchalantly. "Asa, I told you to stop saying that. Mary, let's get you in the house and get settled. It's been a long day for everyone." She took me by the hand, and I glanced over my shoulder to the barn, but there was no sign of Tom or any light. An emptiness and sadness overtook me.

Later that night, I laid in our bed, with my children cuddled in on either side of me, as I read them Robinson Crusoe, picking up where I had left off before the trip. As my children fell asleep, I settled myself into the down mattress with the gaslight glowing. I heard the footsteps of Luanne and Asa heading up to the loft. The following sound of silence threatened to suffocate me.

Chapter 34

The sun rose and set, and rose and set, but with Luanne gone that summer, everything was different, and I was so lonely I thought I would die, for Luanne was my heart. Some days I would cry, missing her so badly that I actually got sharp chest pains, and my heart would sometimes flutter like there were a million butterflies inside it. We wrote letters, but when I read them, I would cry even more, because I could no longer see her face. A few mountains away and far down in the Piedmont now, Luanne might as well have lived on a different continent. To visit in person was a luxury that time and space didn't afford us. She now had her own husband and farm to care for. Her time for taking care of me was over, and my soul felt it sorely. I remembered how she bathed me the first night I came to Tom's house. With her gone, I would never feel that type of tenderness and care from another human again. The love she gave to me was the love I gave to my children, and no man can top that love, as it is pure. A good thing that chores kept me busy, especially now that I was doing them alone. Tom resigned himself to Luanne's marriage, and we even went to Tom's mother's house for a family celebration of the event. It was so sweet to see Luanne, but she was different, more grown up or something, and she was not mine anymore.

Tom was busy early and late and not much of talker when he came in for the evening meal. If he was cutting hay, he often went back out and kept working after eating supper and I would clean up the dishes while Evie chattered on like a parakeet. Colin was going to school steadily, as Tom had promised him a new shotgun if his grades held. After I helped Colin with his homework, he often went to the woods or out to help Tom. With this new shift in our household, and Tom being too tired for relations, half of me was relieved, as I didn't want another baby, but half of me was worried. Perhaps, this was married life, yet I was so lonesome.

As the dog days of summer came on, I fell into a routine that provided comfort in its regularity. A sweet spot in my day was around midafternoon. I would get the old red mare, place Evie in the saddle and walk the woods to the creek and little swimming holes that still had water. While I rested on an old quilt I had brought, Evie, buck naked, splashed in the creek and threw pebbles. Sometimes I would join Evie in the cold mountain stream, and she would squeak with delight as we splashed each other. It was in these moments that I felt she was my child. As the mare dozed, I would rest back on the blanket, listening for a call from the pileated woodpeckers. Solace and peace would descend upon me as the creek gurgled, and the sunlight poured through the trees and my daughter was a picture of innocent perfection. But one evening, in the last days of August, we got word from Elkton in the day's mail. The letter said,

Dear Mary,
Enclosed are some funds for you to hire a car and come visit your mother. Mother is ailing and has been asking for you.
Daddy

"I can take you to town tomorrow, and we can get a car," said Tom. I looked at him and nodded.

"I can manage Evie, I think," said Tom, as he looked at her scolding her brother in the back yard. He put his hand on my knee as a way of comfort.

"They need to see their grandparents. I'll take Colin and Evie with me. Would you go see what is going on between them while I go pack?"

With a sense of urgency, even though I wasn't leaving until the morning, I set about packing our good clothes, discarding here and there items that were faded or had a hole that I hadn't had time to mend. In my turning over the bedroom, I uncovered the brocade-wrapped parcel that Adams had given me so many months ago. I stared at it as if this package had fallen to earth from another planet. Slowly, I reached for it, and I undid the red silk ribbon, and the velvet covering opened up to reveal two leather-bound books with gold letters: *Troilus and Cressida* by William Shakespeare and *Madame Bovary* by Gustave Flaubert. A note on Adams's monogramed letterhead fell to the floor.

> She walks in beauty, like the night
> Of cloudless climes and starry skies;
> And all that's best of dark and bright
> Meet in her aspect and her eyes;
> Thus mellowed to that tender light
> Which heaven to gaudy day denies.
>
> One shade the more, one ray the less,
> Had half impaired the nameless grace
> Which waves in every raven tress,
> Or softly lightens o'er her face;
> Where thoughts serenely sweet express,
> How pure, how dear their dwelling-place.
>
> And on that cheek, and o'er that brow,
> So soft, so calm, yet eloquent,
> The smiles that win, the tints that glow,
> But tell of days in goodness spent,
> A mind at peace with all below,
> A heart whose love is innocent!

Quickly, I folded the poem up and put the books back into the trunk, Tom's ex-wife's trunk, which was now my trunk. I somehow thought this was fitting for both me and these books. As I buried the books and note under the folded clothes, wanting to be rid of Adams and his leering, I could not have foreseen that I would need Adams, too, before the end of things, but I didn't know it then.

Without further thought, I hurried to finish packing, and by then I heard Tom upstairs putting our headstrong daughter to bed. I heard snippets of the conversation, which mostly was of her excitement about going to town. Coming into our bedroom, Tom looked at me saying, "Good grief, she is a live wire. Now, where did she get that from?" Not expecting an answer, he began undressing and threw himself down on the bed like a man exhausted. As I brushed my hair out and put on a clean linen chemise, I slid in beside him. I knew that sleep would not come, as my heart was racing about the trip.

"Here, turn over," said Tom to me, and as I did, he began to rub my back with his rough but comforting hands, and for a moment, I forgot all my worries, and I remembered that he was my person now that Luanne was gone. His caresses got slower and slower until I heard him softly start to snore. Hearing the train way down in Stanardsville, before dawn, I rose. Dressed and ready, I had breakfast laid out for my family as I stared down our lane to the valley below.

Before Tom had even got the wagon ready, my children were dressed and clean, clothes and body. As we made our way off Hightop Mountain, Evie was looking down the road to town and Colin kept glancing back to the farm as if it would disappear in the morning mist. With dread, I traveled to my parents' home for the first time in fourteen years.

Chapter 35

The Elkton streets were now paved, and the Queen Anne Victorian house I grew up in had subtle signs of invading deterioration that surrounded it as if it were cloaked in a shroud. The magnolia, to the right of the house, had engulfed the entire front window, its glossy green leaves impervious to the decay of what was man-made. Our wicker porch furniture, always a crisp bright white, was peeling, as if the furniture had never been removed from the porch from the previous summers. Leaves littered the front walk. I noticed some of the wood trim was rotted in spots. Yet, Evie was exclaiming it was a castle that looked as if it had a princess locked away in it somewhere, and Colin looked around the street and wondered how people lived that close together.

The driver that Tom had hired placed our bags on the porch, tipped his hat, turned on his heel and left. I took one swipe at Colin's hair, who pulled away, and I straightened out Evie and her dress, who was already posing as if she was meeting the Queen of England. I took a deep breath and entered my parents' home, very aware how many miles I had walked since I had lived there. When I opened the front door, the damp and stale air sucked the breath out of my lungs as my eyes searched the room for a sign of my parents.

"This place is creepy and smells funny," Evie remarked. "I think the princess must have escaped."

"Hush," said Colin, jerking her hand.

I heard a creaking of the upstairs floorboards and instinctively called, "Mom?" as if I had just gotten home from school. There were no cookies and milk waiting for me now. The creaking on the floorboards quickened. "Mary? Is that you?" I heard my father's voice call down the stairs.

"Daddy?"

I walked over to the bottom of the staircase as I heard his footfalls cross to the upstairs' foyer and he appeared above me on the landing. As he came down the stairs, he braced himself firmly by placing his hand on the wall and grabbing the stair rail. I backed up to let him descend, but I also backed up out of horror. My father's clothes looked as if they were two sizes too big, and even though he was smiling, his sunken cheek bones and yellow complexion gave his face a feverish appearance.

"My Mary, I'm so glad you could come, and look at my beautiful grandchildren. He opened his arms and hugged me so tightly, kissing my cheek.

"Oh, Daddy, what's happened?" I said, as tears and panic welled up inside me.

"Can I get you something? Look at how Colin has grown. Would Evelyn like a cookie?" I felt completely disoriented. I walked over to the familiar velvet couch where I had sat with Halsom so many ages ago. Evie took my father's hand and said as loud as she could, "Yes, I would love a cookie, actually, many cookies."

"Well, good. And how about you, Colin? So grown up and a fine picture of a young man."

"No, thank you," Colin replied, clearly uncomfortable, but trying to be a boy Tom could be proud of. If Colin had his way, he would have high-tailed it out of town and gone back up that mountain. Who had he taken after? Me? Halsom? Tom?

My father motioned my children with his hand, and I followed them into my mother's sunny kitchen, and I was relieved to see that there was evidence of life. There was a bread on the counter and an icebox that looked new. I could see clothes hanging on the line outside the kitchen door and a dishcloth that looked wet draped over the faucet. My father opened the kitchen cabinet and took out my mother's favorite cookies, Lorna Doones, and gave two to Evie.

"What do you say?" said Colin to his sister, poking her in the arm for good measure. Evelyn looked to me, and back to my father, knowing what to say but refusing. We all waited.

"Thank you," she finally said.

"Mary, here have a cookie."

"Dad, I don't want a cookie."

"Colin?"

"No, thank you, sir."

"Can I get you something else? A cold glass of water? Iced tea?"

"I'm really fine for right now, Dad. Where's Mom?" My father's face fell, and he placed both his hands on the kitchen table as if to steady himself.

"She's very sick. Dr. Timmson should be by this afternoon. I wonder if the paper is here. Mary, can you go check?"

I looked at my father, who was unnerving me, but I nodded and went out the front porch to see if the paperboy had delivered the *Valley Banner* and the *Daily News Leader*. I could almost hear my mother's voice. *"Don't slam that screen door!"* but all I heard was the *whap* of the screen door hitting its frame. My father was sitting in his chair when I came back in carrying the two newspapers. Evie was eating her third cookie and Colin sat on the edge of the sofa looking as if he wished he were anywhere else in the world.

"Thank you," Daddy said as I handed the papers to him. I heard firm footsteps going across the upstairs foyer.

"Mom?" I looked up expectantly. A woman rounded the stairs carrying a tray and wearing one of my mother's aprons. She descended the stairs with authority. "My, my, my is this your girl?" she said, regarding me.

"Mary, this is Betty from over in New Town. I hired her to help with your mother and the household."

"Pleased to meet you, Mary." She nodded at me with a big warm smile. "Look at these two handsome children," she said as she breezed into the kitchen. "I see someone has gotten into the Lorna Doones." I could hear her place the tray on the kitchen counter, and a second later, I heard the back-door slam.

"That woman has been a Godsend. I don't know how she does it." My father said, staring off into the far corners of the room. "Do you know she refuses to let me drive her home? She insists on walking." I picked up Evie who was playing with my mother's fine China figurines of little Dutch children, windmills, ballerinas, French serving maids, and cherubs.

"Dad, can I see Mom?"

My father looked at me. "She's upstairs."

My children, like ducks, followed behind me with trepidation, as they didn't want to be left with my father who was a stranger to them. Slowly, I began climbing the stairs, looking at the familiar sconce light fixtures, paintings of antebellum homes, family pictures and gold striped wallpaper with urns with roses. My children were at my heels, ogling as if they were in a museum. Evie, seeing a picture of me taken at a photography studio when I was 14 said, "Mom, is that you? What happened?" Colin shoved her in reply, and I told them both to hush.

The door to her room was open and I stepped across the threshold hesitantly and quietly as my eyes took in the sight and smell of the room, which was known, but no longer well known to me. My mother, Mary Elizabeth Jenkins, lay on her bed with her eyes closed and her mouth open; her mouth looked like a black gaping hole in her head, and her beautiful chestnut hair was stringy and plastered to her scalp in greasy folds. I looked around the room. Her dressing table, formerly filled with various creams and make up, was now filled with pill bottles and dark liquids. The curtains and windows were closed, and the smell in the room was sickly sweet and acrid at the same time. Colin started to enter the room and I grabbed him and motioned him to wait. Evie pushed by both of us and walked up to my mother, looking at her.

"Yuck," she said, looking at me, "I'm going back downstairs."

"I'll keep an eye on Evie, Mom," said Colin glad to be putting some distance between himself and the sick room as they both backed down the staircase. Alone in the room, I saw my mother's eyelids flutter and her mouth start working. I approached the bed. "Mom?" I said softly.

She didn't stir but a trickle of brownish fluid leaked out of her mouth. Panicked, I looked around for a cloth and, spying one, I grabbed it and dabbed at her mouth. A faint weak voice seemed to cry inside me, *help.* I was relieved when I heard Betty enter the room. This helpless ill woman is my mother, the unloving force of nature that haunts me. As I was about to hyperventilate, I heard, "Mary, let's get you and your belongings situated."

I, too, backed out of the room, staring with grief and fascination at my mother, and followed Betty into my room that had seemingly been preserved as a shrine since I ran away. It was as if I had never left. The same chenille bedspread, white with pink roses, covered the bed. My grandmother's crazy quilt was folded on a quilt rack, waiting for colder nights. The lace curtains still filtered the light onto the wallpaper. The wood floors gleamed and glowed, and the rug, with its pink, yellow and blue flowers, looked untouched by time. My eyes widened as I saw my schoolbooks still lying on my desk where I had tossed them the afternoon I left with Halsom. I was held for a moment by revulsion, horror, and a sick attraction as I thought of him and my previous life.

"Here, let's open this window," I said, because I was unable to breath. I wanted to stick my head out the window and gulp air like a drowning man. Betty had carried up my bag and began to unpack for me. "I've got that," I said, grabbing it from her.

"This is why I'm here," she said, grabbing it back.

"Betty,"

"Yes?'

"What's wrong with my mother?"

As she continued to unpack and place my clothes in the chifforobe, she told me about my mother's breast cancer and how my mother had not told anyone she was suffering until the stench became so bad that she had to relinquish her authority and a doctor was called. Betty placed both hands on my shoulders, and held me hard, as her deep brown eyes looked at me square. "Doll baby, your mother's dying." I searched this stranger's face, taking this in. "It happens to all of us. It's a part of life." She patted me on the cheek. "The sooner we mortals' figure that out, the easier it gets." I numbly tried to absorb this. Colin and Evie trudged back upstairs, and Evie climbed onto my bed as I sat on the edge wondering why time had not stood still. Evie was delighted that the bed bounced because of the springs. As if in a dream, I watched my daughter bounce on my bed, giggling with glee while jumping higher and higher, trying to touch the ceiling.

"Now, young lady," said Betty, yanking Evie by the arm, "you ain't gonna think that's so much fun when you bounce off and bust your head wide open."

"You can't tell Evie nothing," said Colin as he leaned against the wall wishing, I'm sure, he was back on Hightop. As Betty exited the room, pulling my daughter with her, I pulled a chair over to my open window, and like I had so many lifetimes ago, I sat facing the Shenandoah River, Massanutten Peak and the far-off Alleghenies and stared, wondering how to reconcile my life, this situation, and realizing that at the crux of it, I was somehow to blame for it, for if not me, whom?

Chapter 36

The days in the valley in my parents' home came and went as we waited on my mother's dying, which is a thing, I learned, that moves at its own speed, just like living. Mortals are powerless to control it. I moved around my once-familiar house like a ghost, as I was part of it but no longer relevant. My children, given money each day by my Daddy, were sent to town for ice cream, or to the movies, or to buy something at Conrad's store, or to walk to the park. Why, Daddy even got Colin a fishing pole so Colin could escape to the Elk Run River. Colin was aware enough to realize this new-found freedom and what money can buy, but he missed the mountain, its routine and the person he knew and honored as his father, often commenting, 'I can't wait to tell Dad,' about a big trout he caught or what he saw in town.

Evie thought she had landed in heaven with my father's money at her disposal, and all she had to do was smile and charm to get her way. She always came home from town chatting a mile a minute and showing off her candy or new toy or dress that my father had showered on her as if he had a second chance. I worried for my daughter, who was so much like my mother, but also her own true self and independent. Darwin never covered that, but I am certain it has to do with survival of the fittest. I, on the other hand, helped Betty change and bathe my mother's body in selfless care to make up for all the wrongs I had committed and, in turn, free me from my mistakes.

As Betty and I kept watch over my mother's deathbed, the only sounds I heard my mother make were groans accompanied by grimaces. Betty and I attempted to move her or clean her. My father had disappeared at my appearance and found new life with his grandchildren, only inquiring, maybe once a day, as to his wife's welfare.

I was aghast when I first saw my mother's oozing breast, the smell of it filling the room. The fortitude she possessed to keep this a secret, amazed me, but, of course, she would; it was messy and untidy and not a part of keeping up appearances.

"It's going to be okay, Mom. We just have to get you comfortable." I held her in my arms so Betty could change the sheets.

"Where's your father?" she said out loud so that it startled us.

"He's downstairs. Do you want me to go get him?" But she didn't answer as she went back to wherever the mind takes you to when you are finally relinquishing your mortal shield.

My father never came into the sickroom, but he would occasionally ask how mother was doing. He shuffled around the house with his yellow skin, reading the papers, dozing, engaging with his grandchildren. I sat by my mother's bedside as if lost in a trance and that was harder work than any pig butchering. Only Betty's cooking, the visits from Dr. Timmson and checking on my children punctuated my days. At the end of the week, I became distraught as I watched Dr. Timmson give my unconscious mother a shot, marching up to the poor man, demanding, "What are you doing? What are you giving her? What is going on?" I was panicked and horrid to Dr. Timmson, who had known me since childhood. Betty, who had been in the room, silently left, closing the door behind her.

"I'm trying to make her comfortable," he said with infinite patience. "It won't be long now. Here, let me show you how to do this. You can give her these shots when she looks uncomfortable. You have my permission to give her as much as is needed." He looked straight into my eyes and held my gaze. I nodded as he then explained how to draw in the needle.

"Dr. Timmson?"

"Yes?"

"What's wrong with my father?"

"I suspect he has a liver disease. Betty's been giving him some pills I left."

"I mean, about how he is. He doesn't seem right, and when afternoon comes and night starts to fall, he gets so unsettled. He's just not himself. It's like..." I searched for words, "I don't know, he just isn't right."

The doctor turned and regarded me. He closed up his big black leather bag and snapped the buckle. "Well, so much has happened in such a short amount of time; the business closing and both of them getting sick, you being gone. Just unfortunate events. Sometimes, these types of things cause people to develop dementia of the mind. I'm sorry." He stood up. "I'll check in tomorrow."

The bedroom door opened slowly, and I could see one of Evie's eyes peaking around the doorframe. "Hello, my little girl." She burst into the room with a bright smile.

"That one is a little pepper pot," said Dr. Timmson.

Betty came in as well, and Evie started skipping around her. "Doesn't she ever get tired?" said Betty to me. I shook my head no.

"I told Mary that she can have the shots as frequently as need be now."

"Yes, Doctor."

He smiled and nodded, and Betty and I both stared at my mother. Then we escorted the doctor downstairs as Evie followed on his heels. The sound of the porch door closing behind the doctor, my mother's rattling breath, my children's voices coming from the kitchen, the icebox rattling, and the birds chirping outside made for an odd symphony. I thought about what Dr. Timmson had said about my father's business as I looked at the parlor ceiling's water stains and peeling plaster. I wanted to go home to Hightop, and in my anxiety I thought, what if there is no home left when I get back? What if Tom's been kicked off his farm and he and Belle have just headed out west?

Chapter 37

I had gone into the kitchen to get a drink of tea and see if there was any chicken left from dinner in the icebox to calm my nerves from all my crazy thinking, which seemed to be accelerated by being at my parents' house. Betty had taken both the children to town when she went out for her shopping. My father was napping in his room. When I went upstairs to sit with my mother, I knew the moment I laid eyes on her. "Mom," I whispered.

I looked at my mom, her eyes open and dull, her mouth open, and brown liquid oozing down her jaw. "Oh...Mom," I said softly wiping her mouth. "Oh, oh, oh, Mom, oh, Mom."

Grief took me without tears but with heaviness and weight. I sat and I looked at my dead mother, the first dead body I had ever seen having not been allowed, as a child, to sit with the bodies of my grandparents because of my age and temperament. She wasn't my mom, she wasn't a person, and she was just dead, a thing, as if it never held a soul. If this is death, what do I do now? The certainty of it all, took my breath away. It is nothing, and this thought made my heart palpitate, but there was also a glimmer of freedom.

Finally, I did what was expected of a grieving daughter. I got up and stopped the clock and covered the mirrors. Then I went outside to the porch with a glass of iced tea to wait for Betty. Soon enough, I saw her walking down our street with Colin, who was carrying his fishing tackle, and Evie walking beside them chatting up a storm. Betty had a satchel of shopping balanced in one hand and her pocketbook in the other. She wore a small blue hat on her head, but she still had on her apron. When she saw me sitting on the wicker settee, she quickened her pace. As soon as her foot hit the front step I said, "Mom's dead."

She stopped. "She's in a better place now, God rest her soul." As she placed a hand on her chest and cast her eyes to heaven, I wasn't so sure.

"Did you tell your father?" Betty asked.

I shook my head, no. "He's sleeping, and she'll still be dead when he wakes up," I told her. And this was true. At this moment, I was numb and could not reconcile my mother, her charm, good manners, her dedication to my and our family's future with that wrinkled, smelly, sunken former human lying in that bed. All I could recollect was the hole of not having been held dear by her, never having been kissed or comforted, never told *I love you*. As a mother, I knew, with Evie as my mirror, to always hold my children dear, regardless of whether they sometimes seemed to behave like hooligans.

"Well, I best go and get the doctor. Here, Evie, now you be a good girl." Betty reached into her bag and got out a shiny red ball which she handed to Evie.

"Colin, would you please go into the backyard and play catch with her," Betty commanded. He nodded obediently as he put his fishing gear on the porch. "Go on now, go play, and be good," Betty told them, and I watched Betty adjust her hat and set off again down the road. I watched my children play catch in the evening sun. I realized, with relief, that I could start packing to go home, but could I? What now to do with my father?

The funeral came and went. My father was too weak to attend. I sat in the front row with Betty and my children taking peaks at my mother's friends and our neighbors. They brought food and looked at me with both pity and disdain. The night after we buried her at the Elk Run Cemetery, I was sitting in the backyard helping Colin and Evie catch the last remaining summer fireflies for a firefly lantern. As I turned to go back to the house, there she was standing, Ethel, my childhood friend, holding a casserole. She appeared genuinely troubled.

"Ethel," I said.

She approached me with apparent trepidation, and she held out the casserole to me, only it wasn't a casserole. "I made you your favorite, orange fluff." She looked sheepish. My eyes opened wide, and I looked at her and smiled big and honestly. Ethel, relieved, smiled too.

"I'm sorry," Ethel said, and I knew that she meant it for more than my mother's death. "I've missed you sorely all these years." I nodded at her, and I think we both wished we could turn back time.

"Where's Johnathan Abel? Cause you know how fond I'm of him."

"He's inside keeping your father company. We just got back from Virginia Beach and heard the news. What do you need me to do?"

"Nothing."

"Do you need me to watch your children? You know, for whatever reason, I can't seem to catch one. However, between you and me, I'm sure tired of the trying. Good God, if I never have to have that man heaving on top of me again it won't be a moment too soon." She looked at me and covered her mouth, and we laughed and laughed till Betty came out the back door.

"What are you two carrying on about? Don't you know whistling and laughing women come to no good? Now, get those children out of this night air before they get a chill. Besides, there's food to eat in here. I can't fit it all into the icebox."

"Come on," I said to Ethel, taking the orange fluff. I placed the white milk glass bowl, filled with the orange goodness, in the middle of the table and proceeded to dole out bowls for us all.

"Betty, come and have some," I said. She was taken aback by my offer, and Ethel stiffly made a show of shifting her chair to make room for her. Surveying the situation, Betty said, "I'm going to finish up these dishes and go to bed, but I thank you." Relieved, Ethel scooted her chair back, and I spooned in the orange fluff and served myself a second bowl while Ethel caught me up on our friends, the town, and her life.

"So, are you going to stay here now?" asked Ethel.

"I've got to get back to Tom."

"You're going back? Why, I thought now, with things the way they are, with your mom gone and all, and your father alone, that you might stay. I have to admit, I had my heart set on it. I was looking forward to us, well, us having us again. And I have a car and can drive us around."

I looked at Ethel and smiled.

"But my life is with Tom now. He's my husband." I didn't say this to claim a sense of respectability but because I owned it. Hightop Mountain, Tom, and I, along with Evie and Colin were as much a part of Hightop as the ferns that rose from the summer rains, the turkeys that scratched spaces of the woodland into green fairy mounds, the bear that overturned rocks and stumps for grubs and goodies, the King Stag that claims his territory in November, the American Beauties of violet-pink flowers in Spring, the ginseng's ripe berries in October, the morels glowing in the woodland underbrush in early April, and the moonshine still's curling smoke, stealthily hidden, and quiet.

Ethel regarded me, and she knew me. "I understand." The moment stretched out until she said, "I just wish you lived back home. I wish you'd never run off, and I wish I had never been so so..." she hunted around for the word. "Contrary?" I suggested. She regarded me for a moment, and we both started laughing again.

"Yes," she said, orange fluff flying out of her mouth in a most unladylike way.

I looked at my daughter whose eyes were getting glassier and glassier. It had been a long day. "I better get Evie to bed before she falls asleep where she's sitting."

"You know that child is the spitting image of you. Only I think Evie is prettier." Ethel said this last line directly to my daughter who was eating the compliment up with a spoon.

"Ethel, are you sure *you* aren't really my mother's daughter?" I started to gather up our plates.

"I'm prettier than Mommy," said Evelyn, beaming, "and I don't look anything like her."

Ethel raised her eyebrows. "Maybe that one is really your mother's daughter," she suggested. We both exchanged looks as I started cleaning up our plates.

"Won't your girl get that?" said Ethel, motioning to the table.

"Betty? Why, she is older than I am. She isn't a girl."

Ethel looked at me, exasperated. "Here, then, let me help you." Ethel and I brought the dishes to the dry sink. I washed and Ethel dried, and we went into the parlor to see my father dozing in his chair and Johnathan Abel sitting there holding his Bible. He stood up when he saw me.

"Mary, I'm so sorry for your loss. Your mother was a good church going woman and I know she is at God's right hand."

"Really?" I looked at him. He stared at me, then at Ethel, then back at me as I felt myself going backwards to my childhood as if flying in a time machine. My mother was a professed Christian, but never seemed to act like one. At least, that's how it appeared to me. I never saw her hand out a dime unless someone was watching and would give her credit for it. *Poor people have to pull themselves up by their bootstraps,* she would say, never giving any credit to luck, her luck, or circumstances. All it would have taken was one glitch in time, one hesitation, and her family would have remained indentured servants and renters. Luck, I'm telling you, is just as important as skill in playing the cards you're dealt. My mother had no sympathy or empathy for others, unless they were the right kind of people. She refused to believe anything other than that she was God's chosen. If someone was having a hard time, well, they were obviously damned in some way, and it was best to distance yourself in case it jumped off the afflicted and onto you.

"Come on, John. Grab your hat and Bible. Mary and her daddy are tired. It's been a long day for everyone." Ethel looked at her husband as she picked up her own coat and hat. I walked them out to the front porch. "Mary?" said Johnathan Abel grabbing my elbow.

"Yes?"

"If there's anything you need, you call on me or Ethel. For better or worse, we're your oldest friends." He squeezed my shoulder and looked at me and Ethel meaningfully.

"I hear you," I told him, remembering his unrelenting chasing of me like a young billy goat that is so wound up it pees on itself.

"There is something I'd appreciate, if you would, check in on my father, because I'm leaving tomorrow. And Ethel, if there is anything wrong, you'll come get me?"

"Yes, I'll come get you."

"Wait a minute," he said, looking at his wife. "She's going back? You're going back?" He directed this to me.

"Yes. Tom's my husband. I live up there."

"Well, I know, but I guess, well, can't you get him to come down to the valley? Why, with all this talk about a park, he might have to come down here anyhow. I can get him a good-paying job with the railroad. My uncle is one of the engineers."

"I appreciate that, but there's no one that is going to get him off that farm anytime soon, and I don't blame him. I love living up there," I looked at him, "because, I feel closer to God." I whispered this and looked up to Heaven. Ethel grinned.

Johnathan Abel sputtered and coughed. Ethel grabbed me and held me close. "We'll take care of things down here. You have my word."

"Thank you, Ethel."

I watched fat Johnathan Abel roll down the walk. Ethel, carrying her pocketbook in the crook of her arm, walked beside him to their new car, shiny and black with red leather interior. Even from the porch, I could see the glowing newness of it like it had a halo. I turned and went back into the house, debating whether or not to wake my father from his chair.

"Daddy, come on, let's get to bed." He awoke confused, but willingly let me lead him to his bed. "Your husband is very nice man, very nice man," he kept saying.

I had mixed feelings about leaving my father the next morning as I stood on the porch with my bag packed and my children by my side. He looked so small, frail, and delicate.

"Do you want to take the car home?" he asked.

"Daddy, I don't know how to drive."

He thought about this.

"Are you sure you can't stay?"

My father had never, not once, asked me for anything in his life, and it made me sadder than I can even describe to not have been able to stay.

"Do you want to come back with me? You can stay with me, Daddy."

He shook his head, and I, too, could not imagine his leaving a house he had lived in for over forty years, and all of them with my mother. Betty came to the front porch.

"Here, take these two boxes of Lorna Doones and this chicken. Your father can't eat it no way." I accepted the packages, and as I was finding room in my bag, Betty reassured me that she would be staying with my father as long as he needed her. I put my bags down and hugged and kissed my father as if my life depended on it. I tried to give him the biggest smile I could muster. Colin extended his hand, and my father smiled as he encircled my boy with his arm. Evie extended her hand as if she were a fairy princess, and my father made a great show of kissing it, which made her giggle.

"Now, Colin," said Betty, "you listen to your mama, and Evelyn...I'm not so sure about you. You watch her, she is a little devil, though you would not expect it with all those sweet blond curls around her head."

As I walked to the waiting car with Betty, I felt like I was torn between two magnets. I wanted to stay, and I wanted desperately to get back to the mountain. I took one look back at the once-fine Queen Anne house and thought about Lot's wife as I stepped into the car. With a cough and sputter, my hired car drove past the other shaded Victorian and gabled houses of Elm Street, the choicest street in Elkton toward the bustle of Main Street. Even though I had been in town for a while, I was astonished by all the cars on the road, making the occasional wagon, horse or mule seem conspicuously old-fashioned. As we motored past, I watched as men from a construction company from New Jersey poured sidewalks on Main Street. Soon we were climbing alongside Swift Run, the car backfiring from the pull of the grade. The cool mountain air was a relief, and I turned my eyes eastward. We were headed to Hightop and home and whatever awaited me there.

Chapter 38

To my relief, all was as I had left it, including Tom, who had been busy since I left bringing a fat pile of wood to the back porch. I had not been settled in for even a week when Tom and Colin, coming back from a trip to Ruckersville, brought me the following letter from Ethel.

Dearest Mary,

My heart aches to have to tell you this news. Your daddy passed away on Saturday afternoon. Because of the recent cost of your mother's funeral, we were not able to embalm your father and he was buried quickly, alongside your mother, on Sunday. John Abel is seeing to the headstone for both of your parents (thank goodness he is good for something besides preaching) and is taking care of the immediate paperwork, bills, et cetera, with your Daddy's lawyer, so do not worry about it.

I can't imagine how you are feeling as I know how close you were to your Daddy, and to lose both parents in sight of a week and it must be extremely hard for you, but I hope your children will be a comfort to you.

Do you think you can talk your husband into a phone? John Abel put one in a few months ago and I love it.

May my love surround you forever,

Ethel

I sat on the porch rocker, because I felt as if I was in a spinning vortex. Just like that, I was an orphan and once again a lone body and soul with no earthly ties to anyone except my children and a gentleman's agreement between the man who married me and my late father. I couldn't cry. When Tom came in for his noon meal, he took one look.

"What's wrong?"

I showed him the letter. A deep sigh escaped him as we looked at each other.

"I want my Daddy," I said softly. "I wish I hadn't been such a burden to him and my mother. What have I done? My poor parents."

Tom took me in his arms, and the smell of tobacco, sweat and musk was a comfort. I pushed my face deep into the center of his chest and all that was familiar to me and wished he could swallow me up.

"You'll be fine. I promise. It's better not to suffer, and they were both long ill, from what you have described to me. I knew and liked your father. He was a good man, and you were the apple of his eye, regardless." Tom held me back to look at me.

"Besides, you were just born in the wrong place and time. The way things are going, women won't even have to get married, and, like Belle, they can all run their own lives. Mark my words. Your Daddy enjoyed you like I do most of the time." Later that night, as we were lying in bed, I rolled over and whispered in his ear, "I hope we just caught another baby." I couldn't think of anything else to replace the hole in my heart.

Chapter 39
Christmas 1927, a few months later

A steady snow kept us homebound that Christmas after a year of such enormous change. I couldn't believe, that in one year, I had lost Luanne, lost my parents, found Ethel, and finally been to Skyland. I figured this is what one of those rollercoasters must feel like in Coney Island. But it was Christmas and snowing, which made everything seem magical and mystical.

If there was one thing I knew on that Christmas of 1927, it was that Colin was working more and more with Tom and going less and less to school. That made me angry and would occasionally become the cause of words between me and Tom, though I knew Tom needed the extra help. Tom's body was aching him this winter. "I want him to have choices, Tom, and if he quits going to school now, he might not have any choices."

"He reads, he writes well and can figure numbers better than me; don't you think farming, carpentry, stonework, lumber are enough choices? What do you want? Him to become a lawyer or fancy businessman down in the valley?"

So, we didn't get very far in our conversations. Even so, the weather kept Colin from trudging to the schoolhouse anyway. Evie, on the other hand, loved to get all dressed up for school, have her hair just so, shoes shined, and was always one step ahead of whatever schoolwork she was doing. She seemed to be making up for both of them.

Deep, white, cold, and silent the snow fell in the days before Christmas. On Christmas Eve morning some bewitchment must have fallen over me. Hunkered down under my warm quilts, I slept and dozed and slept. I remember Tom getting up before the gray light came silently creeping through the front windows, and I felt the mattress shift as he got out of bed. The last thought I remembered before drifting to sleep again was the sound of the stove door opening as he filled the stove with wood.

I woke with a start, having dreamt that all my teeth had fallen out. Worried that it was now quite late in the morning, I still had to fight to get out of bed. It was one of those moments when I knew that all was well and not a thing needed my attention. Women do not have many of those moments in life. Colin stomped into my room, shaking snow everywhere.

"Mom, the snow is over the window," shouted Colin

"Shh.... don't wake your sister." Too late. We heard her footsteps trudging upstairs.

"Little Evie," Colin hollered through the house anxious to have a playmate in the snow. I was up now and was suddenly filled with a need of rushing to catch up. I caught sight of myself as I passed the mirror, my hair all wild and goose feathers sticking out of it. I didn't even brush it. I let the cats out, but they simply stared at the snow as if personally affronted by it. In came Tom's hound. I got the stove roaring and poured myself some coffee as Evie ran outside in her stockingless feet dancing around the yard. "It's Christmas! It's Christmas!" She laughed joyously. She immediately began pelting her brother with snowballs.

"Well, children, there is an apple pie and side meat in the chest. Maybe later, we will have snow ice cream."

In came the cats, circling my heels, and out went the hound again. As the snow fell gently around me, I tightened my robe, and the cold, wet snow reminded me that I, too, had not put on shoes. My children and I are from the same tribe; that is for sure. The only shoes I have ever liked were high heels for dressing up. Otherwise, I'd rather have my toes touching the soft earth, and I allowed my children out in bare feet so they could feel the snow, body, and soul.

When I finally got to tend to the chickens, they were all pushed up to the fence in the henhouse as if admonishing me for the snowfall. They were hens with an attitude, but they were good layers and the chickens pecked at the snow, tilting their heads, and refusing to go outside. They had quit laying for a while at about the time my parents passed, and then the light faded, and they were molting. I know I shouldn't have done it, but I was so mad about not having any eggs for twenty-four birds that I kept telling them I was going to eat them. The young ones finally started laying again right before the winter solstice.

My milk cow was already by the barn looking to be fed and let in, as were the sheep. I have those animals well trained. As I opened the gate to the barn, my cow went to the left and my sheep went to the right, each group waiting patiently by their feed trough baaing and mooing. I separated the calf from her mother so that I could milk.

The cold air had me feeling thoroughly alive. I brought some wood into the house with one arm as I balanced the milk jug with the other. Tom was helping with butchering a cow this morning which was why he was gone so early. Everyone always asked Tom to help, not just with butchering but with everything. He was one of those men who could always get the job done, slowly, methodically and in his own way, and it would be done, and done right.

Lately, I sometimes would get so caught up in the day that I would forget to think. Perhaps this was a good thing because Tom was always telling me that I thought too much. My thinking sometimes felt like a bird caught in a house who could not get out. It contained a bit of panic, rushing thoughts, and frenetic energy which was not wholesome and didn't lead me to a place of peace.

Realizing I would not have to rush, as Tom would not be home until much later, I took a breath, steadied my mind, and looked back to the barn. Tom had taken his black horse who was big, fast moving, and steady. He would be able to make time and carry weight with him; I calculated that my husband would not be back until after dark.

That relaxed me a bit as I knew my day would be my own without need for laundry, darning, or checking to see when he wanted his supper. I knew what I would do today; I would go on a walk in the woods, and hear myself think, with the children snuggled onto the old red mare, if they wanted to come, which they probably would. And we did venture out to the woods while the snow fluttered down around us like cotton balls and the forest was silent, magical, and otherworldly in its deep blanket of snow fall.

When the children and I got home, I let them pop popcorn and make snow ice cream. I went down to the cellar to get some of Tom's blackberry wine. With a dram in hand, I began my baking and waited for him to get home. With the house filled with cooking aromas of bread, snickerdoodles, chocolate chip cookies, with sugar plum and fudge on the table, I sat in my rocker by the warm crackling stove, knowing these were the days that I would always remember, and that life can be sweet. For once, Colin and Evie were not bickering but playing jacks and pick-up-sticks.

As night started to fall, I began glancing out the front window, hoping to see his silhouette against the snow sky and tree line. In winter, dark came early, by 5 p.m. Finally, I saw the specter of his horse far down the lane. It reminded me of that long-ago day when I had first laid eyes on him at Sandy Bottom, a shadow in the light. How far I had traveled since that time. We had both had been shadows then, for it seemed that our years together had made us more real, whole, and steady. When I saw the lantern glow at the barn, I put on my shawl and went out to the porch. The world was blue. The rose-colored moon had risen, and the snow had stopped falling. The hound followed me out and bounded into the snow and down to the barn kicking up great powder puffs behind him. I went back into the house and moved the cider that I had heating for him to the back of the stove where the heat of the fire was strongest. I put the soup beans I had cooked back on the fire too. I uncovered the cornbread and butter and took out the nice hunk of cheddar cheese that we had from the store, and chow chow canned from summer.

By the time I went back out to the porch, Tom was moving through the snow. Two saddlebags were slung over each shoulder. He had been gone almost sixteen hours. Slowly he climbed the steps of our house. I went to reach for the bags to help him. His eyebrows, beard and mustache were hung with icicles. As he kissed me, the ice melted against my face. "You proud to see me?"

"I'll show you later how proud I am to see you."

"Good, and I'll show you what I have for you," he replied, putting his hat on the peg by the door.

I helped him off with his coat and placed it on a drying rack I had out by the stove for our winter gear. He placed his saddlebags on a chair and eyed the table, laid out with his dinner and Christmas goodies. "You're mighty fine, Mary." With that he reached into his pocket and pulled out a green velvet box about four inches square. "Merry Christmas."

I was so surprised, having always gotten practical gifts like a new apron, that I put my hand to my mouth and just stared at the box in his hand. "Aren't you going to open it?"

I took the box gingerly and slowly lifted the lid. The wheat of gold chain gleamed golden and caught the light in brilliance as if the metalworkers had dipped the chain in the sun. I looked at it, mesmerized, as if it had the power to melt all the snow and bring back summer. "I've never seen anything like it," I finally said. It was true. I hadn't, and my mother had acquired a lot of jewelry in her day.

Tom took the box from my hand and removed the chain, placing it around my neck. With my hand touching it to make sure it was real, I walked to a mirror. The braid of wheat was thick and lay framing my clavicle like a Celtic torque.

"Where did you find this?" I asked turning to Tom who was admiring me in the mirror as well.

"Apollo told me to give it to you. He said every goddess deserves one."

He left me there at the mirror, and I heard him move his chair to finish eating his supper. With my hand still on the necklace at my throat, I went back to the kitchen.

"I have gifts for Colin and Evie. Do you want to see what I brought them?" Still not able to speak, I smiled and nodded.

Tom took out at a shaving kit for Colin, his first one. We had remarked to each other just the previous week about Colin's light peach fuzz on his face. Tom also brought a nice plaid coat in the bomber style that I knew Colin would feel proud in. I often remarked on my son, inching his way to manhood, and I wondered what type of man he would become. When he would steadfastly refuse to go to school, I would inwardly cringe, remembering Halsom's defiance and catch my breath, worried it was innate. When Colin figured numbers in his head quicker than a jackrabbit ran, I would remember my father. When Colin would look at Evie softly and patiently, untying her fishing line or picking her up when she fell, I praised God for Tom. Yet, where was I in my boy except in his golden-brown hair?

Tom had bought his daughter a new dress as red as red could be with white lace trim around the collar, wrists, waist, and hem. He also brought her a Tiny Tots and ladies' high- fashion paper doll cut-out book. I remembered that when I was Evie's age, my mother had bought me fancy clothes and a Chinese doll in a kimono. Mother took no time admonishing me when I kicked the creepy doll, but my father had snuck into my room later that Christmas night and gave me the sling shot I had really wanted.

"It will be a good Christmas for them," I laughed.

"And for us, too," he said, pulling me over to his lap. As I turned to put my arms around him, I saw the mail poking out of one of the bags. A white envelope from the United States Government peaked out from under the *Greene County Gazette*. I pushed the bag to the far end of the table.

Chapter 40

It was second Christmas, January 7, when the weather cleared, and we were able to see Tom's family. The snow had settled enough for the roads to be passable, and Tom had hitched up the team to take us down the mountain. It was slow going, but his Percherons made easy work of it, as they were carrying only the family and not a load of logs and construction materials. They carved a path in the snow as if they were parting the Red Seas.

I could not wait to see Luanne again, and I was looking forward for festivities, gossip, and the comfort of people. I wasn't disappointed. People I knew, people I didn't know, people I had last met at my wedding crowded in and out of the house, the men gathering at the summer kitchen to smoke and drink and relax without women and children. I noticed Tom's mother, Ruth, seemed to be limping more, but she was not a woman to complain. In fact, she had made a bowl of rice pudding just for me. Often, she sent Tom home with a mason jar of it, knowing how I much I loved it. Looking around, I was disappointed that Luanne was not there. "Is she not coming?" I said to her sister.

"I don't think so. She and Asa had to travel up the country for some job he got on the railroad. But she did send this for you."

She went to the mantelpiece and brought me a box and stood there while I opened it. Pulling the tissue paper away revealed a picture of a flapper with red hair and a daringly low-cut blue dress sitting on a smiling crescent moon framed by twinkling stars. It was a hand mirror. Inside was also a note.

For Mary,
May always see yourself as you truly are.
Your best friend and sister-in-law, who loves you bestest, Luanne

At that moment, Tom came up beside me. "What you got there?" I showed it to him. "From Luanne."

He smiled and nodded at me and walked back to the men. I twirled the mirror around and regarded myself in it and I could see the hint of gold of the necklace peeking out from the top of my blouse.

We left late that night to head up the mountain and home to Hightop. I was surrounded in warm blankets and a bear skin that kept out all cold. The children were hunkered down under quilts and deer skins. Pulling the bear skin up around my head and neck, I felt safe in its cave-like cocoon.

"People will think I have kidnapped me a shapeshifting bear witch," said Tom as he looked at me.

"Good," I replied.

"Did I ever tell you the story of fair Colleen?"

I looked at him, intrigued. "No."

He kept on driving in silence. The horses' snorts and steam from their nostrils filled the air in front of us. The new moon hung over the forest and the stars twinkled brightly in the frigid air. Snow covered the earth in quiet. Finally, I couldn't stand it. "Well, are you going to tell me the story?"

"I can't tell a witch story until you ask. Now that you've asked, I can tell you. Many, many years ago, in these parts lived a young man, and he had himself a cabin far away from anyone. He made his living hunting and trapping and trading with the Indians, and his cabin was warm, and he had plenty to eat, and he had meat drying in winter. But his Indian friends would chide him, telling him he would grow old and gray and never have himself a woman, but this young man didn't mind. He would just smile and laugh and tell them that there was no woman that he had found that was fair of face, fair of voice, and fair of temperament to please him. 'Then you will die an old man without any woman because this woman does not exist,' they told him. But he didn't mind them and kept on with his life, hunting and trapping. But one cold winter evening, on a night like this, he took his pipe and went outside his cabin to look at the stars. As the full moon shone down upon him, he was filled with a longing that he had never known before, and in a moment, he realized he was lonesome. He looked up at that big full moon and he said, 'Oh, lady of the moon, if you can hear me, send me a woman fair, and I will provide for her and love her like a good husband should.' And with that he went inside and went to bed.

The next morning, he rose as usual and set out to check his traps when his dog took off running and barking and making a racket crashing through the laurel thickets. Calling after his dog, he raced to keep up with him, and when his dog went to baying, he knew the dog had found some quarry. As he came around a huge chestnut oak, standing in a mountain waterfall was a beautiful young girl. Her skin was as white as snow, and her hair was as black as the bear skin that was lying beside her, and her hair fell all around her body as shiny as moonlight on the water. Keeping his eyes upon her, he slowly reached down and picked up the bearskin, and the girl gasped and reached for it, but it was too late. The young boy had it. He held out his hand to her and the young girl knew she had no choice. Resigned, she took his hand, and followed him back to his cabin.

In the days, weeks, and months that followed, she did all that a good loving wife could do, and he brought her all her heart's desires, which mostly consisted of fruits, nuts, and berries of the forest. He would also bring her fine cloth from town, white sugar and flour, and China teacups, but she had no interest in such things. She would often ask for her bearskin but that was the one thing he refused her. His Indian friends were amazed and tried to trade him goods, pelts, and guns for her, but he would smile and say, 'No.' He knew he was a very lucky man, for he had caught a bear woman, a goddess of the forest.

She bore him five children, and their lives were filled with peace, plenty, and happiness. Then, one day, he told her he was going on a long hunting trip with his Indian friends and would be back in about a week. He asked if there was anything he could buy or get her before he left. She smiled, kissed her husband, and just wished him a safe journey. With one long look back, he waved at her, blew her a kiss, and, with his long rifle slung across his back, he headed out. She closed the door of their cabin and busied herself with her children and chores.

A few days later, she set her mind on giving the cabin a good cleaning, as the day had gotten warm, and she could open the doors and windows and sweep all the winter dust and soot away. As she was cleaning, she stood on a chair to clean the rafters of cobwebs when up in the log beams, she spied a package wrapped in muslin cloth. Standing on her tiptoes, she used her broom handle to push the package loose. Stretching her fingers, she was able to grab the corner of the package and pull it down. Her hands were shaking as she folded back the muslin to reveal her bearskin. Tears fell down her face and made a puddle by her feet. Later that night, she tucked in all of her children and kissed them each tenderly on the tops of their heads. Wrapping the bearskin around herself, she stepped into the cool night air and looked to the sky and the full moon.

When the young man came home the next day. He found the clothes she had been wearing in a pile on the kitchen floor and his wife nowhere to be seen. He then spied the muslin cloth on the bed."

The winter night surrounded Tom and me as I pulled my bearskin around me, enchanted by the story and wondering why Tom had paused.

"Well, what happened? Did she come back?"

"Why, no. Of course, she didn't. She had found her bearskin." Tom turned to look at me steadily as if I were plain silly to ask. "In fact, many years later, he saw a big bear at the corner of his property, and he had lifted his gun to shoot it when he realized it was her coming to check on her children. You see, she had everything except her freedom." The fall of the horses' footsteps in the snow made a crunching noise that reverberated in my ears, and my eyes filled with tears that froze on my cheeks. The moon illuminated our white farmhouse glowing moonlit blue ahead of us. I narrowed my eyes. "Tom, someone's on the porch. Look," I said, as I pointed at the figure.

And as we drew closer, the shadow who had been sitting on the porch rocker stood up. "It's about time you all got back. I'm freezing my ass off." It was Belle.

"You're a sight for sore eyes!" said Tom, perking up. "Is the new year going to be a good year for you, Belle? Tom asked as he pulled the wagon to a stop in front of the house.

"Why, yes, and no, but the dark of the night is not the time to discuss it. I'm going to help you unhitch that team so we can all get some rest. Especially me."

With my children following behind sleepily, I regarded Belle and her black braid that swung to below her belt, telling her, "Luanne's place in the loft is all clean for you. It's been waiting on you."

I was too tired to think of anything except bed and getting Evie settled.

"Colin, honey, you work on getting the stoves nice and hot."

"Yes, ma'am."

Colin soon had the house warm; Evie went meekly to bed holding her teddy bear, and Colin headed to his room without pleading to stay up. I finally climbed into bed to the sound of glasses clinking in the kitchen and the voices of Belle and Tom rising and falling. I pulled that bear hide tightly around me and fell fast asleep.

Chapter 41

I awoke the next morning to Belle and Tom in a heated discussion at the kitchen table as if they had never gone to bed. I heard Tom say, "Goddamn it, Belle. You don't know everything and I'm tired of arguing with you about it. I know one thing for sure; they ain't going to take my land."

Hurrying to put on my robe over my nightdress, I was pulling it on and shouting from the next room, "What's going on?"

As I entered the kitchen, Tom and Belle looked at each other. Belle pushed a brochure, newsletter, and large document across the table to me. I picked up the brochure that had Shenandoah National Park Association on the cover with a picture of a waterfall and mountains all highlighted in colors that had been enhanced to the point that they looked garish, as my mother would say.

"Read it," Belle said.

"It says the landscape is thrilling," I read, as I looked back and forth at the both of them.

"Keep going."

For here was fought to the finish of a celebrated feud in which three men were shot to death over moonshine. Many years ago, the Blue Ridge was a haven of refuge for bandits and desperados who preyed upon the neighborhood settlements.

I looked at her as I flipped the brochure over, trying to make sense of it, after placing it on the table. "Are they talking about you?"

"I liked how it said there were acres of virgin timber and a landscape untouched by man," said Tom. "I can count on one hand the trees that are over 100 years old."

"They have started surveying the lands in Rappahannock and Madison County. They're coming," Belle said.

"I'd like to see a surveyor step on my 200 acres," Tom said as he waved the brochure around.

"They'll arrest you if you try to keep them off."

"Like Hell they will. They can't just march on a man's land. They don't have a right to do that."

"Yes, they do. Governor Byrd has established some state commission, and President Coolidge has signed a bill. Why Coolidge has even proposed a summer White House on the Rapidan down from Skyland as part of this park."

"A park? A park to do what?" I asked.

"So, people from the city can drive here and relax in the mountain air."

"They can relax in the mountain air somewhere else," Tom said.

"A park? Like Yosemite?" I directed this to Belle.

"I suppose, except there's over 500 families living where they want to put this park, and there has been no mention of that and no worry about it, either."

"How do you know all this?"

"I've got my ways."

"You been up to see Adams?" Tom asked.

She nodded and told us of Adams's push for the project and his new telephone lines and electricity to encourage the Washington officials. It was all being funded by a group of rich men, and she knew this because she had been seated at the bar at the Willard Hotel in Washington, D. C.

"The Willard Hotel? What you doing there?"

Belle just grinned like a cat in response, and I wanted to knock the grin right off of her, only because I was so jealous of her ways, how she appeared to always be in control and never getting any retribution.

"They're not going to come this far down," Tom said, sounding like he was trying to convince himself.

"Like Hell they're not. They are talking about over 500,000 acres and building a road running from Front Royal to Waynesboro right down the spine of the Blue Ridge Mountains. I'm telling you, Tom get out now, while you still can."

"You getting out?" He asked pointing his finger in Belle's face.

"I've not made up my mind. It will depend on where these lines of the park go and who's out and who's in."

"I still don't believe you," Tom said, and I was not sure if he meant about the park or her staying.

"Well, you can go up there and see for yourself. Adams gave me this for you." With that she took an official envelope out of her breast pocket and handed it to him.

"What's it say?" I asked, looking frantically between Tom and Belle.

Tom opened the envelope and put on his reading glasses. Scanning the letter, he said, "it says the horses are well and fine and being used by all manner of men that he is entertaining up there. He has asked me to bring him about six more and the best spirits that I have by the beginning of April and that he is able to pay extra and to bring all that I've got."

"How does he have money to pay with creditors nipping at his heel at the same time?" I asked.Both Belle and Tom looked at me as if I were a simpleton.

"Why, that's how he works; he borrows from Peter to pay Paul," Tom replied.

"What are you going to do?" I asked. Both Belle and I regarded him closely.

"What I'm going to do is bring him six nags and see for myself what's going on."

Belle leaned back and smiled as I ran for the outhouse feeling the waves of nausea rise through my gut.

I didn't concern myself much about Tom's plan for his visit with Adams, because all that winter and early spring my exhaustion and morning sickness consumed me. I'm the sickest person I know who is basically healthy as a horse. When Dr. Timmson's syrupy potions only made it worse, Tom carried over Granny Hite for a visit. She put me on a diet of raspberry leaf tea, peppermint tea and this delicious restorative drink that she learned from some Indian professor from India, who came through Browns Gap and Bacon Hollow traveling with Cecil Sharp, the song catcher. Granny said they got Birdy to sing into some machine that recorded her voice.

Tom had to get the ginger root from an apothecary in Charlottesville that still stocked herbs and roots along with all the pre-made medicine. This pregnancy was going to kill me, I often thought, and being sick with it was a full-time job that winter. So, I could not be too concerned over Tom and his plans to leave with Belle when the ice began to melt. In fact, I was a bit relieved, and I was even more relived that Colin had gotten his school grades pulled up, and Tom, being a man of his word, was taking my son with him.

By the time Tom left with his horses and gear, along with Belle and Colin, they were carrying the finest homemade wine, brandy, and moonshine in three counties. I was excited for my son, who was on his own horse that Tom had given him for his last birthday, along with a bridle Tom had made in his leather workshop that said COLIN down the side; Not one of them waved good-bye, and I thought being the one left is not as good as the one doing the leaving, but that thought soon passed. I was mostly back to my old self. In fact, I was better than my old self having come to peace more with what is and was in my life, so much so, that I no longer mustered shooting daggers out of my eyes at the back of Belle as they rode away. It was a freeing thing to realize that the only thing I had control of was myself.

"My, Evelyn, we are in beauty land now, just us girls," I told her as we went back in the house.

"Good," she said dramatically.

Our days were actually sweet together, and I enjoyed my time alone with my increasingly headstrong daughter, cherishing this time and knowing what the third baby would bring to my life. Evelyn slept beside me, and we rose about seven, as the morning daylight was a reminder of the growing season. We picked mayapples to store for Tom and Sweet

Woodruff flower. I harvested some of the cabbage and picked flowers of the redbud and ate them like candy. I milked my Jersey cow, kissing her sweet side as I buried my face in her flank. I planted tomatoes, peppers, cucumber, acorn, butternut and pattypan squash seeds. I walked Evie part of the way to school and then met her on the way home and Evie reveled in all my attention, especially brushing, doing her hair for school and ironing her dresses and stockings to her orders. She would have been very happy as an only child.

We napped in the afternoon by the stream, and in the evenings, I read to her from the *Treasury of Children's Literature* that Ethel had sent me. The days passed so quickly that I was surprised when I heard a horse whinny from the woods. Looking up, I saw my family emerge from the line of pines on the far edge of the field, scattering the red-winged blackbirds from the grasses as they approached. As much as it pained me to acknowledge this, Belle was my family, too, because she was a part of our lives like the sister you loved and stuck your tongue out at behind their back. My eyes searched for her.

"Mama!" I heard Colin call. He was waving excitedly and wearing an Indian headdress and brandishing a tomahawk that I could only assume Adams had given him. Tom swung down from the saddle. "He has hit me in the head at least twice with that thing while practicing throwing it," but Tom was smiling.

"How did Colin behave?" I asked as Colin slid off the saddle giving me a bear hug.

"He actually held his own and gave Adams a run for his money in the charm department." Tom dismounted as I smiled down at my first born.

"Where's Belle?"

"She stayed up there helping some surveyor that has taken a shine to her."

"So, it's true?"

Tom looked at me, his face hard, firm and resigned. "I'm pretty wore out, Mary. How's about we talk about this later. How have you been feeling? You're looking good." As he said this, the glow came back to his face and he pulled me close, kissing me gently on the mouth. "I swear, you're the best-looking pregnant woman I have ever seen. I'm afraid to take you to town anymore. Last time I took you, that man in the store stared at you like a schoolboy."

"Stop it," I said blushing.

"I'll be up to the house directly." He patted me on my bottom as Evie raced from the house and into her father's arm. He swung her around as the air filled with her peals of laughter. That night, as we were sitting on the porch, I was surprised to see Tom take out his fiddle. He played for a while as darkness fell and the whippoorwills added their calls to his melodies. I rocked back and forth with my cat on my lap and my head resting back on the chair. We were at peace, and it felt like the world was at peace too. When he put his fiddle back in its case, he stared out into that darkness a long time before he spoke.

"Adams said to send his regards but completely understood the circumstances of your not being able to travel. In any event, he has no time for romance now; he's running around like a banty rooster in a barnyard full of full-sized cocks."

This made me laugh. "Are you going to tell me what's going on now and why he is running around like a banty rooster, I mean more so than usual?"

Tom turned to me, looking like an old man. Maybe it was only the way the lantern light was hitting his face.

"The Commonwealth has passed, or is getting ready to pass, a condemnation act so that land can be bought at a fair market price and then donated to this new park."

"No! You're kidding. Right?" The cat jumped off my lap in alarm.

"Why, the Shiffletts told me they heard of some people being offered seven dollars an acre. I also heard that people might be able to stay, other people said some have already sold and moved down to the valley. I also heard that special use permits might be granted. There's a lot of speculating and what ifs and I tell you, all those government men and rich folks that have their hands in the pie that Adams's got up there, *they* don't even know what's going on. At one point I heard the park was going to be 500,000 acres. Then, the next night I heard that it was going to be 300,000 acres. One thing for sure, they don't even know what's going on."

"What are we going to do?"

"Adams assured me that we would be fine."

"You believe him?" The baby began tap dancing inside my belly and kicked so hard I could see my belly move.

"I don't know." Tom let out a big sigh and looked at me, trying to smile in what I'm sure was his way of reassuring me.

"Don't you worry, Mary. The only way they are getting me off this mountain is feet first. Come on." He grabbed my hand. "Let's go to bed so I can snuggle up to that sweet bottom of yours."

Chapter 42

I was delivered of a baby boy that September in the University of Virginia Charlottesville Hospital, which Tom insisted that I go to a week before the baby was due, not wanting a repeat of when Evie was born. He told me his nerves could not handle it. What a difference between my first delivery in the dirty coal camp with no doctor or granny woman, my birth in the field like nature's first woman, and now I felt like I was in a first-class hotel. Everything was sparkling clean. The nurses wore nice white uniforms and little hats, and I got to visit with the other mothers and mothers-to-be on the maternity floor. In fact, my birth was so easy on account of some shot they gave me that when they handed me my clean, disinfected baby to hold, not a hair on my head was out of place. We named him Benjamin, and people came to visit me like I was a celebrity.

Luanne and her husband, Asa, Ethel, and John Abel, and of course Tom, who brought me flowers, all paid their visits. I didn't want to go home. Belle came by on the last day I was there. The nurses gave her the stink eye, what with her trousers, men's boots and man's shirt unbuttoned to mid chest that when she moved you could see the outline of her breasts. She had rings on her fingers and various bracelets, which made her look like a gypsy. She smiled at me, held the baby, and I suppose to be funny, handed me a card and a little brown paper bag that when I looked inside had some rubber cup that looked like it was for the kitchen sink. She told me it was called a cervical cap.

I liked her too much to be mad at her, for she read my heart, and thereby knew my truth, sometimes before even I had acknowledged it.

Then, I was back home, with my baby, Evie, and Colin. Within a month, I had lost all my baby weight and then some, because I simply never had time to eat. And so, time sped by like a hamster wheel, hours, days, weeks, months flew by, and we seemed insulated from trouble with the world at large. Black Thursday came, and we heard John D. Rockefeller say on the radio, *"These are the days when many are discouraged. Depressions have come and gone. Prosperity has always returned and will again."* Yet, while bread lines were happening in the cities, it didn't affect us much on the mountain since we kept on living like we had been living. We still had no phone or electricity, but now the world had airplanes, Communists, and the Great Depression.

In the fall of Ben's second birthday, September 9, 1931, we still felt safe from the park and the Depression way up on Hightop, but one day that all changed. I was on the porch stringing beans, a methodical and slow work, while Benjamin napped. Each time I was done with a string, I would stand up and stretch my legs while I hung the string on the beam that Tom had made me. Then I would rehang the beam on the porch rafters. I would sit back down and start again. I only once forgot to bring the beans in that week, exhausted from being up at night with the baby who had had a cough. The beans got damp, and we fed them to the hogs.

Up and down, in and out went my needle. Farming could be sweet work, just like nursing a baby, and sometimes the monotony of it would put me into a bit of a trance, a half-asleep and not-in-this-world type of place, a place beyond calm. I was trying to keep myself from slipping into such a state when I looked up and saw Stonewall, Tom's big Percheron, emerging from the woods at the edge of the field. He was like a vision holding his head high and stepping slowly into the field, his logging harness straining under his huge frame.

He was pulling no log and there was no Tom walking behind him. I stood straight up, the beans falling all around me onto the porch as if stars were falling from the sky.

"Colin," I said, my voice loud, but calm. I walked slowly from the porch, or it seemed slow. It felt as if time were dripping like water off of leaves.

"Colin!" I yelled now for my son. He came around from the side of the house.

"What's wrong? Hey, can I go fishing?"

"Go get that horse."

"Why do I have to get that horse? Where's Evie? I want to go fishing!"

"I said go get that horse and then get back here and watch your sister and the baby. I'm going to look for your father."

And then I ran. Following the trail that the horse left was not hard. He was a big horse, and he made his mark on the earth. I knew that horse would just not up and walk away. Tom's horses stood, plain and simple. I ran, and I tripped, and I ran far into that forest on foot, already starting to pray to I don't know who, bargaining with myself that all was okay. I came upon his lunch pail and haversack, and I saw some of his work tools. I looked around frantically calling his name. A woodpecker answered me.

"Tom!" I cried, my face and body covered in sweat. I was panicked. He would be mad at me for screaming like a fishwife. He will come up behind me and tell me that at any time now. "Tom! Tom!"

And then I saw him. He was lying on the ground. Dappled autumn sunlight played around him, as if in a tableau, surrounding him like a church-stained glass window.

"Oh, Tom," I said as I knelt down beside him. I could hear my heart thumping in my ears, long, loud, and slow. I looked around, from my husband to the woods, to the tree, to the twilight sunlight low and slanting gold through the tri-colored leaves of red, orange, and yellow.

A strainer had come loose when he had sawed though a tree, and he was lying under it now. His head was all mashed in till I could make no sense of the pieces of his skull, and there was so much blood and white matter, I felt as if I was outside myself as I took off my apron and wrapped his horrible bloody mashed skull and stroked his swollen face. "Tom, I'm here. I'm here."

He didn't open his eyes. He didn't groan. His chest rose faintly under his sweaty work shirt. I laid his head softly down pulling the leaves and bits of bark from around his face and skull and brains.

"Tom, I'm going for help and then I'll be back."

I would get help. We would get the doctor. He was breathing. He was a strong man. It would be all right again. This was a man who had split wood with one arm when he had torn his shoulder muscle. Everything is going to be fine. I thought this, yet knew his head was like Humpty Dumpty's. When I met my son half-way back to the farm, Colin was wild eyed and scared.

"What's happened? Where's Daddy?"

"Now, you listen to me. You go back to the farm and get on a horse and go down that mountain as fast as you can and get help from the first person you see. I'm going to need help getting Daddy back to the farm and they need to send for the doctor. Tell whoever you find that Daddy has been in a logging accident and a limb struck his head. He is breathing but is hurt bad. You have to go fast. Hurry!"

"Mom, no! no!" Colin was grief-stricken and would not move.

"Just go, it'll be all right. We can't waste any time." I kissed him on the head, but I was crying and pushing him forward. "Take my horse and gallop the whole way."

I ran back to the house, where Evie was playing with Benjamin. I promised Evie more candy and a cut-out book if she watched her brother till I got back.

"What's happened, Mama?" She looked at me expectantly.

"Daddy's been hurt." Evelyn's shoulders dropped, her face fell, and her eyes got as big as silver dollars. She knew.

I rode the red mare bareback carrying a blanket, water and towels to Tom and I stayed with my husband providing the only comfort I could. I used this water to try to gently wipe the blood from his eyes and neck. I held his lifeless hand and I talked, and I sang and begged him not to leave me. I begged him. I begged God. I rocked and cried. I sat stupefied. I watched the evening birds begin to flit and fly around us. I listened to the leaves rustle as a buck deer came down to scratch his antlers against a tree, completely oblivious to us. The squirrels jumped from tree to tree. There was just me and him, the forest and God. It was peaceful in its horror. Finally, at near dark, some men came with lanterns and a sled. Colin was with them, and he stared at his father and went pale.

By the time we got Tom home, the doctor from Stanardsville was there. He had cleared off our kitchen table and laid out all his instruments. Tom's mother was rocking Benjamin, and Luanne was carrying Evelyn. When Luanne put Evie down, she was sucking her thumb like a baby. My sister ran over to me, wrapping her arms around me. I pushed her away.

"We need to get word to Granny Hite," I whispered to her.

If anyone knew any magic to turn back time and fix this it was she, but she was dead. I was losing my mind. As the doctor worked, Luanne, Ruth and I cut Tom's shirt off and we ran for water and heated water, blood-colored colored water spilled over my floor until I could watch no more, and I went out to the porch looking into the darkness. The men on the porch made way for me. They were quiet, smoking. Colin stood in a dark corner of the kitchen, his back pressed up against the wall, watching it all, knowing it was the end of things, yet stuck in a time warp of other worldliness. This must be dream world, I thought, for reality could not possibly be this terrible.

I sat in my chair and rocked hard, fast, and deliberately. Someone handed me a drink, but I shook my head. Faceless people now. People whose faces I could not remember. It was like I had been hit on the head. I heard the screen door open, and Luanne stuck her head out. "Mary, the doctor wants to talk to you." I went inside, steeling my face. Tom's mother was holding her son's hand. His head had been bandaged with some white cloth. It was so white, it seemed blinding. A large red blood stain had already seeped through that cloth.

"Mrs. Dodson, Mary, I have done all that I can do. His skull is fractured, and his brain is swelling. I'm going to leave you with this, and if he wakes up, you will need to give him these morphine shots. We could move him to the hospital in Charlottesville, but I'm not sure he would survive the journey. I'm also not sure what could be done for him there. He is in very serious condition. If he does wake up, there is a strong possibility that he won't be able to take care of himself anymore;

at the very least, he might not be able to walk." He finished wiping his hands and rolling down his shirt sleeves.

"Luanne, go get the men and let's move Tom to bed where he can be comfortable and rest," I told her.

The doctor came over to me. He put his hand on my shoulder. "I'm sorry, Mary." He gave my shoulder a squeeze. "Here," he handed me some pills, these will help your nerves."

I nodded as he placed the pillbox in my hand. I went to our bedroom and got the bed ready for Tom, putting more pillows for his head and neck, smoothing out the sheets. The men laid him down as if they were laying down a baby.

"I've got it now. Thank you," I said. They nodded to me and backed out of the room. I pulled a chair over and sat facing Tom.

"It's fine now, Tom. You're in our bed. You can rest." I patted his shoulder, which was still well muscled and strong.

"Mary, I'm going to stay with you," said Luanne.

"I turned to her and matter-of-factly told her, "I won't be needing any help, Luanne. Go home to your husband." Luanne and her mother exchanged glances.

"It will be all right now. It will be all right. I can take care of him and my family. There is nothing you can do, absolutely nothing."

"Well, I'm not going."

"Send me word," Ruth said, as she buttoned her coat.

The days crawled slowly by, and I didn't know if it was morning or afternoon. Luanne watched the children, did my chores, and would come and bring food. Ruth came by, and I would hear her and her daughter talking in murmured voices. The preacher who married us came as did the neighbors and friends. I would not even look at them. I wanted the world to go far away along with all the people in it. Darkness would come, then daylight again.

At night, I would lie down beside Tom and tell him about the day. The children would come in and regard him then ask if they could go fishing or to the church social or get a piece of cake. And I was amazed, for the second time in my life, at how alone I was in my pain and horror and that the earth kept spinning.

He died on the third day of the third week at 3:00 a.m. I know, because I was there, awake and watching him. His eyes had opened, and he had blinked a few times.

"I'm here, Tom. I'm right here. It's Mary." I held his hand and squeezed. He squeezed back.

The right side of his mouth, the side of him that was not paralyzed, lifted at the corner. He blinked again. His breaths were coming deep, long, and so slow now, his eyes wide open and clear. I watched him. Tears began pouring out of my eyes as I watched Tom die. He took a deep breath and a rattle escaped from his throat. Then his chest and face sank, and the light slowly faded from his eyes, and he went flat, and he was Tom no longer. His body sunk into the bed. I sat, amazed, and shattered, as I regarded his face and his quiet and his deadness. Our cat came into the room and circled my feet then sat with me until the dawn light when it left, and I stood up.

I never looked the same and never was the same again.

Chapter 43

Tom's mother and I washed his body. Luanne covered the mirrors, and the bells in the Methodist church rang for each year Tom was alive. A coffin was built especially for Tom, as individual as homemade bread by the men who had carpentry skills. All contributed the wood. Others, with pickaxes and shovels, dug the grave at the Dodson cemetery.

I sat with his body which was laid out in the house, his house, our house. I held my sides, rocking back and forth all night, and the rocking was a comfort. Evie peered into the coffin as if she were inspecting a biology specimen. Colin went to the woods, and Benjamin jumped off the table, scrambled onto the roof, and hung from the coffin lid, not in that order. If that child had been my first, well, he would have been my last.

When the men went to nail down the lid, the dismay, grief, and finality of Tom's death sucked all the oxygen out of my lungs. I was in disbelief. I was out of my mind. Maybe he can wake up? Maybe this has not happened and I'm in a nightmare? How can I go back in time? How do I make this stop?

Luanne pulled me away so I couldn't watch. A neighbor woman came up to me. "You still have your children." I looked at her wild-eyed as Luanne yanked me away as the casket was placed on the wagon. When we got to the cemetery, the men carried the casket slowly to the waiting hole in the ground.

"Dear Friends, neighbors, wife and family of Tom Dodson," began the preacher. *Jesus said, 'I'm the resurrection and the life, he who believes in me, though he will die, yet shall he live, and whoever lives and believes in me shall never die.'*

"Friends, we have gathered here to praise God and bear witness to our faith. It is true that we gather here with grief in our hearts as we acknowledge our human loss. But may God grant us grace, that in pain

we may find comfort, in sorrow we may find hope, and in death we may find resurrection in God of all creation, of all that is and has been and will be. We praise you. We praise you for the great company of all those who have finished their course in faith and now rest from their labor. We praise you for those we love so dearly whom you have given us in this life and whom we name before you now. And we praise you for the life we shared with Tom Dodson, whom you have now so graciously received into your presence. Shine your eternal light upon him and all those we hold dear. Help us to believe that which we have not seen. Guide us with your presence. Lead us through all our years until we at last join those who have gone before us in the joy of your home. Through Jesus Christ our Lord, we pray. Amen."

The preacher came around to me and put his arm around my shoulder as the men began shoveling the dirt onto the coffin. I looked at him as if he had leprosy. Thwart, thwart, thwart went each shovel full of dirt as it flew from the shovels and onto the pine lid, ringing light, final, and clear. I shrugged off the preacher's arm and went up to one of the men to take the shovel out of his hand. He held resolutely to it.

"Give me the shovel," I said firmly. You could hear a pin drop on that mountainside, as no one knew what I was going to do, not even myself, but when he relinquished it and I had that shovel firmly in my hands, I knew. Purposefully, I sent the blade into the earth, lifted the soil, and let it fly into my husband's grave.

The family went home. The friends went home. The neighbors left. I knew where the cash money was hidden. I knew where the liquor was curing. I knew I had to raise my children and milk the cow. I knew I hated God and he must hate me. How else could he have suffered me to live against so much? I felt as if the universe felt I was not worth the energy to spit on. I raised my fist to the sky. "Goddam you, you son of a bitch." That was all I knew. Colin and Evie went to school, and I refused to leave the farm for any reason, and I would send Colin and Evie to the store. When Ethel and Johnathan Abel came up to check on me, I let them take my children back to town with them for a visit.

The children seemed happy to be headed away, and I was relieved to swim in my grief and bitterness.

The vultures and coyotes waited until early spring of 1933 to descend, but like any tricksters, they came with offers to help, or with food or with wood as these men asked me questions about how I was getting along and how much land Tom had and was I interested in selling tools or horses or myself. Disinterested, I let them court me because they were bringing me things I needed, but I wanted none of these men. I let them sit on the porch and talk to me as if everything were normal, and they didn't seem too bothered that I never spoke. I cursed Tom for leaving me unprotected to deal with this.

As the leaves began to turn to another autumn, their visits had fallen off based on my disinterest, but then one day, after a week of cold rains, the sun came out from behind the veils of mist and clouds, granting an Indian summer. I had just polished off my second glass of Elderberry wine and was staring at a ham that was sitting on my kitchen table that William Dean had brought me. He was the most persistent and last of the suitors. He sat, with his big belly bulging over his belt, across from me at Tom's kitchen table.

"You got to make a life for yourself, Mary, while you're still young and you got your looks." I stared at the ham wrapped in muslin and listened to the price I was paying for it.

"You need to think on what type of man is going to come for a woman with three children. Hmm?" William Dean looked at me, expecting an answer. I just wanted him to leave and take his ham with him.

"These mountain folks ain't going to be able to stay up here forever. Why William Carson is at work right now to condemn people's property. And another thing, there is no way you can keep this place running by yourself. It's just not right. Now, I ain't telling you that you got to love me or even like me, but I have me a five-hundred-acre valley farm. And I ain't farming with horses like Tom did; my farm embraces progress. I'm set up with the farm cooperative, and I just leased myself another 100 acres and bought myself my second John Deere. Your children would go to a real school and church down in the Valley." William Dean paused to see if I was taking this all in. I wondered if I could get myself another glass of wine and what he would think about that.

"That boy you got is a nice hard-working boy. I could use a boy like that on my place, teach him a thing or two about *real farming*."

"Would you like a drink, Mr. Dean?"

"What? Oh, sure, I'll take me some iced tea."

I poured myself a glass of wine and handed William Dean a glass of tea with no ice.

"Plus, I have electricity, refrigerator, washer, a phone, indoor plumbing, and a new Model 40 Ford. Have you thought how backwards and unsafe it is living up here without any modern conveniences?"

"Did you hear something?" I asked him. I thought I heard a car and wondered if that was Ethel bringing my children back. I had sent word to her a few days ago.

"I didn't hear anything. But you know what, I also have me a new Sears radio. Sounds like people in the radio are talking right to you. And I will buy you three new dresses a year."

Well, damn. Maybe I will come live with you then, I thought as I looked to see Belle striding through my door, grinning from ear to ear. The look of surprise, disgust and dread that swept over William Dean's face didn't stop Belle. "How ya doing, William? Selling out or selling yourself?"

William Dean looked at me as if Belle were not even in the room. "I just never dreamed that you kept company with her." He kept talking as if she were not present. "I don't like to tell anybody their business, but hanging around with the likes of her is going to come to no good." He looked out the window. "Why, she's even gotten herself a roadster! Now, don't tell me you bought that."

"Well, if Miss Earhart can fly, I can own a car."

"Oh, you think your smart, don't ya? I know how you came by that money, and it wasn't honest."

"As honest as swindling people out of their land when their crops fail, Bill Dean? I know the likes of you, too."

William Dean looked from Belle to me and back to Belle, his big belly heaving like a bellows, and he was so red in the face, I thought he might explode. Finally, he said, "At least I didn't get what I come by, by lying flat on my back."

Before he took his next breath, Belle's fist crashed right into his face as I screamed, and blood came flying out of William Dean's nose. William Dean was no longer a bellows, as the punch had sent him falling over backwards in his chair and his eyes were wide in terror as he cupped his face. "She hit me! She hit me!" He hollered in disbelief as he sat on the floor.

I ran to get him a towel, thinking there would be no electricity, refrigerators, or valley farms in my future now. He grabbed the towel out of my hands as he struggled to lift his fat body off the floor, pushing me away as I tried to assist him. Belle was staring at her fist, opening, and closing it and wincing, not paying any mind to William Dean. Spying his ham on the kitchen table he lurched for it, but Belle reached it first and held it high in air away from him like a child's game of keep-away. I had to turn from looking at his bloody face and sideways nose. His steps were hard, heavy, and final as he left.

"I may have broken my hand," said Belle matter-of-factly, "or my wrist." She placed the ham back down on the kitchen table. "But at least I broke his nose." She smiled.

"I have no ice." I was so glad to see her I thought I would bust.

"I've heard."

"You didn't come to Tom's funeral." I placed her hand in a cold pan of water. I was looking to her to comfort me, for it was she who loved him, and knew the man Tom was, like I did, and it was she who knew me.

Slowly, she looked up at me and regarded me. She had the unnerving quality of looking into the eyes of anyone she was talking to, her blue eyes flecked with brown and her pupils so dark and intense that they resembled the heads of bullets. "I didn't think it was a good idea. Plus, I didn't realize how much you would need me, till now." She looked at the bottle of wine.

"Why?"

"Because." Her voice was slow and hesitant and trailed off like mist in the morning.

For maybe the first time in her life, Belle was without words.

"How are you getting along, Mary?" she asked, her face now soft while wrapping her arms around me and holding me so close to her chest I could feel the thump of her heart. I think this was the first time she had ever spoken my name.

"How do you think?" I sobbed into her neck. A dam had broken loose, and this dam was holding back more than Tom's death.

She nodded at this, gave me a squeeze, pulled out a chair and sat down. I poured her a glass of Tom's wine. "How much have you had?" she asked me.

I held up three fingers.

"Where your children?" she asked, looking around.

"They're in town with my friend, Ethel. I expect them back any day now."

"And Luanne? Did I hear right that her husband sold out and they settled over in Culpepper?"

My heart opened with another load of grief. I missed Luanne so, and she might as well be in France; our paths didn't cross at all now. Belle and I sat in silence for a while.

"Farm's going to hell."

"Yep."

"You got to get out of here before they condemn and take the property."

That is when the fire rose in me fueled by the wine. "I don't have to do a damn thing, and I'm going to stay here till they run me off. What am I going to do in the valley? How am I going to live? Why didn't you come to the funeral, Belle?" I screamed in her face now. I may have even spit on her by mistake because I was out of my mind again. She didn't flinch.

"I'm telling you this as true as I know anything in this world, and believe me, there isn't too much that I don't know for sure. Tom loved you, but he also loved me, and I didn't feel it was my place to come to the funeral." I sat down; gut punched by the truth that I had known all along.

"Then why didn't he marry you?"

"Really?" She looked at me bored.

We sat in silence for a while. My mind rolled around different thoughts and played with them like sand dollars on the beach, and each wave that came turned them over and took some closer to shore and some it swept out to sea.

"I want to die."

Belle regarded me.

"I can't bear another day. I go to bed at night fighting sleep because I don't want another day to come and have to face another day. Then, the panic comes and my heart races, and I feel like the earth is opening up and swallowing me, and I hold onto one of Tom's shirts that still smells like him, because I haven't washed them, and I have to go take a pill that the doctor left." I started sobbing again, big gulping sobbing till I started choking and wailing, and finally, whimpering. This meltdown took some time. Belle got up and stretched her legs and walked over and got another big pan of water and submerged her hand again.

"I know what loneliness is, and it's not a demon I like wrestling with, either. I don't know despair though. I figure if I still got breath, I still got fight." She took the pan of water outside and I followed her to the porch.

She looked at me and said as she bathed her swollen hand, "I got pleurisy a few winters ago and by the time I was too sick to bring in wood, I was too sick to sleep much either and that left me with myself. I got real low. Especially when I realized I might die, and no one was going to be there, and it might take days. Hell, it might take a week or two before someone got a notion to check on me. I wondered if my dog would eat me. I would have given my right arm for the devil to have sat beside me and held my hand, but no one came, not even Jesus. Ain't that right, Mary?" and I knew what she meant. "No one comes and certainly not God. But I did." She regarded me and smiled, and I wanted to crawl into her lap, down her throat and into her bosom and stay there.

"What am I going to do?"

"We'll talk about it in the morning."

"Did you really run some man out of your cabin with a bear?" I asked her. Belle seemed surprised by this and turned to me with a laugh. "Who told you that?"

"Tom." She threw her head back hooting, cackling, and snickering, and watching her filled my heart with what I recognized was joy. "It's late. Go to bed and rest," she said.

"I can't rest. Will you tell me the story of it?"

Belle motioned for me, and I followed her to my bedroom.

"Get in bed and get comfortable."

For the first time since Tom's death, I pulled back the sheets and climbed into bed. Belle laid down next to me, putting her hands behind her head. "You ready?" she asked looking at me.

"Yes."

"Well, once there was this man, and when he and I looked at each other, well, I mean sparks flew. He had hair the color of copper and the bluest eyes I have ever seen. When he kissed me, long and hard, I forgot my name. I was on fire for that man and he for me. Soon enough, we would spend days going back and forth between our respective homes, and that added to the excitement of seeing each other, you know, riding through the mountain to get to him or he to me, riding with a mission and spurring my horse to go faster. Well, we lived on love for months, sometimes doing it three times a day. But one morning, I began to sense that something was changing. Perhaps, it was the tone of his voice when I asked when he would be back over to see me, and he wouldn't know and kind of put me off, or the way he was avoiding my eyes. I left his cabin one night to head on back home, but my women's intuition told me to wait and watch. So, I rode about a mile away, tied up my horse, then I crept ever so quietly back down to his house. I settled myself with my back to a tree and waited. Before the moon had completely risen, he had himself a fine curly headed blond woman come knocking on his door. I watched the door close behind them, then with my blood boiling so strong I thought my brain would explode or that I would kill him, I got a better idea. It took some planning. I waited there all day and all night till I watched them leave from the house. Then, when I was sure they were far gone, I snuck in and took his rifle and shotgun, and put them in his woodshed. Then I went to the bee man and got me a gallon of honey to go with a sack of corn and laid me a bear trail of corn straight to his front door.

I got myself ready by the wood line and sat with the patience of a cat watching a bird. When he and his new woman were asleep, I crept around that door like a pooka smearing the honey around the window and door frames and I then I used the corn to bait the biggest black bear I knew." Belle chuckled to herself for a good long while and it made me laugh and smile too just to hear her. We lay in Tom's bed, Tom's wife and his girlfriend, and for a moment I was saved. Then, in Belle's rich deep voice, she began to sing.

"If you're going to love them bad boys,
be ready to cry
If you're going to love those bad boys be ready to cry
If you're going to love them bad boys be ready to cry
But I know you love that glint in their eye.
I once loved me a bad boy so wild and bold,
Once loved me a bad boy, an outlaw I'm told
I loved on that outlaw, a gun by his side,
When he upped and left me, oh Lord I did cry.
I loved me a Trickster so crazy and wild,
You know he could shape shift to the face of a child
He kept me guessing like leaves in the wind
All that he left me was his coyote skin.
I loved me a grifter he gambled all day.
I loved me a grifter my best roll in the hay.

He smiled and he charmed me, my heart sure did sing,
But he ran out of town with my maw's wedding ring.
So, love on those bad boys oh girls if you must,
Love on those bad boys till daybreak turns dust
Give them a nickel and they ask for a dime
But I take me them bad boys every damn time."

When I woke up the next morning, I realized I had fallen asleep and had slept straight through the night for the first time in six long months. I smelled coffee brewing and for a moment I thought Tom was in the kitchen, but then I remembered. Yet, it was a comfort to see Belle there. I hadn't realized how lonely I had been, and I mean heart lonely not person lonely. She looked towards me and smiled, and I realized that in all the years that I knew her, I had only seen her smile at Tom, and then, only rarely. "Come on, get you some coffee." She motioned to me.

"How's your hand?" I said pouring a cup and boy did she make that coffee strong enough to wake the dead.

"Well, I did something to it but I'm not sure what that something is, but busting Bill's nose was worth it. He's had it coming for a while. You know Tom's first wife use to talk about things like fate and karma. I do believe I was Bill Dean's karma."

I plopped down in a chair at the kitchen table across from her wondering what I did to deserve my karma for as I understood it, from snooping through the first wife's journals, it was some type of divine retribution for your mistakes.

Belle had the newspaper and she had brought up the mail, which sat on the table. All of it was addressed to Tom. The mail was still coming as if he were still alive. After I had a cup of coffee and was going for my second, Belle said, "We've to figure out a plan here."

"I know."

"I've been thinking this morning, let's see if we can knock out some of the chores. I noticed some fence down." I nodded, happy to be given direction.

"Then, we will do an assessment of the items. There is no sense on some of the tools rotting. You need to have an auction."

I looked at her horrified.

"I'm not selling Tom's things. I'll need the tools."

"You plan on living here in a museum?"

I was not sure what she exactly meant. Belle observed me steadily. "The only men offering to come up here to help you have ulterior motives. They want you, the farm, his things, or all of it. What are you thinking of trading for your safety and you and your children's livelihood? Have you taken a fancy to anyone?"

I could not go there again. "Nope, don't want me a full-time man ever again, but they are a necessity, a woman needs to get by with them until... until money falls to us from the trees."

She laughed. "Ha, Soldier's Joy."

I grinned at her and I realized I was with a woman who knew exactly what I meant, and it felt so good to be with a kindred spirit and not have to watch my tongue.

"Here are your options. Marry one of these dumb asses or sell everything and go back home before the government does it for you. "

"Home? What home? My parents are dead. How am I going to support myself and my children in town? Besides, we don't know where the park lines are going to be yet. They might bypass us."

"I don't think it's a good idea to wait. Have you gotten any of the letters yet?"

"I haven't opened them." She rolled her eyes, shook her head in exasperation and frowned. "Let me see." I went over to the sideboard and sifted through the mail till I found the ones from the park people and government. "Here." Belle ripped open an envelope and began reading.

Please be advised that the premises occupied or used by you under "Special use Permit must be vacated not later than November 1, 1934. If the premises are under lock and key, we would appreciate the courtesy of mailing the keys to the Shenandoah National Park Office, Front Royal Virginia."

Do you have a permit?" Belle looked up at me as I began stammering in disbelief; I grabbed the letter out of her hand to see for myself.

"I don't know. I think Tom had mentioned something about this a while back. I can't remember. How do I check? It says here if I have a permit, I can apply for another permit to extend the stay. No one from the government has even been up here since Colin ran some man off trying to do an assessment. I think we felt that they weren't going to bother us."

"Well, you're not alone. That's what a lot of people are still counting on but, they have even taken to putting these warning letters in all the newspapers and down by Skyland. It's started."

"What do you mean?"

"Forcing people out and burning some of their homes behind them. There has been this D.C schoolteacher up there round Skyland. She's going around to all the families and asking questions, seeing how they live and writing everything down. Last I heard, she was traveling around with a photographer who has been taking pictures. But they are only going around to the families that are struggling and have been struggling. They are painting a very particular picture of all of us, and it is not pretty." Belle leaned across the table. She stood up and went for her bag. I watched as she rummaged through it and pulled out a folder. Like she was removing a Biblical parchment from its vault, she handed me these newspaper articles.

After I'd read them, I kept blinking to clear my eyes, thinking I could unread it and realizing I had sat in denial too long.

"I have heard some really bad rumors. Real bad. They have even been taking children away from families *for their own good.*"

"No." My head was spinning. I had no control, again, and again and again. I felt like I couldn't breathe, and I started gasping for breath, trying to suck in air and there was no oxygen. Belle looked at me and slapped me. "Quit it! Ya got to keep your wits about you now 'cause it gets worse. There has even been talk about them taking some people away."

"What do you mean?"

"Well, if they think you might be a simpleton or what they call feeble minded or, I have also heard, if you're a woman and not married and have had children out of wedlock, they send you to the Virginia Colony."

"I've heard about it."

"It's a place for retarded people, ya know, people not right in the head. It's an asylum down in Lynchburg. They do experiments on people."

"I can't believe this."

"Believe it."

"Belle, are you sure?"

"You know that *Washington Post* article you just read? What they failed to mention is that two people, the Cave sisters, got carted off to the Colony. Now, I haven't been there when they have carted people off, but I have talked to a lot of the people, to include that surveyor I had been running with. They told me how the government people didn't know their asses from their elbows, and they had not really weighed what to do about the mountaineers because they were thinking about a big East Coast park."

"Dan keeps telling me that the governments got a ten-dollar word for it, eminent domain, but it is wrong no matter what you call it."

"Dan?"

A crooked smile tickled Belle's lip. "The lead surveyor. If you got to find yourself a man, hitch yourself to one that's got some power." She looked me straight on. "And money doesn't hurt."

"What does this eminent domain mean for me?"

"From what I can tell, it's an actual federal law that the government has the right to take anybody's property at any time for public good."

"Are you kidding me?"

"Nope."

"And what's going on with these newspaper articles?"

"If the government paints everybody as backwards because they are," Belle thought for a moment, "well, it's like if they paint everyone like they are backwards and old-timey and just plain simple, then the world thinks that all of the mountain families are like that. They have to be moved off the mountain to be civilized and modernized so they aren't holding the country back from progress." Belle laughed at that comment. "God help me if I ever get that civilized." She took a sip of her coffee. "These reporters fail to mention that there are families with bone china, rugs, books, and nice two-story farmhouses with red geraniums in window boxes. Not everybody is struggling." I sat for a while not even being able to drink my coffee. I finally turned to her.

"I'm going to see Adams."

"And what do you expect he's going to do?"

"I want to get to the bottom of this. I want to see for myself and if I have to, maybe I can strike a deal. He's in thick with all of them and he and Tom did business for over twenty years. He liked Tom. Plus—"

"Plus, what?"

"He was a bit sweet on me."

Belle laughed so hard and loud that I jumped. "Darling, he's sweet on everyone. He will promise you the moon, tell you what you want to hear, sleep with you, then not deliver. And besides, I have heard he has small hands." She grinned at me.

I looked at her and then blushed.

"I'm going anyway." My mind was racing with a million things. I wanted to leave right then. I had to fix this; I wasn't leaving this farm, ever. It was all I had and, more importantly, all I ever wanted, for the mountain and Tom had restored me to who I was meant to be. I felt as if someone was trying to strip me of my religion and my soul.

"Well, if that will make you feel better, go off on your wild goose chase. Take in these mountains one last time before it's all over. But the only thing I have heard that saves you is if you have connections and some money. You can sometimes get yourself out like the Johnson and Hite families are doing down in Beldor. The government surveyed *around* their property. Mary, I hate to tell you this, you have neither connections or money, and you're a woman."

"So are you." I said, as I stood up, grabbing Tom's rifle.

"What are you planning to do with that?"

"I don't know, but I like how it makes me feel."

Chapter 44

For the first time in my life, Belle stayed behind, and I left, riding my horse alone with all that remained of Tom's liquor carrying it through the last of the wild Blue Ridge Mountains. The leaves were turning gold, crimson, vermillion, red, magenta, chartreuse, and the colors of those leaves danced in front of my eyes like a child's kaleidoscope toy. When I laid my head down in the evening, I slept with no tent, no pillow. Finding a pine den, I simply threw down my saddle and covered myself with a blanket, pulling it over my head and wishing I could be swallowed up by the forest.

I rode fast and the bottles clinked like wind chimes reminding me to slow down. I had almost made it to Crescent Rock when my horse threw a shoe rendering him lame. Cursing my luck, he and I began the descent to Nethers where I hoped I could find a farrier. My second worry was having little money. The going was slow as we scrambled over rocks and down trees with me leading him. To prevent any more chipping of his hoof, I tied one of my heaviest shirts around his hoof for padding.

I got to the Nether's post office in late afternoon to find six men and two young girls gathered around the store. A tall man, in slacks, white shirt and photography bags at his feet stood at the corner of the building, his camera on a tripod. He regarded me with no expression but swung his camera to me as I approached closer. "No!" I threw my arms in front of my face as he brought his camera back down.

Walking my way up to the group of people, I yelled to them. "My horse has thrown a shoe. I got it right here in my bag, but I need someone to nail it back on." The crowd was oddly silent and looked, instead, to the tall man who was arranging his camera. My gaze followed theirs and I felt as if I had come uninvited to someone's party. Looking back at the group, I asked again. "Does anyone know someone who can shoe a horse?"

"Who are you?" said one older man stepping forward. He was middle aged and was wearing a beaten old Top Hat, which I thought odd. A dark-haired girl sat on the post office steps with no shoes, and a taller blond girl, her head leaning sadly against the porch post in loose ill-fitting clothes, stared at me dejectedly. The other men remained seated in their washed out and faded clothes.

"I'm Mary Dodson from Hightop."

"What are you doing all the way down here?"

I hesitated a bit. My business was my own, and I didn't like the feeling that I was getting from any of them. It was like nothing I had ever experienced before and I felt, that in some way, this tall photographer was to blame. There was a tension electrifying the air. "I'm checking out the stories I have been hearing about people getting thrown out of their homes. What say you about that?" I looked at them all defiantly. They were all silent, faces blank, staring at me, then the young blond girl spoke up.

"They been moving some people but not us here, 'cause we are cooperating with the picture man. Ain't that right, Uncle John?" She looked up at a gray-haired old timer leaning back on his chair. He remained silent watching me.

"You from the government?" I asked the tall photographer.

"I take pictures, that's what I do. Now, that's a very nice horse you have there. What's a woman like you doing with such a finely bred animal?"

I got it. I looked back at the traitors on the front porch then back at the photographer. "I bet if I had me a mule, you would be snapping photos of me like I was Greta Garbo." Turning my attention to the men on the porch I hollered, "How much is he paying you to pose like that? Huh?" Some of the men looked down at their feet.

"What have you got in those saddlebags, girl?" asked the photographer.

"What's going on out here?" said the postmaster, as he flung open the front door. "Ain't you done with those pictures yet, Rothstein?"

"That's not a name from around here. That's a city name," I said to the photographer.

"Can someone find this girl a horse shoer?" Rothstein said to the men on the porch. He sounded like he wanted to get rid of me.

"Yeah. I can do it. I got my tools back at the house. You can follow me back there," motioned a man in overalls and black fedora.

"All right then." Rothstein called. "Let's get this picture done while we still have the right light."

I watched as Rothstein positioned his subjects, told them not to smile, placed some people in the darkness and some in the light. Two women came up the road to the post office leading a big old brown mule straight up to Rothstein. "Is this what you want mister?" she said. The woman held out to him a black bonnet that was worn probably before the Civil War. I had never seen someone wearing anything like it.

"Yes. That will do."

He rearranged the men on the porch, and the little girls got some coins placed in their hands and scampered away. He instructed one of the men to tie the mule to a post. Then shooting from left to right, I watched as he took pictures of the two women walking up the road, the one woman with an old milk pail and the old timey black bonnet and the other woman with a huge bag of flour slung over her shoulder. The last picture he took was both of the women climbing the stairs to the post office.

"Who are these pictures for?" I asked him.

"I take pictures. That's what I do. "

"Why here? Why now?"

He smiled at me and didn't try to hide the look of contempt in his eyes.

The man who was going to shoe my horse motioned for me to follow him. I led my limping horse away but kept turning back to make sure Rothstein was not trying to steal a picture of me. The man and I walked in silence, and we had probably gone about a mile or so when he led me up a side road coming upon his cabin. A heavyset woman came to the door holding a child and she eyed me with suspicion though I gave her a big smile. The man went around back and returned with a carpenter box. I handed him the shoe. Taking the shoe, he held it on the foundation stone of his house and proceeded to bang it straight where it had twisted. He knocked out the old nails. Pulling up my horse's leg, his big, calloused hand brushed away the dirt and he picked some of the loose chips of hoof away, then rasped it, before lining up the shoe to the hoof. Taking a nail carefully out of his mouth, where he was holding about four of them, he hammered the shoe back on.

"There it is. Should hold on good enough."

I got out my change purse and took out my last two dollars to give him. He looked up at his wife who was watching us closely. He seemed to hesitate a moment. "In better days, I wouldn't be taking it from you but since work has dried up, I'm much obliged."

I nodded and mounted my horse.

"You headed on up to Skyland?"

I looked at the man.

"They got no work up there anymore. Not so many rich folks buying baskets or apples or nothing since the depression. Ain't that right, Wilma?" The woman looked at me not saying a word.

"But I guess there's always a buyer for what you're toting."

I pretended not to hear him. "Thank you for your help." I nodded to him as I pointed my horse up the road.

Making good time now, my horse didn't seem troubled by his new shoe, and I thought about Tom and our last ride together. Tom was even more gone from me now and continuing to fade away. My spirits sank, and I was flooded with many melancholy thoughts from the many dark times of my life. I was getting mean, or as Luanne would say, ornery, and I wondered if too much heartache had permanently changed me; I didn't know what to do about this or about the eminent domain. There was so much I could not control. I was like the leaf falling off a tree, circling, and spiraling slowly downward to the forest floor where decay would take me, and it would all be nothing. These unpleasant thoughts didn't dissipate until seeing the clearing of the Skyland compound and my next challenge; I set my teeth, jaw, and face. I didn't trot into Adams's camp but slowed my horse to a walk trying to get an idea of where things were at for Ole Harry and Skyland.

The first thing I noticed were all the telephone and electric poles and that there seemed to be less guests and a lot more men milling about who looked at me curiously as I came into camp. Dressed in pressed and clean clothes with close-cropped hair and no beards, they were definitely outlanders. I was glad to be arriving in early morning, and I rode my horse straight up to Adams's cabin. As if by a sixth sense, he was already standing on his porch, carrying his bugle with Ole Fletch strapped to his hip. His hand was on his revolver, and he took a menacing jump off his front porch.

"I told you people I'm giving you blankets," he shouted at me.

I tried to make sense of this. I removed Tom's hat and as my hair tumbled out, Adams's gaze widened.

"I know your face," he said to me hesitantly. I was not so sure he did, and I eyed him warily.

"Mr. Adams, it's me, Mary Dodson, Tom Dodson's wife."

His hand left his revolver and he walked over to me on my horse. "My, my, my, to what do I owe the pleasure?"

"Business." I placed my hand on the saddlebags and looked him straight in the eye.

"I see. I see. Where's Tom?"

"Dead."

"Oh, well now, I'm so sorry for your loss. He was the last of his kind, honorable, and I mean that sincerely." Adams's face softened then and, I saw a brief hint of genuineness, but it quickly shifted as he became focused on his own agenda again.

"You come at a prophetic time, Mrs. Dodson. As we speak, I'm awaiting a troop containing the Governor's party coming up from Luray. Your sunshine will be most appreciated. But you must be worn out from your travels. Let's get you settled, and your horse stabled."

I slid down off my horse and did my best to keep up with his quick and easy gait. Adams always seemed to be sprinting. He led me to the far east of Skyland by Kagey Spring, and I was relieved to not be staying at the Trout Cabin. Like a phantom, one of his Negro servants appeared and was sent by Adams to get cabin 24 ready immediately. With subservient nods, the man took off in earnest in the direction of the facilities shed as Adams kept up a light chatter with me. I was trying to register what was spoken and unspoken, but he talked so quickly, always seeming to combine fact with fiction, so it was hard to know where reality and his reality met. When we approached cabin 24, the same servant was waiting and ready to take my horse. Adams helped me with my saddlebags, and it took all three of us to bring all that liquor into the cabin. As the servant left with my horse, I turned to Adams,

"I understand that you are busy, Mr. Adams, with the Governor and all, but I'm hoping to have a few minutes of your time before I head back home."

"Please, call me Henry, and I would be honored to visit with you, Mary, and will do my best to find some time, as well as relieve you of your burdens that you toted across the wilderness." He placed his hand on my saddlebags. "If you are so inclined, I would welcome your company tonight at dinner. My Grimsby has an incredible menu planned. Now, I will let you get settled." And with his little bow, he backed out of the cabin, closing the door behind him.

I immediately stripped off my clothes and got in the bath and I watched in amusements and slight horror as the water turned brown. Wrapped in a towel, I brushed my hair that had grown so long and seemed to get more and more wavy with each child I had born. I looked at my tan face in the mirror. I had this unsettling sense that I didn't know who I was. I was seized with a panic, and I wanted to go back home at any cost. Trying to stem the anxiety, I unpacked the few remaining clean clothes trying to steady myself, but my mind raced. Who was I? Mary, the daughter, flush with small town possibilities? Mary, the wood spirit, only at home in the forest? Mary, the young girl in love, adoringly following Halsom? Mary of the coal camps, cold, thin, and starving? Mary, the young mother clutching children to her breast? Mary, Tom's wife, trying to be good despite it all? Mary the envious, resenting Luanne and Ethel and Belle? Mary alone, stripped naked and without a compass.

I found one of the peach brandy bottles, opened it, and took two large swigs. I sat myself in a chair and tried to control my breathing. I moved to the bed with the beautiful clean white ironed sheets and laid my head on the pillow, knowing honey would never again flow from the rock.

I woke with a start to the sound of shouting voices and for a moment I didn't know where I was. Sitting up, I glanced around the room and sprung out of bed with an urgency. I drew on a clean pair of pants and a chambray shirt with my chemise underneath. Pulling on the high button knee length boots Belle had given to me, I opened the door to a commotion at the North gatehouse. A group of mountain folks were shouting and gesturing at Adams, and I slowly approached to watch.

"I told you Caves that there was no more work up here. I gave you that work clearing the brush in exchange for winter blankets out of the goodness of my heart so you all would be warm this winter." Adams shouted to the group of mountaineers assembled before him.

A shaggy looking man with a three-day growth of beard yelled, "Well, we don't want no blankets. We want cash and we want it now and we ain't leaving until we get it."

I looked at the bedraggled lot of them, women with hard faces, children with empty eyes and angry men. They looked like they were all hurting. I knew how quickly life could get so desperate. Cave hollow had never been a forgiving place under the best of circumstances. The land was poor, rocky and its proximity to Skyland had made all the Caves dependent on Adams for generations; yet they were the best basket makers in the Blue Ridge.

Sam Irwin, Adams's manager, ran up beside Adams and mentioned something. Adams nodded and I turned east and saw what I assumed was the Governor's party halfway across the Skyland field heading our way. This was going to get interesting. Adams rushed into his house and came out with his Colt 45 and blowing his bugle.

"The next bugle notes you will hear will mean charge! Now, damn you, run, run, and don't stop running until you get to the other side of the dining hall where Mr. Irwin will give you blankets." To my astonishment, Adams stormed right at them his gun firing in the air and the whole group of men, woman and children stampeded desperately in all directions. I was ashamed for them, and I didn't like the feeling. Suddenly, Adams noticed me.

"You have to understand, Mary these hollow folks have to be dealt with accordingly. I have had a liberal education from them over the years, and if I gave in just once to their many demands, life would be intolerable at Skyland." Putting his gun and bugle away and smoothing his clothes he turned to greet the Governor's party, who were arriving on the horses that Tom and I had brought up to Skyland when life was still generous.

"Quite the journey to arrive here from Luray, Henry, but a beautiful one. We'll get the CCC boys working on opening up that road for cars soon enough. Right, gentlemen?" Governor Byrd dismounted from his horse and introductions were given all around. I was introduced to many important looking men dressed in heavy tailored wool clothes and wearing brand new riding boots and some with yellow calfskin gloves with fringe. Why, they were dressed up like they were cowboys. They held themselves all plumped out like peacocks.

In addition to the Governor, I was introduced to Arno Camerer, who was the Assistant Director of the National Park Service, members of some conservation committee and Ferdinand Zerkel and a Colonel Smith representing the Southern Appalachian National Park Commission. I was feeling intimidated by these important men even as I realized that I got what I came to Skyland for. God had delivered me to an audience and now that I was delivered, I wasn't sure how or if I was going to find my voice. But I knew I had to and would. I was my mother's daughter, and I had not been through hell to lose strength at this moment in my life.

"Well Gentlemen," Adams slapped Zerkle on the back heartily, "Mr. Carson will get you all settled in the Shenandoah Cabins, which have been made ready for your ease and comfort. I will see you all at the Dining Hall at 6:30 this evening, and tomorrow we will begin our tour of my beloved Stony Man and Big Meadows."

I watched as Carson directed Adams' servants to tending to horses, people, and baggage. The arriving men seemed to be in high spirits and Adams was all kinetic energy from his encounter with the Caves and the Governor's party.

"Come, come, my Mary, let's sample what you have brought and see what terms we can agree on," he said putting his arm around my shoulder and drawing me close.

"I don't need blankets." Adams turned to me, and his look of shock melted to a laugh.

"No, I expect not," he said, clapping his hands and bounding off ahead of me. I had to walk double time just to keep up with him. He waited for me to open the door to cabin 24, and I was hotly embarrassed, hoping people didn't think this was some type of rendezvous, and I looked around to see if anyone was watching. The Governor's party was on the other end of the camp, but I was staying in the cabins with the worker men, and some looked up as we went across the porch.

"Who are those men?"

"Why some of them were sent here by the government, some will be working for me as I get ready to run the concessions for up here."

"What is going on up here, Henry?"

"We're getting ready to undertake the biggest public service on the East Coast." He pushed open the door to the cabin and following behind him I said, "And what is that?"

"Shenandoah National Park. An oasis of land that runs from mountain to mountain all the way from Front Royal to Waynesboro. And Skyland will be at the center of that universe." He was beaming almost maniacally, and beads of sweat glistened on his brow.

"But what's going to happen to all the families that live up here, not just the Caves, but my family in particular? I can't leave my home, Mr. Adams."

"Well, they'll move everyone to civilization down in the valley or resettlement homes with electricity and indoor plumbing. And while I'm sure it has been a struggle since Tom died, you will see how much better you'll be living among..." He paused searching for the words, "polite people."

"I don't want to live in civilization. I want to stay on my farm."

"Well, your children will be better off in town where they can go to school, be around people, get jobs. You'll see. We are in the age of progress, Mary, the age of living in the mountains like backwards frontiersmen and renegades is over. Plus, this Blue Ridge must be preserved for the benefit of the people, for society, for rest and relaxation from all of this American progress. Don't hard working Americans deserve a beautiful Sunday drive in these mountains?"

"We're in the depression. I'm not certain how that's progress."

"All the more reason that people need a break from their troubles with a beautiful drive in our mountains."

"Well, I guess, but can't they drive around me? I won't bother them." I sounded meek, not liking the finality of any of what he just told me.

"Let's see what you brought me, as I have a bulging pocket..." he smiled slyly... "of cash." He winked at me, ignoring my concerns because they were not his concerns, but I couldn't let it go.

"What can I do? Is there someone I can talk to? Tom's farm is all I've got."

"My dear, there in nothing you can do. It's called progress. I'm sure you have heard that you can't stand in the way of progress. This park is progress. Progress for you and me and America."

"America?"

"Do you want to be a part of the hollow folk that are holding America back? These quaint lifestyles are relics from the past. Industrialization is transforming us into a modern society. Cars, electricity, automation, and airplanes. And people will need relaxation and respite from all this industry, and they will come here to Skyland and beautiful Stony Man. Now, let's see what you brought me."

I hesitated a moment and slowly walked to my bags realizing I was caught like a mouse by the cat in more ways than one. I would take whatever he would give me, or I would be hauling all these bottles back home, run the risk of breaking some, run the risk of highwaymen, run the risk of having to peddle it, run the risk of having no money. I had no agency.

"I have peach brandy, mayapple wine, grape wine and shine."

"Let's start with the wine."

I uncorked bottle after bottle and he smelled, swirled, and tasted it like he was at a fine restaurant, and I wondered if his show was for me or himself. "I will have my man come by and retrieve this so we can enjoy these libations tonight."

He was getting ready to walk out the door and he had not mentioned compensation. I followed him not sure what I should do or say.

"Mr. Adams?"

"Why, Mary, we are old friends, you should call me Henry." And with that he put his hand to the side of my face cradling it. His smile was so sweet and genuine, his face so boyish and charming, I felt myself soften.

"Henry," I said stepping back from him. "What about recompense?"

"Of course, of course. What type of man do you think I am, Mary? I deal fairly with all the mountain folk, and I have a very soft spot for women...especially you."

"How so?"

He looked at me taken aback. Regaining his composure and smiling like a fox, he slid out the door. "Maybe I'll show you before the night's out." And with a wink he was gone.

Chapter 45

The huge fireplace in the dining hall was roaring with half a cord of logs and near the kitchen entrance there was an American Flag which hung from the rafters and nearly touched the floor. I was the only woman seated around the table, and I did my best to not appear small around all these city men. I kept my chin up and shoulder's back, but my red chapped hands remained in my lap, hiding them. Adams served what he called Page County relishes with names I never heard of like Ant-Neurasthenia grass, snake root, mountain run cress and Irish Plums. There was trout, potatoes, Pippinmash, cabbage slaw, a shellfish salad and my husband's wine. After the main course had been served, a large group of colored singers exited the kitchen shouting and clapping their hands singing in camp style, *Little Children, Get Onboard.* Circling the room, they formed a crescent at the fireplace and sang more spirituals in beautiful harmonies. With their faces shining with perspiration, forcibly popping their eyes, hands clapping, and some of them jumping up and down, they were a spectacle as they began shouting, "Glory to the highest for the Park and Hurray for the Governor."

Adams then called for the electric lights to be dimmed and said, "Mammy, show them what've got." His large female cook jumped from behind the flag shouting, "Whoopee," and singing at the top of her voice, "when I feel the spirit moving, moving in my heart, I pray." And she led a line of colored kitchen servants to the governor as she carried a huge glistening chocolate cake. She bowed and placed it before him, and he was laughing in delight. I watched this with a mixture of horror, disbelief, and the increasing realization I was in the court of the Red Queen from Alice in Wonderland. It was a spectacle of discordance.

When the hoopla had died down and we commenced eating our cake, which was the best I had ever tasted, as the cake was moist and the chocolate buttercream frosting was smooth and creamy, I briefly forgot my troubles and wanted more. The governor turned to Adams wiping the chocolate from his face. "So, Henry, tell me what you have planned for us tomorrow, and I would like another piece of that cake."

"After a hearty breakfast at 8, governor, we will commence an inspection of my 6,000 acres, for which I will accept any price the commission will set with rights to the concessions, and you will see a fine sampling of our mountain land and beautiful scenery as well as local color, I might add." Adams made a great show of pulling out an elaborately drawn map, which he placed on the cleared table. All the men bent over it as if they knew what they were seeing.

"We'll come down through Red Gate and to the Big Meadows section of our Park." He traced his finger across the map. "We'll then head to Peterson Hollow and the Peterson school house that I had built for the children of the hollow folk and meet Miriam Sizer, a teacher and social scientist from Washington, who has been working with the local population. If time allows, we will then head over to Hoover's Camp though he is, as I'm sure you know, currently in Washington. I'll get you to the best and most beautiful scenic overlooks, which our cartographers seem to believe will make wonderful vistas for the motoring cars. This is a public service for all Americans to share in the beauty of our mountain paradise."

"Splendid, Henry. Just being in this mountain air makes me feel invigorated."

"Maybe it's just my husband's wine," I said in a loud voice, drawing everyone's gaze as the table went immediately quiet.

"Gentlemen," said Adams recovering the moment, "may I introduce to you, Mrs. Mary Dodson, who has brought you these fine libations this evening." I overheard a man whisper and chuckle, "I thought that was his girlfriend."

"Maybe so," said the other man, taking a drink and smiling at me.

"Now, Adams," said Mr. Crammer, redirecting the conversation away from me, how many of these mountain folks do we have to deal with?"

"Oh, not many. They are scattered like the wind in these mountains and are of no account and are looking forward to moving. You'll get an opportunity to visit with some of them on our tour. Without visiting these people in their homes, one cannot begin to conceive of their poverty and wretchedness. Moving them off this mountain is for their own good."

The men nodded accordingly and by watching these powerful men, I immediately realized how it was done, and it was what I saw the next day that made me realize what I, and all of us here, were up against.

True to his word, Adams took us on a beautiful scenic ride the next morning regaling his party with tales and adventures, sometimes talking of himself in third person. As we passed through a hemlock grove, he began shouting so all could hear, standing up in his stirrups to face his audience. "You know, when the engineers were here late last winter, I came up from my apartment in Washington to help them flag some of the pegs. It was a cold and dreary Saturday afternoon, and I went alone as the men would not be back till Monday morning. Setting off at about three in the afternoon, Ole Harry left with his brown wool suit, and it took considerable effort to locate those pegs and by the time I reached the Hughes River, a snowstorm was blowing. I had just descended into the rockiest place in the whole park, Free State Hollow, and I knew I was surrounded by dangerous cliffs. I had no flashlight and suddenly, Ole Harry was surrounded by a whiteout. Should he go down the mountain and try to find the road that was being built, lose his way, and freeze to death? *No!* Should he try to navigate the upper section of the Hughes River, and break his neck on the cliffs? *No!* Finally, he figured to go up the mountain, yes, up the mountain because that way there was a level plateau and a wagon road leading to Skyland from the peak. The wind was blowing very cold, and Oh God, what a trip."

The squirrels and birds scattered as we rode passed them. I noticed a deer out of the corner of my eye that froze and stared at the party passing through its home. The men didn't notice, neither did Adams as his voice droned on and on.

"Poor Henry struggled up that mountain for over an hour as twilight came and sweat rolling down his body so that he had to pull open his flannel shirt and revealing half his chest to the frozen air. *Up, up...up.* he crawled with every few steps, his legs driving down into holes that had been covered with snow and brush, his heart beating so rapidly that he could not go on for longer than ten minutes at a time without resting. It was dark by the time he stumbled into the field cabin at Skyland. Rousing my cook, I called for hot broth, a warm toddy, and after a deep sleep, I woke to the rising sun and good health."

The men cheered.

"I hope we'll not have such an adventure today," stated one of the men.

"Henry, these mountains suit you. How lucky we are to have you as our guide and host," said Governor Byrd.

I couldn't help but roll my eyes. Adams smiled, very pleased with himself. He was a cunning court jester. After taking the men to some of the vistas that looked out and down to the west and then east side of the mountains we broke for lunch. As the party rode a trail east, Adams said, "Now, we'll have the social science bit of our tour gentleman." Adams was in the lead, and I was taking up the tail end of this trouping party, as we descended down into Cave Hollow. Abruptly, he stopped, as if he remembered something. We were all in a line, nose to tail. Adams stood up in his stirrups and turned back to the line of men and me. He held up his hand as if he were a preacher laying on a blessing.

"Gentlemen, I have employed many of the mountain people over the years and those of Cave Hollow have depended on us at Skyland since the late 1800s for their livelihood. We gave them market for their baskets, payment for fruits and berries and employment cutting wood, working the gardens, clearing the trails. But we also have had to chase them off from begging as times have grown hard. Now, these hollow folk in particular and *all* hollow folk, in general, are probably no different than any other Anglo-Saxon, but these mountaineers are ignorant, usually have some sort of chip on their shoulder, can be possessed of bulky strength, cantankerous, simple, prone to settling their matters over a fight, and usually with guns. We are getting ready to meet a few of them right now. But I caution you gentlemen, try not to be too shocked by what you see."

Our party rode over Indian creek and Adams signaled our approach by yodeling. We then came upon a clearing and a dilapidated one-room cabin with one window, two small outbuildings leaning to the left and dirt for a yard. Two children peeped out of the bushes, and they held out dirty hands, crying, "Mon, mon." It took me a minute to realize they were asking for money. Of all the places to go. Well, he'd made his point, I suppose. If he could get everyone thinking that we all were like this, people would think they were moving us off the mountain for our own good. I was so angry I started to give myself a tension headache. About then a man about 70 and his wife came on to the porch to greet us. He seemed as if he were ailing as his hands were trembling and shaking and he had to take hold of the porch railing to steady himself.

"Halloo, Basil," said Henry

"Howdy."

"Basil, I will hand you a dollar if you tell the Governor the story of how and why you killed Clark Johnson."

Basil's eyes lit up and he hobbled into the house and returned carrying an old gun. Then in a trembling, squeaky and sometimes husky voice Basil began his story. "Well, that Clark, and some of those Peterson boys, came on up here all likkered up and hollering for my two girls to come on out, and not being able to get them to come out, they went on over to the orchard and passed out. Why, they woke up later that night and came back a hooting and hollering again and I was sure mad by this time so I got out of my bed carrying my Army musket, and when that Peterson boy would not leave, I gave him a blast of shot between the legs. Now, that sent him hollering and a running. Well, I went on back to bed, and next thing I know I hear the Clark boy breaking down my fence and threatening me. So, I got me out of bed again and slid this gun through the window and I warned him if he didn't leave why I would shoot him too. That damn boy ripped open his shirt, stuck out his chest and hollered, 'Shoot then, goddamn you, shoot.' So, I did." With that Basil spit over the side of his porch railing. "He died right over by that spring." And he pointed to it.

The men shifted uncomfortably in their saddles, and we all looked up to the spring imagining the dead and dying man lying there.

"My, my, my, that is quite a story. I'm not quite sure what to say," said the governor wide-eyed and a bit taken aback.

"I've got to tell you, Governor," Adams said, "after having over 50 bird shot picked from his nether regions, the Peterson boy turned over a new leaf. I've employed him at Skyland and he's one of my best workers and has never touched a drop of liquor since."

Adams rode over to the side of the porch and handed Basil his money. Upon seeing Adams reach into his pocket, the two children, who resembled the silhouettes of famine and ignorance, held out their hands again calling, "Mon, mon." One of the men from the party reached into his pocket and threw some coins at them. The other children dove out of the bushes like chickens after corn, and I turned my head and looked to the sky, not wanting to see this.

Leaving this gothic scene, we turned our horses down the Hughes River and over to the Peterson schoolhouse where we found two fat women, one old and one not so old, standing in the schoolhouse yard to greet us. They were dressed in black skirts that came to just above the ankles, button down blouses, stockings, and dark shoes. Their hair was short and fashionable, revealing plump faces that melted into their necks. Thin strands of pearls lay buried in their neck creases. Spectacles sat on the tips of their noses. They looked as if they never smiled.

"Hullo, Miss Sizer, Miss Weakly, who is no relation, by the way to the hollow Weakleys," shouted Adams.

"We've been waiting for your party and have some fresh lemonade and sugar cookies. Please tie up your horses by the outhouse and stretch your legs," said the older dark-haired woman.

As I rode up last, I saw the older woman suddenly squint in my direction and she crossed her arms in front of her large breasts. I dismounted and smoothed my hair. I walked over to the water pump and after four pumps cold mountain water gushed from the spicket. I splashed my face and cupped my hands to drink the sweet water. I dried my face on my shirt sleeve. Walking over to the schoolhouse, I joined the party that was already inside. On the teacher's desk were laid out the glasses, cookies and lemonade, and the men were eagerly crowded around the table for refreshments as the woman held out glasses and plates of cookies for them. I was offered neither, but I waited for everyone to be served and got myself my own plate and drink anyway. The older fatter lady motioned or us to take our seats on the wooden benches.

"Gentlemen," began Adams orating at the front of the classroom, "I would like you to meet two highly esteemed women who have labored long and hard to instill education and learning among these hills and hollows. This here is Susan Weakly, schoolteacher and Miss Miriam Sizer who has worked in these hills as a social scientist." He then introduced everyone in our trooping party by name except me.

After pleasantries were exchanged, the older woman, who appeared to be in charge, stood up in front of the men, who were seated in the benches at the front of the class. I took a seat in the back of the classroom close to the door, which they had left open. I turned and two young boys were peeking their heads in through the open door beside me. I smiled at them, and quietly they slid inside and sat on the bench next to me.

Miss Sizer walked to the front of the classroom with authority.

"For two months this summer I taught a vacation school at Old Rag, Virginia, near Skyland. Here I studied both educational and sociological conditions," began Sizer. "To show that my education, professional experience, and background have been such as should enable me to form reasonably accurate judgments, and to reach fairly intelligent conclusions, I'll give you a brief summary of my preparation and professional career. In 1924 I received from the College of William and Mary the B. A. degree; in 1928 I received from the University of Virginia the Master of Arts degree. While teaching in the Norfolk City Elementary School, I conducted classes for the adult foreigners in an

Americanization school. I taught in the Academic School at the Naval Base, near Norfolk. This was work with the illiterate and near-illiterate sailors. I might add, in both instances, I found the adults interested and teachable, unlike the inhabitants of these mountains. I have been working for the Washington School of Science both as a teacher and social scientist for the last two years, and currently have based many of my field studies of the families in and around Skyland."

Beads of perspiration formed on Sizer's temples and began to run down her face, trailing down her neck and disappearing into her bulbous bosom. Despite the open door, it was hot and stuffy in the classroom, and I yawned loudly. The little boys next to me giggled.

"This one-room school has been in session three months last winter and two months this summer, making a total of five months. With approximately seventy children of school age, thirty-seven were enrolled with an average daily attendance of nineteen. Some of the causes of non-attendance are conditions that make it unwise to enforce the compulsory education law. For example, the ignorance of the parents renders them practically non-responsible for their children's training and education; Also, the idleness of the men throws the burden of labor on the women and children, who then cannot leave their chores to come to school. The children have no sense of citizenship; there is no school flag, and neither children nor parents, until this summer, had ever heard *America* sung, until we introduced it."

The men clucked and grumbled among themselves while making faces of horror and disbelief.

Mr. Zerkle spoke up. "Miss Sizer, can you tell our Washington friends a bit about the background of these mountaineers?"

"Certainly. Descendants of the original settlers of the Americas, cut off from civilization by environment, neglected by the State, the population of the proposed park area, several thousand in number, represents a static social order. These mountaineers have aptly been called 'our contemporary ancestors.' They are a modern Robinson Crusoes, but without his knowledge of civilization. Steeped in ignorance, wrapped in self-satisfaction and complacency, possessed of little or no ambition, little comprehension of law, or respect for law, these people present a problem that demands and challenges the attention of thinking men and women." Looking to the back of the classroom Sizer gestured to the two children sitting with me. "Come here boys."

Sheepishly the children shrank down where they were sitting and I could see the hesitation and fear, yet their need to follow what they were told.

I whispered to them, "It's okay," patting the one closest to me on the knee.

Barefoot, they padded to the front of the room and stood in front of the gentlemen.

"Here are two specimens from one of our mountain families. Miss Weakly, I will let you explain. The younger woman stepped in front of the men hands clasped in front of her as if she was going to sing.

"While they have attended our small school sporadically, I'll let them demonstrate their abilities." Handing a piece of chalk to the taller of the boys, with a forced smile she said, "Now, show the men how you can write your name."

The young boy's lips trembled. The younger of the two boys spoke up. "If I write my name, can I then get cookies?"

All the men laughed and Miss Weakly pursed her lips holding the chalk out to the boy, and it seemed to float in the air as if in an abstract painting and just when I thought the boy would never reach for it, he gingerly took the chalk and walked to the board. Time passed slowly as he stood facing the board. I wanted to jump up and run and shield his little body from all this. He looked so small and vulnerable. Suddenly, he threw the chalk to the ground, spun, and ran out the door.

The younger boy picked up the chalk. "Here, I can write my name."

Miss Weakly jumped in front of him. "I know you can, Give me that." The boy smiled and pushing a shock of hair out of his eyes, went up to the table, reached out a hand with nails as black as tar, put one cookie in his mouth and stuffed two cookies in his pocket and sauntered out of the classroom.

"I would say, this is an excellent example of what we are dealing with in these mountains. From inbreeding and lack of connection to the outside world, we have a solid community of half-wits."

"Good God!" said Mr. Carson. "I cannot believe this Dogpatch place that we have seen today."

"If the Government can spend its wealth to save a race of Chestnut trees, can it not spend its wealth to save a race of man?" said Sizer dramatically.

"Miriam, tell them about that child," said Adams.

"Ah, yes. I was doing a survey in Cave Hollow, and I came across a family of six that had been subsisting on cabbage and potatoes. The woman of the household, and I say woman, instead of wife, because many of these mountaineers fail to marry, brought out to me her youngest child that I thought had to be about nine months old. To my horror, she told me that child was two years old, and I realized the child had been stunted due to malnutrition. One only expects to see these things in darkest Africa. We," she motioned to Adams, "did what we could, and I am happy to report that the child is doing well and is in much more favorable circumstances away from this family. I might add, that in addition to surveying these people, I did do my best to educate the women about family planning and the importance of education, which brings me to my next point."

Mr. Zerkle looked at the men present and spoke. "I simply can't understand why they have such big families when they cannot afford to feed them as well as put their lives at such risk by bearing so many without proper medical conditions."

"It is my claim that these women do not feel the same level of pain and discomfort as their more cultivated brethren. It is my firmest belief that we must do our part to preserve the moral fabric of America with thoughtful social engineering to protect ourselves, and others, from this horror. Our institutions like the Virginia Colony and the Staunton School are fine examples. Why, I received a letter last week from one of the doctors there..." Sizer, went to her desk and removed a manila folder taking out a letter that she had placed inside and, putting her spectacles on, she cleared her throat to read it.

"We saw in the clinic this week, Miss Cave, and found her to be well down to the imbecile level. Certainly, there is every reason in the world why this woman should be sterilized. We found no physical defect except some impetigo. However, as the husband and wife are both minors and the wife obviously feeble minded, we cannot get the gynecology department to sterilize her. So, we will have to get her committed to the Colony. We will just need some support letters of which you are familiar. I think it is too bad that she cannot be sterilized without all this trouble. Thank you for sending her down and we will be glad to help in any way we can." Sizer seemed pleased with herself, and she passed the letter around for the men to see.

Zerkle stood up facing the men.

"Time will show that this park will be one of the greatest steps forward for mankind. Plecker is one of the foremost thinkers on this." I was not sure if he was referring to the park or commenting on Miss Sizer's plan of survival of the fittest.

The Governor spoke next. "Do these people even comprehend that a park is being developed and they have to move?"

Sizer pushed into the men's conversation. "The attitude of the people toward the park acquisition by the Federal Government is one of passive acceptance. They are known for a fatalistic approach to their conditions. Yet, this is the uprooting of a whole population permanently attached to the soil, an event unique in the history of America. It means the scattering of a people who have a primitive comprehension of what law means and who have little sense of the responsibilities of citizenship. It means the casting abroad of men largely a law unto themselves, a majority of whom do not have the habit of work, who gamble and above all, who know how to make alcoholic liquors. It would seem that if these people are sent out without some preparation, a majority may become either paupers or criminals."

"Henry?" The governor looked alarmingly to Adams, who was getting increasingly red in the face, and who was not pleased about the direction of the conversation.

"Gentlemen, Miss Sizer is very concerned for the welfare of her wards, as she should be, but I assure you, while some of the population is indigent, the majority are looking forward to resettlement and compensation for their farms, and I'm confident that they will become law abiding citizens and enjoy the modernity that civilization will bring them. Plus, their children can be forced to attend school, thus stopping this vicious cycle of poverty and ignorance."

Sizer jumped back into the conversation, apparently not liking being interrupted. "Some of these mountaineers have been so isolated from the world that they still speak in an Elizabethan English, which me and Miss Weakly have taken the trouble to write down, so fascinated are we by these social idioms. I do agree with Henry that the resettlement and sterilization of these lost and wayward families is for their own good and the good of America's future." As she said this, she passed around the plate of cookies.

I stood up slowly, as I was trembling, shaking and little dots were appearing before my eyes. I wondered if I was having a stroke. I put my hand on the wall behind me to steady myself. My throat was as dry as if I had ridden for days without water. Slowly, I moved, towards the front of the one-room schoolhouse and towards Miriam Sizer, who slowly realized I was coming for her. With her plate of cookies in hand she backed up her fat frame till her back was on the chalk board and her plate of cookies shielded her chest as the cookies dropped to the floor scattering at her feet. Her round black eyes were as wide and unseeing as doll's eyes and got rounder and rounder as I walked with a now unwavering and purposeful gait towards her. All the men shifted in their seats and turned around to look at me approaching.

Abruptly, Adams jumped in front of me and grabbed me and gave me a good shake, spinning me around. "Mary, why don't you see to our horses. We have a fine meal waiting for us at Skyland tonight, Gentlemen."

"Oh, no," I said smiling and shaking my head trying to pull myself free so I could get at Sizer.

"Here, let me help you." And with that, Adams grabbed me firmly about my waist and shoved me in front of his body as he grabbed the back of my shirt and pushing me ahead, he escorted me out of the school, off the porch and then gave me a final push, and I went flying and falling onto the ground.

"What do you think you're doing?" I shouted at him on my hands and knees.

"What do you think *you're* doing my dear girl? Do you want them to have more proof that you mountaineers are common?"

I scrambled to my feet.

"How dare you?" I lunged at Adams.

He s raised his fists and sent a punch flying towards me. "How dare *you,* you stupid girl. I suggest that you get yourself home." He threw a handful of money at me as he turned and walked back to the schoolhouse. I looked at the coins and dollar bills scattered in the dirt, and I was forced to get on my hands and knees to pick it up as the men, Sizer and Weakly all watched me from the front porch.

"It's not true. What she is saying is not true. Gentlemen, don't believe any of them. Adams is a swindler, and that fat old woman is a liar." I yelled at the direction of the schoolhouse.

Adams stepped back of the porch reaching for his gun.

"Henry!" shouted one of the men.

"I know how to handle them," he said to the group assembled now on the schoolhouse steps. "Mary!" he turned addressing me as I was now standing and looking at him square on. "Get yourself home. You are not fit for our company." Turning to the men. "See, gentlemen, even the women are without propriety." Putting his gun back into its holster he ushered the men back inside the schoolhouse. Sizer shot me a look of contempt as she slammed the school door shut.

Hour after hour I rode home only pausing to sleep when the moon was high and, before daybreak, I was saddled and mounted again. Even as the sun shone, my heart felt as if it were as dark as two a.m. when all is silent and there is no succor. The deer, turkeys, bears, squirrels, bobcats, and owls were strangers to me now and I passed them as if they were monuments. As I began the ascent to Hightop, my horse picked up speed, as was his way, for he too knew we were close to safety and rest. To my delight, my children were home, and they came onto the front porch when they heard my horse whinny to his pasture mates.

"Mommy," yelled Colin who bounded off the porch. Evie's face lit up and Ben jumped up a down.

My horse still had enough energy to spook at this, but I did a flying dismount, dropped the reins, and ran towards them as if my life depended on it, and it did. Sweeping them into my arms, I covered them all with kisses as tears ran down my face.

Colin said, "Mommy, we have to stay together. Uncle John and Aunt Ethel's house was fun, but we all wanted to come home, except maybe Evie. They spoiled her."

"I promise. We stay together from now on."

He looked at me as seriously as I'd ever seen him. "And I don't like town all that much, too many people and cars. You know the first thing I did when I got home? I went squirrel hunting. I even made myself up a new recipe for frying them."

Evie hugged me tight then pulled away to talk to me. "Oh, Mama, I'm so glad you're home, but did you know they're building a department store for new clothes right in town? And Aunt Ethel said she is going to take me back-to-school shopping."

I smiled at her as I scooped up Benjamin and swung him around.

We walked, hand in hand, to the house, and I was never happier than at that moment in time, and I decided that we would be safe here and they might never find us. For one moment, I forgot about how much food we had or didn't have, if the animals were alive or healthy, if there was enough hay and wood. Luanne came onto the porch.

"Well, hello stranger. How much you get?" she said with a smile as she dried her hands with a dishcloth. My heart was about to burst on seeing her. I climbed the porch stairs carrying my youngest.

"Mama, you left your horse in the field," said Colin.

"He's fine. I'll get him in a minute." I put Benjamin down.

"Why don't you do that for your mother?" said Luanne to Colin. Colin frowned but did as he was told.

"Twelve dollars and 36 cents."

"What?" Luanne handed me a glass of cold water her face incredulous at my being paid less than half of what Tom's liqueur had been worth.

"And Adams threw it at my feet which I expect is what they are going to do when they pay us for our land."

"Thank God Tom is not alive, and I expect he's rolling over in his grave. Oh, Mary," said Luanne holding me close. "What are you going to do? And I suppose it does no good to say I told you so."

"I'm not giving up."

"No, I mean about getting through the winter? That's not near enough."

"I'm going to have to start selling Tom's things off, but I don't want to think of it now."

"Asa is coming up tomorrow. He and Colin are going to do wood."

I nodded. "Thank you. I appreciate his help and I'm sorry I need it."

"We're family, Mary." Luanne went to the cupboard and handed me three envelopes, all from the government. When I didn't take them from her hand, she put them on the kitchen table.

"Thank God Tom is not alive to see these days," she said again. I looked at my beloved sister. "But I am."

Later that night, I had just laid down in the bed when Colin and Evie, who was holding Benjamin, appeared by my bedside. "Mommy, can we sleep with you?"

I pulled back the covers and nodded as they piled into the bed and so began our new sleeping arrangements. I was surprised at how much their warm bodies comforted me. Pulling the quilts around us all, I savored this moment and I willed myself to not fall asleep so I could keep tomorrow at bay.

Chapter 46

In early winter, the auctioneer came from Ruckersville. He assured me he would advertise as far away as Charlottesville and as close as Elkton. I debated about Elkton because I was embarrassed. By the day before the sale, I was so heartsick I didn't care. All week I had worked with Colin to round up the cattle, hogs and horses and I did my best to clean the equipment, harnesses, and trappings. Running my fingers over Tom's leather-working tools I thought about how his hands had touched them and how he had crafted so many bridles, bags, mended shoes, and belts, but when I saw his reading glasses, still sitting on the bench, I fell to my knees crying. Quickly, I wrapped up his gear and his little glasses and held them to my chest as if they were precious jewels. Running out from the barn as if it was on fire, I bounded into the house and gently placed them in my chifforobe.

I explained, as best I could, to the children about what was going on and why we were in this predicament. Benjamin was too little to care, Evie was hoping that this meant we were moving to town, and Colin bore his sorrow in his heart for the rest of his life and never got over it. The morning of the sale, Colin took Tom's gun and went off in the woods hunting.

"Mama, do you need me to bear witness to this with you? I can stay and will stay if you want me to," Colin said.

"No, my dear boy. Stay as far away as you can today. This is a black day; I don't plan on coming out of the house myself. I'm sorry Colin." Somehow, I felt responsible for all of this, as if my bad luck had brought bad luck to this entire mountain.

"It'll be all right, Mom. At least we get to stay on the mountain, and I will be old enough to get a job soon."

"And remember we will still have our milk cow, Bella, and the two horses and our two hogs," Benjamin said.

Colin feigned a smile and went out the back door. As I listened to it slam, I was gripped by an awful thought. I pushed it out of my mind quickly and stubbornly and said, "No," to myself and the universe as I looked at Colin's back trudging up the mountain and all I could see was the metal of that gun.

"Colin," I shouted. "Colin, are you...." my voice trailed off as my throat closed.

"I'm fine, Mom." And he turned his back to me and disappeared into the woods.

Tom's hound started barking and I knew the auctioneer had arrived with his men. I listened for his footsteps on the porch and soon he was knocking on my door. Stealing myself, I opened it.

"Mrs. Dodson? I just have a few things to go over with you before we get started." He spit tobacco juice over the porch rail and came in. I tried to not look past him at the people already arriving and I closed the door quickly. Evie walked in and eyed the fat auctioneer suspiciously.

"You the one selling my daddy's things?" she said with her hands on her hips. I shot her a look, but Evie didn't care. The auctioneer ignored her.

"You sure you don't want to let go of some of these items in your house?"

"I told you no. Just the livestock that is penned up and the farm tools and equipment."

"This paper states we get 30% of the sale and we will cut you a check when the sale is completed."

"Can I see those papers?" Evie asked with authority pulling them from the auctioneer's hands.

"They say they have a right to more percent if they have no sales." Evie looked at me and back to the auctioneer.

I nodded and hoped that they wouldn't steal from a widow woman with three children as I signed and dated the document.

"We got to do what we got to do now, Evie."

Evie shook her head as if she were scolding me.

"Well, looks like we are ready to begin." He tipped his hat, and I opened the door to usher him out when I caught a glimpse of his men leading out Tom's beautiful, stately, and fine-looking draft horses Stonewall and Lee, and I slammed the door with such force I thought I had broken it. Leaning my back against the door my eyes filled with tears again. To stop the tears, I slapped myself in the face. Evie came up and regarded me.

"What wrong with you, Mom? They're just horses." If I had not known it before, I knew it then, and I was immediately thankful that Evelyn was nothing like me.

"I suppose you're right. Well, I decided I can't stay here all day hiding. Let's go for a walk and find some persimmons and acorns and we'll have us a persimmon pudding tonight."

"I'll go get Ben. He's in the dining room coloring on the wall with the crayons Aunt Ethel gave him."

Not even caring about that, I went to my cupboard and got out a bottle of Tom's wine to carry to the spring to cool then thinking better or it, I grabbed two.

We ate in silence that night. Colin came home at dark with a turkey hanging from his shoulder. Ben immediately went to work helping his brother clean it and they all worked together to make Ben a turkey feather headdress, so he looked like an Indian chief. I watched them, rocking in my chair by the stove, sipping my wine and plotting my next move.

Chapter 47
Harrisonburg Virginia, East Market Street, 1934

With the money from the sale, I hired a car and retained a lawyer in Harrisonburg confident that with money, I could fix anything. I had not been to Harrisonburg since that day I met Halsom, ending my life as I had known it, embarking on a life of horror and yet, beauty. What a long road it had been.

Remembering my own mother, I laid out and ironed my best clothes for my children and myself and we walked down Hightop mountain carrying our polished and clean dress shoes. The car was waiting for us like I had arranged, and we arrived like a proper family at the lawyer's office. My children followed me like ducklings, all four of us walked to the courtyard of the brick house. I held Evie's hand for strength as we walked up onto the porch. Colin tried to keep a tight hold on Ben who had already tried darting into the street several times.

"Who's this man, Mom?" asked Colin.

"He's someone that might be able to help us keep our land."

"He's a lawyer, Colin. He reads things carefully and tells people what to do," said Evie as we rang a bell at the front door.

The office smelled of leather and it was clean as we were ushered into the brick building by a middle-aged woman as crisp as a piece of new paper. The dark wood shone, and the secretary peered over at us from behind her glasses. "Can I help you?"

"I'm here to see Mr. Hayjack. I have an appointment. I'm Mrs. Mary Dodson."

The secretary forced a smile.

"I will see if he's available."

"I have an appointment," I said to her back.

She disappeared up the stairs. Evie was looking at the books on the shelves, peering around the corner of the waiting room and into the other law offices of Mr. Hayjack's partners.

"What's that?" she asked, pointing to the framed pictures.

"Those are diplomas. Those are the lawyer's law degrees. They have been to big universities to study."

"Who's that?" she pointed to another picture of a man standing beside a pleasant looking woman seated in a chair, holding a baby and a young boy in a sailor suit seated with his dog on her lap.

"That's Mr. Hayjack and his family." She regarded the picture.

"I bet Mr. Hayjack's family doesn't worry about losing their house." I looked at my solemn daughter.

"Shhh. That's because they made good choices, remember that."

"How much do lawyers make?" said Evie looking around the office with its gleaming new furniture and polished wood floors.

"Oh about $3. 00 an hour." I said, not wanting to remind myself of this.

"That's a lot of dolls."

The secretary was headed back down the stairs and Mr. Hayjack followed behind. Ben was jumping up and down on the couch and I grabbed him and gave him to Colin. I whispered, "Keep your brother from breaking anything and Evie, you help him. If you all stay quiet and don't cause trouble, I will buy you all something from the five and dime."

"Hello, Mrs. Dodson. How are you doing today?" He said, holding out his hand to me.

"Thank you, and I'm fine." I wasn't fine but I shook his hand firmly anyway.

As he led me up the stairs, he said in his smooth Virginia highborn lilt, "That's a very flattering dress you are wearing. Very becoming." This was true, of course. If you had looked at my family and me, seated in that lawyer's office, there would have been no resemblance to what Sizer and Adams had described, but the lawyer knew nothing of that. He was a Southern gentleman, gentle, gracious, polite and deferring.

He motioned for me to go inside his office. I sat on the chair facing his desk, and then Evie was at my side, seating herself on another leather couch. She smiled politely and placed her hands in her lap, crossing her legs at the ankle and regarded our lawyer. I looked around the room at the heavy mahogany furniture, tall brass lamps and numerous leather-bound books. There was a framed drawing that caught my eye. It was a sketch of a lawyer striding out of a courtroom, his nose pointed in the air, and he was followed by a weeping woman, her head in her hands and holding a handkerchief to her face. The caption said, *Well, madam, at least you had the pleasure of hearing my argument.*

"Mrs. Dodson, I had a chance to look everything over. Unfortunately, we have a few problems against us. First, I was unable to find any record of your marriage to Mr. Dodson in the Greene County or Madison record books." I got ready to protest, but he held up his hand silencing me.

"I know what you told me about the minister and the ceremony at the house and what I'm thinking is the minster forgot to file the record or perhaps it was lost. Now, that is not consequential to this matter as a whole, because I could prove a common law marriage for you and Mr. Dodson. The bigger issue is legally, you are seen as a tenant by the Shenandoah National Park Association and therefore you have no legal rights to the property. I may be able to do something with the State Commission for Conservation and Development, and get a special use permit, but even so, you must be vacated no later than November 1, 1934."

"Now, according to the paperwork I reviewed, Mr. Dodson owned two hundred and sixty acres that comprised land on both Greene and Rockingham County. The Database of Land Records that was commissioned by the State and Federal Government shows 50 acres under cultivation while the rest remain unimproved. Listed here are a two-story frame farmhouse plus two barns and numerous small outbuildings."

He was reading to me above his spectacles which were sitting on the tip of his button nose. He thumbed through some papers. He wasn't completely impervious to my plight, but my plight was not his plight or the plight of his beautiful family in the photograph on his desk.

"Yes. I suppose that sounds correct," I said, but it didn't sound correct. It didn't mention that the house had two chimneys laid by Tom's father and because Tom and Tom's father were such exacting men, the whole house was as plumb as could be and airtight. Or, that he had built a porch in front and behind the house and a beautiful river rock fireplace. The Database of Land Records didn't mention the springs or fruit trees or even my flower garden.

"Let's see, they have appraised this at $1,442. That is a fair price for that mountain land. I have heard that many are not getting that much." He stared at me to make his point.

"Of course, they are willing to move some of the residents to the resettlement homes. They have some available houses in Elkton, Grottoes, and Ida over in Page County. I expect if we petition, we might be able to get you into such a home, but they will be looking at your ability to maintain and make payments on such a home before they allow you to move into it. But it will have electricity and running water and I'm sure these conveniences would be a considerable improvement."

He was looking over his glasses at me. I sat as straight as I could with my shoulders back. My lips were a tight smile. I clutched my purse in my lap. Evie was nervous, I could tell. She looked back and forth from me to the lawyer, and back again.

"I understand that some residents have been given extensions on that special use permit. Why, Mrs. Peters has been given lifetime rights to her land. Now, what do I have to do to get lifetime rights? If you prove that I'm legally married to Tom, whether by records or common law, why can't we continue to live on our property? I would cooperate with the Park people. I would never bother them at all. They would not hear or see us." My voice was cracking.

"I understand your sentiments, Mrs. Dodson. This must be a very tough adjustment for you. Now, I was looking through your paperwork, and I see that you rightfully have inherited a house on 260 Elm Street in Elkton? Is that correct?"

"Yes. That's my parent's home. They were married 48 years. Can you imagine? And they died one week to the day of each other." I kept thinking that the more that I said of this story that I would make sense of what it meant to be married so long.

"It was left to you free and clear, Mrs. Dodson. And I'm thinking that a woman in your circumstances might take advantage of that situation before a lot of significant and costly litigation with the courts."

I nodded. It didn't matter that it was not my home. It was my mother's home, and it was for a woman who had the advantage of being maintained. And the house was in disrepair when my parents died. I could not imagine what state it was in now. I would not have the money to live in that house with my children; we would live in genteel poverty, or worse. I didn't want to leave that mountaintop. I didn't want to move to the valley. I didn't want to be around people full time. I could deal with being alone on that mountain, but surrounded by people, I could not bear. At my home I knew where and when to pick the berries and the ginseng; I could raise what we ate. I would be able to milk my cow and butcher my hog. How would I support my children in town? What would we eat? Tom's home was the only home I had ever had.

"What will I do to support myself and my children down off the mountain?"

"Remind me how many children that you have?"

"I have three children."

"What are their ages?"

"Sixteen, ten and seven."

"Well, they'll all benefit from being moved down to civilization and getting a proper education though I can see that you are no mountain woman, Mrs. Dodson. With your husband dead and the park condemning the land, I don't see any choice for you. I'm sorry for your loss, but remember, God does not give us more than we can bear."

Oh yes, he does, I thought, heat beginning to rise in my body until I felt my face flush. "Did you hear about Mr. Cliser?"

"Yes, I did."

"They dragged him out of his mountain home in handcuffs and he was singing *America the Beautiful* the entire way to the Sheriff's car."

He regarded me.

"And what about Mrs. Peterson? Those men dragged her out of her home when she was seven months pregnant. Then they set her house on fire right in front of her." I had to bend over to stop Evie from kicking me, but I hoped that didn't dilute the point I was making.

"I understand, Mrs. Dodson. And they will be doing the same to you if you do not leave. They have started building that park whether you like it or not. I know this is a hard for you and your family, but ultimately, the greater good will be served, and you will come to see your children will be much better off in civilization."

"Do you think they realized how many families were up there? Did they think about what it would mean about displacing those families? Displacing my family?" I was getting a bit hysterical. My hands were shaking.

"Between you and me, and I did sit in on a few meetings of the Shenandoah Land Association with Adams and Zerkle, I believe everyone was under the impression that there were just a few families of little means and moving them would better their situation. Many of those farms are owned by well-to-do farmers in the valley and many of those people are just tenants."

"With all due respect, I'm not sure if that is exactly true. There are a lot of untruths being printed in the papers. It's not right what they print in those papers. It is just not right. Saying everyone cannot read and are feeble minded, and from what you are telling me, that they don't even own the land. Do I look feeble minded?"

"I'm sure no one would think you feeble minded, Mrs. Dodson. You are a very capable woman."

"Well, thank God I was not considered feeble minded, or they would have dragged me to the Virginia Colony and sterilized me like they did with the Caves. Isn't that against the law somewhere?"

Mr. Hayjack started squirming and cleared his throat. "Actually, it is not, but we are getting off the point. Ultimately, this decision is up to you. I'm just telling you my sound legal advice on your specific situation. You can leave by choice, or they will drag you out by your boot heels."

It was over for me, and I knew it. After a few years gone from the mountain, would it feel like I had dreamt it all up?

"I appreciate you taking a look at my paperwork and advising me what I need to do," I said as I stood up.

"You're welcome, Mrs. Dodson. Let my secretary know what you decide to do."

I was standing and moving towards the door. "Thank you, I will."

"Now, there is the matter of my bill."

Evie and I walked out of his office with Evie talking a mile a minute, telling me what I should do with my life and all of our lives in this predicament.

"Mom, this here is plain silly. Let's just take the money and move to town, because I have made up my mind I'm going to be a town girl and be a lawyer."

Colin, who had overheard this as we descended the stairs, said, "You can't be a lawyer, Evie. You're a girl." Evie looked at her brother with her face as smooth as glass and regarded him like Mr. Hayjack had regarded me. As she passed her brother by, she looked him square in the face. "Watch me." She didn't smile as she headed out the door in front of us all.

"Evelyn, wait a minute," I called after her.

"Mom, are we moving to town?" Colin said, his brow furrowed.

"No. Yes. I don't know right now, Colin. Let me think. Where is Ben?"

In a panic, Colin, Evie and I rushed out the door to find Ben way down the street swinging on a street pole.

"We going to the five and dime now? Can I get a soda?"

"Yes," I said, relieved to have found him.

We walked the remaining block to the five and dime on North Main. I could not think straight, recalling what the lawyer had said, plus trying to keep an eye on my children who had, luckily, forgotten our plight as they looked at all the toys. I got them ice cream sodas and hamburgers at the soda fountain before we left, like I was a real middle-class woman living in town with a husband whose job could afford such luxuries.

By the time we got home many hours later, I fell into bed, my mind swirling with exhaustion and worry.

Chapter 48

"Mary, here let me hold done these blackberry canes so that you can get back and on into those bushes," Tom said. Venturing into the bushes with some trepidation, I found a cache of beautiful blackberries that the birds had not gotten to yet.

"There better be no snakes in here, Tom," I said as I picked.

"Snakes are looking for birds, not you. You're too big to eat."

"Well, in any event, how many bushels are you going to need?"

"At least thirty."

I had already picked what I was selling at the store in Ruckersville. Then, I had picked what our family would eat and can, and now, we were picking for Tom. Slowly, steadily and with a fixed determination, Tom and I picked with sweat dripping down both our faces and backs.

"Lookie there."

I stood up and stretched my back. "Where?"

"Look at those chestnuts."

I looked at the stand of chestnut trees.

Tom said, "They're dying."

I woke up with a start and looked around my dark bedroom and then I reached out to the empty place beside me in bed. I had been dreaming. My reality hit me like a freight train at 3 a.m., and I closed my eyes tightly trying to will myself to go back to sleep and back to dreaming that all was all right. That, of course, didn't work, so I got up and rooted around in the chest of drawers until I found one of Tom's shirts. Clutching it tightly I crawled back into bed. I buried my face in the shirt, my only comfort, as I waited for dawn.

I always make a blackberry cobbler every year with whipped cream. That morning, I found a jar of blackberries from the last time Tom and I had gone picking and made a cobbler. I ate it with such sadness; I didn't finish it.

I must admit that when it came to the blackberry's, I would sometimes not put in enough sugar. They can be a bit tart. It always seemed just too much to add more than 1 cup sugar. Because I no longer gave a damn after Tom died, I put two cups of sugar in so that my children would eat it. Tom and I used to eat blackberry cobbler for breakfast and as a snack until it was gone.

Chapter 49

October 13, 1935

Dear Mr. Lassiter, Shenandoah National Park Superintendent

I'm writing about my recent case of Mrs. Mary Dodson and her three children who live in a remote, yet beautiful farmstead on Hightop Mountain. Her property is in both Greene and Rockingham County. As Family Selection Specialist and Home Economist employed by the Federal government to assess loans for resettlement housing, I interviewed Ms. Dodson after she tried to shoot some of the CCC men. This woman, about 30 years old, widowed will not be eligible for resettlement or loans due to lack of income and livelihood. The easiest way out of this situation would probably be to grant her lifetime rights or eviction. I don't know if you would be willing to provide her and her children with lifetime rights due to her young age and therefore her possible long-time nuisance to the park. She is a smart woman of good character despite her most recent altercation that I believe was brought on by desperation. Her daughter is verbally aggressive, and her oldest son seems anxious to fight with everyone he meets. Her youngest son seems rather weak mentally as he was unable to sit still and proceeded to throw marbles at me for the entire time of my visit. Finally, Mrs. Dodson, who does seem quick to anger (as her recent dispute exemplifies) ran me out of the house stating, 'I've answered so many questions for so many people. Don't you people ever write down anything and show each other what you write down?'

While I don't see social welfare issues as part of the function of the Park, yet, as we have it thrust upon us anyway, we will have to make best of it for a little while. I will not travel up there to see her again and whatever you decide to do with her, and her family is the Park's call.

Sincerely,
Mozelle Cowden
United States Government Family Selection Specialist

December 19, 1936

Dear Mrs. Dodson,

This permit, enclosed herein, was signed by Deputy Sheriff Lucas of Elkton, and was approved by me for the purpose of giving you notice that you must move out of the park and allowing you until April 1 to find a new location and make your move. You are advised to lose no time in locating a place to which you can move, as we do not want the embarrassment of having you evicted from the Park area.

Mr. Lassiter, Superintendent, Shenandoah National Park

January 1, 1937

Dear Mr. Byrd,

We met at Skyland and I'm writing to ask you, before it is too late, on behalf of myself and three children, if it would do any good, or there be a chance, of keeping my home on the grounds that I (and many of my neighbors, friends, and other mountain residents) were badly misled. All of us believed that we would be able to retain our homes, even after they were sold to the park and not be forced to move. Many of us are of modest means and do not have the livelihood to support ourselves and our families in town. I, myself, am widowed and with no next of kin. Also, we mountaineers and my children were born, reared and love the mountains, so we will never be satisfied otherwise. There are stories of many people forced to leave who have died from broken hearts! I include herein the poem written by John T. Peterson, published in the *Madison County Eagle* last year.

In the old mountain home
For six months more
Where then shall I go
Down in the valley
To perish and die
To leave my mountain home
Is such a loss and grief...
I would rather go to my grave
Than to leave my mountain home.

I beg you, Mr. Honorable Byrd, to not move me and my family. We live on a remote farmstead and are a good bit from the road you are building so we will not bother any of the cars. The recent unfortunate altercations notwithstanding, we are a quite sensible, but now desperate family, who will be in terrible circumstances if we are forced to leave. Please consider my case and plea.

P. S: Time is running out for me so I would appreciate if you could answer at once.

Respectfully yours,

The widow, Mary Dodson

Chapter 50

Belle looked over a copy of the letter I sent to Mr. Byrd, then put it on the table and looked at me. "You think this is going to do something?"

"Maybe. It is worth a try. In any event, I'm not going to leave by my own accord."

"I don't understand why you don't want to move to town. I love being off the mountain," Luanne chimed in, placing her coffee cup on the kitchen table.

"I'm not you, Luanne, and your circumstances are much different from mine, and I would not love it, and I would have no idea how I would support myself and the children. How are we going to eat with no way to support ourselves?" I almost screamed.

"You could get a job doing something. Cleaning houses maybe. I was going to say sewing, but you can't sew worth a lick."

Cleaning houses. Perhaps I could work for Ethel and John, wouldn't that be a pretty picture?

"I appreciate the ham you brought me, Luanne, and all the advice, but I expect you have kept Asa waiting long enough." I wanted rid of her like I had wanted rid of all people. And if I was being honest, I was envious that she had a husband and a house and safety.

"What about your parents' house in town?" said Belle as she stood up.

"The last time I was there, it seemed like it was in poor shape. The real estate agent I wrote told me he would not list it until it was fixed up."

Luanne said, "Well, it would at least be a roof over your head, because if you don't do something soon you will be living in the woods."

I had already laid awake many nights contemplating how the children and I could live in the woods, what we would eat, how we could build a shelter.

We sat there, Luanne, Belle, and me like the three Graces.

"All right, ladies," Belle said, finally turning to Luanne, "I know you are worried as I am, Luanne—"

"I'm no longer worried, I'm furious." And with that she picked up her purse and slammed through the kitchen door, but not without leaving an envelope on the mantle above the stove. Belle looked at me as I hollered after my sister-in-law, "I don't need that, Luanne."

Belle got up to follow Luanne outside. I could hear Belle's heavy foot falls as she clamored down the porch steps. I didn't go after either of them, but I strained my ears to hear, nonetheless.

Luanne said, "I hope you can talk some sense into her."

"You've got to remember that you have not walked in her shoes. Count your blessings and try to understand."

"Well, we all make our beds, too."

"Luanne," shouted Belle. This piqued my interest and I got up to peer out the window. Pulling back the curtain slightly, all 5' 8 inches of Belle was nose to nose with 5'2-inch Luanne.

"Don't you ever say that when you got candy in your mouth. Now, go back down the mountain to your waiting simpleton husband and the farm his daddy left him that you know has some of the best bottomland in Greene county, so it doesn't take him too many brain cells to farm it."

"Thank you for reminding me why I don't like you."

"You're welcome."

As Luanne walked away, she called over her shoulder, "It's not going to be a pretty picture when it happens and you will be far away when it does, Belle, and... and... I just don't want to see her in that situation." Luanne was crying.

I retreated from the window and sat down in the chair. By this time, Evie had been drawn into the kitchen by the commotion.

"You know, Mom, she's right." I thought for a moment wondering which part Evie was agreeing with. "Can I go live with Aunt Ethel and Uncle John until you figure this out?"

"No. We stay together, always." Evie shook her head at me as if I were the child and she the adult. Belle came back inside and joined me at the table and spent a long time looking past my head to the wall.

"I have been racking my brain for all the men I've slept with to see if any one of them has any pull, but I have already used my cards to get you off the hook for that incident you had with the CCC and Colin poaching that deer."

Evie rolled her eyes clearly disgusted with the situation and us. "I'm going to see what Colin and Ben are doing at the barn." She walked out the door without a glance back.

"What are you planning to do now, Belle?"

"Well, by hook or by crook, the government men have circled the boundary around Bacon Hollow so my kin are fine, but I can't stay around here and watch any more of this. I have finally made up my mind about what I'm going to do, and it has been a long time coming. It is not my mountain, my world, and it is not my place here anymore." Belle looked me in the eyes. "I'm going out West, maybe Yosemite where there is still wild and freedom. And I'm going to learn how to fly a plane." Her face lit up as she thought about this.

My heart sank. I would never see her again; everything was going away.

"Going out west hasn't worked so well for the Okies." I told her.

"I ain't no Okie and I got jingle in my pocket, and there will be a lot of factory jobs opening out there."

"We are in a depression, Belle. What jobs?"

"We won't be in a depression much longer. I read the newspapers and my current lover works for a congressman in DC; we will be in a war soon enough."

"War? With who?"

"Germany, maybe, or Japan. Maybe Italy. It doesn't matter."

"What type of war?"

"That doesn't matter to me, as I'm only interested in my personal politics and opportunities to live like I see fit." I thought on this then and asked, "I see you got yourself a new car now?" A smile lit up her face.

"I bought myself a Lincoln Zephyr convertible in red." I smiled at her, forgetting my troubles for a moment.

"How did you settle on that?"

"Because I couldn't buy a plane." She stood up laughing, pushing her chair back. "Looks like your kids are coming back to the house," she said looking out the window. "They are carrying rabbits."

I stood up to look, and my heart sank when I saw they were carrying live rabbits and not dinner. Belle stood up to face me and I looked into her eyes. I would never see them again, and my own eyes filled with tears.

"Now, my Mary, don't you weep. Don't you remember? Pharaoh's army got drowned."

I nodded, weeping anyway, as salt and water, trauma and soul wrenching sadness slid down my face and onto my chest. I was going to miss her so much. We walked outside to the porch; my children were in the distance. She turned to me and kissed me on my lips, and for a moment time stood still.

"I wish you could come down to the new road and see the car. It's a beauty," she said with her devilish grin. Why lookie here. What you all got?" she said to my children who were scrambling up to us.

Colin came up to me smiling. "Look, Mom, we found them over by the barn. They were all alone." Ben showed me his baby bunny the size of a ball of yarn, it's nose twitching.

"Something ate the mama. So, they were going to die," said Evie matter-of-factly. "Look, mine is the perkiest. It wants to jump around." I peered at her bunny.

"Here, Mommy, this one's for you. It's the littlest one." Benjamin handed me the tiniest bunny the size of a shot glass. Its eyes were glassy. I stroked its tiny head and its eyes half closed as it calmed down.

"As usual, looks like you got your hands full," said Belle smiling.

"Mom? Can we walk out with Belle? I want to see her automobile."

"Yeah, me too," said Benjamin.

"Me three," said Evie.

They looked at me expectantly. I forced a smile and nodded. Immediately, they put all the rabbits in my hands, and I had to scramble to hold them close as my children started running down the lane. Evie was waiting to walk with Belle, who was standing next to me. I sat still in the porch rocker so as not to drop the bunnies.

"Watch your brother!" I shouted to Colin.

Belle then crouched down so her face was even with mine. "Remember, Mary, *the world is not flat.*" She stood up, brushing off her trousers while I sat there completely perplexed.

"Come on, Belle. The boys are going to get there before us," shouted Evie.

"Here, you'll need this before the end of things." Belle handed me a wad of cash held tight by a rubber band as she bounded off the porch steps.

"The world is not flat? What the hell is that supposed to mean?" I shouted after her.

As she and Evie headed away, Belle turned and said over her shoulder, "You're not going to fall off. Get in your ship and sail."

Hours later, I heard the shouts of my children as I was frying apple fritters. Wiping my hands on my apron, I quickly went to the front door to see what the matter was. Colin came bounding up the porch out of breath, and I could see Evie running, holding Benjamin's hand. "What's wrong?" I shouted at them and Benjamin who I could see was now crying. Colin was bent over, trying to catch his breath. As I started to head down the steps to go to Benjamin, who I figured had hurt himself, Colin grabbed my dress. "Mom! They are coming!"

"What? What are you talking about?"

"The men! They are down the mountain, and they are coming for us!"

"What do you mean?" But even as I said this, I felt my stomach turn over and the blood drain out of my heart. By then, Evie and her brother had made it to the porch, and I picked up Benjamin and held him to my chest, though he was too old to hold.

Colin continued. "Belle's trying to stall them, and she has her big ole car blocking the road. Oh Mom, they got guns and big cans of gasoline!"

My breath was coming in short pants.

"Mom? Can I have a fritter?" I looked at Evie in disbelief.

"Good God. What's wrong with you, Evie?" hollered Colin, and with that, Colin lunged at his sister. I grabbed him with my free arm. "Stop it," I yelled at all of them. "Let me think." I sat down on my rocker with Benjamin. Then I got up and paced the porch and walked in and out of the house like a crazy woman.

"Oh, God," I said to no one.

"I'm getting the guns," said Colin.

"No. Evie, Colin, start organizing your things just in case. And help Benjamin." I went back to frying my fritters.

"What are you doing?" said Evie. Even Colin looked at me with disbelief as he went to his room.

When I heard Tom's hound barking, I knew they had descended but I was not prepared for what I saw. I opened the door of my house to more men than I could count dressed in dark suits, some with holsters visible under their suit jackets. Their hats were pulled down over their eyes, shielding their faces. There were no deputies or sheriffs and not a face I could recognize. Behind them were men in work clothes carrying rifles, boards, and cans. "Are you Mary Dodson?" asked a man, flicking his cigarette onto my front field and walking towards me.

Suddenly, my children joined me. Colin stood on my left and Evie came to my right. Benjamin went around us carrying his box of bunnies.

"Mister? Want to see my new pets?" Ben tottered down the porch steps. All the men stopped walking, taken aback. The workmen shifted nervously, and just as Ben was showing his box to one of the Federal Agents, the man turned his face saying, "Get away from me, boy." Ben looked at him and his face fell.

The man who was closest to us began talking. "You can go easily, or you can go to jail, but I'm here to evict you off of government property. You are trespassing. Boys!" He shouted to the workers, "start taking it all out."

"Wait! This must be some mistake. I wrote to Senator Byrd. My husband is buried here. We can't leave," I said, my throat so dry I could barely form words.

"Boys!" he shouted again, motioning for them to head to the house. He walked up the steps like a bully, and as he was about to shove me aside, Evie kicked him so hard in his shin that he fell to his knees, and it knocked the wind out of him. He crouched on his hands and knees before us, and time stopped, and all the men stood frozen. One of the workmen snickered. I swallowed hard.

"Lady," he said getting to his feet, "You best get your knickers packed before they are set on fire."

"Get your stuff," I said to the children. "Colin, load what you can on the horses. Set the hogs loose. Take the cow."

Colin nodded, his face set but tears coming to his eyes.

The man lit another cigarette staring at me with disdain. I turned and went back into Tom's house. Sleepwalking into the bedroom, I placed the few personal items I had accumulated over the years into the small bag I had come up the mountain with all those long years ago. I walked into the kitchen and placed my apron on the peg by the stove and I stepped over the threshold of Tom's house to the world outside. My children were coming up from the barn with the last of Tom's horses and my horse, the Giant. Evie was leading the cow and Benjamin had his bunnies.

"Set it on fire boys," he said, smiling.

I looked at this evil man. "You're a son of a bitch and may the sound of my voice and curses follow you and haunt you till the end of your days and beyond," I shouted to him, and then I leaned close and with the breath of a madwoman, I whispered to him, "as God is my witness, you will never get it up again."

He recoiled from me. "Boys," he shouted. The men didn't move but looked down at their shoes.

"Davis," he shouted to one of the men, "get on up here." The man looked sheepish but then he shook his head no and would not move.

"Goddamn it! Smith. I will fire every one of you worthless CCC degenerates." He pushed past his own men who parted, and he grabbed a container of gasoline.

"Let's just board it up. They're headed out," said one of the younger Federal agents.

"I got special word on this one. We are to burn it. Otherwise, what is going to prevent them from coming back? Look at her. She's got nothing," he spat. "She'll be back with her bastards before we're down this godforsaken mountain."

A gun clicked and we all turned to stare at my daughter holding her father's shotgun with her long curly blond hair all around her.

"Mister, you can run us off this mountain, but you can't talk about my mama like that."

"Honey," one of the CCC boys said, walking towards her and putting himself between her and the agents, "you're as right as rain, but please listen to me and put down that gun or things are going to get ugly here."

"Evie," I tried to say calmly, "unload it and put it on the horse." Slowly, Evie lowered the gun.

I walked to my children, and I thought how Dog Patch we did look with our cow, bunnies, the horse. The mangy old hound and one of our cats were standing by us. I tied my belongings to my horse who was getting nervous with all the commotion.

"Come on," I said to my Noah's ark.

The men parted for us as I heard the first crackle of fire as the house caught and I thought about my apron, the apple fritters sitting on a plate on the kitchen table, Tom's clothes, and the deadly fire eating it all up slowly and deliberately. My sons were crying and the CCC boy's faces were ashen, ashamed, yet aloof, for they knew they could do nothing, and for good men, that is sometimes a hard burden to hold.

"Don't look back," I cried to my children, as much as a command to myself as to them. And I walked down the mountain amid my children's sobs as a cold crept into my heart that pushed every ounce of grace from my body and soul. I thought that the heavens surely must have confused me with someone else, someone sinister and evil. Otherwise how could I make sense of this last chapter my life? Our steps were miserable and deliberate.

"You think I can go back and shoot them?" asked Evie after we had walked about an hour.

"No."

"It ain't gonna help now, Evie. Look," said Colin who had stopped and turned around in the road. I gritted my teeth as my children turned to look up at the mountain. I stared straight ahead down the road, refusing to look back.

"Look at all that smoke rising from the mountain. You think they set the mountain on fire by mistake?" Colin said

"Would serve them right," Evie said. "I hope they all get trapped up there and get baked like a chicken."

"Really, Evie?" I looked at her. She smiled at me, and Colin stifled a laugh, but then he quickly grew quiet.

"I'm going to remember this day as long as I live and I will never forgive any of them for it," said Colin. And he was true to his word.

"Well, I'm glad we are moving. I plan on going to school and being a lawyer and tell everyone what's what."

"Women ain't lawyers, Evie," said Benjamin.

"Oh, yes, they are, and I will be one and then I won't give my stupid brothers a lick of help." She made a face at both of them. And her words followed her intent, but she did always help her brothers, complaining most mightily each time.

We walked along in silence, the gold afternoon sun oblivious to our plight as it danced off the springtime leaves and redbuds, blooming mayapples and patches of maroon, white and pink trillium, and I kept repeating over and over as I walked into the spring twilight the world is not flat, the world is not flat, the world is not flat.

"Mom?" Colin came up to me.

"Yes, son?"

"What are we going to do?"

I thought about finding the first man I could meet and getting married, borrowing money from any bank that would lend me some, cleaning houses, finding a barn to sleep in for the night, how long I could make the money from the auction last, how many barns we could sleep in until I found a house to rent, what we were going to eat in the next 24 hours, how long it would take to walk to that house on Elm Street, and if it was still standing. "I guess we are going to sail."

Chapter 51
Elk Run Retirement Community, Elkton Virginia 1971

I had a vague idea that something was wrong. Had it been a month? A year? Days? I could not recall anymore, as I seemed more tired, dreamier now, and the material world didn't concern me at all which, in a way, was kind of nice. I believe I was completely worn out, but not in the way I would be from picking blackberries for days in the summer heat or washing clothes for a family of five or heart pain from what is and can't be changed. This was different. I could not seem to get my strength back for the first time ever in my life. I blinked my eyes to try and clear them. How old was I now? 75? 85?

Across my little room sat my granddaughter, Lily, and her mother, my daughter, Evelyn. Lily was reading a book. Evelyn was paging through *Cosmopolitan* magazine. As I tried to shift my body around in my bed, their eyes went to me.

"Hey there, Grandma." Lily beamed at me.

"How are you feeling, Mom?" asked Evie.

"What's wrong with me?" I asked my granddaughter. Lily looked at her mother for help.

"You're old, Mom, that is what's wrong with you," Evie said, coming over to my bedside. "Can I help you sit up?" She propped me on some pillows with a bit of difficulty, because my body hurt so bad. How long had I been lying here?

"Mom," Evie said in her lawyer voice, all serious, proud, and unwavering, "I'm here so we can help get you organized for your move to the Virginia Mennonite Retirement Community. We will be moving you the day after tomorrow."

My thoughts were clear as a bell now. "You're moving me now? At the end of things?"

"Grandma," said Lily nervously.

"Mom, you will outlive me," said Evie without any humor in her voice.

"I have outlived anyone that has ever loved me, that is for sure." I was not sure if I said this out loud or in my head. "Where's Ben?"

"We sent word. Remember, he is on a ship doing that underwater welding." I thought on this, but all I could see was his impish smile and his lithe and little body scrambling onto the roof of the house to throw acorns at the tax collector.

"Have you talked to Colin? Where's my first-born son?" Evie and Lily exchanged a glance.

"Grandma, I brought you some ice cream. It is one your favorites, blackberry." Lily smiled too broadly. She took it out of a small cooler she had by her side, opened it, and put it in front of me. I regarded it.

"What time of the year is it?" I asked her.

Lily looked at her mother. "Well, Grandma, it is getting towards fall. We have been having some beautiful Indian summer days. The leaves are turning on the mountain. Before you know it, the persimmons will be ripe."

I regarded the blackberry ice cream, wondering what it was doing in ice cream when it was not July. "Are the Milam's ripe?" I asked her.

"Mom, those trees have been gone for years; I can get you a Golden Delicious from Kroger if you want an apple," said Evie sighing.

"I was stringing beans the day daddy got hurt."

"That was over fifty years ago and an unpleasant memory I would prefer not to think about," said Evie.

Lily said, "Grandma. It's okay. You can tell me."

"Why does she have to tell you? Haven't I told you that story?" her mother said.

"You were only a small child, and your memories are different from Grandma's," replied Lily.

"Well, I'm not going to sit around listening to all this. I have to pick up Tommie from football practice and go to the supermarket. Lily, I will swing back around to get you later." Evie looked at me. "I will be back later."

My eyes followed her as she left the room. I turned to look out the window. "Lily, can you open the window, please?" Lily did as she was asked. She opened it all the way. The cheapskate Elk Run Old Age Home didn't have screens on the windows, so the glorious fresh air came in along with a leaf from the cherry tree outside my window. Then, a wren perched on the windowsill. "Look," Lily said softly.

"I see it, sweetie."

The little bird cocked its head right and left and hoped down the length of the windowsill. It stood a moment and preened its feathers and then cocked its head to look at me again. It hopped along some more. Then, with a flutter and a flash, it disappeared. I knew that bird. I knew it like I knew myself.

My granddaughter was smiling at me. "I wish mom could have seen that," she said.

"It would not have come if your mother had been here."

"Grandma," she said looking at me. Her eyes were filling with tears. She laid her head in my lap. She started sobbing. "I'm sorry, I'm so sorry. I'm going to miss you so much."

I stroked her beautiful hair, overcome that there was one human being that loved me completely and totally and would miss me and remember me the way I really was. I had been surprised by a lot in my life and had made some assumptions based on God knows what. There was a time when my children were in high school and we were living in my parents' home, still without electricity because I could not afford it. I was working at the pharmacy and taking in laundry. Yet, I made sure that my children were dressed properly for school, that they had a nickel to get an ice cream. There was food on the table. Did they ever notice that there were nights that I didn't eat so that they could get their fill? No, they did not, thank goodness. But I could never understand their resentment towards me, as if I were to blame for our circumstances. I suppose I was an easier target than God or luck or fate, but it still hurt my heart, for I loved all my children with my body and soul. They were all I had, even though not one of them was easy, heartache most of the way. For despite all my love for them, it was not returned in a way that I expected. I looked at my granddaughter, now silent and holding onto me for dear life, and I thought to myself that I must have done some good in my life to be blessed with her at the end.

The ice cream had started to melt, so I spooned a bit into my mouth, and for the first time in a while, what passed my lips tasted good. I used to make blackberry ice cream. Tom and I would go berry picking together. We were a good team, as we could work long and hard. Of course, Colin, Evie and Benjamin would get bored or eat more than they picked but we could keep right on at it. Those berries were money in the bank. What we didn't put up or use Tom would sell in town.

"What I would give for a Milam apple," I said to Lily. I had no appetite, but I wanted one just the same.

She lifted her head up from my lap. "I could try and find one, maybe at the old homeplace?"

"I'm just wishing is all."

"I wish I could have known Granddaddy."

"He was a good man, a man's man."

"Was he your best friend?" she asked, wide-eyed.

"Best friend? What type of nonsense is that? He was my husband."

"Who was your best friend? "

I thought a minute. "Well, I guess it had to be my childhood friend Ethel or your father's sister Luanne or maybe even Belle."

"Ethel was the one that married your old boyfriend, Johnathan Abel? the one you would go on vacations with when he died?"

I laughed. "Yes. Life didn't turn out quite like she expected either. She just had nicer curtains. You know, he didn't turn out to be such a nice man. It was alleged that while he was baptizing girls in the river, he would grab their bottoms as he was dunking them. Ethel...I remember...Ethel's dead, too."

"You must miss her."

"Yes, but after Tom, then leaving the mountain, I grew..." I had no word. "I'm not sure what happened in me. It was kind of a mixture of being resigned and sadness. I mean, not the type of sadness where you are crying. I went about my day, and to bridge club and made lemon cream pie, but I had been done in a bit by one too many hardships. But, you know what I also learned is that good things and good memories can help. Why, when Johnathon Abel finally died, Ethel took all his insurance money, and she would take us on a trip each year. After watching Humphrey Bogart in *Casablanca,* Ethel booked a trip to Morocco. Then when Ethel went through her Anthony Quinn phase, we went to Greece."

"Grandma, you beat all. A Mountain Girl in Greece, that sounds like it could be a book!"

"Or a porno movie."

"Grandma!"

When I woke up, Lily was gone. It was dark. My glasses were still perched on my head, cockeyed. I turned to look at the clock. It was 4:12 in the morning. Quickly for me, I got out of bed and stood. I felt surprisingly good, like I did when I was young. I was ready to start the day and see what I could get into. Concentrating on my steps, I walked over to my bureau and removed a folded dress. When was the last time I had a bath? I mean, it was not like I was in a sweat or anything, but I suddenly wanted water on me. For many weeks, that was not the case, and I think the nurses gave up on me. The water on my skin had just gotten to be too much.

Slowly, I stepped out of my nightgown and underwear. I ran the water in the sink until it was warm, and I added soap and took an old-fashioned sponge bath. You know, when Tom was in his coma, I would do this for him every day. I found a comb and combed back my hair, which was short now because Evie kept taking me to the beauty parlor and telling them to cut it off. I felt like a million bucks.

After I slipped the dress over my head, which was no easy feat since I had arthritis in both my shoulders, I sat in the chair and decided what I should do about my hose. That seemed like a lot of trouble, so I found some Peds that Evie had bought me, and I put them on and slipped on my shoes. I unpinned the money from my bra and put it in my pocketbook. I decided to put on my white cable knit sweater, because it was always so cold on the mountain in the morning.

Then I left the Elk Run Retirement home. I simply shuffled down the dark corridor and past the empty nurses' station down past the next corridor of rooms and out the side door into the alleyway behind the Elk Run old age home.

I looked around and smiled. Morning was coming. Black had given way to almost an indigo blue in the morning sky. It was a color I could not described, but it was if I had never seen a color so rich or like it ever before. The crescent moon was hanging in the sky along with Venus and a small constellation of stars. The birds had begun to sing their morning song, and the streets of Elkton were quiet.

Down the street I shuffled, past the convenience store, past the pharmacy where I had worked. Mr. Maynard, the pharmacist, was dead now, and I didn't think his family still ran it. I worked there when you still could buy laudanum, and he kept opium for some of the ladies too, but no one was supposed to know that. He kept other things, too, for when the women came in tight-lipped and worried. I was his right-hand man in that store. If I had not met Mr. Maynard, I'm not sure what I would have done for money when we had to move to town. It was a mutually beneficial relationship.

On I shuffled now in a nice rhythm, past the shiftless boys sitting in the abandoned storefronts, past the feed co-op that was not yet open, past the police station, the municipal building, the newspaper office. The few cars that passed didn't slow or notice me. I was invisible. By the time I made it to the gas station by the underpass of Route 33, there were a few more cars on the road, men headed to work. I began my way up 33, and I felt my old strength coming back. By the time I made it to the Bear Store, so called because they had a big stuffed bear on the convenience store roof, it was true morning. The store was open, and I could smell bacon and eggs frying. Now came the hard part, and I was not sure what I was going to say or do. A working man held the door open for me so I could go inside. I was smiling and hoping I looked pleasant and sure of myself. I headed to the attendant.

"Hello, young man, I said to him. He nodded at me. "I'm headed over to Whitehall to visit my relations and I was looking to see if I could find a taxi service or a ride over the mountain this morning. My car is in the shop."

"I don't know." He didn't look up from his cooking.

"Where are you headed, ma'am?" asked the same man who had held the door for me.

"To Whitehall. If I can get a ride to Lydia or just across the mountain, I can meet up with my relations."

"Well, I'm headed to Charlottesville. I can take you." He paid for and grabbed his sandwich and coffee from the counter.

"Thank you." I followed him to his pick-up truck, and it took a bit of energy to get up in the seat, but I made it.

He drank his coffee with one hand and drove with the other. He had on a POW bracelet and a wedding ring. He turned and smiled at me. You're up very early in the morning. My granny always got up early, too. She lives up in Beldor. You know John Hite?"

"Do I know John Hite? Why, I knew his great grandmother."

"Now, that's a long time ago. She lived way up in there, didn't she?"

"Yes, she did. Anyone keeping up with that cemetery on the corner of that ridge?"

"Not that I know. People only go up that far to hunt these days."

"My, my, my," I thought to myself, "it has been a long time since I was up in Beldor and Sandy Bottom and over Swift Run Gap to my home place. I can remember when you still could cross the mountain through the path up in Beldor," I told him.

"When them government people were afraid to try and run them Roaches and Shiffletts out of there, they pipe gated the road and starved them out those sneaky cowardly bastards. Excuse me, I didn't mean to curse," the young man said.

"Oh, that's quite all right. They were sneaky government bastards and not one of them man enough to stand up to those people. Well, I did hear a rumor or two that some of those government men went in there and didn't come back out."

"They are still a tight group up in Beldor. Why, did you hear what Johnny Carson said about us?" He was beaming.

"Yes, I did. I had the good fortune to be watching his show that night."

"The number one murder capital in America. For a small town, I mean."

"Well, perhaps we should not be so proud of that."

"It's because of what they did. It bred resentment and hate and cut off people's livelihood. People who had lived here for hundreds of years then told to leave their places so outsiders could come driving up through their land to look at the scenery? That damn Adams and the rest of them, I hope they are all in Hell. Why, I'm sorry. It just gets me riled up. And, you know, I don't give a damn about those park officials. I keep on hunting on my family's land every year, and they can't stop me."

"You sound like my oldest boy, Colin. He never did get over it... never."

"They should have just left well enough alone."

He let me out at the store in Lydia. He would not accept gas money, but I left a twenty-dollar bill on the side of the seat all the same. He would find it.

My next ride was with a young farm boy who pulled up to the filling station on his tractor. "Young man," I approached him.

"Yes'm?"

"Where you headed with that machinery?"

"I'm raking hay today."

"Well, that's good. I need you to give me a ride over to 810 in Dyke." He stood looking at me like a deer caught in the headlights. "Now don't worry. I can get in that cab; you just hold onto my pocketbook but first I'm going to go into the store and pay for that gas of yours. Do you want anything else?" He nodded no; I brought him out a Mountain Dew.

Down the road we bounced at 15 mph; I was delighted with the backup of cars behind us. Stone faced, the farm boy looked straight ahead drinking his soda and spitting tobacco juice into an empty cup. I was beyond commenting on anything; I was as light as the September air. He pulled over at the corner of 810 and 33 and kept staring straight ahead, glad to be rid of me, no doubt.

"Now, young man you are going to have to get down there and catch me. I'm going to jump." That made him a bit worried, and he swung the tractor into neutral and put on the brake. With my pocketbook in the crook of my arm, I made my way to the fender. He put his two hands on my waist and lifted me up then down onto the dirt road. His hands on my waist, for that fleeting moment, made me feel like a young girl. Maybe I was going backwards in time? Perhaps I was a young girl again. I touched my hair and thanked him. He touched his cap, nodded, and was gone. Nothing could stop me now.

"I'm coming!" I said out loud as I started walking. I was so slow or maybe I was floating, or maybe I was already dead and dreaming this all up, and as I thought on it, I did see ghosts ahead on the road. Two figures were headed my way. I felt the urge to jump into the woods and hide from them. For a moment, I hesitated, then held my ground and kept walking forward. As I got closer, I could see that they were carrying all their possessions on their back; it was a boy and a girl.

"Did the park people throw you out?" I said.

"Oh, no. We are headed to the nearest town to resupply." They smiled at me. Their body odor was overpowering. I stepped back.

"Are they letting people back to their homes?" I asked excitedly.

The boy and girl looked at each other. They shrugged their shoulders. "We don't know about that." They smiled beatifically at me. Tan. Radiant. Innocent. Strong. Muscled. Wiry, just like Tom and I use to be.

"Well, here, I got something for you." I reached into my pocketbook and pressed a twenty into the girl's hand.

"You go to town and get yourself two cold beers. Or two cold cherry sodas or whatever you want." They really beamed now. "You look like you might find this handy," said the boy. He handed me his walking cane. "At night, everywhere we stopped, I carved on it."

I looked at it and twirled it around. Symbols and words and pictures were interwoven around the limb. It was as light as a feather but rock hard like petrified wood. I tried it out and it felt good. "Thank you. This magic is going to help me on my journey." I smiled at the boy.

"Maybe we will see you on the trail." The young girl hugged me, and they moved off.

I thought, as I walked with my new walking cane, I would soon be journeying no more. No more trails for me. This idea kept me going up and up and up the Hightop mountain. Was I sweating or crying? I didn't know anymore. I was not thirsty or hungry or tired. I simply was. I felt lighter. No pain. No age. I felt the most of me I'd ever felt and not me at all.

I was the orange monarch on the sundrop flowers,

The iron weed growing in the boggy field,

I flew on a squirrel's back as he scampered across the road.

When I saw the goats eating bindweed and honeysuckle, I laughed and clapped my hands which caused them to look up at me and then scatter and stop. There was a whole herd of them, big and small, brown ones, white ones, dappled ones, goats with horns, goats with no horns, goats with little tiny ears.

Peering into the woods, I saw a body lying on some pine boughs, a book by his side. I poked this body with my walking stick. The body screamed. He backed away from me as if he had seen a ghost. If I was already dead, I was going to be mad, mad, mad.

"Holy shit! How did you get here?" the young man said.

"I flew on my broom."

He laughed. His hair was long, like a woman's, and he was tan and well-muscled. He wore no shirt or shoes.

"Young man, do you or your people have some type of horse or mule or tractor or something?"

"We sure do. The Three Oaks Commune keeps mules, and I ride all up and down these mountains."

"Go get one and bring it here now. You must take me the rest of the way home."

"I can do that. Can I bring you any food? Something to drink?"

I shook my head no. "Do not mention me," I said.

"Are you on a spirit walk?"

"Yes."

As I watched this young hippie and his menagerie of goats head off, I sat for the first time that day. Because there was no longer any fat on my backside, I had to slide off of the rock and onto the forest floor. Was it my eyesight or the coming afternoon that made the sunlight through the forest look like a colored kaleidoscope? I had been to the woods for love and now for death.

I felt my body come alive as I watched the young man return leading a white draft mule.

"Are you ready?" he asked me. I nodded.

"Okay. Here is what we will do. Let's get you to stand on that rock and then I will get you seated." Childlike, I obeyed. Halsom's body pressed to mine. I'm pregnant. My mother's face. The coal camps. Tom's back. Memories were whirling in my head making me feel like I was going to swoon.

"Young man, for a moment, you reminded me of someone else," I laughed.

"I'm all that has ever been and all that will ever be," he said, and he looked into my eyes and his eyes swirled crazily like the cosmos, and I clutched at my heart.

"I'm going home."

"I know." He smiled at me.

So many times, I had ridden and walked this mountain by myself, or followed Tom's back up, down, across rock ledges, down mountains in the dark with Tom holding a lantern, across streams swollen with rain, to blackberry bushes, to the rock ledge that looked out towards the Alleghenies where Tom and I would strip off our clothes and make love in the sunshine on top of a mountain.

"Mary, Mary, quite contrary how does your garden grow?"

"With silver bells and cockle shells and bluebells all in a row." I answered.

As we came to the home place, the massive chimneys were still standing as was the right side of the house which was weather-beaten. No more glass windows, the porch leaning and caving in on one side. The left part of the house was burned, and overgrown with brambles, shrubs and small trees. He said to me, as I gazed at my beautiful home. "I do believe we will find room at this inn."

Gently, with the most delicate of touches, he lifted me from the animal and placed me down on the soft earth.

"Thank you. Thank you, thank you, thank you." I whispered to the world around me. "You know, I stayed until the last. I stayed even after they put up the pipe gate. I stayed until the sheriff came, not once, not twice, but the third time, the Feds came with the guns. I wish my children hadn't had to live through that, packing up what we could carry, escorted off our home like prisoners of war." He regarded me with such a peaceful and beatific smile that I no longer felt any pain for or about the removal. It was so all- encompassing, every hard moment in my life fell completely away. "Do you need anything else?" he asked.

"No, I need nothing else." I put my cheek on the mule's neck remembering the sweet smell of beasts. I watched him turn and leave disappearing into the woods and twilight.

Time worn time worn into the grey twilight. Yeats. My favorite poet coming to me now across the years.

The forest had reclaimed the farm, just like the park people wanted, but I was able to use the Virginia creeper vines to hold onto and make my way up the front porch, which was still intact.

"Tom?" I called as I climbed the steps. "Tom? I'm home!" I shouted into the house seeing the children come. I was crying tears of joy.

I placed my pocketbook on the sunken kitchen table. I wandered to the rooms that were not burned, running my hand on the walls, feeling the walls that were left. I went upstairs to say goodnight to my children. I went to our bedroom and struggled with opening the trunk that had rusted shut. The bolt came away, as did the handle, revealing the dusty remnants of a life of a woman who was long dead.

The bed was just springs now, the bed where I used to sleep and cry and laugh and elbow Tom when he was snoring. The bed where I gave birth and screamed my head off. The bed where I lay sick with the flu. The bed that used to squeak to high heaven. The bed where Tom died.

I went out the back porch, so tired and holding onto the rail, which gave way in my hands. Losing my balance for a moment, I swayed violently, then righted myself. With the last of my energy, I followed what looked like a deer trail to where I remembered the apple trees were, past where the clothesline had been, past the old garden shed that was covered in Old Virginia Roses until I found the old, gnarled Milam. It was covered with tiny apples, and the limbs twisted and twirled and hung low. Yellow jackets feasted on the dead fruit fall, and deer droppings were scattered; the deer had beaten down a beautiful bower to lie down in.

I sat and took off my shoes. I pulled off my Peds and wiggled my toes in the cool air. How ugly my feet were now was of no consequence. The yellow toenails, the giant bunions. There was a time I would paint them, and Mr. Maynard was always surprised to see those red toes hiding under hose and sensible shoes.

I had made it home! Oh, the sadness and joy mingled together, and I cried for it all. The sky was so blue and beautiful. Had I never seen the sky before? How long had I been a prisoner of war? The clouds floated by, and I laid my head down on the long grass. The smell of earth, autumn leaves, and apples swirled together until it filled my head. Would the deer graze around my bones?

There was not much left to me now. I remember when I went through the changes, and I suddenly got a thick middle. I was appalled. I used to tell myself, "Well, at least I've got my figure." When my figure went, I was not sure what I could call on. Yet, now, I didn't have an ounce of fat. Funny how life is.

I closed my eyes to rest.

After Tom died, whenever I got scared and I was feeling alone, I would put a hand on my belly and a hand over my heart. This would make me so calm. I did that now.

Rising above the apple tree, I decide to fly over the home place. I flew about one hundred feet into the sky before I began to float. Look, the tin roof is still intact! The fields were filled with cattle. Tom always had about ten Angus heifers, big square-built girls. There is the spring house. That water was so cold running though that trough. I should have gone to the root cellar before I started my journey. But here I go over to the barn. There's a big hole that needs patching, or the leather will get ruined. How I love the smell of that hay in the barn loft.

Beauty has lost her collar again. But she was such a good milk cow she really didn't need one. She would stand for milking and come when she was called. Once, she knocked over the milk pail and I punched her. She looked at me, and I felt so bad, but all that milk was on the ground and all over me. When that cow died, I cried as if I'd lost my mother. I laid next to her, stroking her neck.

Oh, I'm rising now. I'm going over Hightop. Now, where is that cave? There it is over by that rocky crag. I'm swooping down so I can get a look. Tom would keep his shine in there, bottled and ready to go. I knew this and got to it before the vultures did. The day after Tom was buried, I collected it all. Then I made the trip to Skyland on that wild horse of mine that Tom could not stand. Even laden down, that horse could cover some ground. It took me 22 hours one way. I was no stranger to long journeys.

Look at this farm! As pretty as a picture. I'm so far up now I can see the whole place laid out as if it were sitting at the hand of God. I'm finally at peace. My, my, my, what a long road it has been.

Who is that? What is my mother doing here? Oh, no, it's Belle, dead these long years, smiling and holding her hand out for me.

Mary Louise Dodson
1900-1971

Mary Louise Dodson was born in Elkton in the year of our Lord 1900. She was preceded in death by her husband, Tom Dodson, and one of her children. She is survived by her daughter, Evelyn Louise Shifflet, lawyer, her granddaughter, Lily May Shifflet, a senior at James Madison University, and her son Benjamin Thomas Dodson, a marine welder in Norfolk. She was preceded in death by her son Colin Dodson, who died as an army radio operator in WWII.

A service will be held at the gravesite at 2 p.m. on Sunday. She will be laid to rest at the Dodson-Hensley cemetery. The Shenandoah National Park will be opening the access gate for the funeral proceedings.

Authors Note

Across the Blue Ridge Mountains is a work of fiction. Any resemblance to people living or dead is coincidental.

If you would like more information on the primary and secondary sources consulted during the research for this novel, or about the author, please visit the website shown below. This website will also allow you to enter Mary's world through photos, maps, recipes, and songs that are referred to in the preceding pages.

msmarangione.com

About the Author

I fell in love with the Blue Ridge Mountains in my early twenties and moved to Virginia from New York. One evening, at the Alexandria Public Library in Northern

Virginia, I came across a display on Shenandoah National Park with photos of the mountain families and books such as *Hollow Folk, the Undying Past of Shenandoah National Park, Recollections, The People of the Blue Ridge Remember.* These were some of the only books available in the mid-1980s, and *Hollow Folk* was highly biased. Yet, the books lit a fire in me to discover more about the people and families who were removed from the Park.

One winter's morning, Mary's voice spoke to me, and I started writing.

I am a Professor of American and Appalachian Literature at Blue Ridge Community College. My poetry has been published in *Lumina* magazine, Sagewoman, and the *North Shore Woman's Newspaper.* Additionally, I have published numerous academic articles.

msmarangione.com